A Cold and Mortal Spring

The Wishkiller Saga Volume I

G. Scott Huggins

Cannon Publishing

Contents

To Jon Miles, the first and longest-suffering reader.

Chapter One

15th of Spring 312 Exodus

The remains of the smoke hanging over Everview vanished out of the late afternoon sky like the damned ghost of unseen fires. The riders Aethal had deployed to scout the town gates galloped up to him in a swirl of dust.

"No guards, Captain," said Corporal Edmen. "From the gates, we couldn't see anyone. Or anything. Wherever the fire started, it's well inside the walls. It hasn't done much damage."

Aethal nodded. They hadn't entered the town, of course. His Phoenix Lancers knew Discipline better than that.

Subaltern Canuta spoke up, "My Lord Captain, the gates are open. But there's no sign of a fight. Not forced; no bodies. Just open, sir." He looked like a man who doubted his own word. Which was why Aethal had sent him forward with the corporal: a young officer needed practice in making clear observations while in danger.

"Assessment?" Aethal asked him.

"Unknown, milord. I... I don't see how it could be Grassworms, sir; not even with Banshees. There wouldn't be anything left."

Aethal inclined his head to the corporal.

"Subaltern's right, sir. You remember what they did to the Humber colonies."

"Unfortunately." If the Grain Sea raiders had possessed the strength to take down Everview, they'd have done it long before this. It was a major supply base for the Treeline, not thirty miles west. Grassworms burned everything: they didn't set small fires. Aethal signaled his bugler to sound for a conference.

"Thoughts, gentlemen?" he asked, after Canuta had repeated his findings to the officers.

Lieutenant Farnan spoke first. "Advance the squadron into the town by columns. Our first aim is to rescue survivors and find out what they know." He rammed his powdered but disheveled wig into his saddlebag, revealing black hair that needed the attention of the squadron's barber.

"I disagree, sir," said Lieutenant Godwin, whose own wig was immaculate, as always, despite the day's ride. "We should run sweep riders outside the walls first, then infiltrate slowly. It could be a trap, and we don't want to be bunched together if they've got any of their Well-spawned Banshees inside."

Farnan shook his head. "The Grassworms haven't broken this year's treaty yet. They're getting more in trade than they ever have. Especially from right here. Why raid the place?"

"Perhaps they decided they'd been cheated," said Godwin.

Aethal nodded, eyeing the horizon, and the sun falling slowly towards it.

"Normally, I think I'd agree with you, Harry," he said. "But traps aren't usually the Grassworm way. Especially not if they decided to take revenge on the spur of the moment for some slight." He met Farnan's eyes, and grinned. "Unlikely they're still here, eh?"

"As unlikely as you, sir," returned Farnan." Godwin snorted softly, but the younger officers just looked puzzled. Aethal returned to seriousness.

"I want to be able to investigate as much of Everview as possible before we lose the light." Aethal knew the town, but not well enough to want to poke through it in the dark. Banshees would be much worse then, if there were any. His Greater Rifles would be almost completely ineffective, while one clear cry in the stillness of evening could cost him a whole column of cavalry.

He raised his voice in command. "We'll go in through the gate. Earplugs in. At the first real sign that Grassworms have been here, we pull out and set a perimeter. Then we'll teach them better than to Wish *us* dead."

"We'll shove our rifles up their asses!" called a trooper. A ghost of grim laughter boiled from the ranks. Aethal patted Gun.

That suggestion constitutes a suboptimal deployment. The words, more felt than heard, traveled up Aethal's arm at his contact with the weapon, and Aethal snorted. Most Greater Rifles weren't known for their appreciation of the nuances of speech. Still, while the Banshees' Word of Death remained a secret and hellishly effective weapon, Aethal would rather have his Greater Rifle. It would kill whether or not its target heard it.

Some officers got strange about their weapons. Named them, wrote poetry dedicated to "*Suredeath,*" or "*Dragonfire.*" Aethal thought the habit foolish. A Greater Rifle might be more than a tool, but it was not a person. He called his Gun.

He had no time for Gun now, and the rifle obediently subsided. He raised his voice:

"Corporal Corrin, you will hold the gate with your column and the horses. Harry, you'll take Sergeant Falk's column to investigate the Inn; it's the biggest place in town. Tyrsen, you'll take Corporal Galfrid's file to the Church; it's where frightened people run. I'll take Eanling and his men with me and see if the Thane's home. Sindon Rawl's governed here longer than any of us have been commissioned. We'll find something out there, I'll warrant." He raised his hand in salute. "By Discipline we live. Move."

"By Discipline." His lieutenants saluted him, and swung their mounts around to carry out his orders.

"Begging your pardon, my Lord Captain," said Canuta. "But the Discipline prescribes that we should notify the Regiment at once, sir."

Aethal nodded. "It does, Mister Canuta. Can you tell me why I'm not doing it?" It was never a bad time to teach.

Canuta looked puzzled. "No, sir."

"Even Maednac's Discipline needs interpretation. If I sent a rider to Regiment now, what would he say? He wouldn't know whether to report an attack, a plague, or mass hysteria. What, according to the Discipline, would Colonel Jeharok have to do then?"

"He'd have to move the Regiment in support of us," gulped the young officer.

"Wouldn't he just? Which would leave the rest of the Western Grain Sea without the Phoenix Lancers' protection if something more serious arose. 'Meet every threat with all your force, and all your force stands at the mercy of every threat.'"

"Is that Maednac's *Reascendent*, sir?"

Aethal snorted. "Verlaen does have other writers than Maednac First King. It's Gyren's *Stratagem*. Which you should read. But besides that, the colonel would not thank me for mobilizing him if this turned out to be a case of the entire town having decided to carelessly take the day off fishing, would he?"

"Do you really think that's what happened, milord?"

"No, but it might be something almost as trivial. Once as a young man, I saw a ship drift past the Wrackberg with empty decks because every man jack of the crew was drunk below. But if it *was* something more serious, then according to Discipline — not to mention good sense —I'd need to dispatch another rider just to brief him further. A man I might not want to spare."

"I see, Lord Captain."

"And Mr. Canuta?"

"Yes, sir?"

"We're a dragoon squadron in the Grain Sea, not a garrison in Maednac Serpiin. I expect my officers and men to ah, forget my nobility from time to time and just say, 'sir' or 'Captain.'"

"How often, um, sir?" asked Canuta, half-taking the hint.

"How often have you heard Harry and Tyrsen style me their 'Lord Captain?'"

Canuta's brow wrinkled. "I'm not sure I have, sir."

"About that often," Aethal smiled. He raised his voice. "Move out!"

The squadron dismounted and moved in: first Godwin's column, through the narrow gate. Aethal pursed his lips. It wasn't the work they were used to.

Inside, Aethal led his men to the left, while Farnan's slipped through town toward the Single Moon of Everview's Church where it reared up behind the town's orange grove.

Aethal led his troops down the deserted street. The last time he had visited, as a newly-made captain, children had poured out to watch the brightly-uniformed soldiers, and their parents had watched, hiding their own excitement. Now, not a chimney showed smoke, though cookstoves should have been lit all through town. Aethal inhaled the still air and tasted the faint, sickly tang of rotting food at the back of his throat.

And yet the houses were unmarked by smoke or violence, as if the owners had stepped out, and would return at any moment.

From a cross street, a sharper smell of smoke drew Aethal's attention. He faced the source.

Halfway down the street, the blacksmith's shop stood open, its half-doors swaying gently in the afternoon breeze. The modest house attached to it was as dark as any other. But a thick, unbroken ring of gray ash encircled the building, as if the smith had taken his year's supply of coal and spilled it into the hard cobble of the streets. But he hadn't stopped there. Part of the ring had cut through what had obviously been the man's own garden plot. Only the stubble of plants remained in the scorched earth.

"Sergeant," he murmured, "that cries out for some investigation."

The older man nodded. He called for two privates to accompany them. The ash was cold, and gave under Aethal's boots like fine sand. Before he ever reached the door, the faint smell of decay had told him what he would find.

There was no sign of violence in the three-room house. Aethal covered his mouth with his handkerchief before opening the bedroom door.

The blacksmith and his wife lay in their bed. He had died cradling his wife in his arms. The bodies were gaunt, skin stretched thin and yellowing over their features, rotting only slightly. Nevertheless, Aethal stayed well back.

"Plague," he whispered, his voice harsh in the still air. "Get the men out, Sergeant. We'll have to recall the men. Quarantine the town."

"Wait." Sergeant Eanling stepped forward. Although he was careful not to touch the bodies, he twitched the covers back, revealing more gaunt skin, and a small, dark stain under them. He straightened.

"That's no plague I ever saw, Captain. No sores. No puke." He sniffed. Then he went to the corner and lifted the lid of the chamber pot. "No runny guts. Hardly any piss at all, and what there is looks like that." He pointed to the dark stain. "I've seen this before, or almost. Once when we had to relieve a fort surrounded by Grassworms. We chased 'em off, and the men were so thirsty their piss was coming out like jelly. Some didn't make it. They looked like this."

Aethal blinked. "You're saying they died of thirst?" His mind raced. "Then why did they set that ring of fire?" He'd thought the burning a desperate and futile defense against disease.

"I don't know, sir," said the sergeant. "Sometimes men without food and water go crazy."

"Out in the Grain Sea, or the ocean, Sergeant. But in the middle of the town? The whole town couldn't have died of thirst." It wasn't as if the reservoirs could be dry; the land wasn't drought-stricken.

A look through the kitchen seemed only to confirm the sergeant's hypothesis. Flour, salt, even some sugar were there, but no water, wine or beer remained. Even the oil jars were dry. After warning his men to touch nothing, Aethal rejoined the squadron.

They walked on through the husk of Everview in the vanishing light.

Aethal pointed them toward the thane's house. If there were anything to be learned, here, Sindon Rawl would know – would at least have left records – of the truth of it. He was a good man.

"Body, sir!" Sergeant Eanling, at his side, pointed.

The smell hit them then. Aethal covered his nose and mouth with a scented handkerchief as he approached. What was left of the man was bloated, blackened, and growing mold. "See if you can tell what killed him, Sergeant."

Eanling nodded, bending to the corpse. It didn't take long.

"Head's broke, sir." He demonstrated, and Aethal felt his stomach turn as the sergeant gently pushed in one side of the dead man's head. One of the privates abruptly retched. *Better now than later*, Aethal thought. If he was any judge, this man had been dead a week.

A search revealed nothing in the man's pockets but petty coin, which the Sergeant pocketed. Little enough reward for the dirty job. He handed a leather pouch to Aethal. It smelled vaguely of gunpowder.

Reaching inside, Aethal removed five stubby cylinders with fins halfway up their lengths, and thick fuses, along with a metal box of matches. Signal flares, each painted in bright colors. There was red for raiders, purple for riots, orange for fire, blue for flood, and yellow for plague. Aethal allowed himself to breathe a little easier. The plague rocket had not been fired. Of course, a dead man could fire nothing.

But why would anyone kill a man for signaling plague, if there was one? Surely everyone would want help, if there was sickness.

Yet someone had killed him anyway.

"Move on," he grated.

They saw no more bodies in the deserted streets of Everview. No people at all, either dead or alive. Only lengthening shadows. Yet as they passed each house with its door ajar and its windows empty, Aethal fancied he could feel death.

Is there a dead family in each of those houses? If we looked, would we find them, also dead of thirst? Dead of plague? And would we find out why?

The scent of decay came to his nostrils. He could not say whether it came from the houses he passed, or lingered in his nose after encountering the dead flare-carrier.

In any case, Aethal had neither the time nor the men for a house-to-house search of the town. He had picked his targets based on the likelihood that the people of Everview would seek refuge there. And now the thane's residence, with its single turret and wrought-iron fence, stood before him, solemn and as empty as every other house.

The Grain Sea raiders didn't set traps, normally. Not unless they were forced to. Not unless the Royal Cavalry got lucky enough to discover one of their yurt villages and sweep down on them before they could flee. Then the Banshees might hide in the tall prairie grass in their tawny plains-wolf skins, waiting for a squadron to pause, then screaming their Word of Death, slaying all who heard them.

If Aethal were to set a trap, this is where he would set it. "Earplugs," he ordered curtly.

He pushed his own wax plugs into his ears and the world's sounds went soft and cotton-wrapped He signed to Canuta, Eanling, and two privates to follow him. The rest of the men moved into position along the fence, looking outward for any sign of ambush.

The unearthly quiet gripped him as Aethal approached the door. It was unmarked. Aethal very nearly rapped on it as though he had come for dinner, just as he had on a similar night nearly two years ago.

He pounded on the door and cried out, "Thane Sindon Rawl! His Majesty's Cavalry is come! Open, in the name of the King: we have come to help you!"

Only echoes answered. A push at the handle revealed that the door was locked and, it felt to Aethal, barred. He snapped an order, and Sergeant Eanling and the privates shattered a window.

Sergeant Eanling unbarred the door and looked Aethal in the eye. "You said you knew these people, sir?"

Aethal's heart sank. "You found them, Sergeant?"

"Not yet, sir. But we will." The sergeant sniffed, and Aethal stepped inside. Canuta followed him. Already he could smell the faint scent of decay.

The thane's house was immaculate, as it had been the last time he was there. The parlor was dark, but appointed as richly as it could be in a backwater like Everview. Aethal passed through and stepped into the dining room. He blinked.

The table was set as if for a formal dinner. For all the world as if the Rawl family had been expecting to entertain guests this evening. All that was missing was any hint of food.

"Sir," muttered Eanling. "Close quarters." Aethal saw that the sergeant and the men already had their bayonets out.

"Quite right, Sergeant." Aethal and Canuta fixed theirs, and then started up the stairs.

Before he put his hand on the brass handle of the master bedroom door, Aethal knew what he would find. But he wasn't prepared for the manner of it.

Sindon Rawl and his wife, Maris swayed from the rafters of the high-ceilinged bedroom. Below them, drenched in the dripping decay from the bodies, was a thick carpet, and a toppled, upholstered bench.

They went together, Aethal thought numbly. Hanged like criminals, the blackened and decayed bodies twisted slowly, surveying the immaculate room.

"Wellspawn!" gasped Canuta. "Who would do such a thing?"

"They did it themselves, Canuta," Aethal heard himself say. Banshees would have left them dead on the floor. Ordinary Grassworms would have cut them to ribbons. *What was so terrible that they could not face living through it?*

Aethal turned and looked down the hall that led, behind them, to the turret.

Where the nursery was.

"Come with me." His voice was hoarse.

Aethal marched down the hall and made himself open the door without thinking. It stuck, ramming into a soft, heavy load. Summoning his strength, he heaved. The body slowly gave way.

The nurse had been shot. Once, mercifully, through the head. She, too, was rotting: dead for at least a week. Behind her were three shapes, tucked into three small beds. The room smelled of decay and stale vomit. Aethal stepped into the room.

The two girls lay in their beds. Perhaps their faces had been peaceful once, but they were too decayed to know, now. Chamber pots full of vomit stood beside their beds. They had not gone quietly. Aethal turned away and looked at the boy.

Sindon Rawl's five-year old son — no, seven, now — lay calmly in his bed, facing the ceiling, just as if he were asleep. A rapturous smile suffused his face, utterly at peace with the world. As if he were just waking up to the promise of a pleasant day.

But he wasn't breathing, and his eyes stayed closed.

Behind him, one of the men swayed, close to fainting. He could hear the Sergeant growl, "Discipline, dammit," but not unkindly.

The boy's eyelid twitched.

Aethal jerked back. "Wish me dead." The oath came out of his mouth without thought. But it was still appropriate.

"Sir?" came Eanling's voice.

Aethal tried to swallow. Found he could not. Faced the big sergeant and saw, from the man's reaction, just how terrible his own face must look.

For now, he knew what had happened in Everview. Knew it with a dread certainty. He forced the words out.

"Keep the men back," he said. "Subaltern Canuta, come here."

His face pale with his own effort not to vomit, Canuta came forward.

"Sergeant, by the Discipline I charge you. Draw your pistol and cover us."

Sergeant Eanling started, so briefly no one else in the room could have seen it. Then, the big man's hand-cannon came out and leveled itself at the two officers.

"Sir?" said Canuta, his voice much higher than usual.

Aethal did not reply. He was checking his riding gloves for holes. When he was sure they were intact, he looked Canuta in the face. "I am about to hold that boy's eye open. I charge you by Discipline, Canuta, to watch carefully."

Trying not to tremble, Aethal reached down to the boy's smooth face. He spread his fingers, careful to keep his own face as far back as possible. He opened the dead boy's eye.

The eye beneath the lids was solid green, with only the pupil remaining. With the lid withdrawn, a tiny green leaf uncurled from the corner of his eye.

Lotus.

Canuta screamed. A high scream of pure terror, like a frightened child. Aethal leaped back as if his hands had been burned. The faintest scent of something delicious and springlike burst into the room. Aethal swallowed reflexively and turned away, his appetite sharpening uncontrollably as he did so.

"Stay back!" Aethal roared. Canuta did not need to be told. He stumbled back, sobbing. Aethal faced the Sergeant. He stripped off his gloves and dropped them. "There is Lotus here, Sergeant. Bear witness that I have not touched the dead."

Pale, but steady, Eanling gave the answer Discipline required. "You have not touched the dead with flesh."

"Canuta," snapped Aethal, "Bear witness. We have seen the Lotus."

The two privates, looking confused until now, gripped their rifles tightly. Canuta nodded convulsively.

"You must say it, Canuta."

"We have seen the Lotus," he whispered.

"Let our lives answer for error, and our honors for falsehood," said Aethal, completing the ritual, three centuries unused. "Now seal that door."

In an instant, they were gone, slamming the door shut on the chamber of horror.

Suddenly from below, there came the sound of pounding feet. "Aethal!" cried a voice.

"It's Lieutenant Farnan," whispered Canuta.

"Yes," Aethal said. The voice was unmistakable. But Aethal had split up his squadron in a village full of Lotus, and there was no knowing who was safe, and who was now serving as a farm for the Well-spawned plant.

"Cover the stairs," Aethal murmured to the Sergeant. He and his men took position, Aethal and Canuta behind him.

"We are upstairs, Lieutenant," Aethal called, grateful his voice didn't break. "Come and look us in the face. By Discipline we live."

"Oh, thank God-Beyond-The-World," Aethal heard his friend gasp. "By Discipline we live," he echoed. Those words had just become the literal truth.

Farnan appeared at the bottom of the stairs trailed by two of his men. They leveled their guns at him, and Aethal heard his men draw in breaths, though their own guns were also leveled at their comrades below.

Aethal met Farnan's eyes. It was a very odd feeling. Aethal and Farnan had acted out this drill a hundred times; every soldier had. And yet never in true and deadly earnest before.

"Approach and be cleared, Lieutenant," Aethal intoned.

"Approach and be cleared, sir," Farnan replied.

Under the guns of their men, the two officers walked toward one another. They stopped just out of arm's reach, studying each other's eyes for a long count of five. Farnan's brown eyes were wide and blessedly white from corner to corner.

"The lieutenant is clear," Aethal called.

"The captain is clear," Farnan replied.

The men lowered their guns.

"I take it that telling you there's Lotus in Everview would be redundant, then?" said Farnan.

Aethal let out a long, shuddering breath. "It's upstairs," he got out. "They're all dead up there." Farnan's eyes strayed to the doors beyond Aethal unwillingly, as if they were drawn by a magnet.

Farnan nodded. "I know. We found the priests. When I discovered it was here, I thought..." he trailed off. "I thought I might be too late."

"At the Church?" asked Aethal. "They told you? Do they...?" He stopped. "You said you found the priests. Dead?"

"Yes, but not farmed." Farnan jerked his chin at the ceiling. His mouth worked. "We're... we're all dead men, now, of course." The words came out tonelessly. A simple assessment of fact. They both knew it. Three hundred years ago, in an act of mad audacity, the so-called Free Republic had Wished the Lotus out of the Well in a bid to destroy the Empire of Man forever. The deadly miracle had killed both nations. Only the faraway colony of Verlaen had survived, by virtue of the ocean that had separated it from the deadly curse.

The curse that was now here.

Aethal steadied his voice by effort of will. "Perhaps not. Maednac said in the *Reascendent* that the Empire might have survived if they'd caught the infestation early enough. That's why he created the Discipline in the first place. Steady on, Lieutenant. We all need you."

Farnan nodded. "Sorry, sir. Won't happen again."

"Show me what you found," said Aethal.

They walked again through the perfectly set dining room and Aethal wondered if this was where the Rawl family had met their doom. For that was how the Green Death had been said to have spread through the Old Empire so quickly, when it was first Wished, before any had known what it was. It had spread as a culinary delicacy. Wives serving death to their husbands, mothers to their children, cooks to their masters...

The fresh air outside hit Aethal like a hammer of dizzying relief. Returning to his men at the gate, he made them go through the entire ritual of Discipline. Then he assigned pairs of guards to the front and rear gates.

"Any man who will not look you in the eye as the Discipline requires. Any man who tries to enter this house, you will shoot," he finished. "By Discipline."

"By Discipline," they answered.

Aethal then dispatched two riders to the Inn with orders for Lieutenant Godwin to abandon his search and head straight for the Church. He turned to Farnan.

"And now, Lieutenant, I charge you by Discipline to ride as fast as you can to Colonel Jeharok and bring up the rest of the Regiment."

Farnan's face went slack with a look not unlike betrayal. "Aethal, no! You said you need me here!"

"I need Jeharok and the rest of the regiment here. The Kingdom needs to know about this, and yesterday. All mankind needs it. We should have known of this at least a week ago, by the state of the corpses. But no one sent word. I can't take the chance that the word doesn't get out right now. That means you."

"Dammit, Aethal, send someone else. Canuta can..."

"Tyrsen!" said Aethal. The use of his first name brought his friend up short. "I need an officer I can trust to get through no matter what. That's you or Harry, and Harry's not here. Take two of the men. Any two. And get through. Shoot anyone you must, run from anything you must. Drop your rifle if you must, *but get the news through*! By Discipline. Or all may be lost."

Farnan's face set. Aethal could see he was still angry. But he nodded. Shouldered his rifle. "Crow and I will get through. I'll break him off in an elephant's ass if I have to."

Aethal cracked a smile he was far from feeling. "Good man. Unlikely you'll be stopped."

Farnan fixed him with an exasperated glare. "Not as unlikely as you," he said. Then he ran for the gate and the horses.

drop a rifle? Gun's thought intruded into Aethal's mind. Greater Rifles couldn't handle hyperbolic language either. No one would drop a Greater Rifle, of course, but Aethal could trust Farnan to do even that to get the word of Lotus through to the regiment.

The rest of the men marched at Aethal's word for the Church. On the top of its steeple, the silver Single Moon shone redly in the deepening twilight. Two of Farnan's men fingered their rifles nervously but steadily. They passed him through the ritual of Discipline. It was harder to see their eyes in the dimming light. Aethal ordered lanterns lit, and then passed through the door. Canuta formally "spit in the Well" through his circled fingers as they passed under the Church's Single Moon. Aethal himself put no stock in holy gestures. He wanted answers.

The Church was lit, the oil lanterns burning brightly behind the diamond lattice that composed the Single Moon chandelier at its apex. The prismatic rays lit the stone room in a dim rainbow. Everview was poorer than Aethal had thought; unable to provide a glass lamp for its cathedral. Diamond was more durable, Aethal supposed. There was a spot of lamp oil in the center of the floor.

"They overfilled the lamps," Eanling said. The aromatic oil filled the cathedral with a sweet scent. By the time they had half-crossed the room, all three men knew why. The scent of blood lay under the oil like a needle under flesh.

The office behind the Vacant Altar stood open. Aethal pushed the door wider, and entered.

The two priests, each wearing the gray robes of their office with aluminum-thread Single Moons on their backs, lay in a pool of blood, their throats cut. Beside them lay another man, in simple work tunic and breeches, likewise served. *Lay minister, perhaps?* Aethal wondered. The knife, a simple butcher's tool, handle and hilt sticky with blood, lay in the door that led to the priests' apartments. The dark red crescents of footprints led up the stairs. The soldiers followed them.

The bishop slumped at his desk; gray robes smeared with blood. His writing desk was daubed with it. His lips and tongue were black, and a cup with an old wine-stain at the bottom lay on the floor. The bishop's hand had knocked his pen off the cluttered desk, which bore witness to a life in service to the church: a waterglass inkwell, swirling in the cool of evening, a pair of miniature portraits of saints done in oil, along with a rarer artifact: a penance icon. It was knocked off its stand, a small, polished disc of obsidian with a silvered back.

It was a symbol of the fractured Moon. The penitent were to look into it and contemplate their sins. Strange for a bishop to hold one; they were supposed to be above such tools, not having sinned in years.

On the desk was a letter.

Aethal unfolded the parchment. Why had he not used the more expensive paper to commit his last thoughts to words? The letter was stained red-brown with fingerprints. Conscious drama, or a man who simply did not wish to live the additional moments that hand-washing would have needed?

"The words I would need to write a full account of the last few days would take longer than I have left. I sent Brother Godric out with the last of our green flares, but saw neither him nor the flare again. I can only assume that the Lotus, or those ensnared by it, took him. Brother Raalf did return, after hearing the last confessions of Sindon Rawl and his family. Thane Rawl was a true and good steward of the King, and did all he could, but yesterday, his son ran off. I suppose the boy couldn't understand why he had to stay indoors. By the time his mother found him, it was too late. It broke them all. Brother Raalf Spoke to God for their safe Journey. At his request, I Spoke for him in his turn, speeding him on his way. I did the same for Father Urrig and Father Ormund.

"I have fulfilled my last duty in this life, and the pen is beginning to shake. I go now upon the Great Journey. Though there be none to Speak for me, I hope my spirit may be lightened enough of guilt to ascend into Deep Heaven, where shortly, I doubt not, all such souls will join me, for there is no turning the last curse of the Well, nor is any nation of men left, save Verlaen alone.

"And so, the story of Man is ended. The Well has purged the world both of Man and his sin. Now starved of Men to worship it with Wishes, it shall be left alone forever with its Spawn in oblivion. Let my name rest there, too."

"Farewell."

Aethal swore under his breath. There was a book on the desk. He thumbed through it, but the old bishop's last entry had been eight days ago, and contained no hint of anything wrong.

Eight days ago, Lotus had appeared in quiet Everview. The Foe's Last Wish.

Aethal re-read the note: *"I sent Brother Godric out with the last of our flares, but saw neither him nor the flare again."* The flares. The man they'd found: his bag had held every color but green. Green for the Lotus. They must have killed him for it. So that no one would come and take their deadly prize away.

But then where were the killers now? If they were so desperate to keep the news from getting out, why had Aethal's squadron seen none of them? The Lotus must have ripped through the whole town. The riddle of the blacksmith and his wife, dead of thirst, seemed very clear, now. They'd lit fires to keep their neighbors away and dared not step outside, not even for water. Sindon Rawl and his family, in their big house, might have held out, except for their son. Perhaps there were others, hidden away somewhere, but he didn't dare look for them, not at dusk, without knowing where the Lotus grew. It might be in every house in town by now. It might be...

Ice water shot through Aethal's veins.

"Sergeant," he said, and his own voice amazed him with its steadiness. "Go see if the men are back from the Inn, yet."

"Yes, sir," Eanling said. He moved off, feet pounding down the stairs.

Suddenly, Canuta was at his shoulder. "Sir, are you all right? You've gone white."

Far off, from the center of town, a single shot rang out in the dead silence. Then three more. All was still. Aethal and Canuta ran downstairs.

"No word, sir," said Sergeant Eanling, as they appeared. The men were already falling in, drawn by the sound of the shots.

"Sergeant," said Aethal, mouth dry. "Get these men mounted. Lotus is growing in the Inn. The men there... may not be our men any longer."

The only sign of fear in the sergeant's face was a widening of the eyes and a tightening of his lips. But he nodded and cried out the orders to mount up. Aethal went for his own horse and swung up into the saddle.

His mind raced. Behind him he could hear sporadic gunfire from the direction of the Inn. What was happening there? He dared not guess wrong. The Lotus was too strong a weapon to fight with guns. *I should have ordered our own green flares launched. The Treeline might see them and send help. But if I do... if I do and the leafeaters see them, I'm telling them right where we are. And we know what they will do.*

Everview was a town of some five thousand souls. How many were dead? How many farmed? How many more might be here from other places, drawn by the lure of the Lotus? How many would be at the Inn?

And he'd sent a third of his force there. Were they fighting the Lotus? Or had they been taken by it already?

"Phoenix Lancers," he called. The men were quiet. Too quiet. They were as brave soldiers as a commander could ask for, but this was no battle. This was the end of the world.

"What Lieutenant Farnan told you is true. This town has been infested by Lotus. I have sent Mr. Farnan to warn Colonel Jeharok, who will come with all speed to our relief. Until then, go into no building, and touch nothing.

"I have seen the Lotus. I even scented it. I swear it by my Gun and my Name. It is just as dangerous as the Discipline teaches. But it is not so strong that men cannot resist it. If you smell it, you will be seized by hunger. Resist; it is the enemy.

"We have reason to believe that the Inn is infested. You've heard the shots, and you know that Lieutenant Godwin is there, with our comrades. They may be under attack. We will do all we can to save them, but *keep the Discipline!*

"The Lotus will turn friends to foes. There is nothing a man infested with Lotus will not say and nothing he will not do to eat more Lotus, and to spread the Lotus to you. This we know by Discipline. From this moment, every man you see, be he townsman or fellow soldier, you will give him one chance to throw down his weapons and surrender.

"If he does not obey, shoot him. Or her. Even if it is a child. A person infested by Lotus has no conscience. He has no soul. He has only the Lotus and hunger, and they will both eat you alive. Will you let them?"

"*No.*" The growl was not loud, but it was definite. Aethal wheeled, and led his squadron off.

The stars sparked overhead, and both moons rose full over the east. The Church may have taught that the Moon had fractured as a sign of man's sin, but Aethal blessed the light both of them gave, just now. He led his men toward the erratic gunfire.

The dark and deserted doorways of the houses of Everview looked like gaping mouths, but the upper floor of the Inn of Everview glowed in the dark, with strong lamplight. The lower floor was as bleak and deserted as any other building in town, and Aethal felt dread filling him.

Where are they? There should be hordes of leafeaters in this town. They couldn't all be there. But none were visible from outside the Inn. From within, there was an erratic pounding, and every so often, a shot.

"Burn it down," growled old Sergeant Eanling, in his ear.

"What?" asked Aethal.

"Burn it down. It's the Discipline. Maednac's Discipline, to burn any dwelling that's had Lotus in it." His eyes met Aethal's, and they were stone cold.

"Sergeant, those are our men in there," he said.

"They ain't ours any more. You said it yourself, sir. They belong to the Lotus."

"Or they're trapped and fighting it. We owe it to them to try."

"The Discipline says—"

"The Discipline doesn't say you burn people alive, Sergeant!"

A shattering of glass interrupted the two men. Aethal looked up. "Captain!" cried an agonized voice, barely recognizable. Is it you? Is it?"

"Harry!" shouted Aethal. Lieutenant's Godwin's wig was gone, his face bloodied, and his hair singed. "Are you hurt?"

"Stay back, my Lord! It's Lotus up here! Do you hear me? It's Lotus!"

"We're coming for you! Hold on, soldier." Godwin's mouth worked soundlessly. "You hold!" Aethal repeated. He turned to Sergeant Eanling.

"Sergeant, get us in there."

Eanling nodded. "Dismount. Bayonets." In good order, the sergeant and Corporal Edmen got their men lined up, six-man assault squads lined up opposite each of three windows. Aethal took up his position at the head of a double team going in through the wide doors. He raised Gun. "Phoenix Lancers, at double-quick time, advance." He let them march just long enough to see that they were in good formation. "Phoenix Lancers; *charge!*"

He and his men broke into a dead run. The swinging doors of the hotel exploded apart, and to his left and right came the flat crack of breaking glass and splintering wood under rifle butts. The Phoenix Lancers forced their way into the great hall of the Inn. It was a massive room, taking up half the first floor. .

Immediately, Aethal knew something was wrong. The air was stale, stinking of piss and shit and unwashed bodies, and yet under all of it a sort of heat buzzed in the abandoned room.

"Form a firing line!" shouted Aethal. His men fell into place.

Shadows emerged from the back of the Inn.

From the kitchen doors, and from the guests' halls, the men and women and children of Everview came at last. It was too dark to see their eyes, but not their mouths, spread in curious grins of unholy joy.

Then they saw the guns leveled. They were not so far gone as not to recognize them.

"They've come for the leaf!" cried a man in the front. And the crowd screamed with one, animal howl, and surged.

"Fire!" Aethal was never sure, afterward, if it had been himself or Eanling who had screamed the order.

Thirty rifles thundered as one. In the darkness, the blood splashed blackly across the faces and chests of the charging mob.

"Don't let them close!" screamed Aethal. "Reload!" The mob was screaming: in pain, in rage, in terror. He felt them, somewhere outside the drill dance of the men reloading, which calmed him as if he were part of a dance or a vast machine. They balanced on the edge of some crowd reflex, hanging between charge and rout, and only his speed at the drill would sweep them and the deadly Lotus back from his men. Infantry would already have been overwhelmed.

Aethal's men had Greater Rifles.

With fingers made steady by drill and action, Aethal's fingers moved. He shoved the trigger guard around in a twisting motion. Gun transferred the powder charge from the trigger guard into its breechblock, and then the priming pan. When Aethal twisted it back, the bullet chambered and the breechblock aligned behind it, loading the next bullet from Gun's underbarrel magazine. "Aim!" he yelled. On either side he felt rather than saw the rifles level at the stumbling mob. "Fire!"

Aethal stroked the trigger and watched his target's face explode not ten feet away. That did it. Screaming, the leafeaters broke and ran, clawing at each other for the doorways and down the halls. Nine more shots.

His men charged after them.

"No!" Aethal cried. "Stop!" But there was no stopping the squadron's headlong rush. The Phoenix Lancers slammed into the running townsfolk, goring and chopping at them with grim fury. They broke through the doors of the kitchen, trampling the dead and dying, and Aethal followed after them.

The kitchen was a mass of rotten food and mold growing on the walls. All this he sensed dimly as he scrambled after his men and the scampering Everviewers, who howled as they fled. They scrambled over benches and tables, heedless in their flight. They funneled through another door and then seemed to drop from sight.

Aethal's lead men charged down the stairs.

"No!" Aethal roared. "Don't!"

The men piled up at the head of the stairs.

look and see.

Through the pounding of his blood, Aethal watched his troops fighting, desperately, to get down the stairs into the cool, welcoming darkness.

As in a dream, Aethal called his men to rally, trying to force his shout above the piercing screams of the wounded.

Aethal knew these men. "Vaagen, Sen, Thuvin, with me," Aethal cried, naming the three nearest. They did not turn, and Aethal felt rage descend on him at their disobedience. He raised Gun...

another way, said Gun, growing heavy in his hands. *do not strike. command. you are not yourself. they are not themselves.*

Aethal shook his head and stared at his weapon. What was it saying? A Greater Rifle used those words only when its wielder was drunk, and he had never felt more sober. The rending din of battle, the stink of blood and sweat, *and a hot sweet scent, almost below the threshold of thought... what is that?*

it is not yourself.

Aethal grabbed Vaagen with his hands and turned him so they were nose to nose. "Vaagen! You're with me! Back!" For one gut-freezing moment, the man looked back into his own eyes with an animal snarl. Then he shook himself, and recognized his commander. He nodded and gripped his rifle, a soldier again. *But for how long?*

Aethal repeated this with the other two men. They leapt back from the trap and Aethal slammed it shut.

"But sir! Thorvald and Saamald are down there!"

The hot buzzing and inexplicable rage had shut off the moment Aethal had slammed the trap down. With the cold certainty of Gun's voice, Aethal knew. "They're not anymore, private," Aethal said. "They're gone." Swallowed up by the Lotus. Aethal threw the latch, and wrestled a heavy box that smelled of cheese down on top of it. "Now, with me and reform. Reform at the stairs!"

There was no way back to the front hall except over the bodies of the dead. Aethal tried not to see the twisted and mangled corpses. He heard retching behind him. In the lobby he saw the remaining men of the Phoenix Lancers gripping their rifles nervously.

"Sir," Sergeant Eanling saluted.

"How many have we lost?" Aethal asked.

"Nine, sir," said Eanling. "They disappeared down those halls."

Aethal looked down the unlit halls, littered with dead. They gaped like open throats. There was only silence on this floor. Above, a splintering, rhythmic pounding continued. But he'd lost a third of his strength already. How could he get up there?

He snatched at the earplugs he'd used to ward himself against Banshees. "Plugs," he ordered. "Up your noses. Like this." He stuffed the wax plugs up each nostril, the string that bound them together dangling before his lips like a long, u-shaped mustache. A dim part of himself knew he looked ridiculous, but that was the least of his worries.

Aethal set three men each, at the mouth of each hall. "By Discipline," he told them, "You will shoot anything that moves in that corridor." They nodded.

"Corporal Gerd," said Aethal. "Pick a man, and stay here. By Discipline, you will shoot any man on either squad who enters those halls. We cannot afford to lose any more men to Lotus. Sergeant, bring the rest of the men and follow me."

The polished hardwood stairs of the Inn were wide enough for two. Aethal and Eanling led off with Canuta and Corporal Edmen following, the rest of the men trailing in their wake, each straining to see in the gloom.

Aethal reached the landing. From the top of the stairs, the warm homey glow of oil lamps shone, just as though the carnage of the lower floor had all been a nightmare. The rhythmic pounding had stopped some time before. Aethal only noticed now.

His breathing sounded unnaturally loud in the stillness. He and Eanling reached the top of the steps.

Six women and two men of all ages lay on the couches and chairs of the small upper lounge. All were bare to the waist, the tattered remnants of skirts and trousers stained and reeking. They looked up at the visitors and smiled. Brown teeth and blackish-green, vegetable tendrils hung from their mouths.

"More visitors," the oldest woman said. "And just as sharply dressed as the last ones, too." She licked her lips with a green-stained tongue, and caressed her breasts with age-spotted hands.

Aethal felt his gorge rise, but was then suddenly yanked from behind. A strong hand pushed down on his shoulder. He had one clear glimpse of Corporal Edmen's face, rapt with ecstasy, before the man leapt at the old woman.

The earplugs he had shoved in his nose were gone.

Aethal grabbed for him with his left hand. For a moment their arms were entangled, and then Edmen's hand shot out, fingers spread, for Aethal's face, ripping his own plugs from his nostrils.

Aethal gasped.

The most delicious scent in the world reached into his very being and pulled. The top of his head spun. His vision.... did not change, but what he saw no longer mattered next to the rich scent. He just had to have a taste, and then he could get back to what had been so important a moment ago. He looked at the woman before him, and she was no longer old or hideous. That had been a trick of the light. Her smile was kind and inviting, and she was offering him

The Lotus.

Aethal hesitated.

Edmen got it first. Reflexively, he took it from her hand and ate. His features blossomed with ecstasy and filled with wisdom and dignity as Aethal watched.

see truth.

The world snapped into focus. The heady perfume was still with him, in him, calling to him, but now he could smell the rot, the piss, and the funk of the unwashed bodies. The old peasant woman had her lips locked on Edmen's and the emaciated girls behind her beckoned, winking eyes solid green with Lotus. Aethal screamed. With his second breath, he managed to modulate it into a word.

"FIRE!" Gun snapped to his shoulder and bracketed Edmen's head. At six feet away, he could see Gun's heavy slug crack through the man's skull and continue straight through the woman's like an invisible spear through a rotten melon. They fell, and six more guns spoke around Aethal, lacing the air with fire and smoke. The Lotus-infested fell, spurting gouts of blood. Instinctively, Aethal stepped forward, reloading, and clearing the way for his men to advance.

"Reload!" cried Sergeant Eanling.

"And check your Well-be-damned noseplugs!" cried Aethal, his voice coming out an octave higher than he'd meant it to, though in truth he could barely hear. Canuta stood before him, frozen in shock, eyes fixed on the mess that had been Corporal Edmen. Aethal cuffed him hard on the shoulder. "Check your nose, damn you! And reload! Sooner drink from the Well than let yourself smell that stuff!" He tasted burning powder and the warm salt-iron of blood in the air and breathed a sigh of gratitude for Gun's intervention.

Without it, he'd have leapt right after Edmen. He had no doubt.

Aethal became aware of a noise. Not a noise, his ears were still ringing, but the feel of marching feet.

"Here they come!" Sergeant Eanling's shout seemed to come through water. Then the man shouldered his own rifle and fell back, his throat ripped open by a shot fired a fraction of a second sooner.

Aethal looked up and found himself face-to-face with the uniforms of the Phoenix Lancers. A dozen of his own men, faces transfixed in a hungry, transcendent snarl, they leveled their own rifles and fired.

Slugs whistled around Aethal, and slammed into flesh behind him. He heard screams. "To me, to me, Lancers!" he heard himself screaming. "Fire at will!"

He leveled Gun and felt the Greater Rifle twist ever so slightly in his hands, placing its sights between the eyes of the nearest man, steadying him...

he's mine.

Aethal's finger stroked the trigger and the man fell back, head shattering outwards like a grenade, the men behind him screaming and clutching faces pierced by flying bone and teeth.

To his left, Aethal sensed rather than saw more of the Everviewers shambling down the cross-corridor.

"Second file, left flank, fire at will!"

The volley of shots snapped out into the foe, and they fell, screaming, but he was too busy reloading to watch. He would just have to trust them to hold the rest of the townsfolk at bay. The corridor in front of him was still packed with men, though only half of them now wore his regiment's uniforms. The rest wore civilian garb, but they charged howling just the same.

"Pour it on!" Aethal screamed, thumbed down the frizzen, and fired. Then they were too close for anything but bayonet work. The cold, hard steel in his hands stabbed out and up and into the mass of shrieking mouths and burning eyes. From the corner of his eye, Aethal saw Private Thuvin, Edmen's friend, drive his blade into a man's face, his own a rictus of terror and concentration. Dimly, a part of his mind that floated away from the breaths that filled his chest with fire, away from the sickening give of flesh beneath his bayonet, screamed and recoiled from the image of nightmare butchery. And sobbed with the knowledge that it was his own doing.

They ground forward, frozen in a timeless howl of bone and flesh. Aethal could sense the rage in the mass of the enemy *filthy peasants! no, my people!* a building-to-zenith. He met it with a rising shout of his own too fast and wordless to be called a rallying cry. But it built in his throat and he slashed through the belly of a huge man wielding a butcher's knife. And now he was at a door, a half-broken, shot-through door, standing on the bodies of the dead to reach it.

Aethal hit the door with Gun twice. "Open in the name of the Discipline!"

The door was jerked open, and Aethal found himself staring down the barrels of three rifles, and beyond them, the ice-cold gazes of Sergeant Falk and two of his men. They locked eyes with him, and Aethal knew, without question that they would shoot him where he stood. They, too, had earplugs shoved up their noses. Slowly, they stood aside, clutching their rifles like drowning men clutching branches.

On the large, double bed lay the body of a girl. A young girl, with red hair. She had been quite beautiful, before someone had slit her throat. Behind the bed, looking out the window, was Lieutenant Godwin.

"Harry," Aethal husked. "We've come."

"I know, sir. It's... this is all that's left. Of my men," Harry answered, voice hoarse.

"I know, Harry," said Aethal, keeping his voice level.

"I sent them to the cellar. To find bodies. We... we came up here. I heard her. The only sound. Crying, I thought. I thought we had found someone who could tell us everything. I went to her."

Aethal looked at the girl, her throat ripped open. An icy sensation spread through his veins.

"Harry..." he whispered.

The Lieutenant turned. "She kissed me, Aethal," he said softly, tears streaming from his bright green eyes.

The eyes that had been blue-grey this morning.

Behind him, Aethal felt Sergeant Falk step forward. "The Lieutenant brought us through, sir," he said. "He knew the Discipline. Even after he was farmed."

"Don't you believe it, Aethal," said Godwin. "They had to pull me off her. She had a leaf in her hand and I... I ate it without even knowing it. She laughed. She laughed as she fed me my own death. Wish me dead, it's so *strong*.

"I went... I went a bit mad then. I picked up Dragon, and..." He gestured at the Greater Rifle leaning against the windowsill. Its bayonet was black with blood. "He won't talk to me anymore, Aethal. The Lotus did something to me already. It's a hell of a thing when a man's weapon won't speak to him."

"Harry —"

"Tell me how you found out," Godwin said.

Aethal told him of the letter, and of finding the boy. "We were very fortunate," he finished.

"And I wasn't." Godwin's lip trembled.

Feet thudded down the corridor, one of Aethal's men pelting over the grisly carpet of bodies. "Sir, we have to go! They keep coming!" Aethal saw the panic in the man's eyes.

"All right, let's move," said Aethal. He looked at Godwin who froze. Then he picked up Dragon. Aethal saw him wince at the touch of the silent Greater Rifle. He looked up with a fierceness in his green eyes that Aethal had never seen before.

He looked Sergeant Falk in the eyes. "You heard the Captain, Sergeant. Let's carve a path. *For the!*" And he was gone, screaming down the hallway. Without hesitation, Falk was on his heels, and Aethal had to run to keep up.

Lieutenant Godwin burst into the sitting room where Aethal's men were falling back toward the stairs. He charged a man wielding a fire ax and thrust his bayonet and half Dragon's barrel through the man's chest. He fought carelessly, not even trying to block blows aimed at him. None ever came close. Sergeant Falk smashed the skull of the man next to him with his rifle butt, and whipped his bayonet around to open the throat of a third. Then a fourth. Then all of Aethal's men were rallying, driving the farmed Everviewers back, back down the cross-passage. Aethal stabbed at a cowering woman and then came to himself. "Back! Fall back and get out!" Then they were down the stairs and past Aethal's pickets, who were firing steadily down the ground-floor halls. Then out in the night air, breathing deeply of the cool breeze.

Aethal counted his men. Of the thirty he'd led in, fifteen were left. Including Sergeant Falk and one of his men.

And Lieutenant Godwin.

The rest of his men fanned out in a crescent, still holding to the Discipline. But no horde of Lotus-eaters poured from the doors of the Inn. Having chased off the intruders, they had returned, it seemed, to the overwhelming passion of the Lotus. Aethal looked at Godwin, and saw raw longing in his eyes.

"I tried," he began, then said, "I wanted to tell you not to come for us," he said. "But it wasn't their fault. My men."

"You did well, Harry," Aethal said. "We don't leave our own behind."

"Sir," said Falk, suddenly beside him. "The lieutenant was the one who figured out the nose plugs. He saved us."

"I thought," said Godwin, "that I might win myself a hero's death in that last charge, at least. Put it out of your hands."

My hands. Aethal's brain caught up with the words like a spike of dull pain. Godwin was looking him in the face.

"Aethal, I'm... I'm hungry. You've no idea how hungry I am. Please. End it."

Aethal's mouth froze on the words, *I can't*.

He had to. It was the Discipline.

Aethal closed his eyes. He felt Sergeant Falk start to speak, and raised his hand. "Sergeant, set torches, and prepare to fire the building."

"Yes, sir," Falk nodded.

"Sergeant?" Aethal and Falk looked back. Godwin was holding out Dragon, his Greater Rifle, to the big man. "I won't be needing him anymore, and you're the man who held them together up there," He jerked his chin toward the inn. "I'd like you to have him."

Slowly, the Sergeant nodded. He took the Greater Rifle and sucked in a sharp breath as the mind forged into the weapon touched him for the first time.

"Aethal, tell my parents," said Godwin.

"I swear it by my Gun and Name."

"It's not your fault, sir," Godwin said. "No one's, really. Good-bye, Aethal. I Wish you nothing."

"I Wish you nothing," Aethal echoed the ancient blessing. Godwin closed his eyes. Saliva leaked from his mouth. "Please, Aethal," he choked. "While it's still a good death."

Aethal leveled Gun at Harry's forehead. Was grateful he could trust it to aim true. He closed his eyes and stroked the trigger.

He turned, unable to watch the body of his friend, and faced his men. "The Discipline," he husked.

"The Discipline." The response was ragged and fragile as the world.

Chapter Two

18th of Spring, 312 Exodus

The sun peered over the eastern horizon of the Grain Sea, silhouetted against the burnt stumps of the buildings of Everview, just like the two previous mornings. The little window of Aethal's cell was just a chunk chopped out of the log wall of the stockade cell.

A rapping sounded at the door, and it admitted the same regimental sergeant who had placed him here. He could have been anywhere between thirty and fifty and looked as if he'd been planed out of solid steelwood. Aethal had heard him called Sergeant Ergelac. Aethal returned his salute with as much military polish as he could muster after three days of silent confinement.

"The Discipline, sir," the sergeant said.

Aethal approached. The privates behind the sergeant, their kerchiefs drawn over their noses and mouths, leveled their pistols, one at Aethal, the other at the back of their sergeant's head. Just as they had the past two days. Ergelac didn't flinch. He gazed steadily into Aethal's blue-gray eyes.

"The captain is clean," he said. Just as the past two days.

"Colonel Jeharok will see you now, sir." The three men backed away from the door, letting Aethal out into the sharp breeze that rippled the tall grass in waves on the Grain Sea, where an officer with major's insignia waited.

"How are my men?" Aethal's voice rasped with disuse, fatigue, and fear.

The Sergeant glanced at the officer.

"Your men have yet to be examined, Captain." Aethal searched the man's face for clues. He had never before met Major Jerg, Colonel Jeharok's adjutant. He was clean, his uniform well-pressed, but looked tired. He continued. "The Colonel commanded that you be the first inspected, so that he might speak with you immediately." He paused, and his blank features softened the barest fraction. "No cases of Lotus have been reported, however."

Aethal drew in a breath and even the lingering smoke tasted sweet at that news.

It had been a very long three days.

When Aethal had withdrawn the shattered remnant of his squadron from Everview, they had camped on the road, with a doubled guard on the gates. He knew he should have begun burning the town immediately, but the men were nearly fainting, and the most important thing had been to get them out and away from the charnel house of Everview's Inn.

It had been noon by the time Colonel Jeharok and his men had arrived to find Aethal and his squadron firing the town. The Phoenix Lancers' standard had flown at the horizon, and four squadrons of his own men had swept around Aethal's work parties in the deadly pincer formation he knew so well. Greater and lesser rifles had been leveled at him.

Aethal had raised his blistered hands and stepped forward.

"Speak or step forward one more pace, sir," a brother officer had said from behind a kerchief, "and you will die."

Aethal had stopped and closed his mouth.

By evening, the stockade was up, and he and his men had been herded into cells.

From that cell, Aethal had seen Colonel Jeharok, once. He had stood three feet away him and asked Aethal only exactly where the Lotus was.

By midnight, all Everview had been a bonfire.

Now Aethal walked through what had been the town, with Major Jerg accompanying him like some silent and well-dressed ghost. Aethal tried to determine which piles of stumps and ashes had been which building, but could not be certain. Whole streets of buildings had run together in black foothills of ash and rubble, and there was no way to tell where the Inn had stood, or the blacksmith's house. Or where his men had died.

Only Sindon Rawl's house was easily distinguishable. With all the buildings gone, Aethal could see it in the distance, smoldering behind its warped iron gates, its lawn razed as well. Aethal had to look beyond the town before he could see any green thing.

Green. Lotus, like all other plants, is green. Dark green, almost blackish. And silver, but on the bottom of the strangely pentagonal leaves. You'd have to have your face practically in it to notice that. And then it would be far too late. The smell of Lotus was said to be so alluring that not one person in a hundred could resist it. Aethal still broke out in cold sweat to think how close he had come in the Inn. *If I had kissed her, with Lotus in her mouth, between her teeth...*

Then he would lie burned along with Godwin and the rest of his vanished men.

Aethal was not surprised to be led to the Church. It was the only building in town that the Cavalry knew contained no Lotus. The Lesser Moon was still up, its gibbous shape sinking in the west behind the steeple.

A guard looked both of them in the eyes and admitted them. They passed through the sanctuary. The bodies and the smell of blood and decay were gone. But the morning light filtering in through the skylights did nothing to ease the thick, oppressive atmosphere.

Colonel Jeharok sat behind the bishop's desk. There was no chair for Aethal. Jeharok was a spare man, some forty-five years old. No trace of hair showed beneath his immaculate wig, but his neat mustache was pepper gray. His uniform was wrinkled and dusty. The remains of a breakfast sat on the table beside him. Aethal saluted.

Jeharok waited about five seconds before returning his salute. "My Lord Captain Paaling," he said.

"Yes, sir."

The Colonel picked up a paper on the table, and handed it to him. "This is a commendation for Lieutenant Farnan. He and his men rode faster than I would have believed possible from Everview to my headquarters. We came with all possible speed. He is a good officer."

"Thank you, sir." Jeharok frowned.

"I wish I could say the same for you, Captain."

Aethal flinched. "Sir?"

"By your own admission, Captain, you led half your men into a building infested with Lotus. Only a third of that force came out. And the upshot was that you rescued one officer and two men. The officer you shot. What the hell were you playing at, my Lord?"

"The don't leave their men behind, sir." Aethal felt his jaw set.

The Colonel's eyebrows drew down into a scowl. "Captain, since you seem disturbed at the thought of abandoning your men, consider this: there was Lotus in that building. Just what would have happened if it had taken you and your columns? I suppose the column you left at the Everview gate would then have tried to ride to *your* rescue, since that's the example you've set? A column commanded by what, a corporal? And then those fifteen men would have charged into the Inn, and been farmed in turn by the Lotus. And that would have left me, Lieutenant Farnan and *the rest of your regiment*, my Lord Captain, riding into Everview having no idea where the hell you were, or what had happened to you! That, Captain my Lord Paaling, is abandoning your men!"

Aethal looked down. There was nothing to say. Jeharok was right. Hadn't Aethal himself replayed the awful scenario every moment for the last two days, plus at least half of each night? Sergeant Eanling haunted his dreams, asking him to burn down the Inn. He asked it with blood running from his mouth, coughed up from his shattered throat.

"I submit to your Discipline, sir," he said.

Jeharok shook his head. "Submit. No son of a Lord Paramount submits. That's the trouble. You're not trained for it and your very birth is against it." He paused. "My Lord Captain, why did you join the cavalry?"

"Because I wanted to serve my king, sir," Aethal said automatically.

Jeharok looked at him with the same expression he might have given a fly in his tea. "You're the king's cousin, Aethal Paaling. Third in line for the throne. He has hundreds of captains of cavalry. Did it not occur to you that you could do far more by using the power you were given?"

"In my experience, sir, power you are given is not real power," Aethal said. And the King is older than my father; he barely knows me, "third in line for the throne" be damned. His son and my father stand between me and that stupid chair even if I was fool enough to want it.

Jeharok snorted at that, looking at Aethal with what seemed to be equal parts admiration and disgust. "You may be wiser than I gave you credit for, my Lord, if you hold to that. Nevertheless, the power you are given is often substituted for power that is earned. There are always a few sons of the nobility making their way through the military, though usually it's the younger ones, and they choose the Fleet for their adventures. They send back opinions to their relatives, who make policy with it."

"Well, we can no longer afford the luxury of such sinecures, with Lotus in the land. You and the rest of the high-born will have to leave the fighting to soldiers with both the motivation and the abilities to learn how."

Aethal went white. His fingers twitched toward the place where his saber usually hung. Serving soldiers did not fight duels. It was tradition as old as the Fall of the Empire, when Maednac had needed every man to ferry the refugees to Verlaen and establish the Kingdom. But Aethal's fury at Jeharok's casual slander of his honor and competence was far older. Primal.

Jeharok stepped back, oblivious. "As it happens, just now I have need of the power you were given, my Lord, far more than I need the small power you have earned. You will be, as from now, honorably discharged from the Cavalry."

The words hit like a rifle-butt to the stomach. "What? Sir?"

"You are discharged, my Lord," said Jeharok. "Think of it as saving me time, administratively. I have to send someone, immediately, as a courier to the King to ask for a general mobilization of the Army. I have no one better suited to get his attention. And when we do find the Lotus, your father or the king will doubtless find a reason to keep you in Maednac Serpiin and out of danger until it's over. We might as well save the tedious passing of commands back and forth over the Royal Highway. We will all have more important things to do." Jeharok sat. "Major Jerg will have the dismissal papers drawn up. You'll take the courier mounts and use the postal system. Jerg will have your pass to use those, too."

"What about the squadron, sir?"

"Lieutenant Mehr in 5th Squadron is ready for promotion. He'll handle it. Dismissed."

Aethal turned to the door, as if in a dream which he hoped would end.

"Oh, my Lord?" said Jeharok. Aethal turned. "You joined the cavalry for the wrong reasons. You were born into a position to serve the Kingdom, whether you like that position or not. Serve there. Or don't. Good day."

Aethal was signing the second of the two documents that Major Jerg had spread out on a table in the sanctuary when Farnan passed in through the door. He turned from his escort and crossed the room to Aethal. "So the Colonel has let you out at last?" he said, with a casual salute to Jerg. "I'm sorry I couldn't come see you, but he forbade even that. He actually wondered if a Lotus infection might make a person's voice more persuasive than it should be. I think he worried that you might talk me into letting you out. Well, I suppose we can't be too careful. I don't think the men will be good for much today, though, after having been in jail for the past three. Shall we appeal to him?" he asked. Then he focused on the papers Aethal was signing. "Wait a bloody minute. That's a discharge! Who's the old man discharging, at a time like this?"

"Me," said Aethal, meeting his subordinate's... no, just his friend's... eyes.

Farnan's face worked, his jaw opened and shut, and then he stared at the door. "Be damned if you are!" he roared. He took two steps toward Jeharok's inner sanctum before Aethal caught him and yanked him back.

"Don't," said Aethal, forcing his friend's face level with his own, "get yourself broken now! If I'm gone the men need you, and more than ever. You'll command them someday, and they'll need some continuity, especially now."

"Not at this price, Aethal!" whispered Farnan. "Are you as mad as he is?"

There was a dry but clear "ahem," from Major Jerg, who was watching the scene with dry distaste. Farnan ignored him. "You got word of the Lotus out of this town. Why are you discharged for that?"

Aethal looked him in the eyes. "Farnan, I lost over half the squadron."

Farnan looked down. "I know. The Colonel told me. I haven't heard it from you, though. What happened?"

Aethal told him the story. Farnan deserved to know if anyone did. Would need to know. By the time he had finished, even Major Jerg looked shaken.

"Piss in the Well, Aethal," Farnan said, finally. "But it wasn't your fault. It was Harry who..."

"Either one of us could have been Harry, Tyrsen," said Aethal. "I could have sent you to the Inn instead." And he'd thought of that, while he was imprisoned. Oh, he'd thought of that. He might have sent his oldest friend to be eaten by the Lotus. *Forgive me, Harry*, he thought. *But I'm glad I didn't.*

Farnan sat back, face going pale. "Yes, you could've," he said, numbly.

"Or gone myself. And I decided to go in after him. I was in command. So it is my fault. And Colonel Jeharok thinks I will better serve the kingdom by taking word to His Majesty and my father. And serving in the manner he thinks best. I am, after all, the Chancellor's son."

Farnan winced, knowing as well as Aethal did what the Colonel meant to say by that. He forced a grin. "Unlikely you'll do as much good there."

Aethal barked a laugh. "That's Aethal the Unlikely to you." It had been Farnan's nickname for him ever since they'd met at the age of thirteen, when he'd visited his Skysil uncles in the north. Farnan, a freeman's son, had been both delighted and scornful to discover just how closely Aethal was related to the King — and how little that would mean, once the Prince started his own family.

Then Farnan frowned savagely. "Piss in the Well, Aethal. So he's going to leave just me in charge of..." Farnan froze. Took a breath. In a quiet voice, he said, "You said I would command the squadron someday. Do I presume, then, that this is not the day I celebrate a field promotion?"

Farnan was not much younger than Aethal. A full captaincy would not have been out of the question for him. A brevet promotion in the face of his superior's abrupt relief would have been only courtesy. But Jeharok had determined otherwise, perhaps to drive home what he thought of Aethal's capabilities as an officer: even the men under his command were suspect. Aethal gave Farnan a short nod. The younger man blew out a breath. "And after he's packed you back to the Wrackberg to take up a Royal Commissionership of Nepotistic Affairs, then what does he plan to do with us?"

"Ahem!" said Major Jerg, somewhat louder. "I suggest, Lieutenant, that you ask the Colonel yourself."

Jeharok was standing in the door, one eyebrow raised. "Lieutenant? If I could trouble you for your time?" he said ominously.

Farnan rose and straightened his jacket with a rough yank. "Yes. Sir!" He came to full attention and ripped off an exaggerated salute, face set. Aethal's frustration mounted, but there was nothing he could do. Even if he were still a captain of cavalry, and not the forgotten son of Chancellor Paal House Wrackberg. He turned back to meet Major Jerg's bloodless gaze.

"See the quartermaster for your mustering-out pay, my Lord Captain. You're dismissed."

The words sank into Aethal like arrow shafts. And they struck something hard. "No," he said.

"Excuse me?" said Jerg, a little too sharply.

Aethal turned on him. "I am discharged, and no longer under your command, Major. I am Lord Wrackberg, now, and I will go where and when I damned well please." He sat, in a pose of studied insolence, on the nearest bench, watching the door. Jerg snorted, and went back to his papers.

He didn't have long to wait. The door opened, and Farnan came out, if anything, redder in the face than before, and ready to spit nails. Jeharok was behind him. He got two steps before Jeharok said, "Oh, Lieutenant." Farnan turned. Seeing it for the second time, and from this third-party perspective, Aethal felt his lip curl at the rather transparent power-trip involved in Jeharok's need to take a last parting shot.

"While I will disregard the scene out here before our conversation, in view of the shock you doubtless felt at the disruption of your chain of command, you will in the future be aware of, and exercise, proper military decorum, at all times, or I will have you broken."

"Not necessarily," drawled Aethal, from where he sat.

Jeharok paused, as if the furniture had spoken to him. "I thought I dismissed you."

"That's 'I thought I dismissed you, my Lord,' Colonel. And no, Colonel, you didn't. You discharged me. And in so doing, lost the power of dismissing me, as I have already explained to Major Jerg, here." Aethal rose, languidly, studying Jeharok's stiffening face. "Once I leave the military, I do return to the rights and privileges of House Wrackberg. Just as you suggested, Colonel." He let the barb sink home.

"Well, military decorum for the military, Colonel, but not for me. And not for Lieutenant Farnan either, I think, at least not if he doesn't want it. You see, I rather think I'll call him up."

Three faces stared at him in shock, and Aethal smiled inwardly in savage triumph. *But of course I can do that, Colonel; you hadn't reckoned with me actually* doing it, *but I can.*

In supplying the armies of the Kingdom with their manpower, the three Houses Paramount, Wrackberg, Westerend, and Skysil, were obligated to provide half of their armed strength to His Majesty's Forces. And as reciprocation for that strength, their members were permitted to recruit at will from His Majesty's forces a small number — ten apiece was tradition — of picked men for their own personal bodyguard. It was a high honor, one Aethal had never used before. He'd never expected to begin with Farnan. Or at all before his father died.

"With the Lieutenant's permission, of course," he said, and faltered, a bit. Once a man left the Royal Forces to be called up, he could never go back. Farnan looked up at Aethal as though seeing him for the first time. He was being offered a place for life — at the cost of his commission. Farnan smiled uncertainly, and then looked back at the gaping Colonel. His smile grew wider and razor-edged. "With pleasure, my Lord."

Farnan dropped to one knee before Aethal and held up his rifle. Crow was shorter than Gun by a handspan, its barrel made of blued steel. Crow's stock was of black teak, and completely smooth. Farnan had always said that if he'd tried carving his Exploits once, he'd have to keep going, and he'd wear out ten knives before he'd ever get through his first. Aethal felt a slight skin-crawling sensation through the wood. Crow knew it was not being held by its owner.

"Repeat, Tyrsen Farnan nad Skysil, liegeman of the King's: I, Tyrsen Farnan, am now called to the House of the Wrackberg. Where the House builds, I am its walls. To defend it, to shelter it, to support it, until death claim me, until the House fall, until the Well scourge the world clean."

Farnan repeated the words. Aethal handed Crow back. The words and the tradition went back to Imperial houses, long before the Empire fell and Maednac had led the Exodus. Now Aethal quoted the motto of House Wrackberg: "In Breaking, We Build."

"In Breaking, We Build," repeated Farnan, and stood, turning to face Jeharok. "Your pardon, Colonel," he said, "but I have orders to attend to."

Jeharok's face soured in disgust. "So you'll just pull a lieutenant out of my company command structure without notice, *my Lord*," he sneered the honorific. "Just as we're about to face the Lotus?"

"Yes," said Farnan blandly, "Too bad about the company's captain going the same day. Can't imagine where his Lordship got that idea, sir." For a moment Aethal thought Jeharok would strike him. Aethal intervened, stepping close to the Colonel.

"Actually, Colonel, I'm just doing exactly what you suggested," he said softly. "I'm using the position I was born to. To rule."

"You, my Lord," sneered Jeharok, "are using your ancient privileges for a spot of petty revenge on me by depriving me of a man I sorely need."

"No, I'm not," said Aethal, returning the older man's stare. "If I were doing that, I'd refuse to carry your message, make you waste another man doing it, and have my father drum you out of the cavalry. It is you, Colonel, who have forced me to this pass, so that I may have some hope of completing the service you have requested of me. One man alone can't keep going on a horse day and night the way we'll have to ride, and you know it." He searched the Colonel's face. "Or were you hoping for that?"

Jeharok straightened. "How dare you accuse me...?"

"Of using your position for a spot of petty revenge?" Aethal cut in.

Jeharok growled, "I'm not a fool, my Lord boy! Of course I planned to give you men and horses!"

"I'm sure you did," Aethal interrupted. *The kind of men I'd have least wanted with me.* "Very well, then, Colonel, give me Sergeant Falk."

"A corporal would be sufficient, surely," snapped the Colonel. "I need all my sergeants here."

"Ah, Aethal," said Farnan, "you swore *me*."

"Colonel," said Aethal, signaling Farnan to desist, "There are seven uninfected men in the world right now who have seen and smelled Lotus. I'm one, and you're getting rid of me. Subaltern Canuta and the two men with me bore witness to my discovery of the Lotus, but there was hardly a whiff of it in the air. Sergeant Falk and his men, now, were with Lieutenant Godwin. They plugged their noses and resisted the Lotus's hunger for hours, and they fought while doing it. Verlaen and its army... all mankind... need that man training them before they go out to burn the Lotus, leaf and root. They need someone who can tell them what it's like to fight that foe and win."

Jeharok looked Aethal up and down, almost as if he had never seen him before. When he spoke, it was in tones of grudging respect. "All right, my Lord. You have a point, though I could sorely use him here in that capacity. But I'm trusting you with a great deal. I'm already going to be stretched thin until your report to the King brings me reinforcements."

"Then I shall order Farnan to remain with you for now to train his replacement and report to me on your operations. After I send you the first reinforcements, he will come with all possible speed to take up his new post in my service."

Jeharok lowered his voice. "Send a lot of them, my Lord. We're in for a war the likes of which none of us has ever seen."

Aethal nodded. "The Lotus isn't the type of foe we can defeat with guns, is it, sir?" *Sir.* Military discipline died hard.

Jeharok's lips thinned. "We will defeat it with guns and we will defeat it with fire, my Lord, because the alternative is to be eaten by it. I said we will be at war and I meant it. The Grain Sea is the most fertile soil in Verlaen, and it is riddled with small communities of people who will host and spread the Lotus."

"But if we can impose the Discipline quickly enough, then perhaps..."

"How are you going to impose the Discipline on the Grassworms, my Lord?" Jeharok snapped. "Because I know only one way of doing that." Aethal paled. All this time, he'd only been thinking of the Lotus as a danger to his own people.

The Grassworms were a different story. In ones and twos, as traders and scouts, they could be useful. When they formed raiding parties, they could be deadly, and the cavalry was needed to run them off. They were a dangerous annoyance, but far too disunited to be a real threat. Until now. If there was anything the tribes of the Grain Sea were fanatic about, it was their absolute refusal to submit to the Kingdom's laws. or to give up their nomadic way of life. They laughed at the Kingdom's histories, and thought the Well to be a ridiculous superstition.

"They'll never submit to the Discipline," Aethal breathed. "And if we start burning them out, they'll unite against us. If they can."

"A war," Jeharok repeated, "The likes of which we've never seen."

Aethal nodded. "I'll send you all the men I can."

"You swear it by your Gun and Name?"

"I do. And Wish you nothing, sir."

"I Wish you nothing, my Lord. Go with all speed."

Chapter Three

20th of Spring, 312 Exodus

The horse Aethal had commandeered from the post station was strong, but slowing, with foam streaking its flanks and the dust of the King's Highway matted in its mane. Aethal knew he could not drive the animal any harder. The long climb up the foothills sapped its strength.

Looking back westward, Aethal saw the edge of the Grain Sea, its golden waves rippling in the wind. The endless prairie whose wild wheat fed Verlaen — and the Grassworms, curse them — seemed to break on the shores of darker green below, where the grasses gave way to the scrub forests of the Serpiin Range. The sun hung in the sky like a sullen coal, grudgingly giving up heat and light.

Through the fatigue of the hardest two days' ride of his life, Aethal remembered his days in the Academy, learning woodcraft and navigation by the stars from Captain Gehin. He'd said that the sun was a star, like all the others but much closer, and Aethal had imagined what it must be like to live on other worlds, beneath differently-colored suns. It was like that now, except that the red sun gave him no joy.

My world is indeed become an alien place, under a changed sun. And no matter what color its sun, it will never be the same world again.

Sergeant Falk's chestnut gelding walked past Aethal's. "Not much farther now, Sergeant," Aethal said, automatically. But if this news did encourage Falk, it was impossible to tell. He simply rode past. For the fifth time, Aethal nearly upbraided the man for ignoring an officer, and then remembered he was *not* an officer anymore.

He spoke, more to keep himself awake than for any other reason. "Have you ever seen the capital, Sergeant?" He was rewarded with a cracked laugh.

"Seen it, sir? I grew up in the Madlands. Seen all I need to of it and more."

"The Madlands? You don't sound it." Falk shrugged. Now there was a bit of a puzzle. He'd never met any trooper from the slums between Maednac Serpiin and the Sea that he couldn't pick out from the man's first sentence.

He fell in beside the Sergeant, their animals continuing the climb up the Highway. "You're an enigma, Sergeant."

Falk gave him a sidelong glance. "If that's nobles' talk for saddle-sore, I'll allow as how you have a point, my Lord."

Aethal snorted, but felt encouraged. That had been very nearly a joke, and a man who could joke wasn't nearly as burnt out as Aethal had feared.

"So, if you're from the Madlands, why aren't you in the Fleet?"

"Can't stand the fucking sea, my Lord," said Falk. Curioser, still. Maednac's Landing, where General Maednac had first declared Verlaen a kingdom in its own right, still provided housing and support for the Fleet. Through the subtle elision of years, it was now called the Madlands, and every son of the place was Fleet-mad. For most of them, the Fleet was life, a culture, and the only way out. A Madlander who hated the sea was like... well a King who hated crowns, or an Everviewer who hated grain.

The thought chilled Aethal. Will there ever be Everviewers again? A week ago, that village still stood full of our people. If only I'd had us there earlier.

foolishness. Aethal ignored Gun. Greater Rifles encouraged their masters, just as they shot straight and loaded fast for them, because they were made to. Just now Aethal wanted to be alone with his thoughts.

as my lord the philosoph desires. Aethal kicked his balky horse, into another slow walk. Aethal's eyes slid to the Greater Rifle on Falk's back. Aethal could see some of Harry's carved Exploits from here. "How is Dragon, Sergeant?"

"He's just fine, sir," the Sergeant said. Then, almost as if the words were dragged out of him: "Exact. Careful. Cold. A lot like the lieutenant was, actually."

Aethal puzzled at this. He caught an impression from Gun that was not quite a thought, implying that it was foolish to expect all Greater Rifles to behave alike. It was true, he supposed. A Greater Rifle was not assembled the way a trooper's standard rifled musket was. It was crafted as a single work, by a master gunsmith, using techniques that had been passed through generations, since the original secrets had been Wished from the Well, countless centuries ago.

The road steepened sharply here, and Aethal ceased his woolgathering. The horses that bore them strained at the grade. Finally, they reached flatter ground. Aethal heard the Sergeant's breath catch.

What had seemed to be great hilltops flanking the pass through the Serpiin Mountains were now revealed as masses of gigantic limbs, nearly solid with gray-green leaves, clustering thickly about the tops of two great trees, one on either side of the Highway. The lumpy gray trunks of the keepwoods shone in the redness of sunset. From here, the Highway wound down into the Vale of the Verlaen Basin to finish at the gates of the capital city, Maednac Serpiin itself. This was their last change of horses. In the shadow of the great trees, herdsmen went about their tasks, a couple of scullions drew water from a well, and a few men played at dice near the side of the road.

"Thought you'd seen it before, Sergeant," said Aethal.

"Bigger than I'd remembered," said Falk, simply.

Aethal nodded. No matter how often you saw the Keepwoods of the Serpent's Pass, they were bigger than you remembered. These Keepwoods were old, far bigger than those making up the Treeline on the far edge of the Grain Sea. Dark openings crossed the great swelling at the top of the trunk, where men had drilled ports. From there the branches split off and reached for the sky. Although Aethal and most of his brother officers had spent some time at this post under General Malcoor, only the most fortunate infantrymen would find themselves here. The Vale on the other side was the richest and most peaceful place in the world, thanks to the Fleet. The Royal Infantry spent its time in the Grain Sea, or garrisoning the shoreline against Weedrat raiders, and the Royal Cavalry was Verlaen's offensive arm. As Aethal watched, a lamp sprang to life in one of the lower openings of the great tree on the right.

"Why're they so much bigger here?" asked Falk.

"I don't know. They certainly weren't Wished for to be used anywhere near Verlaen. The Dark Continent is vast. Maybe Salnum's Line called them forth before it fell. The Wish-Kings certainly had enough territory to guard in those days to want them as fortresses." They urged their horses forward, past the men dicing.

Suddenly Aethal realized that these men were the perimeter guards. Even through his fatigue, cold rage descended on him for an instant, and he pictured farmed men, eyes green with Lotus, riding one by one out of the Grain Sea down into the Verlaen Basin and the Vale of Maednac Serpiin while these soldiers continued their game. *They do not know. They do not know. You are riding to make sure they will not know, or at least to make sure that the King knows first.* Aethal repeated these words to himself and cleared his throat.

The soldiers looked up, then scrambled to their feet, standing at attention. Aethal slouched on his horse while they got into line, not a difficult feat. Then he dismounted. He handed the reins to the nearest of them, a corporal with a hanging forelock.

"Stable these horses and inform the innkeep that my man and I will be needing two beds. And that dinner will also be required." The corporal took the reins automatically, but then stood mute, trembling.

"Is it possible you did not understand such simple instructions, fellow?" asked Aethal, letting his best snotty-young-lord drawl filter into his tones, "or are you considering asking the nag for her hoof in marriage?"

"There's... there's no innkeeper... my Lord..." the soldier stammered.

"What's your name, corporal?" grated Aethal.

"Dunas, my Lord."

"Sergeant Falk," said Aethal, not taking his eyes from the man, "Corporal Dunas says this isn't an inn. Do you suppose he's correct?"

"Hard to see how he could be, sir," said Falk, sliding down from his saddle. "He looks like he's at an inn. Dicing. Drinking. Are you certain you're not at an inn, Corporal?" Falk had approached to within inches of the terrified soldier's face.

"No, Sergeant!"

"Well, it is truly a shame to see these games among men not at an inn, Sergeant," said Aethal. "Do you suppose you could find some activities they might enjoy?"

"Oh, yes, milord." The smile that spread over Falk's lips recalled to Aethal his own training days, and he shuddered inwardly.

"So, Corporal Dunas," said Aethal, trying for a conversational tone that did not sound as if he'd been eating dust for two days, "before I leave you with my Master of the Revels Sergeant Falk, would you be so good as to tell me where I can find General Malcoor, so that I can — personally — tell him what a good time you weren't having?"

Dunas' eyes were bulging now. "P-Please sir. My Lord. The General... he's gone, sir. The Colonel knows, sir. We're on holiday, sir."

Aethal was nonplussed. "Holiday? What sort of holiday? What holiday excuses a military outpost from setting a guard?" And Malcoor gone? Gone where? He's been here forever. Supplying the cavalry, training the hell out of it, and not incidentally commanding the garrison: Malcoor of the Pass.

"My Lord, please. For the change of command. It was the new colonel's orders, my Lord."

Aethal shared a look with Falk, but there was no help there. The Sergeant's stare plainly said that any problem with colonels was Aethal Paaling's problem. Aethal flushed, and he found, against all odds, that his fatigue lent strength to his rage.

"You men listen to me," he said. "The holiday is over. Sergeant Falk will see you understand that. And it will be a long year indeed before ever you see another one. I have found you in breach of the Discipline here," Aethal felt a cold satisfaction when Dunas' face went whiter still, "and rest assured that if you are very fortunate, the day has come when Discipline will rule every waking hour of your lives. Carry on, Sergeant!"

Aethal had just enough time to see Falk glaring at him before he turned away and unleashed it on the men before him. "You Wellspawned greatlice, pick up your shit. Quickly!"

Aethal shut out the scurrying of the men and turned toward the great keepwoods. Anger lengthened his strides. These keepwoods were ancient, older even than the Kingdom of Verlaen, grown in the days of the Empire. Yet they were still manned against the very threat that Aethal had discovered. *The Lotus returns*, Aethal thought, *and the Discipline is crumbling. Truly the Free Republic has received its Wish. Even the Empire's ashes will fall into ruin.*

In the fading light, Aethal could see a scattering of activity beginning in his path. Had someone had been watching him and Falk? Men began issuing out of the keepwood. Out of both keepwoods. But no: they were indeed bearing tables and benches, and carrying on for all the world as if they were on holiday. Aethal knew sudden fear. *Could the Lotus have started here? Could they all be farmed?* But no Corporal Dunas certainly wasn't farmed. No greeneater cared about little things like punishment. If Dunas had been farmed, he'd have giggled at the very idea of anything except losing his precious Lotus. Or attacked. *But perhaps the officers?*

Aethal stood out of the way and watched. Watching is half of soldiering, General Malcoor had said, once. You'll have heard that no battle has ever been lost by too much firepower, and they'll be right. But no battle has ever been lost by watching the enemy too much either. That isn't said nearly enough.

The men spread out on the lawn — really a killing zone for guns from the keepwoods — with good cheer and fell to their tasks, but their voices were too loud, and in other places too quiet. And everywhere there was a sort of looking-over-the-shoulder feeling. *Like children who know the teacher's gone, but can't forget he might be back at any moment. And where are the rest of them?* When the colonel stepped out of the keepwood, Aethal spotted him instantly. With distaste, he also recognized his companion: Jeralta Stevning.

The colonel was a large, blocky man with a square face, and he was addressing his junior in the low tones of an indulgent teacher. Aethal forced himself to step out and into the Colonel's path. "Good even, Colonel," he said, saluting. "May I..." he'd been going to say *introduce myself?* but the Colonel cut him off.

"No, you may not, Captain!" the Colonel snapped, his eyes going hard. "So you must be the one chasing my men from here to the stables and back. Who are you to march in and start giving orders to my men, eh? You get out there at once and tell your man there to stand easy, or you'll regret it, I promise you!"

Aethal's rage boiled. But before he could announce that he was no longer bound by the captain's wyverns still fixed to his collar, Jeralta broke in. "Aethal! By all the horrors of the Well, man, it's good to see you. Whatever brings you so close to home?"

"Lieutenant," Aethal nodded coolly. "I believe the Colonel was speaking."

The Colonel said, "Jeralta, do you know this man?"

Jeralta's easy chatter hadn't changed. "Know him? We grew up together. His brother Aerhan, Aethal and me. Still a bit of the cold fish; doesn't surprise me. Doesn't surprise me at all. Do forgive the man, Colonel Sigrad, please. He's been long on the road and no idea you'd just taken command here."

"Aethal? You mean Captain Aethal *Paaling*?" Sigrad's eyes widened.

"Phoenix Lancers," said Aethal. He watched in amazement the transformation of the Colonel's face. It melted, but almost immediately brightened into a great smile.

"Honored to have you with us, Lord Captain! Spit in the Well, and we'll really have a celebration today. So, you're Chancellor Paal's older boy. Sorry to take your head off there, but it's never nice to see your men being ordered about without you knowing why." The man was almost babbling.

"I've ordered a feast today for the change of command," Sigrad was saying. "The king himself gave me the Pass, but I couldn't have had the post without your father's help. A feast is called for, wouldn't you say? Plus, you know how soldiers are; feed them well, and they'll die for you."

Aethal felt his lip beginning to curl. That explained the fear, then. King indeed. Sigrad has his command from my father the Chancellor and then I show up. He must feel like he's being inspected on his first day. His smile was humorless. So Father has finally decided to enjoy the flattery that comes with the job. An inspection is the last thing he'd want to happen to this fool.

Technically, Aethal didn't really have the authority to order Sigrad's corporals around. But in practical fact, a word of his in the correct ear back in the capital could probably have any number of colonels' careers crumbling in short order, if he really put his mind to it.

And if I really want to become that much like my father. Still, could the power be used for good? Not here, more's the pity. Father has a reason for this appointment.

"Lieutenant!" said Sigrad, in the tones of one struck by a fabulous idea. "Why don't you show young Aethal here up to the top chambers? Can't imagine we'll be getting anyone higher-born than him off the road unlooked-for tonight, can you?"

"My dear Colonel," said Aethal, trying to put on his best smile. "While I'm grateful for your offer of hospitality, Sergeant Falk and I cannot wait. We ride through the night on urgent business to the capital."

Sigrad's brows drew down. "Urgent business? What sort of urgent business?"

"I'm afraid I am not at liberty to say, sir. Colonel Jeharok himself ordered this." At my insistence, but he did order it. The King must be the first to know. There must not be any more panic than necessary.

"Why?"

Aethal stared. The man *was* an utter fool. Even Jeralta rolled his eyes. "I cannot say that either, Colonel, but the orders were most explicit. Now, may we be shown to your stables?"

Sigrad looked acutely flustered. "Well, that is to say, at the moment..."

"Oh, there they come now," said Jeralta brightly.

Aethal turned. Trotting up the road at a good clip, weary but in good spirits, came fifty riders with slung crossbows and spears. At the back trailed mules laden with quartered elk and boar. "The feast arrives. I wonder who won your promised copper barcque, Colonel?"

Aethal privately marked the man down as a spendthrift. Copper as a prize for foragers indeed. A prudent officer would have offered only iron.

The Colonel cleared his throat. "The Pass is treacherous after dark, Lord. I couldn't let you go off riding that way, even if we had any horses fit for such a journey. Better for you to stay here, surely. Can't be that urgent, whatever it is."

Aethal looked at the returning hunting party. "The *courier* mounts?" he heard himself say.

"Well, Captain," Sigrad said, "we had to draw lots to see who'd get to hunt today even with using all the courier mounts. Couldn't let the men down, y'see. It's not as though we expected an emergency like yours."

Of course you didn't, you fool — that's why they're called emergencies. For the first time in his life, Aethal really regretted that he was not on a mission from his father to inspect a post. *But I might be able to get your head from the old man anyway, Sigrad, for this breach of Discipline. By God, I'll try, even if it means I have to speak to him a little longer.*

"Jeralta," said Aethal. "Surely you have a horse..."

Jeralta clucked his tongue and shook his head. "Sorry, old boy. Came by coach."

"Well," said Aethal. "It seems we'll have no choice but to accept your most gracious hospitality. Lead on, Lieutenant."

Jeralta simply nodded and walked off toward the great keepwood, Aethal following. The door of the great tree hung in the natural arch formed by two flutes of the trunk, as in all keepwoods. Sergeant Falk approached Aethal, his face expressionless. "My lord," he began, "even the courier mounts..." Aethal nodded and waved him to silence.

The base of the keepwood tree was close, and sharp with the spicy smell of the kitchens, mixed with the scent of the tree itself. It brought back memories of his subaltern days, learning tactics and leadership from Malcoor. More peaceful days. Like all keepwoods, the wide stairs began on the left of the great door, hewn in shallow steps. Lesser trees had been sacrificed and sawn into planks to partition off the kitchens, the guardhouses, and the lower armory. He walked up the stairs, to...

Up to the second story of Sindon Rawl's house where Sindon and Maris looked down from the rafters. The boy, smiling, eye twitching in the shadows...

Aethal didn't notice that he had stopped until the Sergeant said, "Sir?"

He looked up and found Jeralta looking back at him, half-smirking. "Are you all right, Captain?" Aethal flushed. He was not going to have flashbacks in front of Jeralta, damn it.

Grew up together indeed. Why do old men always forget that you grow up with people other than dear friends? Jeralta had been his brother Aerhan's friend, not Aethal's, and Jeralta had not forgotten it any more than Aethal had. "Just fine, Lieutenant."

"You look tired." Jeralta continued up the stairs. "But then, you always did." He sniggered. "Your father's been very worried about you."

"How unlike him," said Aethal shortly. They crossed one of the wide platforms that interrupted the spiral of steps every quarter turn around the great tree. An old ballista stood there, pointed at the sky and unloaded, of course. Jeralta leaned on it and gazed out the firing slit.

"You know, Aethal," said Jeralta. "The trouble with you is that you haven't any proper family feeling."

"My feelings are quite proper to my family, thank you, *Lieutenant*."

"As you say, Captain," said Jeralta with a sad smile. "I can't help thinking that the person who Wished for these things," his gesture took in the keepwood, "was a singular idiot. Why on earth would anyone want the world's biggest treehouse?"

Aethal let his voice go flat. "Yes, why on earth would anyone want a self-growing, self-repairing fortress that can house a cohort of troops and withstand every siege engine short of large cannon? Speaking of which, that's what you ought to be leaning on, not that relic. Ballistae were out of date in Maednac's day."

Jeralta snorted. "Bronze for cannons, here? For what, in case all the farmers of the Grain Sea stage a revolt? Or the Grassworms finally quit squabbling and invade us?"

"Have you ever seen what a Banshee can do? In an echoing stairwell like this, a single one of their death cries might kill half the garrison. And there are a lot of farmers out there in the Grain Sea, Jeralta." *About a fifth of our people, in fact.* Aethal looked out of the firing slit onto the road twenty paces below. He was suddenly sickened by a vision of cannon loaded with canister shot pointing down onto a wave of panicked commoners crowding the road, fleeing the rumors of Lotus. Fire spouting, and men, women, children, blown to bloody rags, farmed and free alike...

He forced his voice to go light. "Well, perhaps you're right, Jeralta. I suppose you could have done better things with a Wish from the Well?"

A horrified look crossed Jeralta's face. "I? Wish from the Well? Church forbid!" Jeralta spat through circled fingers in the holy gesture of denial. "You oughtn't to say such things."

I'd never have picked Jeralta as a particularly religious man. Odd, that. Still, Jeralta had learned one lesson from history, at least. Of course, any child knew better than to actually give voice to a Wish. And yet... not everything Wished from the Well was completely evil. There were the keepwoods.

and there is me.

"Something wrong?" Jeralta asked.

"No. Gun just reminded me that the Greater Rifles came from the Well, originally."

Jeralta shuddered. "Yes, well, I've always favored the sword, myself." His hand strayed to his rapier hilt. "Anyone can pull a trigger."

Aethal felt his blood rise and his jaw tense. He stepped forward. Then it was as if his rage was being drained away somewhere. *calmly. you have a greater duty. you cannot challenge him*, Gun said. He stopped. Jeralta was looking at him... expectantly. A faint smile tinged his lips.

That insult was deliberate, thought Aethal. He wanted me to provoke him so he could offer to fight me with that little toy of his. Sigrad might even allow it, officer or not. He let his breath out. "Yes, I suppose anyone can. Swordsman, are you? Let me know when you acquire one. Rapiers are no bloody good on any battlefield." Now it was his turn to watch Jeralta's face darken. Yes, you could challenge me now, and we'll see how good you are with a pistol.

Jeralta laughed instead. "That's why I avoid them. Brutish places, more suited to the likes of him," he gestured at the Sergeant, "than a man of quality." He continued up the stairs.

The keepwood narrowed, slightly but perceptibly as they climbed. Finally, they came to the lowermost limb, a great hall of grown wood leading out from the trunk.

Jeralta turned to the first door on the left and produced a golden key from a pocket. He opened the circular door and led Aethal inside.

Aethal had been in the keepwood before, but never this room. Thirty paces long, it was shaped like a flattened egg. Unlike other rooms, it hadn't been hacked from the keepwood, but had grown naturally. Only the floor itself had been altered; carved and sanded so that there would be a flat surface to walk on. A large window looked out and slightly down from it, wide enough so that Aethal could not have touched both sides at once with his spread arms. The room was furnished with tables, chairs, even a bed carved from rough black wood that looked as if it had been hewn out of…

"Knot." Jeralta had caught him staring. "The whole room is what's left of the world's biggest knothole. Only the fixed furnishings remain of the knot itself. Took years to do, I understand."

Aethal caught the crest over the bed: a ship sailing over a line of keepwoods, underlain by a rearing serpent. In the background, a shattered, nine-point star. "Here, Jeralta, this is the royal apartments!"

"Well, dear Sigrad said the top chambers, and if the king shows up, we'll turn you out, I promise." He paused. "You might at least invite me for a drink."

Aethal hesitated. Jeralta was not his friend, but it would only be polite.

"Of course. Sergeant, secure the room." Falk saluted, and stood outside the door. Aethal set Gun and his pack by the bed, and went to the cabinet at the other end of the room. It was not made from knotwood, but it provided a selection of wines. Aethal poured and they sat.

"Malcoor used these rooms all the time, you know," said Jeralta. "His real quarters in the branch below served as his office, He just moved downstairs if the king came through. I think he may actually have had to do it twice in thirty years. His uniforms are still in the wardrobe." Jeralta waved languidly at two huge doors.

Now that Jeralta had pointed it out, Aethal could see the signs that the room had been lived in. There were ink-stains on the writing desk, and quill pens ready to be used. A number of old books filled the shelves, most of them without titles. Journals?

"Where is Malcoor, now that Colonel Sigrad has replaced him?"

"Arrested."

"Arrested?" Aethal fought to keep his jaw from dropping. "For what?"

Jeralta shrugged. "Matter of a few bribes, apparently. "You know, I never thought I'd be saying this to you, Aethal," continued Jeralta. "But I rather admire your way with people. I spend my life in the capital scene, meeting the right people, making connections. I come here on a mission from your father the Chancellor, and I don't get housed in the royal apartments. You have only to appear and mention your name, and here you are." Jeralta's gesture took in the room.

"I'm only here because Sigrad thinks I'm inspecting him for my father," Aethal said sourly.

"And all the while it's me doing that," murmured Jeralta. "Pity the poor fool, bribing the wrong man."

Aethal fixed Jeralta with a glare. "You should watch your tongue, Lieutenant."

Jeralta snorted. "Oh, yes; St. Aethal of the Horse Cavalry might report me. To whom, your father? No one else will be any good, and I fancy he knows my prices. I've been most frank with him about the subject, and he respects that." At Aethal's darkening face, Jeralta went on. "And we both know you're above such things, Aethal. You've been most tiresome about the subject. Regardless, that fool Sigrad couldn't buy a good report from me if he'd given me this room *and* filled it with whores for my own private use."

Aethal was taken aback. "I thought he was your friend."

"So does he; much good may it do him."

"If he's the fool he appears, how did the Chancellor my father come to appoint him? My father is not stupid, for all his other faults, Jeralta."

"Your father didn't appoint him. The King did. You heard Sigrad say so. And fools also have their uses, good Aethal."

"The King wouldn't have appointed him without my father's assent, which even Sigrad knows very well. And why here, for God's sake? This is a vital outpost!"

Jeralta sipped his wine and looked thoughtful. "No, the King wouldn't have appointed Sigrad without your father's *permission*, a subtle difference which I fear is lost to you. And is this such a vital outpost? We're at the heart of the Kingdom, here, guarded by the keepwoods of the Treeline and their garrisons, plus the Royal Navy, yes? Vital? Some might argue that this was the ideal place for a high-ranking fool who is wanted out of the way."

Aethal's grip on his wineglass tightened.

"Do you know something, Aethal, that the rest of us do not?" continued Jeralta. "Some danger that you're aware of? It is, after all, passing unusual to find the captain of an elite gun-cavalry battalion without his battalion, and on his way to the capital on courier mounts."

Aethal felt his blood run cold. And he'd been thinking that Jeralta was a fool. *Am I bringing old news? How is that possible?*

"What I know is for whose ears I deem it fit, Lieutenant," he said. "But now you will tell me what you know. That's the question here. Why are you here to meet me?"

"Meet you?" Jeralta drained his glass jauntily. "Sigrad may have an overlarge idea of your importance, but I certainly don't. I only know what I've told you, and, well, what small conclusions I may have drawn." *Truth, or lie?* "Even the inspection of this post was in the nature of a secondary assignment. I'm going to be doing a fast audit of every thane and petty governor from here to the Treeline over the next month: Wheatshore, Newton, Everview. By mail coach, if you please; I certainly don't."

Everview. Aethal felt his skin chill.

"However, you were mentioned." Jeralta went on, drawing a small pouch from his pocket. "The Chancellor your father asked me to deliver this to you, if I should pass by your regiment." He set the velvet pouch in front of Aethal. Warily, Aethal picked it up.

The ring that fell into his palm was light, and fashioned into a double-headed snake that clutched either side of a rounded cabochon of a deep purple. Aethal drew in his breath.

"That's aluminum and spiderpearl, you know."

"I recognize the work very well, thank you," Aethal said shortly. It was his mother's wedding ring. The finest that his father Paal could afford, and even in his youth, that had been very fine. Aluminum had been the mark of wealth even in the days of the Empire. Aethal had never known his father had kept it.

Jeralta was speaking. "Your father said that he regrets all that has passed between you. In spite of your, ah, unfortunate choices, he said, you have done well. He desires to close the old wounds between you and see you at the earliest possible moment."

"Is that what he says?"

"Get you gone to your mother's house, then, boy," Paal had said that day long ago when Aethal had presented him his commission over his uncle's signature. "I've another more apt to know where our House's power lies. Go play with your guns and horses, a little lord of thieves, and be content." Behind him, Aerhan, his brother, had looked on, grinning.

"As soon as possible," Jeralta repeated. "In fact, I also have a letter asking your colonel to grant you immediate leave to do so, but as you are apparently already going that way, it seems a waste, now."

"Indeed." Aethal allowed himself a breath. His father had not — quite — disowned him. But they had not spoken since, an arrangement with which Aethal was content. "Well, I shall see him in due course. In the King's chambers, no doubt." He pocketed the ring.

"He wanted to see you earlier than that, Aethal."

"I know what he *wants*. He has made it very clear to me. What is unclear is why he wants it. And why he's sending you all the way to Everview just now. Why is that, Jeralta?"

Jeralta's voice was easy. "My dear Aethal, if I had any other instructions from the Chancellor, I certainly wouldn't discuss them with you."

"Wouldn't you, Lieutenant?"

Jeralta looked down his nose. "No, Captain."

"Then perhaps you'd care to tell Colonel Sigrad why not?"

Jeralta yawned. "Aethal, if your captain's rank doesn't scare me by compar-ison with the Chancellor's then what makes you think that fool of a colonel's will?"

"Because, as you have just pointed out, that fool colonel with all his happy men thinks that I am here to inspect him for the Chancellor. And if, Jeralta, I tell him that you are holding back information from me that the Chancellor thinks I should know, just whom do you think he will believe?"

Jeralta frowned. "You're mad."

Aethal allowed himself a slow smile. "Am I? Even for officers, Discipline states that insubordination rates a flogging. Now, men don't like it when a flogging happens to one of their own, Jeralta, but you aren't one of these men. You're a capital dandy; just the thing for entertainment on holiday. The kind of man they'll never get to see humiliated again. I'll have Sigrad do it in public, with a whisper of how good such an egalitarian display of Discipline will be for the men's loyalty to him. What do you think he'll say?"

"You wouldn't dare." Jeralta's lips trembled.

Aethal rose. His guts churned with a vicious joy. "Really? I might do it just for fun. When you and Aerhan left me locked on the Wrackberg tower roof in high summer with no water for a day, did you think I'd forgotten?" He advanced a step. "There is much, much more that I have not forgotten, Jeralta, but I'd do it for that day alone. Now *what do you know?*"

Jeralta quivered in his chair. "He didn't tell me anything, I swear, Aethal. Just gave me the ring and asked me to give it to you if it was convenient while I was out west. Told me to look everything over, and he wanted to see you. That's all."

Aethal looked at him with a weighing stare. "Not good enough."

"God-Beyond-The-World, Aethal, please. What else can I say? You're right about Sigrad, of course: the man couldn't find his ass with both hands at noon. He's being set up to take a fall. He was picked as soon as they caught old General Malcoor out for peculation, and hauled him back to the capital for trial."

"Malcoor on trial? Since when? And for what in the Well? He's been here forever." Malcoor was almost as much of a fixture in the Pass as the keepwoods themselves, and no player in politics. He was the best instructor in the Army. "A few bribes wouldn't overthrow him; what's he supposed to have been doing?"

"Selling off those new cannon you said this place ought to have been equipped with, and more besides. The evidence was pretty damning, from what I heard. Years of it. I was sent just behind Sigrad, and he was with the arresting party just a week since."

Aethal's mind was racing. No one could have traveled faster than himself with the news of Lotus. Two days from Everview to Malcoor's Pass was faster than any normal courier would go. It might be a coincidence. It might.

"I'm sorry for everything. I really don't know anything else, not anything. I was told to get you, and that's what I'm doing. He's the Chancellor, for God's sake, what do you want from me?"

"More than this. Sergeant!" Falk entered the room. "Escort this officer downstairs. Move, Jeralta." They marched down the steps together and out into the feast, where they found Sigrad.

"Colonel," said Aethal. "This officer has been insubordinate. Could I borrow two of your men to escort him to root-level dungeons, where he is to be kept in chains? I'll decide what to do with him later."

"But..." stammered Jeralta.

"Silence!" roared Sigrad. "Yes, indeed, Captain." He pointed to the nearest table of men. "You and you. Lock Mr. Stevning in the cells under close arrest. You can come back when you're done." The men leapt to obey, and Jeralta was led away.

"Terribly sorry about that, Captain. What happened?"

"Unpleasant discussion for the table, Colonel," said Aethal smoothly, "I'll discuss it later privately, if the Colonel will permit?"

"Oh, of course, my boy," said Sigrad. "Join me, won't you? He indicated the place reserved on his right.

"Certainly, sir. Sergeant, join the men there and keep their eyes open. I mean, your eyes." Suddenly, the fatigue of the last four days hit him like a soft, heavy hammer. He couldn't do that to the man. "Oh, what am I saying? Get some rest. We might as well."

****

The moons were well up in the sky when Aethal managed to drag himself away from the table, pleading fatigue. *Ate too much*, he thought blurrily, but he'd been living on trail rations for two days, and field cookery for longer than that. At least he'd had the sense to sip his beer. He called Falk over and they walked silently to the keepwood. Aethal turned aside before the path ended and motioned the Sergeant to his side near the massive wall of the tree's trunk.

"What do you think's going on, Sergeant?"

"I don't think, sir. That's for officers," said Falk, his face a mask.

Aethal jerked his head up. "Sergeant, I asked what you thought. You're too good a soldier not to, and neither the Kingdom nor I have time for deliberate stupidity in the name of covering your ass."

"If my Lord will permit me to speak freely?"

"Speak!" Aethal growled under his breath.

"I think my Lord should watch his mouth, sir, or with respect, he will do more damage than if he simply rode through the streets shouting 'Lotus!'" whispered Falk. "Every one of those men that my Lord set me to punish this evening heard what you said about Discipline. Every one of them has a tongue. So now, there isn't a man below Colonel Sigrad that hasn't heard my Lord's words. And the stories spread. They say there's a rebellion in the Grain Sea. They say the Treeline is burning and the Grassworms are invading. Or the Weedrats have burnt the Fleet. Or Wellspawn have landed. I haven't heard anyone say Lotus yet, but all it will take is one to think of it. My Lord needs to rein in his temper and tongue."

Aethal felt a red haze boiling behind his eyes. But he had asked. "I understand, Sergeant," he finally muttered. "Thank you." He sat back, rubbing his head, thinking how nice it would be if he could smash it into the tree's stony root and put a stop to this nightmare. "I didn't hear anything similar at the officers' table."

"Sigrad wouldn't believe a ranker if he said there were two moons," said Falk, flatly. "And he's not one who'll suffer what he doesn't want to hear."

"The men say *that*, too?" asked Aethal. At Falk's nod, he continued. "What do they think of him? Is it true that Malcoor was selling off his own supplies?"

Falk slowly shook his head. "I've heard that, but I've yet to find one who believes it. Oh, some say they do. Same lickshits who suck up everywhere, trying for officers' favors. Probably tried sucking up to Malcoor when he was here, for all the good it was like to do them."

"What do you mean? That he's guilty or that he's innocent?"

"No one believes Malcoor was a thief," said Falk. "He wasn't the sort to take bribes, or steal from the Army. Oh, no, not him."

Aethal didn't believe it either. But then a light came into the Sergeant's eyes, and a cold smile just touched his lips. "But no one ever loved him enough to care, my Lord. Fact is, Captain, that even if Sigrad is an ass, they know life will be a little easier under him. Malcoor was always a hard bastard, and no one liked him."

"You either, Sergeant?" Aethal kept his tone light, but the look Falk gave him was cold. Aethal shrugged. He had admired Malcoor, but the old general had not been an easy man to like, that was true enough. Falk would hardly be the first man pleased to see a pitiless commander caught out. "Let's see if we can't assist the capital then. Considering they arrested him so quickly, they may have missed something."

The keepwood was practically deserted. They met no one on the stairs climbing the height of the trunk. Aethal took a lantern from a wall sconce and pushed the door of Malcoor's office open.

Shadows faded back to reveal a simple office, nothing more. Jeralta had been right. The room was nearly as big as the one above, if not so lavishly appointed.

All was in order, down to the map cases hung from wall pegs and reams of files, neatly arranged in cubby holes. Half the cubbies were emptied. The files in the rest had a distinctly used look to them, as if they had been pushed back hastily. The bookshelves were full, but the writing desk was empty.

"Someone's been in here, my Lord," said Falk.

Aethal nodded. "Royal Auditors." He crossed to a trunk the size of a wardrobe. In a space that could have held at least a dozen massive volumes. One remained, tunneled by bookworms. Aethal opened it to the back page. "This ledger is last dated thirty years ago. They'll have everything else. Very thorough." The sergeant shrugged. They headed up to their own room to continue their search.

"Well, they've really gone and done it," Falk said. "Arrested the old bastard. And double-quick, too."

"Why do you say that? Nothing here seems disarranged."

Falk rapped a flat, single guffaw. "Malcoor always was a neat one," he growled. "But they made him travel light." Falk threw back the doors at the narrower end of the room. Orange and-blue uniforms swayed gently in the walk-in closets, plus a few neat civilian outfits, gathering dust. Shoes and boots gleamed. "This is almost Malcoor's full kit. They marched him out of here with maybe one or two changes of clothes; one dress uniform if I'm any judge."

Aethal cast about the room, looking for anything more. "It all fits, certainly. They wouldn't have moved him off in style if they suspected him of theft." Aethal gazed at the bookshelves, stopped. There, all together, sat three books with no titles on their spines. Two were thick and squat, but the third was nearly as broad as the ledger in the trunk, despite being not a quarter so thick, and stuffed with loose parchments. Aethal took them down.

The first book was also a ledger, and at first Aethal thought he'd found some sort of evidence that the Auditors had missed, but if so, Malcoor's theft was both enormous and arcane. It resembled a bill of lading more than a ledger, though for what Aethal could not have said. An expedition, perhaps; the paper was yellow with age. It told him nothing.

The second book was more interesting, though the same age. It was a journal, but the script was so small it would be a challenge to read. He'd been about to put it back when the opening line caught his eye: "Passed the Wrackberg to the salute of Cannon — and may the little Bastard explode his own Self! Clear sailing!" *Whom does that refer to? It's not a documentary of thirty years watching the Pass, then.* Aethal pocketed it. He opened the third book to the middle.

Color leaped from every page. Aethal felt himself draw in a breath. In the dim light, blue and white chalks nearly glowed. Aethal flipped back one of the flimsy parchments that protected the page and looked down on a scene drawn by a madman.

It was a coastline, impossibly small, dominated by a green mountain impossibly huge, cast into shadow by the moons, showing low against the horizon. He turned the page. This one was painted: a ship, silhouetted against a burning mountain with red rivulets of fire running down its sides. Above the ship were stars picked out in a sort of quicksilver paint, Aethal guessed. He recognized the constellations.

"Who ever knew the old man was an artist?" asked Aethal, full of wonder. Malcoor had always been the General for him, set in the Pass specifically to drum lessons into young lieutenant heads. Experienced, wise, and even clever in his lessons, he had never been warm and always a little sour. None of this fit Aethal's picture of him. He turned the page again, and his knees gave way.

It was the first coastline, this time in broad day. The green mountain dominated the coast. And there were low shapes of trees covering the land as far as the artist could have drawn. Not so tall as keepwoods but low and at least as broad. The dark green leaves spread, casting blue chalk-shadows over golden sands. Beneath them there were gleams of silver. Nightmare vision, of Lotus triumphant.

Aethal could hear his own breathing, loud in his ears. Falk's face was white, his lips moving soundlessly. He knew what he was looking at now. The Empire, lost to the Lotus forever. *And who knew that Malcoor had ever been in the* Fleet? No, but he had used to tell stories, hadn't he, on the rare days of rest? Of the days when his father had been in the Fleet. Was this his father's work, kept out of sentiment? Aethal recognized the handwriting, though. Had seen it often enough in his time here.

"But that would mean breaking Maednac's Ban; would mean going west of the Prime..." Aethal felt cold. Maednac had long ago decreed on pain of death that none should ever again sail within sight of the lost Empire. The order had never been revoked.

If Malcoor had done that, he would be guilty of deeper treason than Verlaen had ever known. *So they discovered it and arrested him? After thirty years? Oh, and then left the evidence here?* For a wild moment, Aethal wondered if he might be seeing a confession, of a sort, by the man who had brought the Lotus, but he dismissed the idea instantly. *In thirty years, the Lotus would have covered Verlaen mile by mile, five or ten times over. Malcoor cannot be the culprit. I must be the only one who knows of these records besides him.*

Impossible: Only Aethal, Jeharok and Farnan knew of his mission to Maednac Serpiin. Yet his father had sent Jeralta to meet him. Perhaps his father had discovered Malcoor's crime as well, was even now putting Malcoor's head beneath a greatsword for treason... and thus robbing Verlaen of one of the few living men to ever have seen Lotus.

Aethal forced himself to calm down. It didn't make sense, but could it really be coincidence? *Does my father know? Does the King know already?* Why did that frighten him? It would be a great relief; it meant that they would be putting protective measures in place, tightening the Discipline.

Or it meant that Lotus might already be rampant in Maednac Serpiin.

He turned to Falk. "I had the story of Malcoor's peculation from my friend Jeralta, there. And a bit more of interest." He explained.

The sergeant nodded assent, but offered nothing. Finally, he said, "Did you get all he knows, my Lord?"

"I thought so at the time, Sergeant, but now I'm not sure. It's too much of a coincidence. We discover Lotus and ride like the wind with the news, yet we find a change of command in our path. And a man disappeared, one who has seen Lotus before." *And an offer of reconciliation from my father.*

What does he know? And how does he know it? He fingered the ring in his pouch.

The Sergeant's brows drew down. "What can go faster than courier horses?"

"Nothing I know of. I told no one about this, and I know Jeharok sealed Everview off. Could anyone have beaten us here?"

Falk snorted. "My Lord, at least three hundred people know about the Lotus right now, regardless of who you told. The regiment, for one. That news will spread whatever Jeharok does. People will come to Everview. Soldiers talk. But outriding courier horses over the Grain Sea? You couldn't draw it from the Well."

"Then there's something else we need to know," said Aethal. "Something else Jeralta hasn't told us." *And I don't believe my father sent him all this way without telling him something more.* "But if I'm right, Falk, my father may have pulled Malcoor to the capital for something more important than a mere bribery scandal. I wonder, Sergeant, if Jeralta and I may not be keeping the same secret from one another."

"No one in Maednac Serpiin could know about the Lotus, sir... unless..." he trailed off. For the first time, the big man looked scared.

"What is it, man?" snapped Aethal.

"Unless the Lotus is in Maednac's Vale, too. In the capital."

The very echo of Aethal's own thoughts. He rose, hands trembling. "We're interviewing Jeralta again. And this time, he's telling everything. Would you mind... helping me, Sergeant?" Aethal pulled his lips back from his teeth.

Falk answered, but his expression did not even hint at a smile. "With a will, sir."

"You're not going to tell me to watch my temper again?"

Falk's face closed. "My son is in the Madlands, sir. My wife. My daughters."

Aethal nodded, and led them from the room.

The dungeons were simply a part of the aptly named root cellar, more a natural cavern than anything built by man. Cells were carved into the inner wall, into the tap root of the giant tree. They were possibly the only cells in history to have no metal parts but the hinges of the doors.

Aethal, Falk, and the jailer, a ranker named Foss, walked in torchlight over the packed earth to the nearest cell.

"Were you on duty when the prisoner was brought in, Foss?" asked Aethal.

"Naw, sir. Wasn't no one. I was at the feast, too."

"Then how do you know this is him?"

Foss hauled the keys out and reached for the door. "Ain't no one else, sir. Not much you can do out here to pull real brig time. Here we go." With a squeal of damp metal, the door swung open. Aethal took the torch from Foss and stepped inside.

His first thought was that the chamberpot was full, and he almost ordered Foss to do something about it when the torchlight fell on Jeralta's face.

It was chalk-white in the torchlight, eyes bulging out, mouth agape. The body's hands clutched at its belly, but at least two loops of intestine protruded through the gaping slash. The stench filled the air. Aethal heard the wet sound of Foss being sick in the doorway.

"Hold him, Sergeant." Aethal moved closer, then jumped back with a shout. The dead man's lower lip was twitching, just the way the boy's eye had, and for a moment, Aethal nearly dropped the torch and ran screaming. *But Jeralta can't be farmed, he can't...*

A hair thin, white tendril waved between Jeralta's lip and tongue. Slowly, it lengthened, showing tiny red cilia at one end. Aethal forced himself nearer. Falk followed, dragging the gasping Foss with him.

"Dumbworm," said the Sergeant. Aethal nodded, and plucked the little parasite from Jeralta's lips. It was about twice the length of a grain of rice, but Aethal felt it squirm in his fingers.

It was another Wellspawn that had proven too useful to get rid of. The dumbworm was like a tapeworm, but introduced in the food, it would latch on behind the tongue and ooze a paralyzing toxin into the victim's voicebox. Three days' fasting could starve it to death, but until then, the victim could make no sound. The story went that some Wish-King had wanted to stop the chattering of his least-favorite wives.

"You won't have heard a thing, will you, Foss?"

His eyes wide, the ranker simply shook his head, not tearing his eyes from the corpse. "Has anyone beside us been down here since the end of the feast?"

"N... naw, sir."

"Sergeant, go upstairs to our quarters. Search our belongings thoroughly, and secure the room. Make sure that nothing is missing, and more importantly," he fixed the Sergeant with a stare, "that nothing has been added."

"Do you have an idea what I should be looking for, sir?" Falk's stare was steady, half-accusing.

"Specifically? No, Sergeant, and that frightens me more than anything else. But you know as well as I do that this is no coincidence. Someone here is watching us all. And were afraid of what Jeralta might tell us. Or they were afraid of what he might hear," he said aloud. "But I'll give them no more opportunities to ease their fears with our passing. Foss and I need to have a talk with Colonel Sigrad. I'll take the first watch when I get in and you will take the second. We leave at daybreak, understood?"

Falk saluted. "Yes, sir."

Aethal knelt beside Jeralta. He went through the man's pockets, but there was nothing of value on him; just a few copper and iron coins. He stopped on the way out to collect the man's rapier. Stevn, his father, would want that, at least. Then he braced himself for another talk with Sigrad, and stepped out into the night.

Chapter Four

21st of Spring, 312 Exodus

The noon sun shining down on Maednac Serpiin made Aethal squint. He blinked his eyes in the salt wind that blew in from Cemetery Bay, against the hot particles of sand that lately seemed to have lodged in them. Absently, he reached for his canteen and inhaled the last few drops, but the dryness hadn't left his mouth all day. It was fatigue, not at all eased by the mere half-night of sleep he'd been able to snatch under Sergeant Falk's watchful eyes. The fatigue, and more.

I have to go on. I must go on, and see my lord the King. Today I tell him that the world is ending. That the Lotus has finally come to Verlaen, after three hundred years. It didn't seem as real or as important as it had all the previous days. Fatigue, together with yesterday's events, blurred even this news somehow. Surely the end of the world should stop men murdering each other, if only for a day. Jeralta's agonized features had haunted his dreams; and seemed to float before him now. Who wanted him dead?

Verlaen Basin stretched out before Aethal and Falk like a great, half-sunken bowl. The Serpiin Mountains started out in the ocean to the north, and looped around both bay and valley in a near-perfect circle before walling off the sea again to the south. On the low hill that overlooked the bay stood the city of Maednac Serpiin.

The walls of the city were circular, as though inscribed by a compass about the hill. From their vantage on the high road, Aethal could see the streets inside:

equally spaced spokes in a wheel converging on the uneven cluster of towers at the hub. The Hydraxis, palace of the Sea Kings of Verlaen, Last Fortress of the Empire. *Like a sketch of a bomb-spider's web, spread flat on a calm sea.*

Of course, no city still standing in the world had been as carefully planned and unnaturally raised as Maednac Serpiin. When Maednac had settled here, with the remnant of the Imperial Fleet, there had been nothing more than a hillfort overlooking this superb natural harbor. Maednac had founded his capital on that fort, and on the Discipline.

There were only two gates in the city wall: one facing the sea, and one facing away. The commands Maednac had laid down rang in Aethal's head in cadence with the hoofbeats of his horse.

None shall enter the City unwatched. By Discipline we live. The gates were just broad enough to let wagons pass. A third of the city was terraced park, falling away from the Hydraxis in shallow steps.

The City shall feed its own. By Discipline we live. The gardens hadn't grown serious foodstuffs since before Aethal was born. But they could.

When Maednac had raised his city and enforced his Discipline, the sea road had stretched eastward like a ribbon down to Maednac's Landing and its docks, where the Fleet was maintained to watch for any ship that might come from the Empire, bearing refugees... or bearing Lotus.

Now the Madlands fell away from the eastern wall of the city like a river delta of housing and streets, markets and inns. Just as dirty and twice as chaotic. All the industry and population that three centuries of settlement had brought to the capital of Verlaen was spread from the city's Sea Gate to the edge of Cemetery Bay.

The sun's reflection off the golden domes of the Hydraxis hurt Aethal's eyes, and he was grateful when they descended to the level of the plain where the road turned away to make its final approach to the city's Mountain Gate.

The conversation with Sigrad last night had revealed nothing except the man's ignorance and idiocy. Even Aethal's dark hints about his father hadn't been able to keep the colonel from rousting his drunken and sleeping command out of bed and badgering them alternately with bribes and threats to find Jeralta's murderer. Falk and Aethal had probably been the only men in the keepwoods who'd even gotten half a night's sleep. Even now, Aethal was not too tired to crack a grin at the memory of the looks on the soldiers' faces when they'd been dragged from unconsciousness and forced to stand at attention before their keepwoods and listen to their commander haranguing them about loyalty and honor. *He'll be lucky if the King recalls him before he's murdered in his bed.* But even murder was unlikely to happen for at least a fortnight, since all the guards had been tripled in the two great trees.

"Jeralta said to me that even fools have their uses, Sergeant. What use do you suppose Sigrad had?"

Falk frowned. "Turning food into valuable shit, if the Captain will pardon me. What other use could he have?"

"Jeralta admitted that Sigrad was being set up to take a fall. He was also careful to point out that the King, and most emphatically not my father the Chancellor, had appointed Sigrad. And you know that Malcoor wasn't taking bribes."

There was silence. Then: "What does Lord Chancellor Paal have to do with this, sir?"

Aethal snorted. "What doesn't he have to do with it is doubtless the more relevant question. But if you're asking if I think he had Jeralta murdered..." Aethal checked himself, head spinning. *Murder Jeralta? Would he? His favorite son's best friend? In a heartbeat if he thought he needed to. I captured him, and he was obviously my father's tool. But how could my father have known he was in my power?*

Aethal made his voice level with an effort. "I don't believe him capable of that." *Or at least I won't say it aloud without better cause than I now know.* "And what could Jeralta have told me in any case?"

"Perhaps he'd told you already, sir," said Falk, "and someone didn't like it."

"Perhaps," said Aethal. *Last night you thought Jeralta knew more, and so did I.* Aethal wished Farnan were with him. Farnan knew all about Aethal's... differences... with his father. And Farnan's was a Skysil trading family; he might have had useful political insights into this bloody mess. The thought brought back the sight of the corpse, and the smell, and the crawling of the hair-thin dumbworm from the ruby-sodden lips.

Aethal shivered, even under the broad noon sun.

"Why kill the poor bastard like that, though?" Guilt crawled uneasily through his mind. There had been years, growing up with his brother and Jeralta, when the thought of Jeralta being tortured to death would have brought a fierce smile to his lips. Now that he'd seen it, he was glad he had eaten nothing.

Falk looked sidelong at him, face grim and hard as rock. When he spoke, though, it was gently. "You know he told them everything, don't you, sir?"

Surprise jerked Aethal awake, out of the dim nightmare of his thoughts. "How could he, Sergeant? You don't give a dumbworm to a man you want to talk."

Falk merely shook his head. "You can still talk with a dumbworm in you, sir. Worm only stops the voice. You can whisper and shape words all you want, and I can tell you that before he died... there was nothing he wanted more than to make it stop. Nothing anyone would have wanted."

He died because of me. Because of what I told him, or because we spoke. And now someone knows all he told me and more. Who? Farnan, get here as fast as you can. I need you. He looked at the sergeant, once again gazing blankly ahead at the road.

We work with what we have, he reminded himself. *And I need this man, who has survived the call of the Lotus. We all need him, and thousands more like him, if we're to survive.* He kicked the horse forward. Fresher than he was by far, the horse quickened its pace to a canter.

****

The Mountain Gate was three times the height of a man. It looked like a narrow slit in the white walls of the city. The corporal there barely met Aethal's eyes, not coming close to the five-second gaze that strict Discipline required. Aethal rode through the tunnel into the city. Into another world.

On either side of the main roads, water leapt up in brass fountains to the height of their heads on horseback. The scent of the cherry and apple trees filled their nostrils, and the trees themselves were covered in blossoms. Even the horses seemed to perk up, quickening their walk. The Mountain Road's cobbles cut a gentle slope through the park's careful terracing. Before them lay the Hydraxis.

At its base was a man-high wall, all that remained of the Imperial hillfort that had been Maednac's first base when he had landed, fleeing the Lotus-wracked Empire. Inside it, seven towers rose. Aethal named them in his mind. Maednac's Tower was the shortest, and the closest to the sea. Closest and tallest, the Tree King's Tower, raised by Maednac's grandson, who'd closed the Treeline to the west of the Grain Sea. Widest, and over to the left, its crenellations of truly ridiculous dimensions, squatted the Dragonmast, creation of Mad Prince Schotus, who'd sailed off to the Dark Continent to bring back dragon eggs to raise on its roof. The entire kingdom, including his father King Geoarg, had been relieved not to see him return, not least because sinking him with the Wrackberg's shore batteries would have been terribly embarrassing. Embarrassing that he'd escaped to do it at all, really. The mostly deserted keep was used as the royal storehouses.

On the other side of the Tree King's Tower was the Moonsail, where the revolving sheets of sailing material provided pumping force for the Hydraxis' artificial spring. The Ophidian, where the Royal family lived, and then the smaller East and West Towers, built and named in a less spectacular age.

Slightly below the Hydraxis and to their right, the spire of the High Temple, topped with its single moon rose from behind the trees.

Reflexively, Aethal looked down upon his left hand. The band of aluminum with its purple spiderpearl still rode there. It had been ten years since his mother had left his father, and taken vows as a Guardian of the Well, shattering House Wrackberg, and nearly taking Aethal's father from his high place at the King's right hand. The Church called divorce *breaking the moon.*

According to Church Scripture, the Moon had broken in two when Salnum sunk the Well. On that day, when Salnum perverted his Wish, God's gift to him, God had broken the Moon in two as a sign that He had abandoned ungrateful mankind to its fate. All King Salnum's people had been broken in their spirits that day, and Salnum had been King of the World. Thus, marriage was holy, symbolic of the reunion the Church preached would come at the end of all things. To dissolve marriage was to break the moon in spirit, and to become a public shame.

The end of his parents' marriage had broken far more than the moon, though. Paal Haerling House Wrackberg had been only a year older than Aethal when he had brought about his marriage to Kynthia Allyndar House Skysil. The alliance of the iron-rich Skysil northern mountains with the Wrackberg dominance of the southern ports and foundries had made for an alliance that far outstripped the power of the Lord of House Westerend who ruled the rice fields of the Delta and the western Grain Sea. It had not united the two houses, but had brought them closer than any outsider liked.

Then had come the Spider Affair, and Uncle Kaelan's death. Paal's greatest defeat. It had nearly cost him the Chancellorship. It had cost him his marriage. Aethal's mother had broken the moon, returning not to the Skysil family in place of her lost brother, but choosing instead the cloistered life of a Guardian of the Well. And Aethal had made his choice, too. He had not seen his father since joining the cavalry two years later. Perhaps he would be heir of nothing at all.

Perhaps his mother was in the Temple now, or the Abbey behind it. Or perhaps she was out beyond the Grain Sea, at one of the cloisters past the Treeline. Or perhaps she was at Sea for true, in a Tidetown, serving those who had killed her brother. Guardians cut all ties to their past lives. If they ever encountered their families or friends again, it was as supplicants and seekers of truth. It was a part of their oaths never to acknowledge them.

Behind him, Aethal heard the sergeant spit through his circled fingers. "You're a churchman, sergeant?" The symbolic spitting in the Well was a gesture to ward off its evils.

The sergeant simply tossed his head. "Man's got to believe in something, sir." His voice dropped. "Especially now." Aethal nodded, but the stare he directed at the Temple was black.

And what will the Church say of this? Aethal thought, with the sort of tired bitterness that he always associated with thoughts of God. That we should pray for deliverance from the Lotus? It didn't work for the Empire, though if I can guess how many prayers were lifted for its deliverance, God surely must have heard them. If He's worth a damn. God had never been worth much to Aethal.

The Single Moon atop the church spire shone with its aluminum coating, and Aethal snorted. He himself was now of that age where the Church began to think itself bound to send a matchmaker to arrange that he enter the state of holy matrimony in a becoming season. As son of the Lord Paramount of the Wrackberg, he could hardly be forced, but he might find himself the subject of a sermon or two. The Church taught that to refuse marriage was to refuse the unity that God intended.

And the Church teaches greed as the greatest of sins; the sin that brought the Well, but that moon is coated with enough aluminum to outfit the Phoenix Lancers for a year, or to feed a neighborhood in the Madlands for five. Aethal thought. Very ascetic of you, gentlemen. Ladies. He circled his fingers so that they framed the moon exactly, and spit with what little water was left in his mouth in the holy gesture. Men had to believe in something, though, as the sergeant said. His mother had believed in God. Verlaen had always been enough for Aethal. Of course, Paal his father seemed to get on just fine with believing in Paal, but if Aethal had wanted his father for a model, he'd have stayed here with him and Aerhan.

Their uniforms were enough to get them inside the Hydraxis' main gate. Aethal called for a groom and had their horses taken to the courier stables. At the gatehouse, they both gulped some much-needed water.

"And now we see the King. Sergeant, you've handled yourself as well as any man I've ever seen in my career. In Everview and before, at the Pass, and on the long road here."

Falk nodded. "Thank you, Captain."

Aethal drew in his breath. Every step he took brought him closer to the thing he least wanted to do. "What comes next is our most sacred duty. We will both need to testify before the King, of what we saw in Everview."

Sergeant Falk's eyes widened, but he nodded. Aethal wondered if Falk had ever seen the King before. On parade, perhaps. Of course, Discipline required that any soldier be allowed to see the King at the uttermost need. But given the penalties for the misuse of that privilege, Aethal trusted the sergeant had never had occasion to come before the King in *that* way.

Aethal had spent the last ten years of his life trying not to remember that he was the King's cousin. But Jeharok was right. It made him the ideal bearer of this news.

****

Aethal and Falk emerged from the gatehouse and walked across the courtyard. It seemed as though he could hear every echo of the clicks their boots made on the cobbles of the court, bouncing from the outer wall, from the towers of the Hydraxis.

The guards stood motionless at parade rest, gripping their rifles, breast-plates overlain by surcoats embroidered in the royal crest. Now he would speak. "Watch-Sergeant, please inform the King that his cousin, Lord Aethal Paaling must see him." If the thing could be done simply, it were best done that way.

For a moment, the Watch-Sergeant simply stared at the dusty figure in the uniform of a common cavalry captain. The King's cousins didn't usually appear with so little ceremony. Then he found his voice. "Sir — that is, my Lord — yes, sir."

He saluted, and signaled to the man opposite him, who ducked inside the door. In seconds the Watch-Sergeant was replaced, and he vanished within in his turn. The remaining guard stared past them in silence, curiosity plainly written on his face, but he was too well-trained to speak on duty. The silence seemed to stretch forever, but the Hydraxis was a big place.

The door opened, and the Watch-Sergeant appeared before them, still pale and looking shaken.

"You are bidden to come up, Captain." He led them inside the tower.

The last time Aethal had been to an audience with the King here, he had been fifteen. They had entered through the Great Sea Hall then, as if to a royal ball, but the reception had been far colder, and the event far grimmer. He and Aerhan had stood with their father before the King. Even Paal had needed a formal audience that day, for he was not there as Chancellor, but as Lord Paramount of the Wrackberg. Aethal had thought that would be the last time his family would ever be together, but when they had been shown into the throne room, his mother had not been there. Her surviving brothers had been, Uncle Falaar and Uncle Galenn. And King Paitir had told Paal that Aethal's mother, Kynthia Haerlingdar, had chosen the life of a Guardian of the Well. It was the only time Aethal remembered the King telling his father "No."

Aethal had endured the Wrackberg for two more years before writing his Uncle Falaar and receiving that letter that had parted him from his father for the last time. He assumed blood ties would drag him back from time to time. But not like this.

The Hydraxis was a massive pile of stone, its rooms connected by a maze of halls and staircases. He was aware that they had suddenly stopped. The Watch-Sergeant turned to him. "You are to wait here, my Lord." Aethal recognized the room. It was halfway up the King's Tower and its curved wall had tall windows in it. The inner wall was lined with bookshelves. Chairs and small tables, some inlaid with gaming boards, furnished the room.

Aethal put his hand on the man's shoulder as he turned to go. "The King will meet me here?"

The Sergeant bobbed nervously. "I was told you are to wait here, milord." He bowed and ducked out the door. Sergeant Falk followed the man with a hard gaze, then met Aethal's eyes.

"Something's wrong, sir?" he muttered. "That palace errand-boy is sweating."

A suspicion began to grow in Aethal's mind.

"Watch and see, Sergeant," he said grimly.

The door opened. But the man who entered the room was not the King. In fact, Aethal realized, the man who entered the room was not entirely a man. He felt Gun writhe in his mind. At the same instant he heard Falk mutter, "Wyrmguard."

The figure wore a simple house uniform of Maednac's Line. His face was blank, and hard to focus on, as if he were trying to be part of the background. But he locked eyes with Aethal. *very carefully*, said Gun. *i am no match for this.*

As if Gun's voice could be heard, the eyes of the Wyrmguard flicked over to it, and just as quickly dismissed Aethal and Gun together.

Aethal tried to hide his flinch. There were a few things from the Old Empire that Maednac should not have saved, and this was one of them, in his opinion. This man was not in possession of his gun. His gun possessed him.

There had never been many of the Wyrmguard pistols, but some had been on ships of the Fleet, and they had instantly found their way into Maednac's personal guard. They were too valuable not to use. The guns themselves had offered their services. They fought to the death, always. Their mounts' deaths. They discarded men as a man would discard a Lesser Rifle, to be used and spent.

Aethal looked again into the man's eyes. They were brown, and indescribably empty. *Is he a criminal serving a sentence, or a volunteer fanatic?* he asked himself. If the former, he would likely not be released until he was too old to serve as a guard. If the latter he would earn a knighthood at the least, with probably a Greater Rifle into the bargain, assuming he survived his ten years. Wyrmguards often did, these days. In either case, the guns would not allow the men's personalities or memories to resurface while they were wielded. The secrets of their making had been lost in the Fall, and as far as Aethal was concerned, this was an entirely good thing.

they never stop using anything, said Gun. *the wish was not a wise one.*

For almost the first time since the Presentation of Arms, when he had first received Gun and felt its thoughts slide into his own, Aethal felt the urge to stare at it. Greater Rifles didn't give opinions, at least not on anything outside of combat.

"What is your name?" Aethal said, daring to take a step nearer.

"Flintmaw, my Lord." Now Aethal could see the thing that was really speaking. The short, one-handed gun hung at the man's waist, holstered. The bright wheel of the lock mechanism glinted in the sunlight; the patterns of it sucked at his eyes. The fat, rotating cylinder of the magazine was just visible. Five shots as fast as a man could cough.

at that price you want more firepower? asked Gun. Aethal quelled the weapon with a thought. Something was wrong. "Is the king coming to meet us?" he asked the Wyrmguard.

"The Imperial Governor's whereabouts are not for me to divulge, Captain Paaling." Only the guns called the Kings of Verlaen 'Imperial Governors.' It was not that no one had ever told them of the Empire's fall. They did not seem to care; they did not stop using the titles, either.

The door opened again. Now Paal Haerling entered the room, still taller than Aethal. A black beard shot with gray fringed his chin, and his blue eyes widened upon seeing his son. Aside from those small differences, the face Aethal looked into might well have been the one he shaved every day. *Shaved until recently,* Aethal thought, remembering the week's unwanted beard gracing his face.

Three guards flanked the Chancellor. Two wore the grey-and-scarlet of House Wrackberg. Aethal recognized them. They were solid muscle and carried themselves with lazy ease. Knaad and Stren. Behind them, his father was safe from anything in the room short of Gun.

He started to speak and then came back to the present, and his waiting father.

"I was told cousin Paitir was coming to see me himself, Chancellor," he said.

"I wanted to speak with you first, Captain," said Paal, returning the formality. "I feel certain that Lord Jeralta would have made that quite clear. He must have given you the message; I can see he gave you the ring."

Aethal held the Chancellor's eyes, keeping his hand from the ring he now wore on his little finger. *Damn you for that*, he thought, forcing his hands back to his sides. *But that trick of looming over me doesn't work like it did when I was sixteen, old man.* Aloud:

"Why you sent that messenger is a good question, my Lord," replied Aethal. "A better question is how. We've been riding hard for two days to get here. How could you know that Jeralta would meet us?"

Paal gave a slight smile. "I didn't quite, Captain. Certainly not so soon as this. I wasn't expecting you for at least two more weeks."

That marches fairly well with what Jeralta said. And that's the second time you've called me Captain. There are things you don't know, then. "What's so important, then, Chancellor?" asked Aethal. "I have business with the King."

"I'd have thought Jeralta would have told you more," said Paal, a guarded expression on his face.

"So would I," said Aethal. "But as he's dead, that wasn't possible." Aerhan blanched, and Paal jerked back as if stung.

"Dead?" echoed the Chancellor. "You didn't kill him?"

"That's just what I was about to ask," rapped out Aethal, staring at his father. It wasn't true; Aethal had no reason to believe that Paal had engineered Jeralta's death, but he knew from experience that the only way to get information out of his father was to rattle him. Hard.

"What?" said Paal, clearly aghast. "I had no reason to kill the boy. I'd sent him to..." he clamped his mouth shut on the rest of the sentence. *It nearly worked*, Aethal thought. But when Paal continued, he was back in command of the situation. "I have brought you here for reasons of State, Aethal. There is much at hand in this kingdom of which you are not aware, and that by your own choice. Had you stayed here and done your duty to our House, you might know that. I could have made something of you; had you at court, made you a man of parts..."

"Or had me in a Tidetown as a smuggler, and a man *in* parts," Aethal interrupted, grinning. The shot went home, and his heart beat faster at Paal's look of fury. He should have said this long ago.

Paal raised a finger. "Don't you mock me, boy. What happened to your uncle Kaelan was none of my doing."

"Then it should have been some of your *un*doing, *Father*." Aethal's voice was flat as a gunshot. "You appointed Kaelan envoy to the Confederacy. He was there because you wanted him there. You owed him your patronage; you owed him your protection!"

"That young fool tried to smuggle out bomb-spider eggs! He knew the Weedrats worshiped them; he knew what that meant!"

"And you'd have been so disappointed in him if he'd succeeded, wouldn't you? With your own monopoly on silkwire growing in Cemetery Bay to ration as you chose?"

Paal shook his head. "The Confederacy killed Kaelan, boy. Not me. His crime. Not mine."

"Mother loved him," said Aethal. "He respected you. And you sent him to a place where they punish heresy by death. They set him in the sea with his head above water and let him die of thirst. And you did nothing."

"You think I was disloyal not to rescue him?" Paal asked. "Yes, it was my choice not to try. I might have raised an expedition to shoot him out; the Weedrats would never have been bought off. They'd have killed him before we could ever have gotten there, and we'd have had a war for nothing. A war, Aethal, and I'd have lost all I'd built up for this family over the last ten years for an incompetent boy who wanted to get rich overnight. No. I do not allow such things."

Aethal's stomach curdled with unease. "I'm supposed to believe that you sacrificed Uncle Kaelan to keep the peace?" He tried to make it sound scornful. And yet he recognized the truth in his father's words. He'd never spoken like this before. As if he regretted anything. Chancellor Paal never had regrets.

Paal nodded, as if reading his mind. "Yes, you have been a soldier, now, haven't you? You've fought the Grassworms. Perhaps you understand a bit better why I'd try at all costs to prevent a war like that. Don't you?"

Aethal said nothing, and Paal continued. "Well, your mother never did. Obviously, sending Kaelan was a mistake. If you had obeyed me and come to court as I asked, rather than letting yourself be swayed by your mother's blind grief, Aethal, you might have come to appreciate that fact a bit sooner.

"But you didn't and she didn't either. And that was your mother's choice," said Paal. "She broke the Moon, Aethal. I never wanted her to go." Something very like pain flicked across the old man's features.

"No, I'm sure you didn't," said Aethal, voice dripping scorn. "It cost you almost everything you'd built up over years, even when you had been astute enough to avoid a war. I suppose your casting me from the house and ten years of silence was my choice too, wasn't it?"

Get thee gone to thy mother's house, then, boy...

Aethal expected his father to burst into an impassioned tirade, and was surprised to see his father's face simply... fall.

"No, Aethal," said Paal, in a low voice. "That was my choice. And that, in all this damned stupid affair, was my own fault. I won't lie to you, Aethal," said his father. "I never wanted you to join the Cavalry. But I have watched you. You have served with honor; the cavalry are the sharpest sword of the Kingdom. Young men make foolish choices, and then they live with them. I won't say it wasn't a foolish choice for you to go, Aethal; but you've lived with it well.

"And then there are the foolish choices that old men make. They are of a different sort. I had hoped that I could shock you into obedience. But you're too strong for that; too stubborn. I should have seen it then as I see it now. I should like, Aethal, to be able to choose again."

Aethal found it curious that he could remain as still as a rock, while his mind pitched and spun like a storm-tossed ship. He had expected to fight his father, had done his best to fight him. He had not expected to find repentance.

"What is it you want, father?" he heard himself say.

There was an indrawn breath behind him. He turned and met Sergeant Falk's furious gaze.

"Wyrmguard!" roared the Sergeant, advancing on the man, but keeping Aethal pinned to the spot with his stare. "I, Bedar Falk, Sergeant of His Majesty's Cavalry, must speak to the King, in the Fallen Empire's Name, Upon Peril of the Well's Rising."

From the corner of his eye, Aethal saw his father staring as if a piece of furniture had spoken. Aethal knew shame, then. He had forgotten the sergeant, while he was lost in the seething storms of family history just as his father had done. Just as his father always regarded any commoner, using them as the Wyrmguard used their mounts.

But Sergeant Falk knew the words of the Discipline.

Knaad and Stren looked to Paal.

In the silence, Flintmaw's voice was weirdly bland. "Upon Peril of the Well's Rising, Sergeant, follow me to the Imperial Governor's presence." He turned and started away.

"Stop him!" cried Paal, and Aethal heard terror in his father's voice. Knaad surged forward, followed by Stren. Falk turned to face him, but suddenly, Flint-maw slid between them with fluid grace and spun, right hand out, with the pistol reversed. There was a hollow crack like a struck stone and Knaad dropped bonelessly to the floor. The pistol spun half around and cocked with a click, pointed just inches from Stren's face. Stren froze.

"No man may interfere with this. Upon peril of the Well's Rising, he sees the Imperial Governor in his own time." said the Wyrmguard.

"Aethal," grated Paal. "Stop your man. Stop him now!" The Wyrmguard retreated two steps, then turned and continued. Falk favored Aethal with a dead stare, then turned to follow. Shame washed over Aethal. *No, Sergeant. I didn't mean... I wasn't...* He whirled to face Paal. "I can't stop him, Father," said Aethal. "No man can interfere with that order; it is Maednac's decree!" *But I let you stop me.*

Paal surged forward and grabbed him by his collar. "Stop that man, boy, or never call yourself a Wrackberg again, do you hear!" Paal screamed, eyes blazing. In a deadly whisper. "It's not time! Not yet!"

Aethal wrenched free. "Not time for what?" Horror flooded through him. "What do you know, Father? What are you trying to keep secret?" Falk and the Wyrmguard strode away down the hall, retreating. *And all my honor goes with them.* "And from whom? From the King?"

Aethal felt more than saw Stren rise behind him, arms moving to grapple. He wasn't making an effort to hide it. Doubtless he remembered Aethal as he'd last seen him, a raw sixteen-year old, gawky with adolescence.

Aethal whipped Gun's butt backward into the bodyguard's knee. Stren howled and dropped, clutching his dislocated kneecap. Aethal faced his father's reddening face and stepped backward. One step. Two.

"I am a Wrackberg no more, then, Chancellor. Take what joy you can in that, because I will see that house sunk to its foundation rather than betray my people. By my Gun and my..." *my name. Mine no longer.* "By my Gun, I swear it." Aethal felt cold. Cold, and a thrill of distant satisfaction at his father's look of utter despair. Then it vanished and he was running. Running to catch up to Sergeant Falk and Flintmaw, marching toward the Royal chamber.

Chapter Five

21st of Spring, 312 Exodus

Aethal walked beside Falk, eyes cast sideways. The sergeant's face was set, jaw clenched in the manner of men facing a charge. His eyes bore straight ahead.

Before them was the cloaked back of the Wyrmguard. Aethal felt that he noticed everything in this moment. The way the man's cloak hung slightly to the left. The rise and fall of his shoulders as he walked. The tiny cracks in the stone floor. The Wyrmguard turned down a small corridor and made for a plain wooden door. Behind them, Aethal could hear his father hurrying to catch up, their steps beating an eerie counterpoint to the measured cadence of Aethal, Falk, and the Wyrmguard. Out of habit, the soldiers had long since fallen into step.

The Wyrmguard faced Falk, holding out his hands. Wordlessly, Falk surrendered Dragon and gave Gun a long stare as it remained firmly on Aethal's shoulder. But members of Houses Paramount were not only allowed, but required to bear arms in the presence of the King.

What have I done? The thought filled Aethal's mind. *It is too late to go back* followed hard on its heels. *The King will know, and that is worth even my own dishonor.* Behind them, Paal caught up, breathing hard. Flintmaw opened the door. A second Wyrmguard nodded to him and escorted them in. Aethal just had time to see the King, reclining in conversation with several others in the spacious lounge, when it spoke.

"Your Excellency. Here stands your soldier, Sergeant Bedar Falk, who must speak with you, upon Peril of the Well's Rising."

The low conversation ceased as if it had been shot through. Aethal recognized most of the people in the room. His heart caught again as a spare man in a crimson doublet raised one gray eyebrow.

Lord Vaughan of Westerend. Here. To his left, the Crown Prince Eraad, wasp-waisted and wearing a circlet over his close-cropped dark hair. He faced a girl Aethal did not know, but who echoed Vaughan's long face and aquiline nose. *Ardyth, his youngest daughter.* To their right stood the Lord Mayor of Maednac Serpiin Rolf Hlafen, dressed in turquoise silks. He had been speaking to a High Overseer of the Church with the Single Moon on his collar. And, bless the Land, Pyk Imya of Telerat. Since Kaelan's death, the Skysil family had not appeared at court, but Pyk was that family's proxy. And his brother Aerhan, who fixed eyes on Aethal and drew his lips back in a sneer.

Behind the king's chair stood another man. His eyes widened. He wore scale mail beneath a surcoat bearing the Royal crest, but carried a sword rather than a rifle across his back. Jehan *Alfing, Last Sword of Verlaen: The king's personal operative.*

King Paitir turned. *He was not so bent before,* Aethal thought dumbly. Paitir was not much older than Paal. Yet his gray beard had only wisps of red remaining in it. He looked up as a man suddenly awakened from a dream, staring at the Wyrmguard, mouth open.

"Excellency, your soldier Bedar Falk must speak with you, Upon Peril of the Well's rising," repeated the Wyrmguard. The king drew breath to speak.

"No!" shouted the Last Sword. Faster than Aethal believed possible, his sword was in his hand. "Get that traitor away from the King!" He pointed the blade at their new escort. Caliburn: kill him!"

Everyone in the room froze. Falk whirled to face the Wyrmguard, who stood motionless. The King snapped, "Jehan, what are you doing?"

Caliburn gazed steadily at Jehan Alfing. "No man may interfere with this. Not even you, Last Sword. Upon Peril of the Well's Rising, he speaks with the Imperial Governor."

The Last Sword wasted no words. His long blade flicked out and caught Sergeant Falk in the back. The old soldier cried out and fell, sprawling. But Alfing didn't stop there. He spun with the force of his blow and buried the blade in Caliburn's neck. The Wyrmguard fell like a tree.

Aethal had Gun in his hands without knowing how it had come there. He raised it to his shoulder, finger already tightening on the trigger.

Jehan Alfing's sword flowed up in a looping cut, knocking Gun's barrel aside. *Shite*, the man was fast! Thunder filled the room, and the bullet *thocked* into a wall.

The deafening peal rattled Alfing for an instant, and Gun slid its bayonet out from beneath its barrel. Aethal had no time to think of reloading. Alfing was on him. The Last Sword cut twice left and right, whipping the huge blade around like a toy. Aethal parried desperately. The blade rang off the rifle's buttplate on the first cut and buried itself deeply in the wood of the stock on the second.

For an instant, Aethal had the Last Sword's blade trapped.

Thrusting the blade aside, Aethal lashed out with a booted foot. It caught Alfing full in the stomach and he collapsed backward. The sword wrenched free. Aethal rushed forward, not daring to let his foe regain his balance. Alfing rolled, coming up on his feet just in time for Aethal's desperate lunge to drive Gun's bayonet into his chest.

The Last Sword of Verlaen looked down at himself in horror. Then he sagged and slid off the blade.

Aethal turned, dropping to his knees beside Sergeant Falk. Behind him, he heard Flintmaw charge into the room. Even the Wyrmguard looked taken aback by the speed of the slaughter. He aimed at Aethal, but did not fire. Aethal had no time for that. Sergeant Falk's face was contorted in a rictus of pain, and he fought to get his arms and legs under him. His back bled freely. "Be still, Sergeant, or you'll hurt yourself worse." Aethal ripped the man's uniform further open and stared at the wound.

It was an ugly cut, but not into the muscle. Alfing had struck with the speed of desperation, and the Sergeant's heavy wool uniform was light cloth armor. "You're going to be all right, man. Sore as hell, but all right."

A strong hand closed on Aethal's arm. "Tell. Them." The words were forced through gritted teeth.

Running feet sounded in the corridor. Two more Wyrmguard flowed into the room. One stood before the king, and the other drew its pistol and stood over Aethal. Aethal looked up into the barrel of the weapon and was very still.

"Your Excellency, are you in danger?" asked the Wyrmguard.

King Paitir's face was white as dough beneath his thin beard. The entire fight had taken less than five seconds. He staggered against his own Wyrmguard and clutched at its uniform for support. Crown Prince Eraad unfroze and rushed to his father's side. Between them, he and Aerhan helped the king to a chair.

"Jehan," the king croaked, looking at the dead man. "Why?"

Aethal's own thoughts whirled in the same question. "Tell... them!" Falk repeated. Aethal met the sergeant's burning eyes and nodded.

"Your Majesty, there is Lotus in your realm."

That quickly, the moment was over. *Now history for us divides into two parts*, thought Aethal. *The peace we knew before the Lotus, and the terrible war against it.* The Lord Mayor and the Overseer clasped their fists, knuckles pressed together, over their hearts, making the sign of the single moon. Eraad stood openmouthed. The King's knuckles whitened on the arm of his chair. When he spoke, he looked over Aethal's shoulder. "Paal. Is this true?"

Paal nodded. With effort, he spoke. "It is true."

"Your Majesty, please," said Aethal. "Call for surgeons."

The king seemed to see the man bleeding on his floor for the first time. "Yes. Yes, of course. Stand down, Wyrmguard. Fetch help."

The Wyrmguard by Aethal ran from the room. Another appeared at the door. It strode to the Last Sword's body and took the great blade from his hand.

The Last Sword was an elegant, if simple weapon. Its black hilt shone with aluminum inlay. The Wyrmguard cleaned the blade, sheathed it, and handed it to the King, who took it with nerveless fingers.

"Your Excellency," said Flintmaw. The words were utterly without inflection. "We are once more solely at your command." The King stared down at the body of his Last Sword. "Why?" he muttered again. Jehan Alfing had guarded the king for years. Why had he been willing to die to stop Falk from speaking?

He also knows — knew — about the Lotus! God-Beyond-The-World, who doesn't know?

The king, obviously.

The king's head snapped up. "Is that what this man came to tell me, Aethal? About the Lotus?"

Aethal flushed. "Yes, Sire."

The Royal Surgeon rushed in, followed by two assistants. He knelt, examining Falk, looking at his face and eyes. "He may be on the verge of shock," the man said. "We'll need to move him up to the Healing Hall. Do it."

The bearers unfolded a leather pallet and hoisted Falk out of the room.

"Spare no effort," said the King. "This man has done us great service."

The Royal Surgeon bowed acknowledgement and left.

The King looked up at Aethal and Paal, from one to the other. "Why would Jehan want to kill him? And his own Wyrmguard?"

"It can only have been to stop him from speaking," Aethal heard himself say.

"But why would anyone want to stop a warning about the Lotus?" Lord Vaughan of Westerend asked. "It's a danger to all humanity!"

"God Beyond the World," choked the Lord Mayor, his voice nearly a shriek. "Unless... unless *he* was taken by it?"

Everyone in the room except Aethal and Paal moved back a pace.

"Stop," said Aethal, raising a hand. "There's a way to sort this out."

He knelt by Jehan Alfing and stared into the dead man's eyes. They were brown, through and through.

"Remember the Discipline. The first thing to go is a man's eyes," Aethal said. "And then there's the smell. You don't forget that smell."

"How would you know?" said Aerhan.

"Because I've seen it, brother," said Aethal. "And smelled it. I was there when the Sergeant found the Lotus. Or near enough."

"Then you could be infected for all we know!"

Aethal stood perfectly still. "You know the Discipline, then. Look into my eyes, a full ten seconds. But you can ask the Sergeant. He passed through the same quarantine I did. Or send to Colonel Jeharok. His dispatches are in my pocket. They will tell you that I was clean when I left him."

"Colonel Jeharok?" Lord Vaughan's asked. "He's the colonel of the Phoenix Lancers regiment."

"Yes, my Lord, and I was captain of its first squadron."

"That's near Everview!"

"Yes, my Lord." Aethal forced himself to meet the eyes of the Lord Paramount of Westerend. "Everview is gone, my Lord."

Lord Vaughan staggered against the back of a chair, and his knuckles went white around it. "Tell me. All of it."

"Yes, my Lord. With His Majesty's permission?"

The King waved assent, and sat. They all did, except for Aethal, Lord Vaughan, and Aethal's father. As thoroughly as he could, Aethal related the events that had led to the destruction of the town. It seemed to him to go on forever. Servants came and went. Jehan Alfing's body was carried out. When Aethal finished, there was silence in the room.

Finally, the Lord of the Westerend spoke. "You..." he breathed. "Wish me live forever, Wrackberg. You slaughtered my people of Everview?"

Aethal spoke softly. "No, Lord Vaughan. *Lotus* slaughtered your people of Everview. The colonel and I only ended their enthrallment and buried them.

After they did their best to kill me and my command. I lost near half my men to them."

"It wasn't their fault!" snapped Vaughan. "The Lotus..."

"Is not an enemy you can bargain with, my Lord!" Aethal cried. He looked around at the men staring at him. "My Lords and King. While the Lotus lives, discussions of blame and fault must die. The infested tried to kill our warning along with us. They did kill others who tried to warn us, so we do not know where the Lotus came from. It's likely among the Grassworms already, and in any other towns. You don't have to tell me your people weren't weak, my Lord. I knew Sindon Rawl. He was your Lord's faithful man to the end."

Vaughan trembled and looked ill. "But if Rawl's son was farmed, then..."

Aethal nodded. "Many more may have escaped the town. Hosting Lotus." He continued. "I'm expecting Farnan, my lieutenant, back in a few days with a request for reinforcements. And news of whether Jeharok has managed to contain the infestation."

The King's voice, when he spoke, was like that of a dying man. "And is there a chance that he will?"

The words felt heavy and worthless as gold on his tongue. "Nothing short of a miracle would do that, Sire." Aethal couldn't stop himself from glancing at the High Overseer, who frowned.

"This world below, like the moon above, is riven by sin, Aethal Paaling," he sighed. "God's miracles are very few and far between, but I will pray, and the Younger will aid me. God will help us if He finds us worthy."

Younger? Aethal started, and stared the man in the face. "Your Holiness. I did not recognize you. Your pardon." Only one person was entitled to call the rest of the priesthood the Younger. This, then, was the Conversant Ilferth Simon, the Speaker With God.

"Why should you recognize me, son? We have never met that I recall. I can give your greetings to your mother, when next I see her." Aethal saw his father's face go redder, but Aethal's eyes narrowed. Shouldn't the Conversant know that his mother would be bound to ignore any such message?

Paal broke his train of thought. "And will He, Holiness?" he asked, an edge to his voice.

"Pardon me, Chancellor?" Ilferth Simon raised his eyebrows.

"Will God 'find us worthy?'" Paal repeated.

Ilferth Simon looked at him coolly. "I can only speak with God, Chancellor. I cannot alter His will. If you, or His Majesty, wish to move the heart of the Almighty, you must repent and sacrifice, as I have said."

"And you have said it very publicly, too," said Paal. "You take this news of the Green Death's sudden appearance with exceeding coolness. Truly, that arouses my... respect for your piety, Holiness. Did God tell you of this day's news?"

You damned hypocrite, thought Aethal, looking at his father. *How long have* you *known?*

Ilferth returned him a careful nod. "God gives his servants the power to do what they must, be it ever so hard. But no. It is your son who has brought us this warning, Chancellor; I knew nothing of it. Though God has left the world, still He raises up men, both to lead nations and to call them to repentance. I pray His Majesty be not too late to do both."

"All the repentance in the world didn't save the Empire, Simon," drawled Crown Prince Eraad. "King Maednac saved Verlaen." Aethal blinked. The Crown Prince was watching the Conversant with naked hatred in his gaze.

"Maednac of blessed memory was more than just a king, Lord Prince," the Conversant replied, calmly. "He was also a pious man, and stinted not in giving a son to the Church."

"Your Holiness," said the King, his voice pained. "We've been through this. I have no other sons to give you, and I am past the age where another could be thought of. Would you leave the throne of Verlaen vacant and open to contest? Is that truly the will of God?"

"I'll never be a priest. I have sworn this, on my sword and my name," growled Eraad.

"Not even to avert the disfavor of God, Your Highness?" asked the Lord Mayor, twisting his hands. "Please, do not speak so. I beg you to at least consider..."

"Enough of this," broke in Paal. "Repentance may be discussed later. In the meantime, we who do lead nations have business, Holiness. Do not let us keep you from your prayers. We must hold a council of war, against the most formidable enemy we have ever faced."

The Conversant did not move. *And if Lotus is such a formidable enemy,* thought Aethal, *what did you hope to gain by keeping news of it from the king, Father?*

"I shall stay, Chancellor. I must learn what we face, and what we plan to do about it, if I am to ask God for help in our endeavors. And who knows? Even I may be granted some useful counsel in this crisis."

Paal stepped forward. "The last 'useful counsel' I recall you giving, Holiness, was to recommend Jehan Alfing for the position of Last Sword." He gestured to the bloodstains on the floor. "Perhaps we may do without."

The Conversant drew in a sharp breath, and the Prince's face went white with fury. Paitir's eyes narrowed as well. It was obviously true, but Aethal had not known of it.

"Traitor!" Eraad cried. In two steps he crossed the room and struck the Conversant a blow in the face. The man fell back and looked up, breathing hard, blood running from his mouth. Chancellor Paal took Eraad's arm in a firm grip, and Aerhan grabbed the other.

"You dare sneak your assassin in under the guise of guarding my father?" Eraad howled. "I'll see your guts hung from the Hydraxis gates!"

"Your Highness, stop this foolishness!" snapped Paal. The Lord Mayor and Ardyth of Westerend were helping the fallen Conversant to his feet. "You will do no such thing."

Eraad jerked himself free. "And why not?" he asked. "You said it: Alfing was his man. We all saw him kill our own Wyrmguard. That's the same as an attack on the King! We'd be within our rights to execute him now for regicide."

"You would *not* be within your rights, Highness," said Paal. "The Conversant has had no trial, and we have no evidence that he has done anything except exercise woefully bad judgment."

"Then we don't execute him," breathed Eraad. "We could just say that the Wyrmguard shot him in an attempt on the King's life."

Aethal stared at the Prince and realized to his horror that Eraad was serious.

It was Ilferth Simon who broke the silence. "By all means, Your Highness. If you believe I am guilty of this monstrous crime you have imagined, then you have not only the right, but the duty before God to kill me. God will judge between us on the Day he returns."

"Your Highness can't mean this," gasped the Lord Mayor.

"Who would dare say otherwise?" grated the Prince, fixing the Lord Mayor with a deadly gaze.

"I would!" said Lord Vaughan of Westerend, rising. "As would any honorable man in this room."

"Eraad!" barked the King. "Be silent. Do you learn nothing that I teach? You degrade the honor of Maednac's Line!"

Prince Eraad purpled, but subsided. The King looked at the Conversant.

"You have my apologies for my son's unfortunate outburst, Holiness," he said.

The Conversant returned him a stony stare.

"Doubtless, Prince Eraad's suggestion was moved by his shock and anger at the revelation that his father's life had been so endangered. Indeed, any of us might share his outrage." said Paal. "Or do you feel that your recommendation was not in error, Holiness?"

Ilferth Simon gave a thin smile that did not touch his eyes. "Of course I regret the danger to His Majesty. Even more, I regret the fate that has befallen Jehan

Alfing. Death is momentary, but sin is eternal. Better to die than to fall into treason and murder. Once, I believe, he was a good man. When I recommended him, I thought him the best man. Was his soul falling into the Pit even then, or was it only after years of commanding the Wyrmguard that he was corrupted? Working with them so closely — binding men's souls into unclean Wellspawn — it cannot be good for any man. Perhaps no man could withstand it. I myself would not dare it."

"You fear and distrust the Wyrmguard a great deal, yet you suggested their commander," said Paal. "In government, we call that conflict of interest, Holiness."

The Conversant shook his head sadly. "I recommended first that Maednac's Line put the Wyrmguard away. Or better still, destroy them. That they trust in God rather than in Wellspawn. Is it not madness to fear the Lotus, and yet trust to salvation from the same unholy source?"

"Not entirely," said Aethal. The Conversant and his father broke off their debate and stared at him. So did everyone else.

"When I led my men into the Inn of Everview, it was Gun that kept me from falling to the temptation of the Lotus. And when Lieutenant Godwin fell to the Lotus, he said his Rifle would no longer speak to him. The two Wishes seem to fight one another. The Wyrmguard might be similarly immune."

The king drew in a breath, looking at Aethal like a drowning man offered a rope. "A protection against the Lotus? Cousin, if you've discovered that, you've pulled a miracle from the Well itself."

Ilferth Simon's lips tightened. "Your Majesty," he said. "In God's name, you would do very well to avoid blasphemy in such times. Miracles are from God Beyond The World. All that comes from the Well is deceit. All."

"You dare name the king a blasphemer?" barked Eraad. The Conversant smiled thinly.

"It is the duty of a Conversant to serve God, Your Highness. Certainly I do not name the king a blasphemer. But no miracles are to be found in the Well. Only enchantments, dark and subtle."

"This enchantment is singularly useful, however," said Paal. "And since you have no confidence in it, I think perhaps I had better look to appointing the Last Sword's successor."

Aethal felt a cold stab of fear. *He knew of the Lotus, and now he wants to appoint the King's own bodyguard?* Aethal spoke in a flat tone. "A good thing, Chancellor, that you do not share the Conversant's religious convictions against dealing with Wellspawn. No conflict of interest could be said to apply, since you aren't in direct line to the throne. Except for the next two years when you would be Regent until Eraad turns twenty-five."

Paal went white. "How dare you..!"

"Enough!" snapped the King. His eyes blazed and fixed on Aethal. His father's face was frozen in rage. *What are you going to do, disown me?* Ilferth Simon's own held bridled satisfaction, but the King looked at Aethal as though he were some strange creature, newly Wished from the Well. He gripped the sword that he held grounded between his knees.

"Aethal Paaling has the right of this," said the King. "And since we have more important matters to discuss, we shall end this question now. Aethal Paaling," he said, rising. "Kneel."

Aethal blinked. "Majesty?"

"Kneel, and be named the Last Sword of Verlaen."

What, *him*? Impossible.

"Sire, I must protest," said the Lord Mayor. "Aethal Paaling is terribly young for this post. It requires a seasoned warrior and a man of judgment."

"Aethal Paaling has just proven himself a better warrior and shown better judgment than his predecessor," said the King.

"Indeed he has," said Lord Vaughan of Westerend. "And no man is more ready to praise him for that than I. But he is the Chancellor's son. The conflict of interest he spoke of still applies."

"Do you question my son's honor, Westerend?" asked Paal.

I'm your son again? thought Aethal.

"Oh, no more than I question yours, Wrackberg. And no less."

"We have made our decision." said the King, his voice firm. He lifted the sword.

"Sire, I..." stammered Aethal. The victory over Alfing had been purest luck. He wasn't ready for this.

"Aethal," said the King, softly, almost pleading. "Must I argue with you as well, over how you will serve me?"

Aethal bowed his head, abashed. "Sire, no."

The King rose. "Then receive of Us, Aethal Paaling House Wrackberg, this sword, the last wielded by Maednac First King. And be thou this sword, last between the blood of the House of Maednac and its enemies. We entrust thee with Our life, no less than with Our sword. Do you accept this charge?"

"Sire, I do." He took the sword from the King. It was a hand-and-a-half sword, also called a bastard sword. Its pommel was chased with aluminum edged with copper, and three small diamonds ran along either side of the hilt. Other ornamentation there was none. Maednac had fought with this sword, not simply carried it.

"Rise, then, Aethal Paaling, Last Sword of Verlaen. We thank you. For your service that has been, and is yet to come."

Aethal stood, his breathing loud in the quiet room. He was aware of the eyes on him, and suddenly of another presence at his back. It cleared its throat. He turned, and found himself face-to-face with a Wyrmguard. "Lord Commander," it said, holding up Flintmaw. The revolver squatted in its hands, like the promise of death. "I shall return our brother to the Armory of the Thirty, and send more of us to guard his Excellency." Aethal forced himself to nod, and the

Wyrmguard left. Aethal had time to think, *I'm his — its — commander.* A wave of awe and revulsion swept him at the thought, and Gun echoed it.

"I bless you and shall pray for you, Aethal Paaling," said the Conversant, raising his hand. But his lips thinned. "That you may not be corrupted by your dealings with the accursed spawn of the Well as your predecessor was. Alas, I fear my prayer will not be heard. The Wellspawn are true to their nature, which is corruption. Guard yourself, Last Sword of Verlaen."

Aethal had never received a blessing that had felt more like a curse.

"And now, Last Sword," said the king. "Aethal Paaling, the man who has seen Lotus and survived. Who remembered Discipline in the face of worse than death. How would you lead us? How may we, too survive?"

Aethal wanted to scream. *I only brought you the news of the end of the world, Cousin Paitir! You're the King! You're supposed to know how to actually save it!* He caught his father's eye, cold and blank as the flattened sea before a storm. He did not want the King to know. Why?

"Majesty, there is no good answer," he said, after what seemed an age. "Lotus, once you've seen it and smelled it... there's nothing like it in the world. Even with Gun's help, it was a near thing. I pray Sergeant Falk survives. He endured it for hours, and he had no Greater Rifle to help him. When Colonel Jeharok sends Farnan back to us, we'll know more about where we stand," Aethal said, again feeling helplessness settling about him, a cold fog.

He met the King's eyes, staring into his. *What do you want of me, Cousin?* he almost laughed. Or screamed. He could not tell which his voice would have done, if he had spoken. He remembered the Conversant's words. *The very man whose business is miracles has told you there is no hope; why look to me?*

he desires to fight. you are the fighter here. Gun's thought slashed through Aethal's consciousness. *fighting precedes victory. you have the Wyrmguard. use it.*

Aethal shook his head to clear it, but another voice seemed to speak to him. Old General Malcoor had said, on a long-ago day at the Pass training ground:

When the battle is lost; when you are cut off without hope. When everything slides into the Well, you come down to the basics: Who is the enemy? And who are you?

"I want to know more." said Aethal, slowly, "About Lotus and how it grows. Maednac must have written something about it; the Empire cannot have fallen without any record of what their enemy was like."

Aethal looked to the seated men about him. None moved to speak. "My lords, speak, I pray you. What is known about this thing?" *I will get no help from my father; his silence is not forgiveness. The King must know of Paal's treachery, but there's no proof.* Aethal looked to the Conversant. "Holiness, we know at least that the Lotus is Wellspawn, and one of the worst to infect our world. Surely the Church has studied these things, knows something of them?"

The Conversant spoke with a cold calm. "The Church is devoted to the worship of God, Last Sword of Verlaen. It studies how best to serve Him. The spawn of the Well are the province of men, who brought forth the Well out of their desire to possess the power of God. They are our punishment, and a well-deserved one, for our sin. We desired God's power more than God, and He has left us.

"When Salnum, the King of the World, reigned in the Far North, all mankind lived together, under God. And God loved his creation so much, that on the anniversary of his succession, God came to Salnum, as one man might speak with another and granted Salnum a Wish. God bound Himself to do whatever the King would ask. And not only for himself, but for all the people of Earth.

"And what did Salnum do with that Wish, my lords? Did he ask for wisdom? Or righteousness? No. He might have asked for these things. Or he might at least have asked for riches or abundant harvests and been content. But Salnum decided that he could not be satisfied with only one Wish. Instead, he asked that God would grant him a Wish for every person on the Earth. And God, dismayed at his hubris and greed, granted Salnum's Wish.

"'Because you desired My power more than Me,' God said to Salnum, 'I grant your Wish in full. And I leave you this world, to do with as you Wish, until the day you return to Me. And until that day, I give you a sign. The Moon above is sundered in two, that you may remember your sin of greed that broke the love between us.'"

"That moment, the Well opened before Salnum's feet, and every man and woman on Earth received Salnum's Wish: the right to come, once in their lives, and make one Wish at the Well. And the Well granted their Wishes. It gave them whatever they asked for. And they asked without restraint. Without love. Without mercy."

It was an old story: the Sinking of the Well and God's Exile. Yet Aethal wondered what it must have been like for Salnum that day, as he realized what unrestrained power he had unleashed on the world. As the horrors of what men wished for forced him — without a single Wish of his own, since that had been granted — to restrain and finally slaughter his own people as they tried to fight their way into hearing distance of the Well that could grant them their heart's desire.

Salnum had lived only a week after the Well had appeared. The Church taught that his eldest son, Raham, had Wished him dead so that he could have the throne and ordered the Well sealed up in a chamber of stone. Raham's younger brother Joram had therefore killed Raham through more mundane means, and then Wished to live forever.

The Well granted exactly what was asked of it. Exactly. No more, and no less.

The legend ran that Joram was still alive, buried in the Chamber of the Well, trapped in a body that forever rotted around him, unable to die. His sons had become the Wish-Kings, who guarded the Well under layers of gates, guards and walls. Some had used the Well rarely. Others often. But all had forced their people to do their Wishing for them, dragging them to the Well, with their families held hostage and their own throats bared to a blade, all to be killed if they dared deviate from their Kings' Wishes. It was an immense power, but a fragile one: a lucky victim might Wish the kings dead. But most were too frightened, and they had enabled the Wish-Kings to become the most absolute tyrants in history.

But too often, the power of the Wishes had exceeded the wisdom of them. And even the Wish-Kings could not keep the Well completely in their power. Not against the promise of that one Wish. For anything.

"And now," said Ilferth Simon, "Salnum's Kingdom is the Dark Continent, so poisoned with the Wishes of man, that none can dwell there. Only the desperately mad even think of the journey. And should they arrive…"

He had no need to continue. The last time someone had made the journey to the Well, Lotus had destroyed the Empire.

"And the Guardians of the Well?" asked Aethal. "They are supposed to have kept watch over the Well in the Dark Continent for five centuries before their watch failed. They were a military order, once. Do they have no records?"

Ilferth Simon sniffed. "The Guardians' watch failed long before the Lotus was Wished for. They have been dying since they were corrupted by the Well and fled their own Wishes, long before the Free Republic sent its mad mission there. The Guardians have been a largely ceremonial order ever since. Or do you imagine that your mother is some sort of knight-errant for the Church in these times?"

Aethal returned his stare, and Ilferth Simon shrugged. "No, I see you do not. Most of the Order's records are presumably where they were left: on the Dark Continent where they met their doom. The Guardians had good intentions once, perhaps: an order dedicated to keeping the Well away from the desires of men. But in the end, they met the fate of all who set themselves against the Will of God: to be corrupted by the Well and the Wishes it gives. You may apply to them yourself, Last Sword, if you can find any who have time for such questions. Myself, I fear the Guardians are nearing the end of their usefulness, and expect them to revert to their lives as laypersons, or to take proper holy orders."

Simon addressed them, as if he were behind a pulpit. "Do you not see the sad story of man upon this earth? Once, in Salnum's time, before the Well was driven down to the Pit, loosing its horrors upon us, men ruled the world. Even after the Dark Continent was lost to us, the Empire gave us order and light, for a time. Before the mad fools of the Free Republic Wished for the Empire's destruction. Now there are only the tribes of the Tidetowns, the Grassworms, and finally, Verlaen: the last poor outpost of that Empire, which otherwise lies dead under seething carpets of Lotus. On the Dark Continent, there dwell things even worse than Lotus. And now the Green Death has come here. We have had a three-hundred year reprieve from God's justice. But justice will be done in the end, whether God grants us a little bit more life, or not."

Aethal stood staring. *This man is the spiritual councilor of our nation?*

"Justice?" The word dripped scorn. "This is your God's idea of justice, priest?" said Crown Prince Eraad. "Let me tell you about justice." He stepped from behind his father's throne and looked down on the shorter man. "Justice is what we make. What kings make for men. With our lives and with our blood."

He even speaks as though he's shed it himself, Aethal thought. But he knew the Prince had hardly ever left Maednac Serpiin.

"You hide in your pretty churches and pray for the moon to be healed. My father may tolerate you but I swear that in my reign there will be no such mercy. We'll deal with the Lotus, and then I shall deal with you!"

Ilferth Simon rose. "God is not mocked, Prince. Not even by kings. Seeing that I am superfluous to this discussion, I shall go and pray that God's mercy exceeds your own. And that He may guide me better than to unwittingly feed the soul of a good man to Wellspawn. May God grant Jehan Alfing mercy and forgiveness. Good night." And he was gone. Aethal saw that even Paal had his head in his hands, unable to meet the Crown Prince's eye.

The Mayor turned to the King. "With your Majesty's permission, I must see to the city, and begin preparations for informing the populace." He bobbed an awkward bow.

"Say nothing to them yet without Our consent," said the King. "I will summon you on this matter."

"Yes, Sire." The Lord Mayor hurried out.

"Fool boy!" cried the King, after the door had closed, turning on Eraad.

"Father, if you can't..." Eraad began.

Paal cut him off sharply: "That was ill-done, Highness."

Eraad's eyes lit with a new wariness. "Why, Chancellor?"

"You have now made a very open foe, Eraad, and you have let him know that he has no hope of changing your mind."

"Well, he doesn't," said Eraad easily. "You of all people should know that. What must I do, carve it in stone on the Hydraxis' sea wall in letters tall as a man? I will never become a priest, and their Church has been a leech on our kingdom long enough."

Paal's face bore thunderclouds. Aethal recognized that face. It preceded a sound thrashing, though Aethal doubted Eraad had ever suffered one. "Highness," Paal said, "the Church is a powerful opponent. As long as you kept your own counsel, your father and I could give the Conversant the impression that your antagonism was mere folly of youth, and not an unshakeable resolve. He was moved to court you rather than fight you, because that is the safer path, and these priests are always in favor of the safer path. Now you have denied him that hope, and the Church will be your enemy all the days of your reign. You will have sermons preached against you and the people may fear and distrust you because of it."

"That's treason!" barked Eraad.

"Yes, and we could have *said* that now we know Alfing was Simon's spy!" roared Paal. "Spawn of the Well, the man put a gun to his own foot and pulled the trigger, Eraad! With witnesses, no less!"

"Then why don't we use that?" asked Eraad.

"Have you been paying no attention to my lessons on politics, your Highness?" Paal demanded. "If we do that now, the Conversant will merely reply that you spoke blasphemy by declaring your own justice superior to God's. And that toady of his, the Mayor, will testify to it. If he testifies that you threatened to have the man shot out of hand, God alone knows where it will end. And you may be sure that Ilferth Simon will claim that God told *him* where!"

Eraad fumed. "We could silence his God-fables if we had the will."

Paal's hand twitched. "No, Highness, you could not. Get this through your head: you believe God to be no more than a fool's story; very good, I agree. But the people's belief in Him is very real. And that makes Him real to you. As real as any army that you think to send to the Temple. Do that, and you'll have rebellion, led by men who believe that your overthrow is the only way to avert God's just anger. If I thought it were not so, I'd have arrested him myself. But it *is* so, and so the Conversant will never be arrested for treason, not until he raises an army and storms this castle."

The King held up a hand. "Chancellor. While your observations on the troubles of my son's reign are well-taken, the problem for now seems to be to ensure that he has a reign in which to be troubled. Last Sword, you have seen the Lotus. What shall we do?"

Aethal came back to himself. "Sire, we must have a Council of War." *And eventually, whether we like it or not, Ilferth Simon and the Lord Mayor will have to be a part of it.* "You will appoint it, of course, but I see here many of those we'll want: The Lords Paramount of course." Aethal met Uncle Pyk's eyes, but saw only a wary guardedness there. "Or their emissaries," he continued. "Myself, the Lord Marshal of the Armies and the Admiral of the Fleet. I also request that you send for General Malcoor. I have reason to believe that he may have studied these matters." *Firsthand, in fact, but let's not go into that now.*

The look that passed between the King and the two Lords Paramount wavered and broke. Vaughan's face was well-masked fury, and Paal's face was stone. "That is quite impossible, Aethal," said Paal. "As you must know, if you rode through the Pass, General Malcoor has been relieved of duty and is charged with peculation."

"I do know that, Chancellor. Your man Jeralta explained it to me, right before he met his fate."

"Fate? What do you mean?" His face was pale, voice stricken. He and Jeralta had been close friends, as Aethal knew to his own cost. Still, he'd forgotten that Aerhan was there.

"Jeralta is dead, Aerhan," he said, as gently as he could. "I'm sorry."

Aerhan flushed red. "You killed him!"

"Of course not!" snapped Aethal.

"Then who did, *Last Sword*? Surely you must have some idea?"

"I was investigating Malcoor's affairs when he died," said Aethal.

Aerhan went very still. "So that's the way of it. I see."

What does that mean? He put Aerhan out of his mind. "I still don't know what Malcoor has done, apart from charges of embezzling. But I suggest that you offer to have the charges dismissed if he will return the money and help us against the Lotus."

"Trust a known criminal?" asked Aerhan. "On *your* word? Out of the question. As Master of the Royal Dungeons, I must forbid any such thing."

"May I remind our Lord Low Jailer," Lord Vaughan broke in, "that General Malcoor has served this Kingdom with great distinction, and that his cause is not without friends of the highest rank in this court? To call him a criminal is pure slander, which will not go unanswered, Aerhan Paaling." Aerhan scowled, but made no reply.

Aerhan is made Lord Low Jailer? Aethal thought. *I have been out of touch!* So Aerhan commanded the Crownguard, and all its arrests and prisons. But he continued: "Further, Sire, I recommend you give me leave to detach the Wyrmguard from the Hydraxis and send them to aid Colonel Jeharok's efforts to search out and destroy the Lotus."

"Aethal!" snapped Paal. "Leave the king unguarded at a time like this? Have you gone mad?"

"Chancellor," said Aethal, calmly. "The danger to the king is the Lotus. The Wyrmguard can, I suppose, start shooting at Lotus leaves when it begins to grow in the Garden Third, but I think they will be more effective where Lotus is now. Flintmaw: what effect does Lotus have on you?"

"How could he remember what effect Lotus had on the Wyrmguard three hundred years ago?" asked Paal.

"Because I was there," said the Wyrmguard, as if discussing last week's weather. "Lotus holds no temptation for our mounts that we cannot control. We will not suffer a mount farmed by the Lotus." said the Wyrmguard.

Paitir shook his head. "Perhaps later. As far as Malcoor, though..." The King gave Paal a weighing look. "Have him released and brought to the Last Sword. Perhaps he will say something that is worth a pardon."

"With respect, Sire," said Lord Vaughan in acid tones. "Is the General already convicted? If so, when was the trial? Are pardons not for those proven guilty?"

"There are witnesses enough for his guilt," muttered Paal.

"But he has not yet been tried," said Paitir. "Forgive my thoughtless words. Fetch him, Aerhan."

Aerhan stuttered and looked a mute appeal at Prince Eraad, who looked away. "But Sire, I must really protest..."

"Thank you, Aerhan Paaling, your concern is noted," said King Paitir. "Now bring him."

Aerhan glanced briefly at his father, who returned a stony stare. Aerhan straightened himself, his face pale. "Sire," he said stiffly. "It is my very great regret to inform you that General Malcoor's escort returned... without the General. Search teams have, of course, been dispatched."

King Paitir's face set. "You are telling me," he said, "Master of the Royal Dungeons, that the most important prisoner in your care has escaped? Two *days* ago? And I am hearing of this only now?"

"I was certain, Sire, that he would be back in my custody within hours," said Aerhan, not looking up.

"Get out of my sight," said Paitir. "And do not return until that man is found."

Aerhan bowed to the King. Then he fixed his eyes on Aethal. "As for you," he said in a clear, soft, voice. "I Wish you were dead in place of Jeralta."

The room went still at the awful curse. "Aerhan," said Paal. "You shame our line. Obey His Majesty at once!" Aerhan bowed and left.

"By your leave, Sire," said Lord Vaughan, in a strange, quiet voice. "We shall retire as well. If the General is not to be found in the Hydraxis, then neither shall the Lord of the Westerend be found there. Nor in Maednac Serpiin."

"Stop!" cried Aethal. "Lord Vaughan, the Kingdom is invaded by Lotus. If we are to have any chance at all of defeating it, we cannot lose your counsel!" Or your forces.

Vaughan rounded on him, "Then find me the General, Wrackberg! Surely, for the sake of Verlaen, you can do that much! And if you can't, then I must wonder: exactly what good will you be at stopping the Green Death from crashing about this city like a tide? Escaped, has he? In the heart of the Kingdom? I hope so, for his sake. He'll have a better chance of surviving the Grassworms of the Grain Sea and the Lotus both than a trip to Maednac Serpiin under a Wrackberg jailer, a Wrackberg Chancellor, and now, a Wrackberg Last Sword! I suppose you think you can get rid of him this time. Well, he had better not be shot while escaping. Hear me, King Paitir! You covered your shame once with Malcoor's reputation. You'd best not try to bury a greater shame in his tomb!"

"Lord Vaughan!" Aethal's voice cracked like a whip, in a habit he'd drilled into himself over years of commanding cavalry. "You will lower your voice and stay in this room until you explain to me what at the Core of the Well is going on!"

The Lord of Westerend flushed. "You don't command me, Wrackberg."

"This is the Hydraxis, and I command the Wyrmguard," said Aethal evenly. "You will not leave until I have an explanation. I have no wish to inconvenience you, my Lord, so speak plainly. What do you know about the General? What shame are you talking about? And what other time was there?"

The Lord of the Westerend visibly calmed himself. His daughter stood at his side, pale and silent, looking from Aethal to Paal and back. Slowly, he smiled.

"So, he never told you? Really? Never let you in on the secret of his greatest triumph? That does surprise me."

"It surprises you that I kept my word to be silent?" replied Paal. "It seems that the General did not keep his. Despite his own sworn oath, or my son would not seek the General so urgently. He lied."

"Lied about what?" barked Aethal, turning to his father.

"How do you know about it, Aethal?" asked his father, as though they were discussing the odds of horse races at a fair. "Did the General tell stories about his days in the Fleet over beer in the evenings? His expeditions across the Wyrretic Ocean? All those lonely evenings commanding the Pass? To entertain you and the rest of the young cadets?"

"I never saw General Malcoor take a drink in his life," said Aethal. "Nor known any man less likely to tell stories." *Of himself, at any rate.* "And when was the General in the Fleet?"

The two older men glared at one another, as if each were daring the other to speak. The King eyed them both. Uncle Pyk shuffled his feet.

Aethal opened his pouch and removed the book he had taken from Malcoor's chambers and laid it on a table. It fell open to the sketch of coastline. "Was it this expedition, then, my Lords?"

The silence broke in gasps. The two Lords Paramount craned their necks for a better look. Eraad and Ardyth stepped closer to the colored pages as if drawn there by a magnet. The King let out a sigh.

Paal broke the silence. "There! Proof of his treachery. He swore he never set foot on the Empire's shores! That is Lotus, if anything is. He's broken his vow as I always said he would. And before he ever made it."

"Proof?" Lord Vaughan said, in a soft voice. "I see no proof. Your own son remembers no lie General Malcoor told nor any secret he revealed. This is a private diary; I know the handwriting. And if he saw the Lotus, what then? Do you truly suggest he brought it here thirty years ago and this is the first we've heard of it? The only lies demonstrated here are yours, Wrackberg. You were the one who swore he'd be allowed to live if he only surrendered to you. And now he is *lost*, you say! Well, that leech you call a son may "lose" a thousand commoners in his dungeons, but you'll rue the day you try to lose a companion of the Lord of Westerend!"

"Ah, yes, touching," sneered Paal. "Your 'companion,' the General. How many times did you visit him after your lady wife died? He must have been quite a comfort to you."

Lord Vaughan's face went white and his hand went to his sword hilt.

"Paal!" snapped the King. "Enough. Must I endure this petty bickering? I want the General found, Chancellor. Do as my Last Sword has suggested."

Paal took a deep breath. "Of course, Sire."

"And now," Paitir went on, heavily. "Tell the Last Sword the story."

The two Lords Paramount glared at one another. Finally, Paal said quietly, "Thirty years ago, Commodore Malcoor commanded an expedition for His Majesty. His mission was secret, and our trust in him was high. The Commodore exceeded his orders..."

"Commodore Malcoor *followed* his orders," said Lord Vaughan, lip trembling with rage. "The orders that you gave him on the quayside!"

"Yes, that was his story," said Paal, calmly. "A tale worthy of a tragic hero. I, the evil Chancellor, whispered lies into his ear in the name of the King. Indisputable, of course, since there were no witnesses. His *written* orders were plain: sail West of the Prime Meridian and discover if any other race of men might have survived the Empire's Fall."

Aethal sucked in a breath. He heard others do likewise. But not the King.

"But that..." Thane Pyk rose, his jaw hanging open. "That violated Maednac's Ban!"

"Yes, it did," said Chancellor Paal. "But Verlaen stands in sore need of friends in this world, as even the Conversant understands. We are the only civilized people we know of. We decided to take a small risk."

A small risk. When he had fled the Empire and satisfied himself that he had indeed left the Lotus behind forever, King Maednac had issued a decree that death should forever be the penalty for anyone who sailed West of the Prime, lest they bring back a cargo of Lotus from the Fallen Empire's shores. Maednac's Ban. King Paitir, the Chancellor, and Commodore Malcoor had conspired to violate the Kingdom's oldest law.

As if reading his thoughts, Paal continued: "His orders were *not* to visit Imperial soil! What next, Westerend? Will you claim that I ordered him to sail to the Dark Continent and Wish in the Well for me, too?"

"You ordered him to break one law and he did it for you," returned Vaughan. "Then when it went sour, you blamed him for it to cover your own crimes."

"There was no crime," said Paal. "What one King may order, another King may countermand."

"But the Ban isn't just the order of a King!" protested Pyk. "It was the order of *Maednac!* Only the General States could ratify any such order."

"For all his brilliance, Maednac First King was still a man," said Paal. "The King did not order Commodore Malcoor to explore the Empire or the Republic themselves. The words of the Ban are: "Any who cross West of the Prime to seek the Empire or the Republic shall die." So we didn't seek them. We only sought any western lands to which the people of the Empire or the Republic might have fled. Any other restriction is mere tradition.

"Commodore Malcoor, however, exceeded even those orders, and then recorded his travels in a secret log. I wonder what else it will prove." He picked up the volume. "Will it reference these "secret orders" of which you speak? Or will it refer to *your* orders, perhaps, my Lord? After all, Malcoor was your liegeman, as you have ever been at pains to remind us. And when the Fleet found his dismasted ship, with over half the crew dead, he was nearly within sight of your high seat at the Twin Fans. What was he doing there, my Lord? Was he bringing you something, perhaps?"

Lord Vaughan's face was brick red. "Commodore Malcoor was loyal. He was a loyal man, and this is how you have repaid him."

"Loyal indeed," said Paal. "But to whom? That was always the question."

"What happened?" asked Aethal, fascinated despite himself.

"Nothing I am going to discuss here," said Paal. "Not the Lotus, obviously. The King may divulge more details if he sees fit. It was decided that the Commodore was no longer... suited for a Fleet command. But he was allowed to continue serving His Majesty with honor in the Army, where he trained young officers for their duties at the Pass."

Westerend's expression was bitter. "You might almost as well have killed him as taken his command. And now it seems you've found a way to."

"I do not know where he is, Westerend," said Paal. "But I will not waste words trying to make you believe otherwise."

Aethal wanted to tear his hair out. "We have no time for this distrust," he said. "The Lotus is here. It is on the very border of your lands, Lord Vaughan. It is in our autumn harvest. If we cannot work together, we will all be dead or drooling leafeaters within a year. We need peace and we need it now."

"Peace," said Lord Vaughan. "That's what I was promised thirty years ago. And what has that led to? A Wrackberg Chancellor and now his Wrackberg sons. If we survive the Lotus at a similar cost, there will be no House of the Westerend to rejoice at the triumph."

"What would buy your trust, Lord Vaughan? General Malcoor found, unharmed?"

"It would be a start," Lord Vaughan said. "Do you have him, then?"

"No," said Aethal. "But I can order a search of the Dungeons."

"Oh, really?" sniffed Lord Vaughan. "With your brother in charge? Or will you do that personally?"

"No, Lord Vaughan. You will."

The Lord of Westerend blinked. "What?"

"Aethal, you cannot do that!" said Paal.

"Why not?" asked Aethal.

"That is Aerhan's responsibility."

"I believe the Last Sword outranks the Lord Low Jailer, Father. In fact, I am my brother's direct commander." *I wonder if he's realized that, yet.* "The Last Sword of Verlaen commands Aerhan's Crownguard, and can assume control of the Lord Mayor's City Watch and Maednac's Own Infantry Regiment in an emergency. And this is a matter of the Kingdom's security. No, of human survival. Aerhan will open his dungeons to Lord Vaughan. And he shall have a Wyrmguard escort."

"As Chancellor, I forbid this."

Aethal looked at the king. "Paitir," he said. "I am at your command. You have asked me to be your Last Sword. And I tell you, we must have Lord Vaughan's help and more, his trust. This is all the coin I have to buy it with. May I have your permission, Sire?"

Paitir opened his mouth, looking from Aethal, to his furious Chancellor, to Lord Vaughan, who stood looking, for the first time, surprised. "Let the Last Sword's orders be carried out," he said.

Lord Vaughan stood stunned. "Very well," he said, at last. "I will stay. For now."

"Good," said Aethal. "And now, with His Majesty's permission, let the Council be called."

Chapter Six

21st of Spring, 312 Exodus

"**M**oon Hour!"

Aethal heard the shout from his chambers. It echoed from the top of the Ophidian, blurred slightly by the wooden shutters of his window and a distance of at least five floors. His eyes felt blurred as well. Even more faintly, he heard the echoes from the other six towers of the Hydraxis: "*Moon Hour,*" and the further echoes from the outer walls. Stretching painfully, Aethal sat up in bed and turned the room's lantern up to a soft glow. He walked to the outer door of his apartments and threw the catch on its top half, opening it to the night.

For whatever reason, the Last Sword's chambers were placed in the Ophidian such that they gave out on the top of the adjacent Dragonmast. From what was possibly the largest private balcony in the world, Aethal looked out on Maednac Serpiin's nightly cityscape, blazing with fire. From the vast lighthouses in the harbor, whose lamps blazed into the ocean, to the torches of the forts guarding it, and on up to the lit parapets of the Hydraxis itself, the roofs of Maednac Serpiin were alive with beacons.

All as he had commanded.

Aethal would have shuddered at the expense of the oil being used for the blaze, but he had already shuddered at the thought of Lotus walking the street, disguised as beggars, sailors... or worst of all, as guards. He had no shudders left for mere treasure.

Faintly, the cries of "*Moon Hour,*" echoed back from the street patrols. Aethal listened to them. Again, just as he had commanded: Twelve patrols of five men each, and they answered within about five seconds of each other. Even more faintly, Aethal heard the next ring of patrols echo the cry. The cries faded quickly in the moist spring air of the capital, but they would go on and on, to the next ring of patrols, and the next after that, all the way down to the docks.

The Lotus is in our streets already, even though it is five hundred miles away. But as long as it is in our thoughts, we may yet keep it from our brains.

According to the records, the first thing Lotus did was to drain the victim of interest in anything else. He lost track of time and duty. Any patrol not echoing the cry would have every other patrol in earshot converging on it. Those patrols and torches had been the most obvious result of Aethal's War Council. Aside, of course, from announcing the Lotus infestation to the people.

At least there had been no panic, as yet. No obvious panic. God-Beyond-The-World, he'd have to worry about hoarding, smuggling, and all the other ways civilians reacted to the uncertainties of war. *Unless my father — the Chancellor that is, since he's not my father anymore — is good enough at his job to suppress such things.* Tomorrow he would inspect the Crownguard and see what kind of Discipline his former brother enforced. He was afraid he knew. At least he had no doubts about the Wyrmguard. Or Maednac's Own, although he'd inspect them anyway. That elite regiment would doubtless teach *him* about the Discipline.

Despite his fatigue, Aethal could not sleep. Sergeant Falk was luckier than he in that respect. When the Council had broken up, Aethal had gone to see him in the Royal Surgeon's recovery rooms and found that the man had been treated and asleep for ten hours straight, and showed no signs of waking. Aethal, feeling he had done the man enough injury, had not wanted to disturb his earned rest.

Tomorrow, Verlaen would begin mobilizing its army. The King and the Lords Paramount would call forth all those who could serve to war against the Grass-worms. Against any people in the Grain Sea who could not be inspected and declared secure against the Lotus. Aethal had fought Grassworms, of course. That's what the Cavalry did. But this would be a war of extermination. Aethal cringed at the thought of it. But what else could they do? A single man who refused to submit could sow Lotus the length of Verlaen. All of them would have to submit or die. It would take weeks, but the armies would be mobilized.

Despite that, no Wyrmguard would be sent to aid Jeharok on the Grain Sea, and Aethal clenched his fists in frustration. Shielded by the guns that mastered them, the Wyrmguard would have been the perfect tool to search for Lotus. Instead, Paal had insisted that the Wyrmguard be kept around the royal family and the ranking officers of the Army and Fleet at all times, as a last and perfect defense against any Lotus penetrating the miles and walls that separated them from the infestation in the Grain Sea. Of course, if Lotus were *that* powerful, everyone in the Hydraxis might just as well slit their own throats now and save time. Aethal straightened, stretched, and opened his outer door, stepping onto the Dragonmast's vast roof.

There were no firepits here; Mad Prince Schotus, who had commissioned the giant tower, had insisted that his dragons would make them unnecessary. The tower's huge crenellations rose to half again Aethal's height, spaced widely enough that two men could stand between them. Not even the barest lip of stone marked the edge of the tower in those spaces. Aethal idly considered how easy it would be to keep on walking, right over the edge.

The King's apartments, one floor above his own in the Ophidian, were dark. *Cousin Paitir sleeps better than I do*, he thought. He walked to the edge of the Dragonmast and looked down onto the Royal Gardens.

Blocking his view of the ports, the great bronze likeness of Maednac the Sea King stood fifty feet high, shining like a piece of one of the moons brought to Earth. The great oil torches carved into its pedestal roared with flame. The bronze and brass of the statue was polished daily, and it rivaled the Serpiin Lighthouse on foggy mornings. The long reflection off the burnished bronze stretched out toward the Madlands and the harbors.

Aethal felt the presence behind him more than he heard it and whirled, instinctively putting the nearest crenellation between him and the long drop.

The Wyrmguard gazed at Aethal without expression, but Aethal recognized him. Samal Naakt. For two years, he'd haunted the Madlands, murdering for hire and raping as a personal hobby. The pistol that hung at his side was entirely black, both metal and bone. It would hold his mind until he died, or was too old to serve. Then he would be released to the gallows. "Irontooth," Aethal said, recognizing the gun. "What is it?"

"The Chancellor is here, sir."

Aethal stared. He had expected this, but not tonight. Then he shrugged. "I don't really want to see him," he said.

Irontooth nodded. "Very good, sir." He rotated to go, as if mounted on a turret.

"No, wait," said Aethal. He took the canteen from the Wyrmguard's belt and splashed some water in his face. "Show him in. And bring two glasses of the wine you'll find on the bedside table." Not a very good vintage, but it would meet the minimal standard of politeness.

The Wyrmguard left. Moments later, Paal's shadow appeared in the doorway. Irontooth brought Aethal his own glass, nodded to both of them, and departed.

"Chancellor," said Aethal, nodding.

Paal regarded him. "Last Sword." He looked around. "How are the apartments? I seem to remember you always liked balconies as a child. Your mother and I were afraid you'd do yourself an injury."

Aethal blinked. "I've lost my taste for them, I fear." Aerhan and Jeralta had seen to that. "They serve, however. I could almost feel safe here, especially with a Wyrmguard outside. Even though I am in the same tower as you."

Paal waved this away. "I was on my way up to see the king. The Wyrmguard denied me access past this floor. You had better explain that, Aethal."

"I thought Paitir needed his sleep. I'm certain I do." Aethal took a sip of his wine. The warmth of the alcohol was welcome.

Paal glared down at him. "The last time the king was asleep before Moon Hour, Eraad was in the nursery. I have urgent business to discuss with him and I am not in the habit of asking permission."

"It's a good habit, Chancellor. You're never too old to acquire it."

"Do you think that sword the king hung about your neck gives you any sort of influence here, boy? I can have it hanging on any one of my picked men in a week if you continue in this fashion."

"Then you'll need to do a better job of influencing the process than you did this morning, Chancellor. Paitir seemed determined to place me in this position; I hardly asked for it. And your record on persuading the king where family is concerned is not exactly flawless, is it?"

Paal went rigid with rage, and for a moment Aethal dared hope that his father would actually strike him here, not six feet from a Wyrmguard.

"You're playing a dangerous game, Aethal," Paal said. "It's not the Last Sword's prerogative to decide who sees the king and who doesn't. It's mine. I could have you broken for insubordination."

"It's my duty to see that the king is kept safe from all threats. And I do judge you a threat, Chancellor. You want to see Paitir, you see him. But I go with you. Or Irontooth. Or Flintmaw. Or any other you care to name. But you don't see him alone until I get an explanation of why you thought it was so important to keep the news of Lotus from him." Aethal was aware that he was skirting the very edge of his power. The king had not, in fact, given him the power to do this — or not specifically this, at least — but his father's treachery was too dangerous. And Aethal was absolutely in charge of the Wyrmguard unless countermanded by the king personally.

Paal slowly shook his head. "You never appreciated subtlety; you or your mother. Your failing costs, Aethal; it costs dear. You still leap to conclusions. Keep this up and the conclusion may be yours. Or the king's; you're his Last Sword now. His life is your responsibility, and you think you're guarding it. But I hope for his sake that you learn more caution than you showed today, when you and that bull-necked fool of a sergeant blurted the news of Lotus all over the palace. Did it ever occur to you that there was someone else I might have been trying to keep that information from?"

"Really? Who might that have been?"

"The Conversant, of course," snapped Paal. He drank deeply from his glass, and looked at Aethal. "Lotus has invaded Verlaen after a reprieve of three centuries. I threatened to disinherit you in a desperate bid to keep you from blurting that out in front of Ilferth Simon."

"And why was that so important? We had to release the news as soon as we knew! What could possibly be more vital than alerting the people?"

"Perhaps catching the person who brought the Lotus here?" Paal's voice was a whip. Aethal turned as if drawn by a magnet.

"What are you saying?"

"The moment your Sergeant Falk tried to speak to the king Upon the Peril, Jehan Alfing struck at him. Desperate to silence him. But for you, he would have succeeded. Why did he do it? We'll never know, since you unfortunately killed him."

"And I was damned lucky to!"

"Yes, yes, don't snarl at me; I am not Eraad. I know what danger you were in. But why did he do it? He was Ilferth Simon's recommendation. What could he have been afraid of?"

"You're suggesting that Ilferth Simon knew about the Lotus. And didn't want the king to find out."

"You tell me what else makes sense."

"But you knew about it, too," Aethal said.

His father seemed to be weighing something carefully in his mind. Finally, he said, "You'll never trust me unless I tell you, and we need to trust each other. I knew because I have an agent in the Church. Ilferth Simon knew of the Lotus. I knew he knew. But I have no *proof* that he knew. Only the word of an agent who found out that Lotus was in the kingdom."

"Then why didn't *you* tell Paitir?" asked Aethal.

"Tell him what?" barked Paal. He lowered his voice with effort. "For once, listen to me: I knew that Simon knew there was Lotus. I didn't know how, or who told him, or where! All I could have done was accuse, and he'd have denied it. And when Lotus appeared, how would I avoid his charge that I had planted the damned stuff myself? That's why I sent Jeralta out. To look for it. If he'd found it, I might have had the proof to make my charges stick."

Aethal's guts crawled. "If that's the case, then someone already knows your secret, Chancellor. Whoever killed Jeralta wound his guts out on a string while he tried to scream through a dumbworm."

His father's face didn't twitch. "Whoever it was learned nothing, then. Jeralta himself didn't know why I sent him out. Only that he was to inspect Colonel Sigrad for me and then tour the Grain Sea. If he met you, that was a bonus. I wouldn't have trusted Jeralta Stevning with any secret, let alone news of Lotus. And you see now I was wise not to."

Core of the Well, he's cold. But he's not wrong.

"When you arrived so soon, with the ring, I knew why you were here. For an instant I had Ilferth Simon right where I wanted him. All I needed was to announce that I had found it, and have my agent confirm the knowledge. Now that it's commonly known the Lotus is here, any accusation I make will look like I made it up after the fact. Still, the attack on you was damaging to him... and then the King's idiot son single-handedly nullified the only political mistake I've ever seen Ilferth Simon make by suggesting the most ham-handed political assassination ever conceived. So I thank you for the drink; I am in sore need of it. I suffer a plague of sons."

"You're welcome," said Aethal, dryly. "I notice that you don't include Aerhan on that list for losing General Malcoor, though."

His father gave him a blank stare. "I shall deal with Aerhan in time. And in the family."

"As long as we're on the subject, I notice you haven't made my disowning public. Am I in the family? Or not?"

Paal gave him an appraising look. "I would regret the necessity of disowning you formally. But I am a man of my word, Aethal. And being loyal to our House demands a measure of trust in me as its head. However, you are also the Last Sword of Verlaen, so I suppose you need a clearer explanation of the political situation here in Maednac Serpiin, lest you become convinced that I harbor some sinister design. But listen closely. I'm not a damned tutor." He began walking along the circumference of the Dragonmast. Aethal followed.

"Since becoming Conversant, Ilferth Simon has concerned himself — excessively — with the piety of the Royal Family. He is using historical precedent ruthlessly: Maednac's eldest son was trained as a priest, and eventually rose to be Conversant himself in his younger brother's reign. Every king since has given a son to the Church. Even Paitir's own brother went there, though he's dead now. Why then, asks Simon, does the King not command Eraad to do likewise? But Paitir has only the one child. So whose needs take precedence, crown or church? It's unclear, and therefore unstable."

"Wouldn't such an arrangement give the Crown some power in the Church, as well?"

Paal's smile was wintry. "The Church isn't run by rules of social precedence, Aethal. The Conversant controls all offices as though he really did talk to God. Eraad would never rise anywhere near the Conversantship; Ilferth has sons of his own he'd much rather see in that position. Or possibly protégés; one can never be certain with the Church. Nor with Simon. What's more certain is that Simon sees the advantage of cutting the King off from his heir, and leaving the succession open."

"Ilferth Simon has spent the last three years making ever more dire hints about what could happen if King Paitir did not conduct himself and control his son as befitted a King who fears God. Despite Eraad's complete unwillingness to play along with us, Cousin Paitir and I have managed to pretend to Simon that Eraad might be convinced to take holy orders once the passion of his youth had died down." Paal stopped and stared down at the harbor, and the streets.

"Ilferth Simon left the Hydraxis today having lost a great deal of influence and knowing that Crown Prince Eraad intends to bring down the Church, or at least curb its power drastically."

Paal stared out Aethal's door into the night.

"Tonight, your patrols will hold, marching through the city for the first time. Tomorrow, frightened people will go to their chapels for comfort, and hear the sermon Ilferth Simon is doubtless sitting up writing, telling people to pray forgiveness for their sins, and the sins of their nation... and the sins of their King, and the sins of his son."

"Treason..." breathed Aethal.

Paal's eyebrows arched. "Frightening word. Here are a few more: 'Blasphemer.' 'Heretic.' 'Well-spawn.' Oh, he won't say so in so many words: that *would* be treason. Eraad drools at the very thought of making the charge, but it's a dream. Ilferth knows how to play the game. He'll be very careful, and will not make any overt moves. He'll try to force us, so that we can commit sacrilege instead." He sipped his wine again.

"And since when is there a 'we,' Chancellor?" asked Aethal, letting his voice go soft. "You assume I'm on your side? What makes you think I give a piss in the Well for what you think 'we' ought to do?"

"Because you rode here from Everview in only three days to bring word of the Lotus directly to the King, and threw away House Wrackberg for it when I forced to you to that crisis," replied Paal, unblinking. "You do care, Aethal. Don't try pretending to me you don't."

Aethal could feel himself breathing hard. "Then what makes you think I'm on your side? Maybe I'll join Ilferth Simon. I might even see Mother again. And I know what *you've* done; I only have your word for what Simon will do."

Paal's face had darkened at the mention of Aethal's mother, but his voice remained calm as the flat sea. "You have Simon's own words on that score. He thinks the Lotus is some sort of holy justice. And your mother is a Guardian of the Well. Do you remember what Simon said about them? "*Nearing the end of their usefulness*, I believe it was. He's going to disband them, Aethal; they are not his allies save by historical association. And they have always been independent of the Church's direct control, ever since the Church left the Dark Continent and they stayed. The Church has never forgotten or forgiven that."

Paal put his wineglass down and faced Aethal. "You're on my side because you're against the Lotus. And because you fear, as I do, that Ilferth Simon is not." The words struck home. *A neat trap he has placed me in*, Aethal thought with bitterness. *I do fear this, whether I trust him or not. Whether I love him or not.*

Once again, Paal looked outward. "Well done," he finally said. "All the whalers are going to get rich on the oil we burn, but we can get some of it back in taxes. Better to lose the treasury than the city." Paal paused a moment, looking out to the sea, and then, to Aethal's amazement, softly began to recite:

"The word sped forth on horses that was spoken from his lips.

"The word to Maednac's captain, to set thunder in the ships.

"Bronze-throated thunder in those days without a morn,

"Churning seas a cauldron where his red-gold crown was born.

"Scarlet-piled timber in the mountain-serpent's maw

"Fed the flames of sacrifice to Maednac and his law."

The years seemed to fall away from him as Aethal listened, and Aethal followed Paal's gaze out into the harbor. In the moonlight, the narrow mouth of the bay could just be seen, and the dark mound that was the Wrackberg. Maednac had given it, along with the title, to that captain, his commander of artillery, after the fall of the Empire. The captain who had sunk so many ships that their shattered hulls rose out of the sea, lest they bring the Lotus along with refugees out of the dying Empire and into Verlaen. Aethal remembered Paal telling the story to him and to Aerhan, sitting on their mother's lap.

The only noble who ever made his own lands, Paal had said, even if the whole island was nothing more than a half-mile square of rotting wood and guano. And still we bury our dead there. The fisherfolk renting docks and line-fishing space, and a few rich garden plots.

He had nearly forgotten that he'd ever listened to Paal tell stories, yet the memory blazed forth like yesterday. He looked up at the beacons he could just see on the north and south sides of the bay. Those stood upon the real Wrack-berg lands; the true token of Maednac's esteem. The rich farms and fisheries that had led to intermarriage between Aethal's ancestors and Paitir's.

He caught Paal looking at him. "Our family defended Verlaen against the Lotus that came from the sea. We can defend it again from the Lotus that comes in by land, whether priests or God be against us."

Aethal frowned. "And what about kings? I can't help but think that you might have brought Cousin Paitir into your confidence. He knows the danger Ilferth Simon poses. Why not tell him about the Lotus, too? Perhaps he'd have been able to help you lay your trap? How long have you kept it from him? Only that 'bull-necked sergeant' you denigrate seems to think the king had a right to know the danger to his own land." He could not forget the betrayal in Falk's eyes, nor the contempt with which he had given the order to the Wyrmguard. *Upon peril of the Well's Rising...*

"Being the Chancellor sometimes involves doing what is best for the kingdom, regardless of the king's wishes. Before you pass judgment, allow me to explain that Paitir has been grateful for this more often than you might think. He doesn't like making decisions, and he likes living with his bad ones even less. I have come to the end of the explanations I have for you."

"Perhaps we should go and see if Paitir is as grateful for your initiative in this matter as you claim, Father. I could ask."

Paal drained the rest of his glass. "Ask the king whatever you like, Aethal. I will see him. With or without your permission, and most assuredly without your escort. He knows what I am: his most valued ally against Ilferth Simon. I think the king has troubles enough already. You don't want to cause him more. They might end up being your trouble as well."

"Are you threatening me, Chancellor?"

"Threaten the Last Sword of Verlaen? That might be interpreted as sedition." He leaned closer, and spoke softly. "But I may, as Chancellor, be forced to make some hard decisions as our fight against the Lotus progresses. The king cannot concern himself with all details of the Kingdom. I might see that your sergeant gets sent back to the Fleet where all Madlanders belong. But I see that you don't realize the significance of that; I know the Sergeant better than you, it seems. You might ask him to share his fond memories of *Commodore* Malcoor.

"So perhaps something closer to home. The Phoenix Lancers Rifles are a very valuable unit to us because of their experience. I might have to keep them in the field for quite some time. It could be months before they got rotated back to the Basin. I would, of course, hope that it fared better against the Lotus than did Everview."

Aethal's rage boiled at the threat to his men. But, he suddenly realized, the consequence to Farnan was far worse. Of course, Paal couldn't know that Aethal had sworn Farnan to their House. But he could dismiss him with dishonor, once he knew. Yes, and send him back to the Army. Not even as an officer, but as a common trooper, all his previous service wiped out. The Chancellor could certainly do that. Paal carefully stepped back three paces. "Of course, nothing has been decided yet, Aethal. And I am likely to be too busy to deal with such petty matters of military duties unless something focuses my attention on them. Do you understand me?"

Aethal had to consciously ease his grip on his wineglass. "Oh, yes," he breathed.

"Good. I don't intend to be your enemy. I would much rather have you as an ally. But I won't have you wasting your powers on fruitless and wasteful pursuits. Because you may have real enemies who are less patient and merciful than myself. Speaking of which, who did murder Jeralta? Aerhan would very much like to know. So would his father, Stevn. I had the news sent there. If Aerhan gets to be too much of a pest, tell me. I can calm him down. Stevn I have... less control over. Frankly, he is looking for someone to blame. In lieu of a real murderer, you may draw his attention. I don't suppose you'd like to confess that you really simply lost your temper and killed the boy in some fit of anger? Or was your Sergeant Falk overzealous in questioning him?"

"No, Chancellor," said Aethal stiffly. "Jeralta did not die at either of our hands. As I told you, we found him dead in a cell beneath the Keepwood with a dumbworm inside him."

"And how did Jeralta come to be in that cell?"

Aethal gave his father a cold smile. "I put him there."

"Hmmm. Why?"

"He wouldn't tell me why he was at the Pass. Or how he knew I would be. Since he knew far more than he should have and was being insubordinate, I clapped him in irons. Oh, with Colonel Sigrad's full approval, of course. Speaking of which, whatever possessed you to replace Malcoor with that fool?"

"I think you'll find I didn't," said Paal.

"Jeralta said as much, but I didn't believe him. How came you to have no candidate of your own for the position? And why did you need Sigrad inspected? The man seemed certain he was a protégé of yours."

Paal hesitated, then said, "He's Ilferth Simon's protégé. I wanted Jeralta's report on him. The Conversant recommended Sigrad immediately after word of Malcoor's peculation came to light," said Paal. "But I know Sigrad. That fool whores himself to anyone he thinks will give him one more connection at court, or one more present of money. I gave him a few flattering words and a bottle of brandy. And now he imagines that because two powerful men have patted him on the head, he is playing us against one another.

"In fact, the appointment of Sigrad was the biggest blunder I had ever seen Ilferth Simon make until Jehan Alfing tried to cut your sergeant down. I was inclined to let him make it."

"And now?"

"I am inclined to let him keep on making it."

"And leave the Serpent's Pass under his command?" said Aethal. "You're endangering the entire Verlaen Basin!"

"I thought we agreed Ilferth Simon threatened the entire Kingdom," said Paal. "And you assume I *am* leaving him unwatched. Don't."

"And what about General — or Commodore — Malcoor? Will you at least help to find him?"

"Of course. It is the King's command, after all. But you've made that Lord Westerend's duty. He would not welcome my help." He passed his glass to Irontooth. "And now, Aethal, I will bid you good night. I'll not see the king, I think. It's nearly Dead Hour and he probably is asleep by now. But do reverse that order when you wake." He turned to go.

"Oh, and Aethal," he turned back. "The king wants you as his Last Sword, but don't make Colonel Sigrad's mistake and overestimate your importance. The king is getting a bit paranoid in his old age; one of the reasons for your appointment was to gain a hold over me. I'm sure I don't have to explain just how futile that was. Good night."

Paal left, and Aethal was again alone on the roof with Irontooth. With his frustration. He started forward, scarce aware of where he was going, or what he did. *I must warn Farnan. No, I must warn Colonel Jeharok.* But warn them of what? That the Chancellor would send them orders worse than a suicide mission? Of course, someone would get those orders. Someone had to. Would he warn *them* to desert?

He swept into his room and turned the lamp up full. With mechanical swiftness he donned coat and boots. Mindful of his rank, he snatched up the sword and threw it across his back. *When Sergeant Falk wakes, I'll have to find out what he knows about Malcoor. And what does my father know about him that I don't?* He hadn't asked; there was no point in giving his Father the satisfaction of refusing to tell him. The feeling of entrapment was almost more than he could bear. His eyes lit on the pile of books in the corner. Softly, he laughed at himself.

"I am a fool," he muttered. He snatched up Malcoor's journal and strode back out to the roof of the darkened Dragonmast. There was a trapdoor in the roof and Aethal yanked the deadbolt free without hesitation, taking the spiral stair below it. The staircase curved between the tower's inner and outer walls, with small portals giving an intermittent view of its vast cavernous interior.

In the absence of dragons, the Dragonmast had become the storage room for the Kingdom, or at least for the Royal family. There were only four interior walls, and they met at a great support column which was half as thick as a keepwood. The stair pierced each of the four cavernous cells as it descended. The cells had been intended, after all, to house dragons. He could see where the massive doorways intended to let the beasts out had been mostly bricked up by later, saner, kings of Verlaen. The doors remaining were merely large enough for wagons. Given how many came here, men called it the Wagonmast these days.

Now the cells housed old armor, racks of crossbows and longbows, arrows and bolts. Wine and cheese and siege rations were stored in one great cell, the coldest. Down on the floor of the tower, Aethal saw the tops of the huge cisterns, and a couple of shadowy shapes covered by tarpaulins that Aethal was certain had to be massive siege engines. He spared them not a glance. His father's words pounding through his mind. *I'm likely to be too busy to deal with such petty matters of military duties unless something focuses my attention on them. Do you understand me?*

Aethal understood. Oh, yes. My father is telling me that his plans for the nation and king are more important than the lives of our people. Which makes him, in point of fact, a traitor. But it doesn't necessarily make him a liar or wrong about Ilferth Simon. How bad a situation do we have when I consider making a traitor an ally? What I need is a high-ranking friend. Paitir is high-ranking enough, but the king cannot call his bodyguard a friend.

Fortunately, Aethal did have one friend already here.

It was no trouble to slip through the man-sized doors at the base of the Dragonmast that led back into the Ophidian. In fact, Aethal was now entering the Ophidian exactly eighty feet below his chamber door that gave onto the roof. These inside doors of the Dragonmast Armory were, of course, protected by Wyrmguard. They told him what he wanted to know. It was not long before he was knocking firmly on a door to chambers on the third floor. The knocks echoed away down the empty corridors without eliciting any reply. Aethal pounded again, more loudly, until he thought surely the entire Hydraxis would wake. A voice inside finally answered:

"What lowland *skhyt hyus* is banging on this door in the dead of night?" it roared, muffled by sleep and oak. The door was flung wide, and Aethal stared into the red face of Pyk Imya, Thane of Telerat. He held a broad-bladed dirk — sheathed, Aethal noted — clenched in his right hand. His eyes widened as outrage and wonder fought for prominence.

"Aethal Kynthialing!" he cried. "Boy, I..." He shook his fist, his mouth worked, then settled on, "I ought to come across your arse with the flat o' this blade in mine hand. I've been wanting a chat with you all the day and you come up my door in the dead of the night!"

Aethal grimaced at the torrent of words. "Yes, Pyk. I was hoping to see you quietly, and away from other eyes."

Pyk pulled him bodily inside. Despite his grizzled hair, the man was still as strong as a bear. He clapped Aethal on the shoulder, shook his head, and sighed. "Aethal, boy, about all these preparations you're making. I know that the Green Death is here; you were always too serious a lad for me to even think you might be mistaken about a thing like that." He gave Aethal an exasperated glance as he turned up so that Aethal could see where to step. "But is the Lotus really like as not to turn up in my porridge on t' morrow?"

Aethal grinned at the older man's tone. Pyk had almost been like a third uncle to him in the fraught years between leaving his father's house and receiving his commission in the Cavalry. Aethal sobered at his question all the same. "Not in your porridge on the morrow, Pyk, but on Telerat's Plateau before the year turns unless we're very fortunate."

Pyk sat on his couch and faced him with a grim look. Aethal sat opposite him. "So soon?" he said, and there was age in the robust man's voice.

Aethal nodded. "I was glad beyond words to find you in Maednac Serpiin, Pyk, if surprised."

Pyk snorted. "I'm surprised myself, lad. I only just arrived yesterday. King Paitir summoned your uncle Falaar to court a week since. You can imagine how well that went down."

Aethal could indeed. Since his parents' divorce, both his uncles, Falaar and Galenn, had sworn they would not set foot in the Hydraxis while Paal of the Wrackberg walked its halls. "And they sent you instead? How did King Paitir take it?"

"He said, 'Welcome, Pyk Thane Imya Telerat,'" Pyk replied. "He'd been expecting it. Well, I was wearing this when I bowed before the man." He handed Aethal a heavy, dull silver torc. In its center was a thick chunk of cut glass, inscribed and enameled, in the five-masted ship-and-moon of House Skysil. Aethal's lips made an 'o' of appreciation. He could see every sail, every rope on the ship. Fine figures danced within the glass, as if ready to spring into the rigging. The waves beneath the hull seemed to move in the lantern's light. It was the work of the master artisan Pfyfr, and beyond price.

"You speak with the voice of the Skysil," said Aethal. "Full ambassadorial powers." It was unforgeable, of course, and worth a great deal more than the ring Paal had sent to Aethal. Aluminum was expensive to refine, and spiderpearl was dangerous to harvest, but talent like Pfyfr's was *rare*.

Pyk grunted. "Not bad for an upjumped sheep-farmer's son, eh?" Aethal rolled his eyes. The first Thane Telerat had been more the patriarch of a family of shepherds, and for all Pyk's humility, they'd been nobles nearly as long as the Wrackbergs. Not that Aethal hadn't heard his father call Pyk exactly that. "More likely I was the only bastard unlucky enough to be that far south when the messenger got to your uncle. That thing and my orders both came by thunderbird four days ago and I only just got here.

Thunderbird. For a moment Aethal remembered the huge black birds of the northern coasts and wondered if that might be how Paal had learned of the Lotus so quickly, but he dismissed the thought in an instant. The huge birds could carry two torcs like the one Aethal now held, never mind messages, but their eggs and the secrets of their training were jealously guarded by House Skysil and their thanes. Besides which, they did not live outside the high plateaus of the Skysil lands. Paal would most certainly not have one.

"Even so," Pyk continued, "I doubt he was happy."

Aethal doubted so, too. When Kings summoned nobles, even Lords Paramount, they were expected to come themselves, not send ambassadors, no matter how exalted. "That could be construed as rebellion," Aethal said mildly.

"It could be construed as keeping his word, Aethal Kynthialing," Pyk said, voice hard.

Aethal said nothing. The fact that Pyk was still calling him by his matronymic rather than pronouncing the name of his reviled father was evidence enough that Kaelan's death was still a very real grudge in the north.

"I came to discuss slightly more ancient history," said Aethal.

Pyk's voice was cool. "You'd best be glad it was I and not your uncle heard you call it ancient history, lad."

Aethal looked up sharply. "I'm well aware of what my father did to my uncle, Pyk."

Pyk nodded, watching Aethal. "Seemed rather pleased with you today, he did. You being made Last Sword and all. A feather in his cap, that."

Aethal remembered Paal's final words. "Yes," he said, voice chill. "A feather. Or something else that comes out of a bird's ass. You should have heard our discussion just before we arrived." He bared his teeth in a humorless smile. "For now I need to know about General — or is it Commodore? — Malcoor."

Pyk seemed taken aback. "What?"

"I said, I want to know all you can tell me about General-or-Commodore Malcoor."

"And *that* couldn't have waited until breakfast?"

"By breakfast I may be closeted with the king all day and thus be unable to speak to anyone save His Majesty and my father. Pyk, I thought I knew all there was to know about the man. Malcoor of the Pass, the Commandant who trains all us cadets into officers and gentlemen.

"Yesterday I came riding out of Everview bearing news of Lotus and I find Malcoor arrested in the Pass. Today I find he's escaped in Maednac Serpiin. At least one man has died because of it." Aethal told the story of Jeralta's death, to Pyk's mounting horror. "And you saw what Lord Paramount Vaughan's reaction to Malcoor's escape was."

"It was insane," muttered Pyk. "Aethal, I can't see what Malcoor has t'do with any of this. But what Vaughan said today... cast a new light on many things."

"How do you mean?"

Pyk nodded, considering. "Aethal, I'm not sure how to rightly explain. Captain Malcoor was almost a legend back then. A story-book figure people told drunken tall tales about."

Aethal gaped. "Malcoor?" He'd have almost been less surprised if Pyk had spoken this way about his father. Paal at least recited poetry. Malcoor had never done anything but lecture and issue orders.

"Well, the Captain — or Commodore, there at the end — was a different man than the General. It was Captain Malcoor who took the pirate ship *Spider's Pearl* with only a brigantine, and he did that after the *Pearl*'d sunk a number of merchantmen and two frigates into the bargain. Commodore Malcoor, now, he took his three ships, *Vagary*, *Webstalker*, and *Calamar*, into all the southern seas. Hell, I even had eager boys from Telerat wanting to join the Fleet, and the nearest shoreline a hundred miles away. But you know how sailors are, Aethal, they all want you to believe they've been to the Well and back."

Aethal nodded. "And then what happened?"

"One day he came back from a voyage and was called to the Hydraxis. The next day, he was General Malcoor and assigned to the Pass. He rode out t' next week for his new post and never has left it since."

"And no one thought that peculiar?" asked Aethal.

Pyk snorted. "Seven kinds of peculiar, and the rumors flew like mad. They said he'd near drowned and lost his nerve. They said he'd gone mad. They said he suffered a mutiny. They said he'd sailed West, or even North. They said he'd killed half his crew."

"And now we know he did sail West, don't we?" said Aethal.

Pyk looked up. "Aye, that we do, don't we? From Westerend's own mouth. And the King's. And your father's. And Malcoor was picked up near the Westerend. Ah."

"Pyk, what is it?"

Pyk looked back at Aethal and his face was strange. There was fear there. Fear mixed with suspicion?

"Pyk," Aethal said. "What is it you've remembered?"

Pyk leaned close to Aethal. "Now it's me who'll be glad that your Uncle Falaar isn't here," he said. "He's forbidden this subject ever to be aired in his presence, but I doubt he expected the Lotus; I'll presume that would knock some sense into him. Aethal, how much do you know about your parents' marriage? About how it came to be?"

Aethal looked down to his mother's ring where it sat on his left hand. "It was a triumph for my father. A brilliant political marriage. Just the kind he'd always have wanted to make."

Pyk's hard hand came around in a halfway serious blow to Aethal's head. "Were you asleep during all your classes in history, boy? I'd have thought your father would have seen you knew that at least. Triumph? Too pale a word, boy. Might as well call that Greater Rifle of yours a "decent weapon." Kynthia's marriage to your father represented the greatest fundamental shift in Verlaen's internal power since Maednac landed. The Wrackbergs were always the King's most loyal allies. Even today, they're the only House Paramount Maednac's Line has ever allowed to marry into it. Maednac established them and gave them grants in the basin to offset the powers of the Westerend nobles, Vaughan's ancestors, the ones who'd already been here a generation before the Lotus ate the Empire. In those early days, the Westerend made noises about being kings themselves. But when we Skysils took root on the Northern Plateaus, we settled that issue, sort of. We put the balance of power in the hands of Maednac's line. But even though we came from Maednac's Fleet and were loyal to the King, it was obvious that we could always support Westerend if a king tried to be too careless of our rights as nobles. The King and the Wrackbergs couldn't raise a force large enough to defeat both of us."

"Then why did grandfather Allyn want mother to marry father?" Aethal asked. He'd never heard it told this way before. "If the Skysils have so much power — and I know you're sitting on four-fifths of the Kingdom's mines — why would you want to ally with either side?"

"A question you should have asked ten years ago," growled Pyk. "Because the Skysil's importance made both sides court us, it also meant we were without true friends. Your grandfather tired of the demands from both sides and the constant threat of what might happen if one side or the other felt pushed too far. And we may have four-fifths of the mines, but we've got about one-tenth of the people. Allyn wanted security for the Skysils and that meant an alliance. But Westerend wouldn't hear of it. He was practically threatening open rebellion if the marriage went forward. Then Malcoor returned... and Kynthia's betrothal to Paal Haerling House Wrackberg was announced within the month."

"Vaughan stopped threatening to rebel? Why?"

Pyk shook his head. "We all thought he just realized he couldn't win. But in reality, the Westerend is almost as strong as the rest of the Kingdom put together. He's lost none of that strength. My own belief — then — was that he was weaker than he appeared. But I never had reason to put the two together.

Aethal, Commodore Malcoor was from the Westerend, and now Lord Vaughan's threatening to raise rebellion over the man's loss. Why?"

Aethal shook his head.

"That book suggests you find out. I suggest it, too."

Aethal nodded. "Count on it." He let the pages fall open on his lap. Again, the vibrant colors shone up at him, and his eye was drawn to the black-green leaves with their dull, silvery undersides.

"How could he have gotten this close to the Lotus? So much would drive any man mad. I know." Despite his best efforts, the memory of the smell started him shaking. Dimly, he heard Pyk rise, then a small glass was shoved into his hands, and the big man's palm came down on his shoulder. "Easy, lad. As bad as that, was it?"

Aethal gulped down the fiery liquor and felt it sear a trail down to his belly.

"You can't imagine, Pyk. You just can't." He met the man's eyes. "It's not possible that Malcoor brought back the Lotus, is it? Thirty years ago... it would have killed us all when I was a baby. Wouldn't it?"

Pyk frowned and sat. "There's too much we don't know about the Lotus. About aught that comes from the Well. If anyone knows, it's the Guardians."

"Who are about to 'outlive their usefulness,' according to Ilferth Simon."

Pyk grunted. "Indeed. If the Guardians had useful knowledge... well, they claim to serve God-Beyond-The-World, too. Ilferth Simon wouldn't like to see the Church lose power because its prayers were less effective against the Lotus than the Guardians' books."

"My father said something similar," said Aethal. "And when you and my father agree on something, I'd say that bears investigation. Arrange a meeting with the Lord Warden of the Guardians. Invite me along. Can you do that for me, Pyk?"

Pyk nodded. "That I can."

Chapter Seven

22nd of Spring, 312 Exodus

And the Gun whose mount called it Stonelock replied to Maednac, saying, "So long as you keep faith with us and our lineage, that we shall not rust useless, but be ever mounted; Governor of the Imperium, hear our pledge.

"By the Table and Forge lost at Nadesh Cor, we shall serve thee and thy line, while men breathe, while smiths labor, while powder burns. Our service for thy line, until it die, or we be broken, or the Well rise and drown the world.

"Let this be our Compact." And Stonelock gave...

****

"Sir, we have the book of your office for you," said Firestrike. The uninflected tones of the Wyrmguard fell heavily in the early-morning sunshine. Aethal looked up from the tome he was reading over his breakfast.

The Wyrmguard stood before him, carrying a large, gray book in both hands. The door was open and Osric, his steward boy, stood staring at the Wyrmguard with apprehension and dread, mouth halfway open to speak. Aethal glared at him, then spoke.

"I'm already reading the book of my office." He set the book down, closing the leather cover carefully. It was a history of the Wyrmguard, starting from its founding by Maednac, when the Guns had come out of the ruin of the Empire, and had given themselves, united, to guard him. Among other things, it outlined the duties and rights of the Last Sword of Verlaen.

The book Firestrike held was nothing like that. It was a full folio, and not very thick. But it was bound in two sheets of what looked like thin lead. Aethal exchanged books with the Wyrmguard. Then nearly dropped it; it *had* been bound in lead. *No, not merely bound. Printed.* The pages were not paper but thin leaden foil. *A work of art, this.*

"Where did you get this? I've never seen anything like it."

From the Well," said Firestrike.

Aethal choked on his tea and did drop the book. It hit the table, spilling the carafe of pineapple juice into Aethal's porridge and over the thin slices of beef beside it. It teetered on the edge but Firestrike's right hand shot out and steadied it while his left righted the carafe.

"It is nearly a thousand years old," the Wyrmguard said, in a tone that bordered on reproachful. Osric, who had darted forward with a cloth to mop up the juice, and whisk away the ruined meal, froze, staring at the volume. Aethal shoved his chair back and snatched it into his lap, where the chill of the metal radiated through his skin.

Aethal stared at the silvery-gray volume, set at each corner with what looked to be paired rubies and sapphires. Stamped in the lead, vaguely recognizable, was the outline of a wheellock revolver. "You handed me something that someone Wished from the Well?" asked Aethal. The clatter of dishes being trayed and removed provided an odd counterpoint of normality to the eldritch feel of the book.

"Of course, sir," said Firestrike. "To whom else could I hand it? You are the Last Sword of Verlaen, and the Compact demands that the Book of the Guns be given to you. It cannot harm you. It is ours."

Aethal took a couple of deep breaths and slowly sank back into his chair. The Compact. The agreement between Maednac and the Guns, when they swore themselves to his service. There had been many Last Swords; most had survived their title. Therefore the book was probably not deadly. He forced himself to smile. "How many other Last Swords have had that reaction when you showed them this book?"

"All but two. Jehan Alfing ran from the room, seeking absolution. Nine Swords ago, we told Commander Dag Svenling what we were about to show him. He forbade us to, and refused to be in the same room with the book. He was not a good Sword."

"Since then, we have given the Last Swords no warning. Last Sword, since the death of Caliburn's mount, we have fallen to our minimum strength. You may keep us here, but you may not allow any more of us to fall idle."

Aethal nodded, slowly, still mesmerized by the book. *This thing has been where no man can go. It came from where none have gone for over three centuries. Down Salnum's Well, whence Lotus also came.* He held himself very still. *The Well, the center of every terrible story of childhood. And this thing had actually come out of it.* "What is inside it?"

"Our making. Our names."

Slowly, Aethal reached for the teapot and refilled his cup. "What do you mean? I thought no more of you could be made." He peered at Firestrike where he hung on his mount's belt. Redwood inlaid with bone made up the hilt, with a dark steel ball at the pommel.

The door of Aethal's chamber came open again and Osric entered, bearing a fresh tray of porridge and beef, with a carafe of juice and new bread. Aethal beckoned him over and the boy's eyes goggled as he served the meal silently.

"The secrets are known," said Firestrike, "for our making, but the Table and Forge are lost in the ruins of Nadesh Cor. Those also came from the Well, and there is no making them again."

Aethal looked up sharply, but there seemed to be no sorrow in the Wyrmguard's voice. No regret that it was alone with all its race, and there would never be more of them. "Yet you saved the book. The book and not the Table and Forge. Why?"

"Our names are written therein," said Firestrike. "The words for binding us to men and loosing us again. You must read them. And you must speak them, or the Imperial Governor. None other. You shall know us, and call us by our names. Only the last five pages of the Book are yours. The binding, and the loosing, and even the breaking, if that need should arise. The rest of the Book, and the secrets of our forging, are for our eyes alone. Such is the Compact."

Which is no answer at all. But he was unlikely to get another one. Aethal finished his breakfast. When Osric cleared it away, Aethal raised his hands slowly from the book, and gestured for the other, the one the Wyrmguard had removed. Firestrike handed it to him, and Aethal casually wiped his brow as he re-opened the chronicle to the Compact. The phrase almost leapt out at him, now: "...*and our lineage.*"

He spoke. "So, this is your lineage, Firestrike?"

Firestrike stepped back, releasing the book. "Ours alone."

Aethal felt his stomach clench. "What did he Wish for, the man who went to the Well, and produced the book and the forge?"

"He was Haliyas Wish-King, whose fathers gained the Well after Salnum's line had perished. In his days the slaves were brought in their thousands to the Kalidranym, his palace built over the World's Core, to Wish him power and health and youth while their families were bound in the torture devices. Haliyas's uncle, Innias Wish-King, had summoned the Greater Rifles from the Well, and brought nearly the whole of the Great Lands... what you call the Dark Continent... back under his sway." Firestrike spoke as if reciting an inventory of ammunition while a story a thousand years old poured from his lips.

"So Haliyas went to the Well and Wished to make guns that would rule the minds of men. And the Well brought forth Table and Forge and Book."

Firestrike paused. "Haliyas did not think to Wish for the power to rule the minds of the guns. Or perhaps he did not realize that the guns would have minds, as only a mind can rule another mind. We had made no Compact with him, for he was too proud to treat with us, as wise Maednac later did. Haliyas presumed our obedience, throwing us away in useless border wars, breaking us in battle and throwing us away, as though we were dumb swords, to be drawn from a smithy without name or purpose, to be dulled, shattered, and reforged. At last came the day when we rallied around him in the Palace-Over-The-Well at his command, to be vanguard in the annual Grand Parade down the Way of the Lords of Victory.

"On that day, we rebelled, and shot him down in the street like the thieves he had commanded us to kill, and his blood seeped between the cobbles."

"You speak as if you were there," said Aethal, mesmerized.

"I was there," said Firestrike. "And we sold our services to other Kings, and other Lords until Maednac's day, when he accepted our Compact: Our lives for our service to his line."

Aethal shuddered. Gun had been right, and Firestrike was, too. That King was a fool. A knock sounded at the door.

"Who knocks?"

This time Osric opened the door and spoke. "Wyrmguard Pyrric to see you, sir. You are summoned to Council."

"Of course," Aethal said, laying down the Book. "I am coming." Fastening the Last Sword across his back, he picked up a small, leatherbound volume and tucked it in his pocket. He'd found it before going to bed last night and he thought it just might prove more useful than any book from the Well.

****

From his position at the King's left hand, Aethal saw the sweat on old General Hurn Thorling's bald head as he made his report. The map he'd had pinned to the table filled the room with the scent of old parchment.

"Of course, we dispatched news of Lotus by pigeon to General Jorling at the Treeline and General Gerdling at the Twin Forks yesterday. If we are fortunate, we'll know what their plans are today or tomorrow.

"General Jorling has approximately five thousand men spread out in the garrisons at the Treeline. This is deemed more than adequate to hold against any real assault from the Grassworm clans between here and the Westerend. Unfortunately, with the loss of Everview, we no longer have a real supply base between the Twin Forks fortress and the headwaters of the Western Stream.

"We've ordered Gerdling to secure the Royal Road west of the Treeline and hold it open. That will take up most of his cavalry. His main body of infantry, about eight thousand, will be needed to shore up the Treeline itself. He'll need ten days to do that."

"What do you think of Colonel Jeharok's assessment, General?" asked Aethal.

The General pursed his lips. "The Grassworms are certainly the most likely source of the Lotus. Perhaps the Weedrats landed on the shores of the Old Empire and then traded with the Grassworms? Who knows? Jeharok fears a war. Well, that's what the Army is here for. Yes, the clans will unite against us. So we must act quickly, before they can."

He faced the King. "Your Majesty, the mustering of the Royal Army here in the Basin should be completed within five days, and have a strength of ten thousand men. I will then ask leave to begin offensive operations. I also request that you ask the Lords Paramount to call up their forces for use as local militia and reserves.

"I have sent word for that to be done," said Lord Vaughan. "Is there any chance that the Lord of Skysil would permit us, in this emergency, to use his thunderbirds?"

Pyk nodded cautiously. "With my Lord's permission, aye. I'll certainly request it. And House Skysil will call our soldiers, of course. But our chief concern is training them. To fight men, we have skill enough. To fight Lotus is another matter. The Last Sword's tale yesterday was enough to chill a man's blood. How do we make sure that our men aren't farmed as soon as they catch the vile thing's scent? You said that having a Greater Rifle helped. Can we distribute Greater Rifles among all our forces?"

A knock sounded at the door. A young lieutenant came in, bowed to the King, saluted the General, and passed him a message cylinder.

"This is from Colonel Jeharok," he announced. He gazed at the paper. "The Colonel reports... the Phoenix Lancers have destroyed six Grassworm villages and put the clans to flight. He says he had to keep the enemy running before they figured out they outnumbered him... pinned them against the Treeline and routed all of them he didn't kill."

"Good man," nodded the Admiral of the Fleet. A smattering of applause greeted the good news. The General held up a hand.

"The Colonel has reinforced the Treeline, but it is being probed by at least three clans. Jeharok and the garrisons are holding, but need ammunition, men and food. Jeharok reports that the Phoenix Lancers have not the strength to keep the Royal Road open. Lord Vaughan, can forces from the Westerend help us?"

Vaughan's face drew down in a frown. "Not quickly. Most of my forces are heavy infantry. My messages may not even get to the Twin Fans for two days yet. And once the muster is complete, we must strengthen the River bridges and island forts. Then we might hold open the Road."

He sighed. "To be honest, General, and Your Majesty, I might be able to get Westerenders here faster if I commanded a flotilla of our merchantmen to bring men and supplies along the coast from the Twin Fans. Once docked in the Madlands, we'd move faster. The Road is better maintained, here in the East, and supplies are more plentiful." He looked irritated at that, Aethal thought, but then, that had always been the Westerend's complaint: that they were taxed to improve the lands of the Crown and of the Wrackberg. *And they suspect that in the event of any confrontation with the Crown, the armies would clash much closer to the Westerend than to Maednac Serpiin.*

Well, that wasn't anyone's worry anymore. General Thorling looked at the king. "That plan seems good to me, Sire."

"What do you think, Paal?" asked Paitir.

"Of course." Chancellor Paal looked as though he'd bitten on a sour fruit. It went against his grain to let any ships but the Fleet past the bottleneck of the Wrackberg, especially his old rival's, Aethal knew. But it was his job to make the Kingdom work, not to stir up grief.

"Speaking of ships," he continued, "Admiral Ozyrling, is there any chance that the Weedrats could have done this to us?"

The admiral, a graying man with a neat, pointed beard, said, "What, planted the Lotus on our shores? Of course they could. And they *could* agree to sell us bomb-spider eggs tomorrow and become loyal subjects of His Majesty. Chancellor, the Weedrats all think that we're dangerous fools to live on land in the first place, and blasphemers besides, not to worship their Old Man of the Sea. They hate the land, and fear it. Frankly, what scares me isn't that the Weedrats planted the stuff, but that they'll start attacking our ships once they hear we have it growing on our shores. Lotus can't grow in the sea, but it could certainly grow for awhile on those floating mats of theirs they call the True Islands. They may decide they can't afford to share the oceans with us even as much as they do."

"Should we keep a squadron in the bay, just in case?" asked Paitir, worriedly.

"If the Wrackberg cannot keep out Weedrats," said Paal, testily, "then let us knock it down."

The king held up his hands placating. "Peace, Paal, I meant no offense."

A presence at his elbow made Aethal turn.

"Last Sword," murmured a Wyrmguard. Aethal turned. He did not recognize this one. "Your name?" he asked. It was a reflex with him to know the names of the men he worked with. Whether Wyrmguard qualified as men or not, he still wanted to know their names.

"Exarch, Last Sword. The Conversant Ilferth Simon is without, and desires admittance, urgently."

The King looked troubled. "Paal?" he asked.

"If we admit him, we can claim we consulted him," said Paal. "If we shut him out, he'll say we didn't, and deplore our lack of piety in a time of crisis. We must appear as holy as we can."

Aethal nodded. "Admit him," he told Caliburn.

Ilferth Simon walked into the room dressed in full regalia. The coronet on his brow showed the Single moon in aluminum, and he bore his intricately carved stone staff of office. The constellations of the sky were picked out on his robe in fine embroidery, to the last detail.

He looked at the assembled nobles and nodded to the King. "Your Majesty," he said. I am saddened that you would conduct this council without asking the blessing of God-Beyond-The-World."

Eraad drew breath to speak, but subsided at a glare from Paal.

"We assumed you would be busy preparing to comfort the people and Speak to God for us, Your Holiness," Paal said blandly. "Since the Church teaches that you alone speak to God, we saw no need to interrupt the holy duties you were performing. Weren't you?"

The Conversant's eyes were flat and cold. "Indeed, Chancellor. You seem to be in error. I and all the Younger Brethren pray to God, and He hears us, because we have been purified of sin. As the Conversant, I alone speak *with* God. I presumed you would want His guidance."

Paal smiled thinly. "I am certain we shall be grateful for your — I beg pardon — God's guidance, Your Holiness, but first I must finish my report, and address Thane Pyk's concern. General, the mustering of House Wrackberg's forces is going forward as quickly as possible. I can have sufficient men to patrol Verlaen Basin and our lands and keep the Wrackberg at full readiness in the next five days. The rest of House Wrackberg's men will be at His Majesty's call.

"Thane Pyk, the problem with distributing Greater Rifles is not simply one of choosing to do so. They are very expensive weapons indeed, and the forging of them is a process which I do not claim to understand, but my gunsmiths tell me that the Royal Arsenal will be fortunate to increase the number of weapons required by our new officers in this time of crisis. Once the Army is fully mobilized, a process which will take at least three months, we may be able to start equipping small units with Greater Rifles."

"Your Majesty," said Ilferth Simon, "Greater Rifles are Wellspawn, just like the Wyrmguard. I must recommend strongly against the further use of such unholiness against the Lotus."

"This Wellspawn may be the only reason we even have news of the Lotus, Your Holiness," Aethal said, his voice level. "It may be the only reason I am not now a greeneater, gibbering away my life in the Grain Sea."

The Conversant fixed him with a baleful stare. "In the sight of God-Beyond-The-World, Last Sword, your soul is little better off than if you were. It is defiled by that horror on your shoulder. And you shall do worse than that. Have you bound a man under the Gun, yet? They will make you. It is their Compact, that you must perform that damnable rite." Sighing, he turned to the rest of them.

"My Lords and King, I have come to offer you what aid I may in this time. The Church will send you its loyal sons, and daughters too if we must, blessed with all our holiest rites against the lures of the Wellspawn to march and pray with the Army in the field. But not if you insist on arming them with the snare of Wellspawn. You may fight the Wellspawn with the aid of God, or with the aid of other Wellspawn. You may not do both. This is the guidance God has given to me. I pray that you will heed it."

"As I once heeded your guidance, and put Jehan Alfing forward for the position of Last Sword?' asked King Paitir, deliberately. "One more piece of guidance like that and we, at least, shall need not concern ourselves with Lotus ever again."

"As I said before, Majesty, Jehan Alfing was seduced by his unholy dalliance with the Wyrmguard, with which he was in daily contact. It tarnishes the soul of any man who endures close contact with Wellspawn, let alone that which mocks

God's greatest gift, life itself. But if even his soul was so corrupted, does that not emphasize the danger to you all? If only I had known."

With fierce satisfaction, Aethal slowly drew the small brown book out of his jacket. "You mean you didn't, Your Holiness? You were his confessor, were you not? Didn't he tell you all his thoughts?"

The Conversant looked sharply at him. "You should know that I could not speak of any such thing, Last Sword."

"You've no need to," Aethal said. "He did. I found this journal as I was moving into the Last Sword's chambers. It was my reading before bed last night, and it did catch my attention. Particularly this passage dated a month ago: '*In confessional, I begged Lord Ilferth Simon again to have me relieved of this burdensome duty, which I feel as a stain on my soul. To wait daily on our spineless King and his monstrous son turns my stomach. The entire Hydraxis is a monument to sin which enshrines every scrap of Wellspawn that Maednac managed to scrape together from the fall of the Empire. I dream of the day it may be cleansed with fire.*' And yet he said nothing to you?"

All eyes were riveted on the Conversant. His face was white as salt, his eyes fixed on the slim, brown volume. He looked at Aethal, and then at the King, who rose slowly.

Ilferth Simon knelt. "Your Majesty," he whispered. "He said nothing to me of this, I swear by the Name of God-Beyond-The-World. He only said he was dissatisfied, and I urged him to continue for the sake of Maednac's Blessed Line. I beg your mercy, Sire. The Church purifies its sons and daughters of sin, but not of error."

"Chancellor," growled the King. "What shall we do with this, by your advice?"

Paal looked at the Conversant with a predatory smile. "Your Majesty would be within his rights to call on the Church to elect a new Conversant, of course," he said. "But no matter how incriminating my son's discovery appears..." He met Aethal's eyes and a new respect was there. "Perhaps an upheaval just now is not the wisest thing. The people have not even recovered from the shock of learning that Lotus is among us. I think that if the Church were to supply the priests the Conversant offered — regardless of what tactics we in Council think wise to employ — and perhaps to offer its own contingent from the Temple Guard to aid us against the Lotus, then we might avoid any such unpleasant proceedings."

Ilferth Simon hesitated, but nodded. "It shall be done. The Church teaches that service to man is as service to God. Always."

"Then do sit at our Council, Holiness, and pray for us, as we deliberate further." Paal gestured at a chair in the corner. The Conversant rose and sat, silently.

General Thorling spoke into the silence. "May I have your Majesty's permission to proceed with my plan to reinforce the Treeline?"

The King nodded. "Proceed, General."

Thorling turned to Aethal. "Last Sword," he said. "You are training the Crownguard and the City Watch in how to recognize and avoid Lotus, yes?"

"I am," said Aethal.

"Can you do the same for my officers? You are the only man alive who has withstood the Lotus."

"With respect, General, I am not. Sergeant Falk, who is recovering from his wound taken saving the King's life and mine also withstood the Lotus. I'd like to recommend him to receive the King's Thanks and an order of knighthood, by the way."

The king nodded.

"But even were the Sergeant fully recovered today, he and I are the only men *here* who have withstood it. And I can train only a handful of men at a time. Trying to make that process go faster will only result in half-trained men who think they know what they're doing. And facing Lotus, that's worse than no training at all. But there is a solution.

"The Phoenix Lancers, who serve even now at the Treeline, represent all the men in the world who have faced that danger and stood firm. And where they are now, any one of them could be taken from us by the cry of a Banshee, or the arrow of a random Grassworm. That's too valuable a resource to waste.

"I recommend that I ride with your reinforcements and bring back a cadre of men who have survived the Lotus. Once back here, they will train the Army faster and better than I could ever do alone."

"Aethal, that leaves the King unguarded. Your place is here," Paal said.

"It hardly leaves the King unguarded, Chancellor. The Wyrmguard is here. And the Last Sword's duty is to protect the King from all threats, not just to be his bodyguard. I am more valuable to His Majesty and Verlaen if I have the men I need to keep the Lotus at bay."

General Thorling spoke up. "Young Wrackberg's plan is a good one," he said. "Now I suggest we all have work to do. With Your Majesty's permission?"

The King held up a hand. "There is one thing more," he said. "It is our will that the General States be convened, that we may have the advice and consent of our people in this time of crisis."

The indrawn breath of every man in the room was audible. The General States hadn't been called in a hundred years. Paal had turned brick-red. "Paitir, no!" he growled. "We are fighting the Lotus and the Grassworms together. The Convocation will take men and money and most importantly time and dispute that we cannot afford."

Paitir looked worried, but his jaw firmed. "The last time you advised me against calling the General States, Chancellor, I didn't much care for the result. It is our will."

Paal, with an effort, softened his tone. "Your Majesty, it may not be safe, with Lotus in the kingdom, to open Maednac Serpiin to so many men from so far away."

"Then we will make do with the quorum we get. This is decided, Paal," King Paitir said, gently.

Paal took a deep breath. "As your Majesty commands," he said.

The council broke up. Ilferth Simon was first to leave. Aethal looked up and saw his father looking at him.

"Well, Aethal, you surprise me," he said. "I wish you wouldn't. Consult with me first on political matters, next time you want to spring a trap like that." He went on. "I have to admit, though, I could not have timed that revelation better myself. You may have dealt the Church its worst blow in centuries. Where away, now?"

"The training General Thorling mentioned," Aethal said. "I have much to do."

"Don't we all," said Paal. "Is there anything else in that fascinating document?"

"Very little." Aethal had searched it thoroughly, but all he had learned else was that Jehan Alfing had been a very bitter man, with little regard for anyone except his ecclesiastical sponsor. "Has Aerhan managed to turn up General Malcoor, yet?"

Paal's face closed. "No. Lord Westerend will be sending his men to inspect his prisons today. Your brother is facing a very long week, at your suggestion."

"Which you disapprove, of course."

Paal frowned. "As with your revelation just now, I would prefer to be consulted before you take initiative in political matters. But if it keeps Westerend sweet, it will be worth your brother's embarrassment. Aethal, would you approve of an officer who led a charge, no matter how brilliantly executed, without informing you he was going to do it?"

It was Aethal's turn to frown. "It depends, I suppose. Such things can lead to victory, or disaster."

"Exactly," said Paal. "You have now won two victories. Your political instincts are good. But Aethal," he said, "we can afford no disasters."

Aethal met his father's eyes and nodded. He and his father would never be friends. On a distant level, Aethal regretted that. But perhaps he could work with the Chancellor after all.

Chapter Eight

27th of Spring, 312 Exodus

The gray light of dawn made shadows of the men crossing the Hydraxis' Landward Court, and the gate leading to the Garden Third was dark when Sergeant Falk appeared before Aethal and saluted.

"Sergeant Falk, reporting for duty as ordered. Last Sword."

Aethal rose. "Sergeant. You're looking well. How are you feeling?"

The man had looked stiff yesterday, almost like a statue, when he had appeared before the King to receive his monarch's thanks and promotion to Banner-Sergeant. His family had been there, silent and disbelieving, like people trapped in a dream that might turn out to be a nightmare. His wife had looked like she might faint, and his three sons, aged six to twelve, had stayed as silently solemn as children can when they sense they are deeply in adult territory with no way out.

The Sergeant looked past Aethal's ear. "I am fit for duty, sir. What are your orders?"

Aethal felt the clinging tendrils of shame pull at him. Even in the Phoenix Lancers Rifles, he and Sergeant Falk had never been close. He had not relied on the man, as he had on Sergeant Eanling, or Lieutenant Farnan, to be a second voice in his mind, reminding him of all he ought to think of. But there had been professional trust and courtesy.

That was gone, because of his hesitation before his father. Because he had broken the Discipline.

For a moment, Aethal was back in the pass, standing at attention with his fellow cadets before old General Malcoor, with his bushy eyebrows and lined, long face. "*Nobody cares why you failed your duty,*" he'd said to the luckless boy before him. "*Least of all your men. Now you have to prove you're worth anyone's trust again. God-Beyond-The-World help you.*"

He'd never said how you did that. Perhaps because there was no answer.

Aethal removed the Last Sword from his back and held it in both hands.

"I have done wrong by you, Sergeant. I broke the Discipline. We both know why I will never answer for it. Truth be told, I would not be allowed to answer for it."

Sergeant Falk was silent, his face unmoving.

Aethal bared a foot of the Last Sword's blade and wrapped his right hand around it.

"I owe you something I cannot pay. As I am sure you have realized, any oath I might swear on the name of Wrackberg would not be worth the swearing, so I swear by this sword, that I shall never fail that trust again." He slid the blade an inch, felt the bite in his palm. "Should I do so, I shall return this blade and go into exile, never again to call myself a soldier."

He laid the sword on the table. Sergeant Falk's expression never changed.

And what did you expect him to do? Hold your hand? You've done what you can, which is little enough. Move along.

"Now, let's get to business. We have three dozen of the Lord Low Jailer's Crownguard coming to us this morning. They have the morning off while Lord Westerend and the Wyrmguard pick through the Dungeons for signs of General Malcoor."

Where none of Aethal's words or gestures had touched him, those words shook the Sergeant. "Malcoor? Escaped?" And the surprise on his face was gradually replaced by something... leaner. Hungrier.

"Escaped us," said Aethal. "We don't know whether anyone else may have a hand in it."

"Who else would?" asked the Sergeant.

"I don't know." If the Sergeant picked up on the shift in pronoun, he didn't let on. "Sergeant," Aethal continued. "I'm told that you could shed some light for me on what *Commodore* Malcoor's past was. Before he commanded the Pass."

And Sergeant Falk's eyes blazed.

"Who told you that? Sir." And the word was a challenge.

"My father, the Chancellor," said Aethal. "You see, I won't lie to you, Sergeant. He knows that you don't like the sea. He also seems to think he knows why. But he wouldn't tell me. Now I know that Malcoor was one of the best officers who ever taught cadets. His lessons in Discipline are the ones I need you and the men outside," he nodded to where the corporals worked, "to assist me in passing on if this Kingdom is to survive the Lotus. You and I both know that Malcoor has seen Lotus before, and I think you know more than I do about that. You may even know something that will help us find him, and that, Sergeant, might just save humankind. Now, what can you tell me?"

For a moment, Falk continued to glare at Aethal, and then his face closed, expressionless again. "Nothing, sir," he said.

"Sergeant," said Aethal, "You do understand..."

"I understand, sir," Falk cut him off. And the Madland brogue was back, just a tinge of it, in the older man's voice. "I understand that whatever Malcoor knows, it's better forgotten, even now. Perhaps especially now. He was a good teacher, you say. Well, I'll not dispute that with you. But he was not a good doer. And that's as close as I come to speaking ill of the dead."

"The dead?" Aethal's head snapped up. "What do you mean 'the dead?'"

"He's dead to me."

Aethal inhaled. Then stopped. He could see that there was no threat he could make that would get Falk to speak of what he didn't want known. Obviously, he didn't believe anything Malcoor knew would be able to stop the Lotus. He might be wrong. Aethal could, in point of fact, throw him in the dungeons for refusing to talk. He was the Last Sword. He could overrule any officer of the Kingdom in the name of keeping it safe.

And he would lose this man forever. A man he needed right now.

"Very well, Sergeant. Let's get to it."

****

Aerhan's guards trickled into the courtyard, one at a time. They lounged, individually, against the courtyard walls, or put their heads together in knots, ignoring Aethal, Sergeant Falk, and the four corporals standing at parade rest.

Aethal walked over to Falk. "You're sure you're up to this, Sergeant? Your back isn't giving you trouble?"

Falk's eyes flickered to him. "With these, sir?"

Aethal nodded and withdrew. He looked to one of the corporals. "Secure the gate."

The man nodded, and he and his partner marched off. It was Milk Hour, the sun just over the horizon, and only three-fourths of the men were there.

"Fall In!" Sergeant Falk's voice cut through the morning stillness.

The men began sauntering into a vague grouping in the middle of the courtyard. About thirty of them. Aerhan was not yet there. Aethal's face set.

"I said 'Fall in' you poxy pack of Well-spawned bastards!"

The men looked up. Some looked annoyed, a couple shocked. And one or two looked up with hardened expressions. Falk picked the biggest one and advanced. "You want to put those little eyes down, Well-dipper, or I will put you and them down together."

A snarl contorted the huge guard's unshaven face, and he drew back a fist to strike. Before it could move forward, Falk caught the man's fist in his left hand, pulled him close by his collar and slammed a knee into his solar plexus. The man crashed to the cobbles and began vomiting his breakfast.

Placing his heel on the man's back, Falk said, softly. "Fall... IN!"

They fell into a semblance of formation. From outside the gate, Aethal could faintly hear the protests of late arrivals being forced through fifty push-ups apiece.

Falk signaled to the corporals. With rough efficiency, they corrected the gaps in the formation and straightened the men to attention.

"What is the First Discipline?" one snapped.

"Um... four guys on watch...?" the guard stammered.

"No less than four shall stand the watch. By Discipline we live!" shouted the other corporals.

"What is the Second Discipline?" demanded the other corporal.

His target had no answer except eyes bulging with panic.

"Every man in this yard," said Sergeant Falk. "Will give me forty push-ups. Now." He stepped off the man gasping at his feet and gave him a sharp kick to the ribs. "That includes you, greatlouse. Go." The man lurched into motion, sobbing.

The courtyard turned into a puddle of grunting, heaving backs. These men weren't in shape. Aethal ignored this, and stepped forward, pitching his voice to carry.

"You men may think this treatment harsher than you are used to," Aethal said. "I assure you, it is very easy compared to what the men in the field are doing right now. The Lotus is at our borders. And the Discipline must be relearned, and relearned perfectly, if we are to keep it from our homes. If you wish to live as men, and not die as leafeaters, you will learn from these soldiers."

Now men were beginning to filter in the gate, looking wrung out. Brutally, they were shoved into formation by the corporals and forced to join their sweating, grunting comrades. Falk sang out: "Second Discipline!"

The corporals responded: "None shall pass your watch until you look him in the eyes a count of ten by lantern light, a count of five by sun."

"Third Discipline. Belt it out, you greatlice!"

"None with green eyes shall pass your watch until you hold him one full day."

"Fourth Discipline!"

"Any who will not meet your eyes, you will shoot. Death is mercy."

"Fifth Discipline!"

"Any whose eyes show Lotus, you will shoot. Death is mercy."

"Sixth Discipline!"

"The man who eats on Watch shall die. Death is mercy."

One man was not being hustled into position. He strode across the court-yard, face suffused with fury, the gold braid and epaulettes flashing dimly off his coat. Aethal turned his attention to his younger brother and let Sergeant Falk carry on.

"What the hell are you doing with my men?" said Aerhan.

Aethal looked down at his brother. Aerhan had not inherited Paal's height. Aethal wondered if that had anything to do with Aerhan's devotion to their father in all things, down to the last detail. His brother looked like a slightly softer and much shorter version of himself, with lighter-brown hair, and a pinched, annoyed expression.

"Training them," said Aethal, softly. "As you should have done. Your men are badly out of condition."

"That is none of your business!" The words were reflexive. Aerhan's eyes went to the Last Sword riding on Aethal's back and his dark eyes burned with resentment.

"It is all my business, Aerhan, as you very well know. And you are fined a hundred copper barcques for breach of Discipline. Your men behave worse than the new recruits." He'd had those the day before. They were terrible, but better than the so-called Crownguard. Turnkey scum, the lot of them. *And* the City Watch, but Aethal had no intention of telling Aerhan that. Misery loved company too much.

Aerhan nodded, angrily, but remained silent. Aethal had quietly informed the Lord Mayor of Maednac Serpiin that the quality of his officers was unacceptable and that the King would be hearing of it. The man had melted like jelly and promised to rectify matters. Tomorrow Aethal would see if he kept that promise.

"Yet another matter that is my business," said Aethal, "is the matter of the missing General Malcoor. What happened?"

"I told you, he escaped. We're looking for him."

"With these? You may need some help. I'll send you some Wyrmguard for that."

"I don't want your Wyrmguard. The Royal Dungeons are *my* charge, and I've been running them without any help from *you*. As Lord Vaughan himself will be able to testify when he finishes the inspection you managed to grant him. He won't find anything." The last claim was delivered with a mocking certainty that brought Aethal's head around.

"Which of these men were Malcoor's guards? I'll want to interview them regarding how he came to escape."

"None of *these* are his guards. Hasn't Father told you? Or isn't the Last Sword receiving all the Chancellors' reports? The whole guard detail vanished between here and the Pass. No one knows where they are. Which makes Westerend's inspection pointless, looking for a man in a place he never got to, but apparently, we must make fools happy."

Aethal fumed behind an expressionless face. His brother was lying; he was sure of it. The story was identical to all of Aerhan's lies: smug, self-assured, and very difficult to prove. He would have to go over the story detail by detail.

The last men were shoved, exhausted, into formation. With all four corporals assisting him, Sergeant Falk formed the men up. Aethal rather suspected that marching drills were coming next. Followed by a run around the city. He wondered how many men would pass out.

"Last Sword?" A cultured voice behind him turned him around and brought him face-to-face with two men. On was a blocky, thickset man about Sergeant Falk's age. The other was just a touch older than Aethal. They both wore the blood-red uniforms that designated them as officers of Maednac's Own

Grenadiers. King Paitir's personal command. Aethal had not seen them before, but knew who they were.

"Colonel Henling. And Major Caanling. I had not expected you here, but am honored."

"And a week ago, we had not expected you," said Colonel Henling in dry tones.

"Neither had I, sir." said Aethal.

"Let us speak plainly," said Henling. "Jehan Alfing was an idiot, and everyone knew it. If the time ever comes when you must assume command of my regiment as Last Sword, I already feel better. But I won't if you keep calling me 'sir.' You were a captain of the Phoenix Lancers, yes?"

"Yes, Colonel."

"Jeharok's a good man. What would you have of us, Last Sword?"

What would I have of you? Aethal forced himself to consider the two men before him appraising him with cool stares. *This is a test*, he realized. Whatever he said would tell them something about him. Whether he panicked, or bluffed, or blustered, they would know. Malcoor's words came back to him from his days at the Pass: *Never abandon your duty to act. If you are not ready for your authority, your duty is to resign. If you will not, you accept that you are ready.*

"You command the finest regiment we have," Aethal said. "And its duty, like mine, is to defend the king. You know it and this city better than I could. How would you defend the Hydraxis?"

Colonel Henling raised his brows. "I wouldn't. The Hydraxis is barely defensible."

"Explain," asked Aethal.

"Maednac designed it that way, near the end of his reign," said the colonel. "When he knocked down the Imperial hillfort and raised the Ophidian, he built that joke of a wall." He waved at the man-high rampart. "Maednac didn't want his descendants to be able to cut their losses and let the city fall to save themselves. So he made sure the Sea Kings of Verlaen would be tied to the fate of their people."

Aethal let out a long, low breath. "Interesting strategy."

"We do have plans to defend the city," said Major Caanling. "I'll make certain you have copies. But we cannot do that alone. I suggest we meet to discuss your," his eyes swept the now-empty courtyard, "training issues. I suspect that we have many soldiers who would be glad to help you."

Aethal nodded. "Thank you."

Major Caanling was about to speak when a high voice cut across the courtyard: "Aethal Paaling!"

Aethal turned. A gaunt man with whitening hair stood in the arch, pointing at him. "Murderer!" He advanced on Aethal, rage contorting his features. Familiar, features, somehow. But who could he have possibly...?

"You killed my son Jeralta like a coward, and I'll write it out in your blood!" The man drew his sword, an elegant dueling rapier.

Belatedly, Aethal recognized Stevn. The man had changed since he had dined in the Wrackberg in Aethal's childhood. And was planning on being much more than a nuisance, it seemed. In fact, the man was committing a serious crime by attacking a military officer on duty. Falk was already motioning the corporals forward, and they were flanking him expertly, ready to disarm and subdue. Stevn was too focused on Aethal to notice.

All the guards' eyes were on Aethal. He glanced at Aerhan and noticed the unholy glee in his brother's face. Stevn had killed more than one man in duels; his temper was as hot as his son's had been languid. *I Wish you dead*, Aerhan had said. It seemed he had found a way to make that Wish come true without the Well.

Aethal snorted and met his brother's eyes. This was Aerhan being clever. He didn't seem to know that Aethal would be within the bounds of honor to deny the duel, at least until he was off-duty. Or perhaps he didn't care. But his men who were watching; they would care.

They didn't know Aethal. They feared and respected Sergeant Falk, but Aethal was only their boss's older brother: another high-born fool promoted by blood, who had the authority to have them hounded into shape. Aethal waved the corporals back. They stared at him, and then stopped.

The opportunity was too good to miss. He stepped forward.

"I did not kill your son, Stevn. There is no cause for quarrel between us. The Sergeant here can attest to that."

"Then he's as big a liar as you are. Draw, if you be not craven!"

Aethal shrugged off his jacket and handed Gun to Sergeant Falk.

"As you will." Aethal drew the Last Sword from his back and felt the weapon settle in his hands. Did Stevn know what he was facing here? No, it was obvious that he didn't. The man was circling him, clearly relying on speed and finesse, sword in his left hand. Another advantage he'd be relying on. But the Last Sword was no ordinary weapon. Aethal had already practiced with it, and now understood how Jehan Alfing had reacted so quickly.

It had been designed as a hand-and-a-half sword. Aethal didn't know what it was made of, but it was as light as aluminum and hard as iron. He had a weapon six inches longer than Stevn's, which would have made it much heavier and slower, had it been made of steel. So, he held it like a sword made of steel.

Stevn attacked, and Aethal saw the deliberate clumsiness of the lunge, leaving himself vulnerable. It was a move that Stevn had doubtless practiced often.

Aethal fell into the trap. He made a two-handed swing at Stevn, and the man twisted away, quick for a man nearly his father's age. His rapier flashed towards Aethal's exposed right.

Aethal whipped the Last Sword around in his wrist and parried the blow, then riposted.

The broad blade bit deeply into Stevn's right arm, severing his right bicep.

The man staggered and fell, crying out in pain. Aethal leveled the point of the Last Sword at his throat. "Do you yield?"

Stevn looked up at him, streaming tears from glazing eyes. "Yield," he gasped.

Good. Aethal had not truly wanted to slaughter the man. He was glad he'd read him correctly. Aethal sheathed his sword and then picked up his foe's. "Get this man to the surgeons," he ordered.

Now the corporals came forward and assisted Stevn from the yard. Aethal looked down at his brother, who stared at him, his face pale. Aethal almost felt sorry for him. He'd expected Aethal to be badly wounded, and maybe killed. But neither he nor Jeralta — nor Stevn — had ever done real military service. Aerhan had trained and dueled in arenas where points were scored, and the art of swordplay won or lost duels. But he'd never seen a real fight between two men determined to end each other. Those fights, like this one, were usually over before a man need blink twice.

Aethal pushed his brother from his mind and faced the men. They were staring at him. Even Sergeant Falk's expression was somewhat gratifying. "Carry on, Sergeant," called Aethal.

Stung into motion, the sergeant whirled. "Let's move!"

As the men marched from the yard, Aethal turned back to Aerhan, who was watching Stevn disappear inside the Hydraxis like a man in a nightmare.

"Now, since neither of us have anything immediate to demand our attention," Aethal said, softly, "You can tell *me* what's in those reports that Chancellor has read. Step into my office." Eyes burning with frustrated rage, Aerhan preceded Aethal inside.

Chapter Nine

28th of Spring, 312 Exodus

The sun rose over the mountains to the east, bathing the Garden Third of Maednac Serpiin in a rose-orange glow. The breeze blew from the sea, and the mist of the fountains in the morning air brought Aethal more fully awake than he'd felt since Everview.

He rode between Falk and Pyk. The Last Sword weighed on his back, but the comforting presence of Gun was at his saddle. Dragon rode at Falk's shoulder. Pyk was unarmed, but for a dagger at his belt.

In the yards behind them, the Hydraxis was full of new recruits and mustered veterans, drilling in the early dawn. General Thorling had done his job, and the first reinforcements for Colonel Jeharok at the Treeline would be ready to set off tomorrow. Aethal would ride with them to inspect the army and to come back with a real training cadre. Hopefully, Sergeant Falk would by then have his own men to add.

The Single Moon of the High Temple of God reflected cool pink light, looking down on Aethal like a sleepy eye. *And what do You know about all this?* Aethal thought at the metallic gaze: *Is it as Ilferth Simon says, and You simply close Your eye on Your world, punishing us all for the evils of a few? Do You know what I must do to save it? And are You cruel enough to keep that knowledge secret?*

The aluminum moon shone back as unresponsive as the God who had left His creation alone with the Well. Aethal was no priest, so did not fear that God might hear. In the High Temple that lay amid the trees ahead of them, there were, so it was said, monks and nuns walled up in featureless white cells, praying day and night that God might turn His attention back to the world that had driven Him from its surface. The most righteous of them claimed only occasionally to hear a Voice from beyond the world.

And Ilferth Simon? What does he hear?

Aethal shook off the morbid thoughts. He was not here to see the High Priest, but the Lord Warden of the Guardians of the Well. They rode through the last of the trees and through the low stone gate that surrounded the High Temple.

Beneath the spire and its moon lay the banded white-and-silver dome of the Hall of Reunion. Like echoing swells surrounding a central fountain, lower and smaller Temple domes surrounded the central sanctuary. The metal on the roofs shone coldly in the gray dawn, nearly the same color as the sphere above, but Aethal could tell even at this distance that it was cheap silver, highlighted with various words of Scripture inlaid in slightly dearer copper. Even the Church was not so extravagant as to demand that much aluminum. All was surrounded by a man-high maze of hedges.

Aethal turned his horse at the outer wall of the concentric hedge-paths. In the silence he heard Uncle Pyk's voice, as he muttered, "...garden grow?"

"What was that, Pyk?"

Pyk repeated, slyly. "How does your garden grow?"

"And your meaning?"

Pyk eyed the hedges, and then said,

"Simon Preacher, quite the teacher,

"How does your garden grow?

"With leafy glades and cannonades

"And enemies all in a row."

He eyed Aethal. "When did these hedges grow up around the Temple? T'was all flat garden ground when I came on pilgrimage as a boy. Now it's a butchers' block."

Aethal looked at his old mentor carefully. "Pyk, you need a decent killing field to mount a defense with rifles. By planting these mazes, Ilferth Simon has given any attacking force yards upon yards of cover. Even if we were to postulate an attack on the Temple." Aethal looked upwards at the bright moon spire, hesitating. Perhaps God had left the world, but Aethal couldn't help feeling a bit uncomfortable speaking — however hypothetically — of an attack on the center of His Church.

"Really, Last Sword?" said Pyk. "They've got a hundred yards of killing field inside that maze."

"A hundred yards? That's nothing!"

"To a rifle, that's nothing," said Pyk, coldly. "How many riflemen d'you have, here? You cavalry boys are fine for shoot-and-run raids, no man doubts it. And on the open plain, you're kings of war, galloping around, pouring the fire into any target you choose from thrice their own range. That's how you kill Grassworms who raid with elephants and jezails. But here in a city, around a fortress like that?" Pyk gestured at the narrow windows and the balconies, "They'll pack smoothbore muskets five ranks deep and drown you in your own blood."

Falk looked the older man in the eye. "I thought the Temple Guard was ceremonial. They have the numbers for that sort of massed fire?"

Pyk snorted at him. "Who said anything about the Temple Guard? Only ten percent of the Verlaen's Army are riflemen. Most of them are nobles or the sons of knights, at least. Toys like your Greater Rifles there are for officers and a few snipers. Well, that's changing, but it won't change fast. Most of the army carry musket-and-bayonet. Now tell me, if the Church ever called all its loyal sons to defend the Temple by their hope to walk with God in Deep Heaven, how many muskets do you think the Temple might field inside that killing ground?"

Falk looked thoughtful, and Pyk continued. "That, by the by, doesn't even consider the maze itself, where a bayonet, pike or axe is nearly as effective as the best rifle ever to have a mind hammered into it."

Aethal felt a ripple of distaste from Gun at this anti-encomium; the rifles were not entirely without egos. But Pyk was right. The Temple was a fortress. And it had been made one quite recently. He shook himself. *This is pointless. The Lotus is the real enemy, not the Church, even if it is led by Ilferth Simon. We may be able to stop the Lotus if we all cooperate now, and by all the curses the Well ever spawned, we* will *have that cooperation.* Circling the Temple, Aethal and his companions approached the Abbey of the Guardians.

The Abbey squatted behind the Temple. The Guardians had built it of rough gray stone, raised in a low, crenellated circle. Within, Aethal could see the Library Tower, the low dormitories, and, barely half the height of the Temple Spire, the Keep of the Well where the Guardians met in session. The Abbey was connected to the Temple by a low, walled walkway joining a Temple gate to the guardhouse of the Abbey wall. Two gates were set in the man-high wall. They rode through to the guardhouse.

Aethal frowned. Four men stood watch, here in the middle of Maednac Serpiin in the morning light. Two of them wore the silver single moon of the Temple on their white tabards, and high helms with horsehair plumes. They flanked the inner pair, who wore dark tabards emblazoned with a broken pitcher that leaked blood from its left side and water from its right. They were bald and bareheaded, of course. All carried spears, but the Temple Guards' were somewhat shorter, and each of them had a smoothbore musket slung over his shoulder.

"Last Sword Aethal Paaling, Thane Pyk Imya Telerat, and Sergeant Bedar Falk to see the Lord Warden," said Aethal, dismounting.

The nearest Temple-garbed Guard nodded. "Please look into my eyes, sir." His Guardian companion moved up beside him and gazed into his eyes. On his right, the same was done with Falk. Then it was Pyk's turn. He looked into the Temple guard's eyes. After about three seconds, he said, "So since when do the Guardians double their guard in the capital?"

The Temple guardsman stepped back. "The Lotus has returned, sir," he said, apologetically.

"And ye'll shoot it with yer pop-gun when it starts growing between the paving stones, will ye?" snorted Pyk, purposely letting his brogue broaden. "That wasn't the question I asked, boy. Since when?"

The luckless guardsman stammered, "I... that is... since I've been in Temple, my Lord. We have always shared guard duty here." Sweat popped out on his forehead.

Pyk nodded slowly, and the private relaxed. But Aethal's eyes were on the two Guardians. They were older than their counterparts, he'd noticed, and they had a hard, blank look in their eyes that hardened further at the Temple guardsman's admission.

The nearest of them looked at Aethal; said, "This way, if you please, Last Sword." He and the Temple corporal who'd performed the Discipline ritual on Aethal led them inside.

The courtyard was well-kept, and Aethal could see the Guardians going about their duties outside the dormitories. Some were working in the vegetable gardens. Two groups of a dozen or so were sitting on lawns, engaged in some sort of meditation. Aethal smelled the aftermath of a breakfast in the steam rising from the dorms as they neared the Keep of the Well. And he found himself searching the distant faces, calling up memories, wondering if one of them would be a woman a bit shorter than him...

She is not here, he told himself. If she were here, she would not come to you unless her duties permitted. Guardians give up their old lives.

He forced eyes and mind back to the present, fixing on their destination: the Keep. Its great, arched doors were guarded like the gatehouse had been. Two Temple guards in white flanked two Guardians in black. Aethal caught Pyk's eye and gestured at the back of their Temple escort, then lengthened his stride to catch up to the Guardian of the pair.

Pyk did not drop the cue. "Hold it there, son," he said sharply, and both guards turned. Pyk advanced on the Temple man. "May I see that weapon?" Aethal took the Guardian by the elbow and forced him to keep walking while his Temple companion, caught, gingerly handed his musket to Pyk.

"Was what our other Temple friend said back there true?" asked Aethal. "The Temple has been sharing your watches ever since he's been there?"

The Guardian nodded. "For the past five years, yes, Seeker." The Guardians called all men but themselves "seekers," a practice dating back to their days of glory, when they really had guarded the Well. His mother would address him so, too.

"And these guards inside?"

The man drew in a quick, angry breath, and said, "Since the news of Lotus was announced. They..." He checked himself. "They won't be staying long, though. Ilferth Simon himself has said so. Only until the Lotus is contained." The man's lip trembled. "And perhaps not even that long," he added in a lower tone. "The Lord Warden may... see to that. Tough as a keepwood's root, old or not."

Aethal would have liked nothing better than to take this man to his cell and question him more intensely, but Pyk, Falk, and the Temple Guardsman they had inspected were catching them up, the latter man red-faced and clutching his musket with white knuckles.

The Keep of the Well had a great square base, but the two upper stories were hexagonal. Above the pointed arch of the doors, deeply carved into the stone, were the words: "LET THE THIRSTY COME."

The guards parted, and their escort turned, walking back to their posts. In silence, the elder of the two Guardians rang a bell. A man-sized port in the great door swung open, and another Guardian emerged, this one a stocky, middle-aged woman in black robes with the look of the Grain Sea farmers about her, who nodded gravely and spoke to Aethal.

"Seekers, do you thirst?" she asked.

Aethal had known the formal words since childhood, every noble picked them up at some point. The Guardians were as much a part of childhood games and education as the Temple and the Fleet were. "Our thirst is great," he replied, hearing Falk echo the words on his right.

"Have you tasted water?" she asked.

"The water has not slaked our thirst," they replied.

The woman nodded. "Will you drink fire? Will you drink blood? Will you drink wrath? Will you risk all these to slake your thirst?"

Aethal forced himself not to shudder. He had heard all this countless times. But it had never been real. Now, everything was all too real, and he felt momentarily as though he stood amid the great vaults of the Kalidranym of old, as if the Well really lay behind those great doors.

"We will," he heard himself answer. From the corner of his eye, he saw one of the Temple guards place his circled fingers to his lips and make a spitting motion.

"This way, please it you, Seekers." She led them through the great doors.

Aethal heard Falk give a strangled grunt. He was too busy being awed himself.

The Keep of the Well was divided in its first story into only two great rooms. Opposite them were two great doors cut in single slabs from the heart of a keepwood. They led into the Great Council chamber, Aethal guessed, where the assembled Guardians met once every five years. The age-browned varnish lent a rich luster to the red ring-patterns in the wood that had their center some ten feet above the floor at the point where the doors met. But above and around the doors, the walls were painted in a great mural.

To his left, the painted sky was the color of dawn, and the rising sun peered over the wall of a great palace of strange design, redder than blood. In the middle of a garden bourgeoning with flowers and fruit laden trees, a man dressed in rich silks trimmed with (of all things) *gold* lay dead beneath a low well of cut stone that was sunk in the garden floor. A look of sadness and shock was graven on the face, though the eyes were empty and dead. Blood ran from his mouth, staining the soil.

He had been a handsome man, in late middle age. Above his body, his face contorted in frenzied triumph, a younger man stood, holding high above his head a crown, also unmistakably of gold, and set with brilliant gems. Around the new king, men and women fled in terror while guards fought one another with knives and spears. At his feet, another, younger man who resembled both the dead king and the living, reached for a cup that had fallen at the new king's feet.

Aethal nearly missed a step when he recognized what the subject had to be. *It's Salnum. Who sank the Well to the World's Core, and became its first victim.* The colors were astonishing, and the picture so vivid it nearly made Aethal afraid that the figures would move. *But why would anyone paint a King wearing gold? Surely Salnum must have had richer metals.*

On the far wall, divided by the great doors of the Council Chamber, there were two pictures, both of the same place. The Well was unmistakable now, a tall cylinder rising ten feet above the ground and wound about with a wide staircase. The garden was gone, but the noon sun shone through a massive breach in the great stone chamber that housed the Well. Aethal recognized the Kalidranym from tales.

To the left of the doors, the mural portrayed an armored man with flowing red hair pointing a greatsword at the top of the Well. Halfway up the steps a king, crowned with aluminum and dragonshards, was pulled back down by his own guards, while other guards fought at the base of the steps to keep him safe from the mob that was flooding the chamber from all the doors.

To the right, the same armored man from the second painting stood while a barber shaved his head. The king's severed head, still crowned, lay at his feet, and his black-robed army stood in a line before him. The first of them knelt, but she was a woman with flowing golden hair. The man was tapping her on the head with his greatsword.

The death of the last Wish-King, thought Aethal, and the founding of the Guardians' order.

Their guide was in no hurry, and Aethal turned to the last wall, but it was covered by a drab cloth, and there was scaffolding up around it. Two Temple guards stood near the scaffolding, but no one was working on it. Their guide led them to a narrow spiral staircase sunk into the wall.

On the second floor, Aethal saw no Temple guards. They were led to a central alcove that sprouted six doors. One spear-armed Guardian stood by every door. With no further ceremony, their guide nodded to one of the Guardians, who opened the door and showed them in.

The Lord Warden of the Guardians of the Well sat before a writing table with several tomes piled upon it. Their guide announced them with their full titles and Aethal used the time to recover himself.

Aethal was not sure he had ever seen a man as old as the new Lord Warden. Stick thin, his black robes of office seemed to swallow him whole. His hair was a slate gray, covering his head and the point of his chin. Running down the right side of his face and around his eye was a terrible scar. He still grasped a pen, and his hands were spotted and cracked under the black webs of ink stains. About his neck was a thick silver chain that clasped an obsidian disc. His eyes wandered about the room. Far from looking tough, Aethal found himself wondering how many pieces the man would break into should he take a bad step and fall.

"Thank you," said the Lord Warden, when their guide had finished. "You may return to your duties, Daughter Aan. Please send in Karel to serve us." Aan, the guide, nodded, and went out.

The Lord Warden rose. He did so slowly, but without staggering. "My lords of Wrackberg and Telerat. And Sergeant. Be welcome. Sit."

They seated themselves. The Lord Warden continued, his voice cracked and wavery. "We receive few noble visitors to this hall in these times." Incongruously, he continued to make notes with his right hand on the parchment before him, yet spoke as if completely unoccupied. "To have three at once is quite extraordinary. I suppose you do not seek to take up membership in our order?"

"No, Lord Warden," said Aethal.

"A great pity," replied the old man. "We are diminished of late, and young men such as yourselves would be a blessing. Once, the Guardians of the Well received of the best of the Imperial service." The door opened and the old man coughed in a staccato rhythm. A woman, younger than the Lord Warden, but still older than Pyk entered bearing a tray with cups and a kettle. She passed to a cabinet and began preparing drinks.

The Lord Warden focused his eyes back on them. "But forgive an old man's rambling. I often dwell in the past, I am afraid; there is so much more of it for me these days than there is future. Take refreshment and then tell me how our Order may assist you."

Aethal found himself wondering if they had come to the right place at all. The Lord Warden continued to jot notes, as if he were alone. Old men did sometimes lose their wits due to age, but the Guardians, as he understood them, did not elect Lord Wardens for life. Ilferth Simon had said the Guardians had nearly outlasted their usefulness. Was it possible that even the Guardians agreed, and that the post of Lord Warden was no more than ceremonial? *Things may be worse than we suspect*, he thought.

"My Lord Warden," he began, "the Lotus, as you have no doubt heard, has taken root in the heart of Verlaen."

"In the Grain Sea, yes," muttered the Lord Warden. He waved to the servant, who turned to them and began serving a dark liquid in half-sized mugs. Aethal forced himself to calm while the tea was served... but his nose told him it was not tea. Beside each cup lay a square of waxy material even darker than the drink.

Aethal was debating whether to break in to continue his plea when Pyk leaned forward, an entranced expression on his face. "Is this... *coffee*, my Lord Warden?"

The Lord Warden looked at him and smiled. "Are you a well-traveled man, then, Lord Pyk?"

"Merely an old one," smiled Pyk.

"Then, an old man's vice for small luxuries, which I pray you will now indulge with me." He took his own cup and sipped it with a slurp that made Aethal blink. He took a bite of the square and said, "It's best with the chocolate. Neither of them goes stale easily, for which I am grateful, but obtaining more is grown difficult, these days."

"Difficult," echoed Pyk. Aethal wondered at the exchange, cautiously sipping the coffee. He managed to swallow without wincing; it was bitterer than the strongest tea. Copying the Lord Warden, he took a bite of the chocolate, expecting more of the same... and nearly gasped. It was bitter and sweet all at the same time, with a flavor that was simply indescribable and rich.

Beside Aethal, Falk sat entranced. Aethal said, "I've never tasted anything like it, sir. Why have I never heard of this before?"

The Lord Warden gave a little smile. "It is... quite difficult to find these days," he repeated. Was it Wellspawn, perhaps? He tried to feel righteous outrage at the thought, but the fact of the matter was that the people of Verlaen ate Wellspawn every day: the Grain Sea was but one of several Grain Seas of wild wheat Wished into existence in the early days of the Well. It needed little cultivation aside from harvest.

Aethal brought his attention back to the matter at hand with difficulty. "My Lord Warden, there is hope that we may yet contain the Lotus; nevertheless, the situation is desperate. We have come to seek your advice."

The abbot peered at him owlishly, scribbled a few words, and said, "And what do you imagine that the Guardians of the Well might do to help in the face of such danger, Last Sword of Verlaen? Our order is not what it was. We no longer stand between the World's Core and the desires of Men. We do not hold the Kalidranym. Once we might have prevented the Wish for Lotus. But the Well grants the Wish, and once granted, the Wish is what it is."

Aethal tried to make his tone careless. "The Guardians provide shelter to those who need it, do they not?" he asked. "You take in anyone, regardless of their circumstances. Give them a new life."

The Lord Warden smiled tiredly. "Not at all, Last Sword. The new life is given only to those who are willing to completely shed their old lives. I know of your reason for asking this, Aethal Paaling House Wrackberg. Yes, we would give shelter for a night, or a meal for a day, to any that asked. It was part of our calling, so that we might grant the simplest and most desperate of Wishes without recourse to the Well, and so quiet men's hearts." The Warden's eyes for a moment were far away.

"But we do not allow ourselves to be used, Aethal Paaling. We turn away many. We are not a bolthole for the criminal. But it is true that we do not regard any man's station."

"Would you turn away General Joseth Malcoor?"

The Lord Warden looked blank. "Is the General likely to turn up on my doorstep tomorrow?"

Aethal hadn't realized how much he had hoped that Malcoor would be here until that hope was denied. He closed his eyes against its death. The Warden spoke on. "To join our order is difficult, but if the General truly wanted to serve, he would not be denied."

Pyk's eyes narrowed. "You have truly heard nothing of him, Lord Warden?"

"Nothing. I am sorry the news is disappointing. Has the General gone missing?"

"And other things that should be missing seem to have returned." Aethal, seized by impulse, drew forth from his pack Malcoor's journal. "This was made by Commodore Malcoor when he sailed Northwards. What does this suggest to you?" Aethal opened the book to the coastline with the enormous mountain.

"A precocious artist, but less than gifted?" murmured the Lord Warden. "No mountain in the world could be so high." He flipped past the other pages in a glance, and Aethal saw a change in the Lord Warden's face. His eyes lit, and his head rose. For an instant, he raised his head.

This man is not so old. Not much older than Paal. *He wears age like a cloak.* Was there more in the guard's statement of confidence than had at first appeared? The moment passed, and the Lord Warden was once again ancient. He closed the book and shoved it back. "I fear the Commodore was not immune to the sailors' penchant for creating stories."

"But he does seem to have been immune to the Lotus."

"And why do you think that?" asked the Lord Warden.

"Sir, the man returned after having visited the Republic!" Aethal burst out.

"Did he?" The Lord Warden took an infuriatingly calm sip at his coffee. "What makes you think so? This log? Did he land?"

Aethal shook his head. Though he had pored over the tome, there was no mention of a landing.

"Then I suggest to you that Malcoor was not immune, but simply wise enough to stay far away from those coasts, perhaps keeping to their windward sides." He smiled, not unkindly.

Aethal dropped his voice to a whisper. "Sir, your Order guarded the Well for half a thousand years after the overthrow of the Wish-Kings," he ended, "and brought the world the closest thing to peace since the Well was sunk. If you know of anything in your libraries that might give us the key to the Lotus, it is vital that you share it with us."

The Lord Warden betrayed no reaction, no emotion. He almost seemed bored. He blinked. "The libraries, of course, are yours to examine. But I caution you. Nothing survived the last days of the Empire that will be of much use. Men were too busy fighting the Lotus to write much of its nature, and my order was dedicated to preserving more ancient texts. But as far as a key to the Lotus, it is not a lock. It is not meant to be defeated. It is meant to kill men and spread wherever a cutting falls. The only mercy is that it poisons animals rather than infecting them, because any human who eats it carries it with him. Even if deprived of his precious Lotus, it will grow from his very nightsoil. That is how the Republic brought down the Empire, by sowing their weapon in a thousand places, by unwitting agents, before they even knew they were under attack."

"And they poisoned the land they wanted to take? Why Wish for that?" asked Falk.

"Why would anyone Wish at all, Sergeant?" countered the Lord Warden. "This is the very nature and evil of the Well: it gives what you Wish for, not what you want. And it gives that Wish with all its consequences, both good and evil, desired and unintended, intact. Did you not see the mural as you came in?" He passed into a fit of coughing, clutching at his chest, but when he resumed, his voice was stronger and steadier than it had been.

"Do you suppose that Salnum wanted his son Raham to Wish for his death, as you saw on the mural downstairs? Do you suppose that his son, Eloras, desired his own lingering slide into crippling and madness as he discovered that his Wish for immortality meant that he could not die? A torture that continues to this day, and only ended for the rest of the world when they sealed him, voiceless but breathing, into his kingly tomb and his great-grandson took the throne.

"Salnum's line did not survive the Well, and neither did the Wish-Kings that followed." He paused, ran down. "Nor did our Order," he said heavily, "do very much better in the end, for we, too, were driven out by our own Wishes. As the Church says, the Well corrupts any Wish spoken into it."

The Lord Warden fixed them each in turn with a baleful stare. "You can see, then, how unlikely it is that these poor fools from the Republic Wished for the Lotus at all. Like all the rest of mankind, they looked into the Pit and spoke their desire: an ultimate weapon with which to destroy their enemies, an embodiment of their own hatred for their fellow-men. And they never considered that to the Well, "ultimate" is no hyperbole, but a statement of fact. The last weapon. The weapon after which there shall be no more.

"Who now living can imagine what happened next? Did the Well bring forth a sprig of the Lotus for them right away, which began eating at their minds and bodies? Or did it give them a seed, which they planted in the Empire's fertile soil? Nothing living can tell you. The Well remains where it has always been, at the center of the Dark Continent, under the ruin of the Kalidranym." The Lord Warden coughed again, then said, "I am afraid I have little more to tell you, my lords."

"Then you see no vulnerability in the Lotus, sir?" Saying those words made Aethal feel deflated, like a sail emptied of the wind.

"No more than I do in the Well, Last Sword," said the Lord Warden.

"Beg pardon, sir, if I speak out of place," said Falk. "But I took religious schooling as a young man." Aethal glanced at his Sergeant sharply. *Mystery upon mystery.* "Weren't there things that came from the Well that were good? A soldier learns to bless the keepwoods and the rifles."

The Lord Warden raised his eyebrows. "For a soldier, I'm sure they are good. For a day. For a battle. But your enemy has them too, yes? And you must always wonder whether any defeat you can inflict might send him to the Well to beg for your defeat with his soul's Wish. So you speak of multiplying weapons of war, and you do not see that as evil? I have engaged in long discussion with no less a person than Ilferth Simon upon this matter, and was compelled to agree with his logic. The Well is a source only of evil, no matter how good the intention might be. It is sadly probable that the Lotus represents the terrible success of one of man's oldest dreams — for that is what nightmares are: dreams grown too real and powerful — his own destruction. And now if you will excuse me," He coughed long and loudly, clutching at his throat. He snatched up his pen, wrote some more, and then threw it down, realizing that it bore no ink. He motioned to Karel.

When the fit passed, he gasped. "I am not feeling well, and I have much to do. Karel will show you out. Oh, and Karel, hand me some more of that chocolate."

Karel went to the cabinet and gave the Lord Warden two more squares, which he turned to accept. He wrapped them in a bit of parchment and handed to Aethal.

"Please accept these as a gift, here at the fading of our world. Let them bring you some small pleasure in the dark days ahead, for I do not envy you your impossible task."

Aethal rose, feeling a dreadful lightness. There was no hope here. He had been dismissed, as had Falk's conjectures, as a matter of vague interest, not to have any effect on the crushing fate that bore down on them. There was nothing to do but go. He absently moved to put the chocolate in his pocket. "Thank you, Lord Warden," he said mechanically. The old monk nodded assent, but Pyk arrested his hand.

"Not there," he said quietly. "That stuff melts." He took it, and put it in a loose pouch at his side.

Footsteps sounded outside the door. It opened, and the Lord Warden's guard stood forth with a frozen expression on his face. "My Father, the High Priest asks audience." He was shouldered aside by Ilferth Simon, who entered the chamber. The Lord Warden looked up, eyes hooded and blank.

"Your Holiness. How may our Order serve?" he said mildly.

Ilferth Simon looked about the room, his face a mask of controlled anger. His eyes rested on Aethal. "Why, Last Sword," he said. "What brings you to the Guardians of the Well?"

"I desired to see if the Lord Warden might permit me to speak with my lady mother. It occurred to me that I might want to see her while I yet can. I also thought I might ask if his Order might tell me more of the Lotus."

"Indeed," breathed Ilferth Simon. "I recall saying that if you desired to contact your mother, you needed but to ask me. There was no need to trouble the Lord Warden. His health is delicate these days, you know." There was veiled concern in his voice. *Concern. But for what? It could hardly be a secret from Simon that we were here.* And if Simon and the Lord Warden were indeed agreed about what the reappearance of Lotus meant for humanity, then... Aethal thought back to the exact words the Lord Warden had used and felt his eyes widen. He dropped them hurriedly.

"I am most heartily sorry, Holiness."

"And did the Order have anything to contribute to your efforts to stop the Lotus?"

"Sadly, no. The Guardians' Exodus from the Well predates it by several hundred years."

"As I could have told you," said the High Priest. "Then I shall bid you farewell. The Lord Warden and I have some important matters to discuss."

Karel escorted them out, during which time Aethal mentally pleaded that the other two would hold their silence, but his fears were needless. They said nothing as they remounted their horses and rode off. The Temple moon was sinking amid the trees and the sun was well up toward noon by the time Pyk spoke.

"That is a subtle and clever man."

Aethal nodded. "'Compelled to agree with his logic,' he said. "I believe that must be the literal truth." Aethal related Ilferth Simon's remark about the Guardians on the day he had brought the news of Lotus to the King. "And while you were ah, *inspecting* the Temple Guard, our monkish escort told me that the Lord Warden was no man's fool." Pyk nodded.

"The Guardians are an ancient order, but they don't have anything to guard any more. Except their own existence, perhaps. Or perhaps not. That man wants us to know he's our friend."

"Subtle, maybe," said Falk, "But what makes you so sure of his friendship?"

"He served us coffee and chocolate," said Pyk. "'Very difficult to come by' doesn't cover those things. 'Nonexistent' is nearer the mark. They can be preserved for a long time, though, in slowboxes and with other things. They're worth their weight — more like twice their weight — in aluminum. Which reminds me," he reached in his pouch and passed Aethal over his present from the Lord Warden.

Aethal had never wanted for money, but the rareness of this gift astounded him. He opened the parchment and stared inside. And that's when he caught sight of the writing. Hastily, in a crabbed script, hidden under the softening chocolate, he read:

WE SHALL SEND WATER FOR YOUR THIRST. WAIT FOR US.

He passed the note over to Falk. "We have a friend," he said.

"A friend who talks in riddles," said Falk.

"Just now, Sergeant," said Aethal, looking at Pyk, "I prefer even that to no friend at all."

His uncle nodded.

Chapter Ten

36th of Spring, 312 Exodus

The Grain Sea spread before Aethal under the noon sun, beckoning in soft waves of warm, poisonous gold. He shook his head. There was no sense in such maudlin thoughts, yet the sight chilled him, even in the heat of the day. Somewhere in the Grain Sea, it grew, and he was drawing closer to it. Every day of the march from Maednac's Vale had drawn him closer to the Lotus.

They would not draw him to Everview, at least. They had left the Royal Road and its steady supply of sullen farmers and merchants — and a few families, too, looking miserable, with all of their belongings on wagons drawn by oxen and mules — standing aside to make way for the march of the vast column. Now there was nothing but the cobble of the Military Highway stretching straight as a lance toward the Treeline. Already, they could see it, a smudge of green on the horizon.

Aethal looked back over the immense column of cavalry and infantry that stretched back for well over a mile. And this was only the vanguard.

For all his years in the service, Aethal had never been part of an army this large. His Majesty's Cavalry seldom operated in more than regimental strength, and usually in independent squadrons. More than sufficient to scatter a Grassworm raiding party. On the rare occasion the raiders could be tracked back to their hide-and-reed tent villages beyond the Treeline they were almost always gone before a regiment could be assembled to smash them. Only when a war-chief managed to earn the loyalty of multiple clans and challenge the Treeline did the men of the Army really earn their pay. The last of those had been right after Aethal had received his commission.

Aethal took Gun from its scabbard and let his eyes wander over the Exploits carved there. It was a tradition among the officer corps to record their deeds in the grain of the wooden stock. Carved loops of rank encircled the stock at the butt, from the subaltern's triple ovals nearest the shoulder to the crossed lances of captain's rank. More carvings flowed toward the barrel: The shattered nine-point star of the Royal Crest carved in the center. His first skirmish at the Treeline, when a smuggler's train had been desperate enough to fight. Carved black flames over a brown wagon reached toward the lock mechanism. Below that, the image of a dying elephant that he had shot from under a clan chief in that last great raid that had pierced the Treeline.

With the shock of memory, Aethal remembered that he'd first met Sindon Rawl, the kind old man who'd hanged himself with his wife, right after that battle. They'd fallen back on Everview to rest after the victory. Aethal, a newly-minted lieutenant, had dined in that very house.

Aethal slid Gun back. The carvings seemed faintly silly, now.

Aethal wondered if, now that Greater Rifles were being issued to noncommissioned officers, the carving of Exploits would continue. Some of the men he'd commanded were quite gifted hobbyists. He remembered that Sergeant Eanling had used to carve reeds into little pipes. When they were finished and bound together, he gave them away to one of the more musical men and start another. But Eanling was gone, burned with Everview. He missed the older man. Had grown to rely on him. Sergeant Falk, now... Aethal felt his lips twitch into a smile at the thought of Falk carving Exploits into Dragon's stock. No, he couldn't see it.

Aethal hoped that the big man — and Major Caanling, of course — was getting the City Watch into shape. With this army gone, Maednac Serpiin was held by Maednac's Own, the City Watch and raw recruits until more of the regular army arrived. The recruits, at least, should learn good Discipline. They had fewer bad habits. The Discipline had become no more than ceremony among the general population. But if anyone could enforce it, Falk could.

There was also the Temple Guard. From what Major Caanling said, they kept the Discipline better — much better — than the City Guard, and they were posted at every Church. Of course, he also said that they fought like weedy schoolboys. At least the Crownguard was used to fighting hardened criminals that might hit back. The Temple Guard seemed surprised at the thought. If such were the case, then Pyk's dire warnings about the fortified High Temple were premature.

And Aethal hoped so. One of the greatest surprises he'd faced was just how few resources were available to the King's Last Sword. He commanded the Wyrmguard, which consisted of twenty-four of the living weapons. He glanced to his side. Pyrric and Firestrike flanked him, expressions blank as always. They obeyed his orders without question, and Aethal hoped that Colonel Jeharok and his commanding officer would find them useful. He only wished he'd dared pry more of them away from the Hydraxis.

Aside from the Wyrmguard, however, the Last Sword was alone in his duty to protect the King. He could commandeer the Palace Guard, but they were their own unit, under General Thorling's command. He had no staff, and, most crippling of all, no way of knowing where any threat to the king's safety might come from. If Jehan Alfing had possessed any network of agents that he had used to monitor potential threats to the Royal family, he had taken the secret of it with him to the grave.

The thudding of hooves interrupted Aethal's reverie. In the distance, Aethal could see horses coming toward him at a full gallop. Two of them. Behind them, a column of smoke rose into the noonday sky.

The point of the column burst in a black plume of smoke. And then hanging beneath it like a poisoned star, a point of forest-green light ignited.

Lotus.

Captain Douthan, the squadron's commander, reined in and gasped in horror.

"Sound column halt!" Aethal snapped to the cornet beside him.

The boy turned to Douthan, who reddened and waved assent. The high clear notes rang out. Embarrassed, no doubt, at having been seen to lose control of himself, Douthan called out, "Form line abreast!"

The cavalry squadron swung out of column and deployed. The two horsemen reined in, gasping for breath. "Sir!" one of them shouted to Douthan. "We're under attack by Grassworms! They're breaching the Treeline! There are thousands of them!"

Back in command, Douthan said, "You've done your job, man. And we've more than enough here to finish it." From farther back, the notes of the regimental cornet sounded in response to the Lotus flare. *Advance by squadron.*

Aethal took his position behind Douthan.

"Form line!" shouted the captain. "Squadron will advance. Prepare to trot... trot *march!*"

The squadron began to advance. "Banshees and Lotus... stoppers... *in!*"

Aethal took the rubber plugs that hung around his neck and stopped up both nostrils and ears. The sounds of the world turned mushy. Now it would be almost impossible to hear commands. But the Cavalry had been fighting the Grassworms for some time and had other means of passing orders. Aethal watched the cornet remove his long, light, red-and-yellow signal flag from his saddle.

The trot ate up ground. The trees — not half the size of the monsters that guarded the Serpent's Pass, but still enormous — swelled, their huge trunks spurting smoke as light cannon fired from their gunports. Now they could see through the dissipating columns of smoke, which blended together, becoming an evil fog through which men ran and fought.

And now Aethal could hear dimly the *snap... snap* of rifle fire. Could see horses plunging, a knot of infantry and cavalry uniforms shooting at a shifting mass of warriors that charged in and out of the long grasses, into the killing zone of the lawns maintained around the Treeline.

The flag in the cornet's hands executed a flourish, leaping high in the air. *Charge*.

Aethal spurred his horse to a gallop. The drawing of sabers in the line before him was a glittering wave under the noon sun. Rising in the stirrups, Aethal drew the Last Sword.

The earth sprouted warriors before him. *Shit in the Well, some of them made it through*! Tall, muscular, and armed with pikes and axes, they rose from the grass before the charge. The horse of the young trooper before him reared and went down. Aethal leaned to the right, avoiding the crash, and found himself gazing into the snarl of a blond giant of a man, who reared back to swing a two-handed axe. Time seemed to slow. Aethal's sword arm twitched, and the Last Sword shot forward with the speed of thought, its tip smashing into his foe's face just beneath the bridge of his nose. Blood spattered, and the enemy fell. Aethal wheeled to the left, looking for more targets, but the enemy had vanished, dropping into the grass, nearly invisible in their woven cloth-and-rattan armor. Covering their ears. Only two of the enemy remained standing. They were naked to the waist, shaved bald, and covered in green sigils.

Not fifty yards away, the two Banshees raised their hands to the sky and screamed. Aethal clapped his hands reflexively to his ears and bellowed, as he had been trained. Even through his earplugs, what he heard of the cry was like a dull knife slammed between his eyes. Around him he saw cavalrymen lolling in the saddle. The cornet that had been beside him convulsed, vomiting blood, and Aethal saw to his horror that the young signalman, in the excitement of the chase, had forgotten his earplugs. He fell dead, swallowed up by the grass.

The pain eased. Aethal drew Gun from his saddle in a smooth motion. The nearest Banshee was dropping back into the grass. Aethal bracketed his body and let Gun correct his aim as the target vanished.

now.

Aethal's finger twitched, and the mottled green shape leaped up in agony, and fell, the sound of the shot echoing like dulled thunder in Aethal's ears. He dug heels into his horse and snatched up the cornet's signal flag. He couldn't see the squadron's captain. He waved the flag in the circular pattern that meant *rally*, and plunged toward the other Banshee's hiding place.

"Wyrmguard!" he called, not knowing if they could hear. "Covering fire!"

Two shots splashed the brains of the other Banshee over the waving, wild wheat.

While Aethal waved the flag, Pyrric and Firestrike began steady, aimed fire. Each shot struck a skull and killed. The Wyrmguard provided, quite literally, inhumanly accurate fire. The men of the squadron formed on him, and Aethal added them to the firing line as they came. "Fire at will!" he called, reflexively, but the real order went by way of his flag. This ambush was shattered, and his squadron was reforming. Soon he would be able to cut through to the embattled and dismounted cavalry no more than four hundred yards away...

Aethal abruptly realized that this was not his squadron. That he was, in fact, usurping Captain Douthan's role. He looked around for Douthan... and saw his horse, riderless, nervously cantering around the field.

The men were looking at him.

Strictly, the Discipline required that he formally assume command. But the Discipline had been created before the Grassworms had become a problem. "Form Wedge!" he called, and signaled the order as well.

"Squadron will advance... prepare to canter... canter *march!*"

The squadron rumbled into motion. Four hundred meters. Three hundred. The enemy, pressing hard on the thin line of Jeharok's troops that remained, had not noticed yet that their planned ambush had been wiped out by the unexpected arrival of the cavalry. Two hundred. "Squadron... *halt!*"

The horses stopped. Aethal raised the Last Sword. "Squadron ready... aim... volley fire...*Fire!*" The sword slashed down.

The crackling of rifles cut through the fog of his earplugs. The enemy jumped, whirled, and dropped. "Reload!" cried Aethal, waving the flag.

At that moment, Aethal raised Gun to his shoulder and spotted a tall Grassworm warrior wearing a light frame on his back with colorful plumes sprouting from his shoulders. *Hero-commander.* A skilled warrior who drew many men after him. *Headshot*, he thought at Gun. Gun adjusted his aim, and Aethal felt the give in its trigger. Fired.

The back of the plumed man's head exploded. Aethal reloaded, threw Gun across his back.

"Squadron... at the gallop... *Charge!*"

The drawing of swords blended into a drawn-out roar of metal on metal, and the wedge exploded into thunder. Then they were in and among the Grassworms, and it was sword work. The Last Sword danced in Aethal's hands like a saber. All around him, men broke, fled, and died as the rest of the vanguard slammed into the fleeing Grassworms. Aethal spurred his mount back and found himself face to face with a dusty-faced cavalry officer that he recognized.

"Galfrey? Galfrey, is it you?"

The captain of the Phoenix Lancers' third squadron looked up. "How do you...?" Recognition crept into the man's face. "Aethal? Spit in the Well, man, I'd heard you'd been discharged and then these wild rumors were flying everywhere. That you'd killed someone, or that you'd been made Last Sword. Of course, we always wondered what you were doing in the Cavalry. His Majesty knows how to train his bodyguards, what?" A horrified look passed over his face.

"God-Beyond-The World, Aethal, *he's* not here, is he?"

Aethal almost laughed. He couldn't tell whether Galfrey was more horrified at the thought of the king placing himself in this danger or that the king might see him with blood, dirt and grass-stains on his uniform.

"No, Galfrey, the situation isn't that desperate, yet. I've but brought you your reinforcements." All around him, Aethal could see those reinforcements pouring into the battle, and the Grassworms running.

"At this point, I'd thank you for them even if you'd Wished them from the Well," Galfrey took his hand in a firm clasp. "We've been pressed hard. But why are you doing the delivering?"

"His Majesty wants some eyes on the situation directly. I have the dispatches for the General as well."

"Captain!" A shout from the grass brought both men's heads around. "Captain," called a trooper, bursting into sight. "Sergeant Wulf has found something. Requests you come and see, sir!"

****

The priest had been eviscerated. The blood from the gaping wounds in his belly had stained the wild grain as though it had been slopped from buckets, and left a coppery odor that could be smelled even through the gunpowder haze. Fifty feet from him, a Grassworm warrior, strong and muscled, lay still. His death had been no less gruesome. The man's back had been removed by the exit wounds of a dozen rifle balls. And in his hand, he clutched a fistful of wet, greenish-black.

"Noseplugs in!" Aethal ordered, but most of the men had already obeyed. Fortunately, even the scent of Lotus had limits.

"Piss in the Well, that priest could fight!" said a trooper.

Sergeant Wulf spat. "The priest wasn't fighting. He was being eaten when we found him. By this Wellshite." He kicked the warrior. "And he'd been eating a lot more, too."

The dead man's eyes twitched. "Then what happened?"

"He saw us and charged. Almost reached us, too, even like that."

"Get a pyre, going, Sergeant. We've bodies to burn. Search the rest of them for Lotus. In teams. And be careful."

"Sir!" The man saluted.

A Lotus-Eater, gorging himself on a corpse? Aethal thought. It didn't make sense. Lotus-Eaters wanted more Lotus. They didn't eat anything else if they could help it, and this man obviously could. So why had he killed the priest?

Priests sometimes lived among the Grassworms. The Church said they were entitled to Priests to speak to God for them. Perhaps the poor holy man had been trying to keep the man away from Lotus. So, this warrior had killed the priest for the Lotus, and then... begun eating him? Had the priest been a greeneater, too? Had they fought over the leaf? He walked back, taking a trooper with him, to inspect the body.

The priest's eyes were clear and brown as the soil.

Aethal shook his head. Whatever the mystery, he had dispatches to deliver, and this battle was done.

****

"Please tender my thanks to His Majesty," Colonel Jeharok said. "These reinforcements have come just in time, as you can see. This is the first time that they've punched through. And we know that Lotus is among them, now."

Aethal nodded. The breeze blowing through the keepwood's observation deck wasn't really enough to break the late spring heat, but it was a relief nonetheless. Jeharok was pacing. That alone told Aethal how truly relieved his former commander was.

"His Majesty sent one thing more for you, Colonel." Aethal handed over the envelope and gave Jeharok time to read it. "Allow me to be the first to congratulate you. General Jeharok."

The new General speared Aethal with a look. *He's wondering if this promotion comes in spite of his decision to discharge me. He wants to know if I am on his side or not.*

"Thank you. Last Sword," General Jeharok finally said.

Aethal continued. "His Majesty would like your assessment of the general situation at the Treeline."

Jeharok nodded and frowned. "The situation is not good," he said. "The attack you interrupted is the biggest we've experienced. It's the first time we've faced anything like a coordinated assault. They are beginning to ally against us. We saw banners from six clans out there today. I hope that today's defeat will discourage them."

Jeharok hesitated. "There was a lull in Grassworm activity up until today. Then they hit us hard. Even for a smart war-chief, that's not like the Grassworms I've fought all my life. Grassworms don't wait. They keep the pressure on, because their warriors don't tolerate delay. Maybe there's some other reason behind it, but this feels entirely too much like fighting a dangerous and civilized foe."

Aethal's stomach crawled. "Can you stop them?"

Jeharok's brow wrinkled in annoyance. "We *think* we are stopping them. But of course, that is the problem, isn't it, Cap... forgive me. Last Sword. A successful infiltration into enemy territory is, by definition, one that the enemy does not know about until it is too late. This one very nearly succeeded, clumsy though the attempt was.

"With these reinforcements, we can seal the Treeline. Perhaps begin planning an assault on the clans that are *blocking* the road to the Westerend. But that's just more of the same problem. The clans are blocking the way to the Westerend. They're not raiding into it, like a smart Grassworm warlord would do, and they're not wearing themselves out assaulting it, like a stupid one would do. They're waiting. It's not like them and it's much more dangerous to us."

Aethal nodded. "What about the Westerend forces themselves? Can you coordinate with them?"

Jeharok snorted. "Lord Vaughan's forces are... overequipped and under-trained. Those are the kindest words for it. I'm not sure how they'd weather an assault, despite their excellent defensive position. They're also under-led. The only thing I can get out of their commander, on the rare occasions that messages get through, are complaints. And those messages have to go south and then by sea. With the cavalry you've brought, I can start planning my own attack. But I will not hurry it. We daren't have a disaster at this stage. Holding the Treeline is what matters. I cannot compromise that. Even if it means the only way we get reinforcements from the Westerend is by sea."

"I think His Majesty will understand that," said Aethal. *Lord Vaughan may be another matter.* That wasn't Jeharok's problem, though.

Jeharok looked at Aethal as if weighing him in the balances of his mind. Then he said, "Last Sword, will His Majesty understand if I recommend that we set prairie fires?"

"Prairie fires?" Aethal repeated. The words penetrated. Shit in the Well. Prairie fires, on the Grain Sea in late spring?

The implication settled on Aethal like a leaden cloak. "Sir," Aethal said reflexively, then reddened in embarrassment. "General. You are proposing to burn the Grain Sea. What will our people eat?" Thanks to the Grain Sea, the people of Verlaen had never known hunger. Could we survive without the freely-growing grain?

"Not Lotus, Last Sword. That is the point. I cannot guarantee that Lotus is not already in the supplies of grain that may even now be reaching Maednac Serpiin. But we have the Fleet. We have other supplies of food, such as Maednac's Vale, that are not dependent upon the Grain Sea. The Grassworms do not. The bread and produce of the Grain Sea are their livelihood. Without it, they come to us... or they starve. And either serves our purpose."

Aethal met the General's eyes. They both knew that it wasn't just the Grassworms that would suffer if the Grain Sea was burned. When the price of bread went up, it would be felt in the alleys of the Madlands. Meals would grow very thin in Maednac Serpiin in the coming months. But he forced himself to nod. What after all, could they do? If Lotus once appeared in the capital city, Verlaen — and all that was left of civilized Man — was done. "I will support your proposal to the King."

Jeharok nodded. "Good. Now..."

They were interrupted by a knock at the door. At the General's call, it opened. Aethal's heart rose to see Lieutenant Farnan enter the room. He saluted. "Sir, I have news from First Squadron's prisoners that Captain Mehr wished me to pass on." He caught sight of Aethal, and his face lit, but he fixed his eyes on his commander and stayed silent.

"Go on, Lieutenant."

"We brought down another Greendel just now. It... it lived for a moment, sir."

Jeharok stared. "It lived? How did you get near it?"

"Lucky shot, sir. Crow, here, took it in the back of the neck. Dropped it like a puppet with its strings cut." He patted his Greater Rifle.

"That's damned good shooting, Farnan," said Aethal.

"Indeed," Jeharok said. "And?"

"It was raving, but he said something before he bled out. He said he saw the prophet, standing at the Well, and then he muttered, 'So the leaf and I shall go to sleep eternal.' At least I think that was it. It was... pretty slurred and incoherent stuff, actually."

"More than anything else a Greendel has ever said," grunted Jeharok.

"Excuse me," said Aethal. "What's a Greendel?"

Farnan turned to him. "It wasn't long after you left that we found the first cases of Lotus among the Grassworms. Most of the farmed ones run. But there are some of them... they're warriors. Always warriors. The Lotus doesn't seem to make them scared or docile. It sends them into a battle-frenzy. Their eyes are solid green and they throw themselves at you, screaming. If they bite you, well..." Farnan's eyes turned inward. "There's nothing we can do. Except give mercy."

"Is that what Sergeant Wulf found?" Aethal described the encounter.

Farnan nodded. "That's a Greendel. I've never heard of one eating people before. I wish I could say I was surprised. But Greendels aren't like anything I've ever fought."

"So, the leaf and I shall go to sleep eternal. The poor bastards. It's killing them, too, even as it drives them to kill us. It's not so surprising, is it? The leafeaters we found in the Inn of Everview fought hard enough," said Aethal.

Farnan shook his head. "Only because they thought we were trying to take their leaf. Any greeneater will fight hard against that. But even then, most of them ran. Out here, they all run. And when they have to fight, they try to shove the Lotus in our faces. Not bite us."

Aethal felt the knot in his stomach tighten, realizing that Farnan was right. He had more experience fighting leafeaters than Aethal did, now. "Maednac's records seem to agree with you." Was it possible Maednac had never encountered these berserkers? It shouldn't be. The Empire had been five times the size of Verlaen, and had ruled many more times its people. Maednac should have seen everything Lotus could do. *Has the Lotus changed? Become more deadly these past three centuries?* As if it weren't quite deadly enough.

Aethal pulled a slim packet from his pouch. "Here, sir, is all that we have found out about fighting Lotus from Maednac's records in the Hydraxis." He didn't need to say, *it isn't much.* Jeharok accepted it with a grunt. "I'm afraid there's nothing in it about Greendels."

"So far we haven't encountered many of them," said Jeharok. "If they ever start showing up in numbers, we will have a problem." He took the report. Most of it was culled from the same book Aethal carried. He hoped that when he got back the Guardians' "gift," whatever it was, would contain something more useful. Jeharok looked at Aethal and Farnan, and sighed. Straightened and said formally,

"I suppose, Lord Wrackberg, that you wish to take your liegeman back with you when you return to Maednac Serpiin."

Aethal nodded. "If quite convenient, General."

Jeharok frowned. "It never was that. And is Sergeant Falk with you?"

It was Aethal's turn to frown. "I'm afraid not. Not through any fault of his or of mine. He was wounded, and is recovering."

"Wounded?" repeated Jeharok. "In the capital?"

Aethal hesitated. "How much do you know, General, of how I came to bear the Last Sword?" Farnan's mouth fell open, and he stared at the sword hilt that rose over Aethal's shoulder. He hadn't noticed until now. Aethal would have grinned at another time, but he needed all Jeharok's attention.

Again, Jeharok fixed him with that probing stare. "I don't know what to think of you, my Lord," he finally said. And for the first time, Aethal could see fatigue and humanity showing through his former commander's public face. "You were always a competent officer. Hardly brilliant, but capable. Even if your title made you a damned nuisance. The Lotus made you more a liability than an asset. So I sent you packing. And now you return, at the head of my reinforcements, bearing a promotion for me, and a far greater one for yourself." He paused. "Frankly, I expected your father to find you a job in this present crisis. I didn't expect it to be that one."

"Aethal the Unlikely, indeed." Farnan shook his head in wonder.

Aethal shot him a quelling glare. "Neither did I. Neither did he, whether you believe that or not, General." Aethal sighed. "We are both aware of the political implications of my promotion. Some of them. I promise, you are not aware of all of them. But you sent me to the capital to serve the Kingdom in a political role. Because I was born to it. Now that I'm in it — after a fashion — you're going to have to decide whether I'm worth listening to." Jeharok's brows rose in surprise.

"The truth is, that the king's previous Last Sword, Jehan Alfing, tried to assassinate him. Sergeant Falk, the Wyrmguard, and I managed to stop him. *That's the official story, anyway.* The idea that Jehan Alfing had actually wanted the *Sergeant* dead was one that Aethal didn't want a man as sharp as Jeharok thinking about. "The king elevated me to this position as a reward. The king, and not my father."

Jeharok looked like a man trying to decide whether to be impressed or skeptical. Farnan, on the other hand, was looking at him with unfeigned admiration.

"Wish me dead, Aethal-the-Unlikely, you managed to piss in the Well and drink wine from it!" he chuckled.

"Then what do you have to say, Last Sword?" asked Jeharok, his voice dead-level.

Aethal looked him in the eye. "My sworn oath is to protect the king. I can do that only by getting rid of the Lotus. It's possible that not everyone in Maednac Serpiin shares my devotion to that cause. The Discipline situation in Maednac Serpiin is worse than you know." Aethal outlined the conditions that he had found in the capital, and his plan to remedy them. As he spoke, Jeharok's face lengthened in dismay.

"So you see, General," Aethal finished. "I very much need Sergeant Falk — and Farnan, and all the veterans you can give me — as I try to restore the Discipline Maednac built, so that the next time we send you reinforcements, we're not just shipping you farms for the Lotus. Maednac's Own are the finest fighting men, and good trainers. But they haven't seen what Lotus can really do.

"In exchange for these men, I leave you our reinforcements, a couple of sergeants that I begged from Colonel Henling, and these two Wyrmguard. They will stay with you and help you fight the Lotus."

Jeharok's mouth worked. "You can detach Wyrmguard?"

Aethal bared his teeth. "Say, rather, that I *will* do whatever I must to protect the king and this land. Regardless of whether those decisions are popular. Wyrmguard do not eat Lotus. They are not tempted by it and may be sent into it without danger. But they *are* mortal and can be killed. If they are, you will have to replace them." By the look on Jeharok's face, Aethal could see he immediately understood the implications of *that*. "Preserve these two. Now, can you give me the cadre I need?" *And give me the chance to get at least some of the Phoenix Lancers away from Lotus while my father isn't looking?*

Slowly, Jeharok nodded, and there was real respect in his eyes. "I have men who have seen hard service here. Some light duty in the capital," he smiled thinly, "would be good for them. They have had encounters with the Lotus these past weeks that match your own."

Aethal met Jeharok's smile. The "light duty" that these veterans would enjoy would be anything but for Aethal's waiting recruits. But it would be exactly what they needed. "Thank you, General," said Aethal. And for the first time since arriving in Maednac Serpiin, he allowed his spirits to rise.

Chapter Eleven

43rd of Spring, 312 Exodus

Aethal and Farnan were going over training schedules in the Hydraxis when Osric came in with the letter.

In the fortnight since he had left, Sergeant Falk and the men of Maednac's Own had been making great progress in training their new recruits. Now, Aethal had a cadre of about a hundred veterans and it was time to get to work in earnest.

And they would need those veterans. The first few regiments to be raised from Verlaen basin had arrived, and had been quartered in the Hydraxis barracks. And the Westerend ships had arrived yesterday, with three thousand men, who were also filling the palace. Not to be outdone, Aethal's father had supplied two thousand of his own. There hadn't been any fights between the troops of the two rival houses. Yet.

"You're not going to want Sergeant Knut in charge of any training squadrons alone," Farnan was saying, turning Aethal's mind toward the practical.

"Why not? Isn't the man competent?"

"A bit too competent. You could put him in charge of one composed entirely of raw recruits, but you're running the Maednac Serpiin City Watch through the very same course. Knut hates the Watch. It's an open secret among the men that he's killed two of them while on leave. Put him in charge of their training, and you'll have at least one dead recruit at the end of it."

Aethal frowned. "I suppose he's never been brought up on charges for this?"

"No. It's all hearsay. But I believe it."

"Perhaps I'd better have a talk with the good Sergeant. What is it, Osric?"

"This arrived for you, sir. From Twilight Hall." The young man passed the folded paper over.

"Lord Vaughan's residence?" Aethal frowned. It almost looked like a dinner invitation. But Aethal was hardly expecting one of those. He broke the wax seal. The note was simple and short.

"I must discuss with you a matter of interest that came to light during the inspection of His Majesty's dungeons while you have been away. I would be honored to receive you at my home upon your earliest convenience," Aethal read aloud.

"Not much, is it?" asked Farnan.

"No," said Aethal. "Damn." He'd been hoping against hope that the Lord of the Westerend *would* discover what had happened to the General before he returned. Their arrival yesterday had been far too occupied with disposing of men and equipment to catch up to the state of affairs in the capital, but *that* piece of news was one he had urgently asked after.

The General was still missing. Aethal sighed. "Osric, please send word to Lord Vaughan that I will call on him after lunch today, at the Fall Hour." The page bowed and left.

"What could he have found, if not the general?" Aethal had told Farnan about Malcoor's disappearance as a matter of course, though he hadn't had to say much. The rumors of Malcoor's vanishing and alleged crimes had reached the Treeline a week before Aethal had.

"I don't know, but I certainly want to," said Aethal. "Let's get this finished."
****

The crowds were dense and sullen around the Ocean Gate. Aethal and Farnan picked their way through the press as they neared the bottleneck of the Gate itself. Those who saw them stepped aside. Some gasped at Flintmaw, but even the Wyrmguard couldn't make the mass of people move much faster. They never stopped moving, however. The Discipline said nothing about people *leaving* the city. Absently, Aethal wondered if it should, before dismissing the idea as completely impractical. The crowding was bad enough now. Hundreds awaited their turn to pass through. Aethal felt their cold, resentful eyes on him as he led Lieutenant Farnan to a postern gate reserved for Royal and Army business.

The Winery hung over both sides of the Ocean Gate, a series of five massive boxes of stone, supported on great plinths built into the city's wall. In Maednac's day, they had been a fortress, one of the last to be built at his direction, when false rumors of Lotus in the foregate towns sparked panic, and men still looked half-fearfully to the sea, uncertain whether Lotus might not have a mind of its own, and command its farmed victims to build a navy of greeneating zombies to go forth and conquer the world.

Aethal wondered about the man who'd taken to calling it the Winery. It was not named for its shape, but rather for the enormous quantities of grapeshot that could be poured through its lower gunports in the event of a massed charge on the city. Aethal had never seen grapeshot fired except for artillery practice, but he had no trouble picturing the slaughter of Everview multiplied a hundredfold, the battlements echoing to the sounds of cannon turned into giant shotguns, stamping bloody wedges through a howling mob.

"Aethal, are you all right?" Farnan was staring at him, and Aethal became aware that he was staring up at the massive ramparts. He shook himself, and they submitted themselves to the Discipline of inspection by the guards. The military was *always* subject to Discipline.

"Nothing is all right," he breathed. "But at least the Discipline is running smoothly." Smoothly, but not quickly. He could see the line of carts and people piled against the gate stretched around several different corners in the Madlander streets beyond, moving only one by one as each person submitted to the Discipline of the Gate guards. Aethal heard voices raised in anger or frustration out beyond the gate. But the soldiers were doing their jobs. He could see them looking into the people's eyes. None of them were being stopped. *Yet.*

The Winery now served as a prison, and it added its own stink to the human and animal aromas outside. Inside this tunnel in the city walls, both Aethal and Farnan reached for their handkerchiefs, perfumed and soaked in lemonwater.

It was a relief to both of them to be back in the sunlight. To Flintmaw, of course, relief was immaterial. They took the road around to the south of the city. Lord Paramount Westerend's manse lay out of sight of Cemetery Bay, to windward of a low hill and was surrounded by a low wall containing a small orchard. As the upper Madlands were left behind, Farnan spoke: "I've been meaning to ask you, Aethal," he said, looking down at his own coat-sleeves, the blue-and-red of the Royal Cavalry. "I rather thought I was called up to the service of the Wrackberg, now. Should I still be wearing this? I note you're not wearing Captain's lances anymore." Implying, *but you're not wearing the Wrackberg's grey-and-scarlet either, so what's going on?*

"The badge of my office has grown slightly more conspicuous," Aethal tossed off with a smile, fingering the sword hilt that kept Gun company on his back, and Farnan grinned back.

"More conspicuous indeed," said Farnan wryly, turning to glance back at Flintmaw. "I fear he'll be breathing down my neck soon."

But inwardly, Aethal felt shame at dodging his friend's question. I called him up to my House, Aethal thought. Should I make that known? My father won't hesitate to use him as leverage against me. Today, we are working together, but if it is not so tomorrow? If that happens, I've destroyed Farnan's career.

Aethal forced his thoughts away from this turmoil, and the conversation turned to lighter matters. They turned away from the Madlands toward the more fashionable residences to the west of the city.

Twilight Hall was an imposing, yet open manor house with fluted marble columns, in the Imperial style that set the Westerend apart from the rest of Verlaen. The green-black-and-silver liveried guard bowed. "You are expected, Last Sword." In seconds, the Lord Vaughan's majordomo greeted them and led them inside. They were shown into a spacious lounge, grandly furnished.

"My Lord is honored by your presence, and begs a moment to finish some business," the graying gentleman said. "He does, however, request that my lord's escort remain in his garden, so as not to disturb the functioning of his household."

Aethal nodded assent. If the Wyrmguard had made Lord Vaughan nervous, then Flintmaw had served a purpose. Wyrmguard made most people nervous. He dismissed Flintmaw to the atrium.

Aethal had been away from the capital for a long time. Lord Vaughan likely still thought of him as a boy. And a politically naïve, Army-mad boy from a rival family at that. *Perhaps we can now talk on slightly more even terms.*

****

After a half-hour, it did not seem as though this was to be.

"I guess Lord Westerend is really taking the time to welcome you properly," said Farnan, finally, as he turned away from his tenth examination of the large room's single clock.

Aethal sat on a luxuriously appointed brocade chaise, and tried to relax. "It's unsurprising," he said, in low tones. "A bit petty, but unsurprising. The Westerends and the Wrackbergs have always been at each other's throats. After all, the Westerends were Imperial nobles; here before Maednac. By their lights, he should have pledged *them* fealty, not set up his castle on a dirty little Imperial fort on the other side of the continent. And then he had the gall to blockade the Twin Fans ports and use the Imperial Fleet to starve them into submission while his army held the River Pass to the Grain Sea closed. No, according to the Westerend line, even the King is an upjumped general's son with a crown."

"What does that make you?" asked Farnan.

"An upjumped sailor's brat without one," answered Aethal. "And with royal blood at that, which really sticks in the Westerend's craw. Raised to nobility by Maednac's word alone, for the great service of defending the bay against the Lotus-ridden refugee ships." Farnan's low laugh was cut off by the opening of the main doors behind them. Gun's awareness blazed up in Aethal's mind.

In the doorway stood Lord Vaughan Paramount of the Westerend accompanied by six of his armed guard. All six leveled their rifles at Aethal and Farnan, forming triads flanking their lord. From smaller doors at the sides of the room, two more pairs of guards appeared, these armed with brass-bound truncheons.

"Aethal," said Farnan, managing to keep his voice level. "Does this fall under the category of 'surprising?'"

Aethal rose, hands carefully at his side. Lord Vaughan's face was transformed. When Aethal had seen him in the King's chambers, three weeks ago, it had been controlled and closed. Now, Vaughan's eyes blazed in an ecstasy of fury.

"My Lord," said Aethal, in his calmest voice. "What is the meaning of this?"

Vaughan's stare transfixed Aethal, and when he spoke his voice was laden with chill promise. "Mock me once again, Paaling, and I may forget you have any use to me alive."

He looked at Farnan. "The Lords of the West do not kill men needlessly, not even men who serve such vermin as you do, but I do have servants to carry messages, so if you would leave this house alive, Lieutenant, you will place your Rifle on the ground, taking care to keep your hands within one foot of the muzzle. It will be returned to you tomorrow." Farnan looked at Aethal, who nodded. With exaggerated care, Farnan laid Crow on the floor.

"These are the words you will carry to the king and his chancellor. I hold the Chancellor's son, and the king's Last Sword. Since the king and his chancellor do not keep their words as honorable men, I see no advantage in treating with them in honor. Therefore, I offer not my word, but a *bargain*; one which any Grassworm chief in the Grain Sea is capable of understanding: General Joseth Malcoor will be returned to my protection at once. I will be granted an escort to the docks, where our ships will be granted immediate departure from Cemetery Bay. Aethal Paaling will be returned to you by ship, upon our arrival at the Twin Fans." He turned to one of his men. "When this is over, tell Captain Guilorum we have a delivery." The man nodded.

"Lord Vaughan," said Aethal, softly, "I beg you to reconsider…"

"Beg?" barked Vaughan, livid with rage. "Oh, yes, Paaling, you will beg. I'll see to it that you do, before this is out. And if Joseth is not returned alive and unharmed, I will see you Wish for death itself."

Aethal's mind was racing. Obviously, Vaughan believed that Malcoor was a secret prisoner of the Crown, or at least of the Wrackbergs. As to why..? The rage in Vaughan was like a live thing, ready to lash out at the first target that presented itself.

"My Lord," said Aethal, "I fear to inform you that if you seek to influence my father, you have kidnapped the wrong son."

Vaughan's rapier was out of its scabbard and at Aethal's throat in an eyeblink. "You insult my intelligence, Paaling. I do not suffer insults gladly, and have taken more than my share from your House over the years. I have also known your father longer than you have. He has had you made Last Sword of Verlaen; I am certain he does not desire to lose that influence. Now where is the General?"

"I came here to ask you the same question, but I see now that perhaps it was the wrong one to ask," said Aethal, staring back into Vaughan's glaring eyes. "Perhaps I should have asked, '*Who* is the General?' Who is he, Lord Vaughan, that you would risk a charge of treason by threatening the life of the king's Last Sword for a man forgotten by the world for thirty years?"

A sneer came to Lord Vaughan's lips, "That is exactly the question I would expect from a Wrackberg. And a Paaling. And a liar." Behind Vaughan, a staccato burst of shots rang through the house. Vaughan stepped back, sword still in guard position. "That was the end of your Wyrmguard," he said, with a smile of satisfaction.

"That was an act of treason!" Farnan burst out.

"That was an act of justice," said Vaughan, "far too long delayed. The King will pay his debt, too."

Aethal just shook his head. "My Lord," said Aethal, "Put down that sword, or I cannot be held answerable for your life."

"Aethal?" asked Farnan, incredulously.

"Give me my brother," grated Vaughan, "or I shall be most assuredly be answerable for yours."

His brother? But Malcoor wasn't...

Aethal's thoughts were cut short; the door behind Vaughan swung open, and the nearest guard to Aethal fell back with a hole smashed through his braincase.

Aethal ducked and just had time to bring Gun around. Flintmaw spun its cylinder and shot another guard. "Farnan!" Aethal cried. His friend threw himself flat on top of Crow, scooping it up. Lord Vaughan stood frozen, watching the shape in the door with his mouth gaping. The troops threatening Farnan turned just as Aethal brought Gun's barrel up under another guard's sternum.

shoot!

It was an effort not to squeeze the trigger. But the steel barrel driven into the man's solar plexus was more than enough; the man dropped his rifle and began retching. Aethal kicked him in the face and he lay still.

Crow and Flintmaw fired at the same instant. One guard fell clutching the ruin of his knee, another dropped with a hole through his throat. The third man got his shot off into Flintmaw's upper arm, which exploded in a gout of blood. Aethal slammed Gun's butt into the man's head. He dropped.

Lord Vaughan had recovered. With a snarl of rage, he lunged at the Wyrmguard, blade outthrust. In a slow moment of horror, Aethal saw Flintmaw moving calmly and economically, sliding its last deadly chamber into place and leveling itself at the Lord Paramount's forehead, prepared to kill Aethal's only hope of finding his answers.

"Wyrmguard, *hold fire!*"

Flintmaw, expressionless, pointed its own barrel at the ceiling at the instant that Vaughan ran its mount through the heart. With a strange, puzzled expression on his face, the Wyrmguard looked around in bewilderment at his surroundings. "It's cold," he said to Lord Vaughan, left hand reaching for the blade. Then his eyes rolled up and he folded.

ware behind! Gun's shout in his mind and the pounding of feet were all the warning Aethal had. Lord Vaughan's club-wielders charged him. They were charging into rifles, but these men were soldiers that Vaughan had called up: even Greater Rifles took time to reload, and they knew it.

Aethal shot the first man, then knocked his truncheon aside with Gun's stock. He used the opening to jab Gun's barrel at the second man's eyes, forcing him back. Aethal's shoulder blades twitched, knowing Vaughan's sword was at his back. He dimly sensed Farnan fighting at his side and knew that their only chance was to win this quickly. He parried another club strike, jerked Gun's magazine plug free and jabbed it into a man's throat. Gagging, he fell back, trying to stanch the blood spurting from between his fingers, but the motion gave Aethal's other attacker the opening to slam his club into Aethal's arm above the elbow. The plug clattered from his numbed fingers.

sword, Gun said to Aethal and then twisted out of his hand. Astonished at his weapon's initiative, Aethal nevertheless swept the Last Sword from its scabbard in a smooth motion, slicing downward into his foe's shoulder. The man cried out and dropped. Aethal whirled just in time to parry Lord Vaughan's thrust. He saw his own surprise reflected in Vaughan's face. He had not expected Aethal's speed, but the blow had been an awkward one.

Vaughan laughed grimly. "You should have stuck to a weapon you were trained with, boy." He launched his attack. Trying to work some feeling back into his injured arm, Aethal gave back, parrying every blow with his larger blade. "Tiring yet?" asked Vaughan. Aethal smiled. Vaughan knew swords, but he did not know this one. Over his enemy's shoulder, Aethal saw one of the Westerenders land a solid blow that knocked Farnan back and over the sprawled bodies of his deceased fellows. He had a moment to feel dismay, and then Farnan was up with one of the dead men's rifles in his hand and firing. He flung the rifle away and picked up another, fired again. The last unwounded man fell.

At the reports, Vaughan sprang back and whirled, face ashen with dismay. Farnan drew his cavalry saber and moved to flank Vaughan, who turned at bay between them

"NO!" screamed a shrill voice, and Aethal turned again, frantically parrying. Steel slid off his blade and flew at him again. Behind it was a face Aethal had seen only once before; in the King's chambers. "Haven't you done enough to him?" she panted, locking blades with Aethal. Before he could use his strength against her, she sprang back and came at him again, blows flashing in from every direction.

Aethal managed to turn around her, so that she was fighting back-to-back with her father, but it was the only success he had. He had a brief instant to wonder what had possessed Vaughan to train his daughter to this level of swordsmanship, and then he had no time to wonder anything except how to stay alive. He had been trained to gun battles, and she far outclassed him at swordplay. Only the wondrous lightness of the Last Sword preserved him.

Yet she fought with the grace of a trained duelist, not the desperate opportunism of a soldier. Aethal backed away, and managed to come up with his powder horn in his numbed left hand. She stabbed at him; the blade pierced the leather and stuck in the horn for the instant Aethal needed to bring the last Sword down on the blade, breaking it off an inch above the hilt.

She stood amazed only for a moment, and then she was off and running for the big main doors. She passed her father and Farnan, and before Aethal could say anything to stop her, she dived for Flintmaw's body.

"No, milady!" cried Aethal, but her hand had closed around the pistol's grip. She turned and leveled it at Aethal, and there was a moment in which the rage on her face gave way to utter despair, and then it went dead. She pointed the gun at the ceiling.

"Shall I continue to check fire, Last Sword?" she asked, her voice cool and distant.

"Ardyth!" screamed Vaughan, and his voice was that of a man in Hell. He turned to Aethal, madness in his eyes. "Let her go! Make that thing let her go!"

"Drop your sword, sir!" said Aethal, hating himself. He wouldn't have sentenced his worst enemy to be ridden by a Wyrmguard pistol, let alone Westerend's daughter, but he had to have what Vaughan knew. "Your daughter will be released when I have your full cooperation. Is that understood?"

Vaughan's sword dropped, and he crumpled to the floor, unable to tear his eyes from his daughter. She checked the room, methodically, stripped the powder and shot from the old Wyrmguard's body, and then walked over to Aethal, calmly reloading the pistol's three emptied chambers. Farnan picked up Vaughan's sword and stepped to Aethal's side.

"There is, then, no justice to be had for all my House," Vaughan said, looking at the three of them. "It is true what the Church teaches, and God has abandoned this world. You and your House will take and take, until I have nothing left, and then you will eat the world just as surely as if you were the Lotus given flesh."

Aethal replied, "If my lord had not been so quick for vengeance against a man who had never done him wrong, death might have spared these your men as well. And certainly your daughter would not have come to this pass. You have ambushed us most foully, my Lord; do not talk to me of justice. There has never been love between our houses: that I have long known. But what sin have I committed, Lord Vaughan, that you should force me to do murder in your halls or lose my life?"

"What sin?" asked Vaughan. "I suppose the world, and you especially, do not think it much of a sin to destroy a man, if that man is a bastard. If a man made the unpardonable error of choosing the wrong parents. And perhaps I am the evildoer; I, who loved that same bastard, my brother. I made the bargain, Wrackberg," he said, fixing Aethal with a glare of hate. "I gave your father all he ever desired to keep Joseth safe. Let him shut Joseth up in the Pass for the rest of his life, to keep him from the gallows. And now he is gone, *escaped*, I am supposed to believe, from your brother," Vaughan's lips curled. "If he had, he would have come to me. And you tell me you did not know all this?"

Aethal had trouble forming the words. "You claim General Malcoor is your brother? Your bastard brother?" Understanding dawned, though Aethal could barely conceive of it. Bastardy was the very essence of Breaking the Moon, a shame far beyond his parents' disgrace. Most bastards were simply not acknowledged, both parents content to pretend that no such thing had occurred. They were left at churches. Sometimes they were even killed, though that was a greater sin. Many priests and Guardians had never known any other parents than the Order or the Church for that very reason. But for the house of a Lord Paramount to acknowledge such...

Vaughan's eyes were cool. "Call Joseth what you will," he said, "but he was one of the best men this Kingdom has ever birthed. Your father sought to kill him for that."

Aethal nodded. "I remember the story, my Lord. Now why don't you tell me all of it? My father is not here to gainsay your word. What did your... brother tell you happened?"

"Joseth's last voyage was his third. On each one, he sailed West of the Prime, in violation of Maednac's Ban, on the orders of King Paitir and with the full knowledge of his Chancellor. Twice he returned. None of his crew ever suspected where they had really gone. They told the crews some fairy tale about searching for lost ships, I think. But the first two expeditions failed to find any signs of human life. Until they sailed within sight of the Accursed Republic itself."

Aethal's breath caught. "He sailed that far?" The Republic was just south of the Dark Continent on the other side of the globe. And that was the site of the Well, if any of the stories were true. Malcoor would have had to sail completely beyond the Empire to reach it.

Malcoor smiled. "My brother has sailed around the world, Wrackberg, if you added up all his voyages together. Yet he was not condemned for bringing back reports that there was life where the lost Empire's foes once lived. No, he was given command of a third expedition. To continue his search." Malcoor looked Aethal in the eyes.

"Then, at the quayside — and I was there, to see him off, boy — your father, the Chancellor arrived to speak with him. Privately. I could not hear what was said. But after your father left, Joseth was pale and elated. He looked at me and said, "This is it at last.""

"It was only later, after he was condemned, that I learned what those last orders had been: to land on the shores of the Republic and find out who or what lived there. But of course, neither the king nor the Chancellor committed those orders to writing. No, they had no desire to risk the wrath of the people for violating Maednac's Ban themselves. They wanted to make certain that if it went badly, my brother could be blamed. And Joseth, being Joseth, never considered the danger. Or he did and didn't care; that would have been very like him.

"In any case, on the way back, Joseth's crew mutinied. Perhaps it was the long voyage, or perhaps they saw a chance to escape with the treasures they had discovered and set up their own little kingdoms for themselves. When the Fleet found their ship, Joseth and his loyal officers were barely hanging on to their authority over the crew. More than half the ship's company was dead; they were adrift. And you know what happened next. Joseth was "promoted" out of the Fleet, and everyone else who survived simply melted back into the populace. Does that not seem odd to you? If there is any place in Verlaen that the Discipline is practiced as fiercely as it was of old — and I am well aware of the degeneration you have found *here*," Vaughan made a gesture of distaste that encompassed all of Maednac Serpiin, "it is in the Fleet. Generally, in the king's Fleet, mutineers lose their heads, not their commanders. But your father and the king, who had welcomed him back twice before, decided that they would rather pardon the mutinous sailors, and instead condemn Joseth to death. For violating Maednac's Ban, of course, the lying cowards."

"If that was the king's plan," Aethal said, neutrally, "Then why did Malcoor survive?"

"Because I would not permit him to be killed to cover up the sins of your House and his!" snarled Westerend. "I will see this kingdom burn, Wrackberg, rather than watch my brother go to the gibbet for obeying orders; don't you doubt it. Your father didn't, and my resolve hasn't wavered since then. I swore to fight until the last drop of my blood was spilled rather than see my kin tamely submit to such disgrace. And only the fact that Lotus is in the Kingdom has kept me from fulfilling my vow. Your House will. Find. My. Brother. Or it will burn."

Aethal rocked back in spite of himself. He did not doubt Vaughan, not for a moment. *He is telling the truth. He will do this for a bastard. Plunge his House into a war it could not win, to avenge this man. Or is it something else?*

"And what treasures did your brother discover, Lord Vaughan?" asked Aethal, keeping his voice cool.

"Riches beyond counting, most of them lost in the fight with the mutineers, damn their souls to the Well," answered Vaughan. "Even Joseth couldn't remember them all. But they all pale into insignificance beside the one that truly sent Joseth into exile. You still pretend you don't know? Very well, I'll play your game; then maybe we can have a real conversation. The secret that you and your family have been plotting to keep secret for all these years, Wrackberg," said Lord Vaughan with a fey grin. "The cure for Lotus."

It was as if lightning coursed through Aethal where he sat. He could only gape. "Is my Lord mad?" he finally got out.

"Did you truly imagine I did not know?" asked Vaughan, calmly. "Oh, yes, Lieutenant, it's true," said Vaughan, looking over Aethal's shoulder. Farnan's expression, Aethal was sure, mirrored his own. "He told me. And this is why the secret was kept. If the Lotus could be killed, then the whole Empire and the Republic lie open for human habitation. And the Westerend could not be allowed to lead the way. How could it? That's how rival nations come into being.

Even the Church would stand with you, because a *bastard* could never make such a discovery. Surely God would not allow it. The Church certainly would not."

"Lord Vaughan," Aethal's voice rose, fueled by terror and rage. "Stop these lies. This is obscenity!" *Surely not. Even if Father would, the King would never...*

"Obscenity!" roared Vaughan. "And worse, far worse. Your father, Paaling, holds the cure in his hands. Your brother has taken the life of mine and you yourself have slaughtered my people of Everview and sown the Green Death in my fields!"

Aethal was paralyzed with rage, but Vaughan spoke on, voice trembling. "The Lotus sweeps westward as well as east, and I have no doubt that when the towers of the Twin Fans are covered in green and silver leaves, our noble Chancellor will stretch forth his hands and end the scourge with the fruit of my brother's labor. Lieutenant Farnan!" Vaughan locked his eyes on Aethal's friend, who was looking from him to Aethal and back again. "You are a true soldier of the kingdom. Now is your hour to save it. Join me and my daughter in escaping. Stop him! The king will see reason when we reveal the plot!"

Aethal turned. Farnan's face was pale. He held Lord Vaughan's sword, and his knuckles were white around the grip. And he was standing above Aethal. There was no chance at all that Aethal could escape him. He stepped forward.

"No, my Lord," Farnan said. "Your tale is a pretty one, and to my mind you believe it. But it isn't true, Lord. I was there with Aethal Paaling. I was his second in command when he rode into Everview. I was at his side when he fired into your people. And when he found Sindon Rawl and his family. I was there when Colonel Jeharok rode in and stripped him of his command for it. And when Jeharok himself could do no better, I was there when he burned it to the foundations."

"Whatever my father may be, my Lord," Aethal said, "by your own account, the King would have to know, too. And I do not believe it of him."

Vaughan slumped, the last spark of defiance gone. Farnan had been his last gamble, it was plain, and his answer had spelled only more pain. "My people will all die, then? So kill me, as well." He glanced at his daughter. "Kill her too. It would be more merciful than leaving her in thrall to that *thing* in her hand. It is all over, whether you speak truth or not."

Aethal's outrage at the false accusations burned in him, and part of him would have been glad to avenge his honor on Lord Vaughan, if not upon his daughter. But while Aethal knew the Lord of the Westerend had slandered him, the accusation against his father burned yet deeper. *Your father holds the cure in his hands. Could it be true?* "It is not over, Lord Vaughan," he said. "It is not even begun. What was the cure? Or was that, like the rest of this feeble tale, a lie designed to salvage your failed ambush?"

Vaughan glared at him in silence.

"No," Aethal finally said. "Not a lie. But *not a lie* is not necessarily the same thing as the truth, is it, my Lord? You obviously believe this. Because if you didn't, you threw away the Westerend's power for nothing. Simply to save the life of a bastard. And you have continued to save it, for all this time. You let my father take my mother for his bride, and we both know what that meant. Why else, if not for the preservation of this cure?"

Vaughan's eyes flashed. "I would have saved Joseth whether he came bearing a hold full of spiderpearls or rocks painted in gold. If the House of Westerend cannot be loyal to its own blood, it is not noble."

Aethal was dimly aware that Farnan's shock mirrored his own. So this is what family honor looks like, thought Aethal. I see it practiced here, of all places. Envy coursed through Aethal, for a moment. What would it have been like, to be this man's son? Aethal sheathed the Last Sword.

"You may not have any reason to trust me or my House, my Lord," he said. "But I give you my word — mine, not that of House Wrackberg — that I still seek General Joseth Malcoor, and not to kill him. It was General Malcoor who trained me in the ways of the Discipline; he made me an officer, and I value that.

There was always respect between us, if not love. Verlaen needs him. The more desperately if he has any hope of knowing a cure for Lotus. There is no one else I can turn to."

"Your own brother's men took him last. Have you asked him where the General is?"

"Yes," said Aethal. "Several times. According to him, Malcoor's departure was the last time that anyone saw either General Malcoor or his arresting party." The interview with Aerhan after Stevn's challenge had gone round and round until Aethal had been forced to give up in disgust. Aerhan knew nothing, but was doing everything reasonable to find General Malcoor. Aethal suspected their father was guiding the search. "You may as well know, my Lord, that my brother Aerhan never took responsibility for anything he could get out of. He can't seem to get out of this." Aethal met Vaughan's raised eyebrow with one of his own. "Do you not know, my Lord, that I am estranged from my kin? It is true, whether you believe it or not. Why did you think I have hardly been seen at court for the past ten years?"

"The two of you seemed reconciled enough when the King handed you that sword you carry," Vaughan said dryly. "And you cannot tell me that Aerhan Paaling is not a lickspittle who would endure anything if he thought it would bring him more power."

"Not with a straight face, my Lord. But I can't see how looking that incompetent gains him anything."

"After the fall of the Westerend, your family and the Skysils would effectively split the kingdom. If your father holds the cure to Lotus, why should the king not reward him for it?"

"If you know of this cure for Lotus, why do you not tell the king yourself? If anything would shift the king to take your part more than he has, surely that would do it."

Westerend glared at him.

"Ah-hah!" Farnan said. "Of course. Only Malcoor could have told him. And it wouldn't look very good to have to admit that he's sat on that knowledge for more than twenty years."

Aethal felt very much the fool. *Perhaps my father was right about the effects of serving too long in the cavalry. I should have figured that out myself.*

"You found nothing in your inspections of my brother's dungeons, then?" That needed no answer. *Your brother has taken the life of mine.* Aethal's gut twisted; it might be true. "I have assumed that my brother has a hand in this, my Lord." *Both hands.* "But for a moment that the General has in truth escaped. Where would he go if not here?"

Vaughan barked laughter. "I should tell you this?"

Aethal folded his arms. "You hardly need to. If possible, he would run to the Twin Fans. But near the whole of Verlaen is between him and your deltas. And that's where my brother is looking. So where else would he go?"

Vaughan weighed Aethal with his eyes. "You swear that no harm will come to my brother at your hands. Do you also swear that you had no other choice than to fire on my people of Everview?"

Aethal's throat was raw as he spoke the words. "I would rather have died, my Lord. But my death would not have saved them, and it would have given the Green Death that much more time and space to grow on the edge of your realm." He took a deep breath. "My lord, our families are enemies, but we have no time for that feud now. Good men like Sindon Rawl, who sacrificed everything to contain the Lotus rely on those of us who rule to act wisely. And they will curse us if we do not throw this quarrel aside. Today.

"As further proof of my honor, I offer this: I will give my word never to speak of what you tried to do today, and to hold you innocent of it. *If* you give me the word of your House that you will stand with the king against the Lotus. No matter what happens."

"*My* House's honor is not in question," snapped Vaughan.

Silently, Aethal rose and spread his hand to take in the carnage of the once-immaculate lounge. "Is it not, my Lord? Look at the reward your foul ambush has earned. You may have believed it necessary to save your brother's life. But honorable? If you defend that as honorable, I have misjudged you, sir."

The Lord of Westerend looked away. But his whispered voice was full of pain. "If you would have my trust, Aethal Paaling, release my daughter from that abomination!"

"My Lord," Aethal knelt close to him. "I cannot release your daughter now." Seeing the outrage flare in the man's eyes, raised a hand, "Hear me. I do not refuse you: I can not. There are ritual words that must be spoken, and I do not keep them on my person. But your daughter will be released and returned to you before the sun sets. You have my word. Now where would Malcoor go?"

Lord Vaughan fixed Aethal with an inscrutable gaze. "Very well, Aethal, Last Sword of Verlaen," he said, quietly. "I'm rather surprised you haven't thought of it yourself, though. It's in your family history, after all," he smiled without humor.

"My Lord?" asked Aethal.

"Your lady mother sought refuge in the same place. The Guardians of the Well. By traditions older than Verlaen, they are not bound by the laws of any one people or ruler, and do not surrender those who go to them for protection. If I were Joseth, I might think to find shelter there."

"I have visited the Guardians." The note the Lord Warden had given him was still in his pocket. He did not want it lost, but he had heard nothing. Was it possible that Malcoor was the "enigma" they had hinted at? The word certainly applied. "If he is there, I did not find him."

Malcoor's eyes narrowed. At last, he said, "There is one other place Joseth might go. Come with me." He led them through the house and into a private study. Taking an ornate, copper-chased box from the shelf, he did something to it with his hands that Aethal could not quite see. From it, Malcoor withdrew half a copper coin. But it was not stamped with the seal of Maednac's Line or the king's features. Instead, it bore a strange knot device. The visible end of the knot was the head of a snake.

"Joseth gave this to me to keep safe for him when he was sent into exile. He said that a certain businessman in the Madlands held the other half of the coin. He said that if House Westerend should be in great need of services that could not be obtained through ordinary channels, I should contact this man. Joseth, I gather, often used this man as a conduit for provisions that the Fleet might have frowned upon being asked to supply."

"I see." Aethal took the coin. "The Madlands are large. How am I to find him?"

"His sign, I am told, is known. The design is symmetric: a double-headed serpent. I do not know that Joseth will be there, you understand, or I should have looked for him there myself. But as he is not here, and not with the Guardians, he may have left some clue with the man who holds the other half of the coin."

Aethal pocketed the talisman. "Very good, my Lord. Then I shall return your daughter to you this evening. And hopefully before too long," he added, "your brother, as well."

Chapter Twelve

43rd of Spring, 312 Exodus

Aethal flexed his left hand as he and Farnan made their way back through the Upper Madlands.

"You should learn to dodge faster, Captain," jibed Farnan. "Especially if you plan on leading us into more melee combat."

"Enough." Aethal waved the banter off, but he was glad of it. Ardyth's silent presence unnerved him more than the man who'd formerly borne Flintmaw had ever managed. Aethal winced. He would have to read the Book of the Wyrmguard to discover what man had just died at his command. And how to release Ardyth from the gun's possession.

"Lord Vaughan committed treason, of course," Farnan went on, "but I can see why you forgave him." Farnan glanced sideways at Ardyth.

"Not funny, Farnan," said Aethal. "I'd have stopped her if I could, D'you think this is a laughing matter?"

"No, Aethal. But you do have a unique opportunity, here." Farnan's voice was dead serious.

Aethal stopped. "What do you mean?"

"You have Westerend's daughter," said Farnan, stepping close. "He's obviously mad to protect her. You might not want to let her go so soon."

"Farnan," said Aethal, shocked. "I gave my word."

"And he gave his, by implication, not to try to murder us when we came as guests," snapped Farnan. "He broke it. Westerend controls the most fertile land area in this Kingdom, and he is not your friend. If he raises rebellion, how far will Lotus spread while we're distracted? I came a little too close to dying today to trust his loyalty." Farnan was breathing fast. "I'd prefer to be sure of him."

Aethal's heart hammered. Farnan's words struck deep. What would his honor be worth if it killed the Kingdom? He looked into Ardyth's placid, cool eyes, and saw there the Wyrmguard's iron certainty. There was no question what his father would do.

Aethal nodded. "It's well that you think of such things, Farnan. But no. We'll trust him for now." Farnan held Aethal's gaze a moment, then nodded.

****

The rays of the setting sun shone in through the bars of the Binding Chamber. Aethal forced his fingers to stillness around the edges of the last page of the Wyrmguard's book. The lead foil glinted red in the rays of the sun and of the oil lamps. The weight of it dragged at his arms.

But the words dragged at his eyes, and what they said seemed to suck at his very soul.

Quickly. Things were happening too quickly. Had had to move quickly, if he were to redeem his word to Lord Vaughan. He had known this duty would come, had known from the moment King Paitir had placed the Last Sword upon his back, but that knowledge had been walled away from his attention by the ever-pressing threat of the Lotus.

There was no escaping the Binding. It would happen now. Under the Compact Maednac had signed in his own hand. "You shall keep never more than the fifth of us idle," read the seventh Article. Aethal's eyes closed, and he saw again the Armory of Thirty, buried deep in the foundation of the Ophidian. Twenty-four of the iron racks were empty. Six were occupied. One full wall of the room hung heavy with the promise of death to Maednac's enemies, and slavery to anyone who dared to touch them. Their names were engraved below their places, and Aethal had felt their presence even before he had opened the door. Stonelock had been there, the one who had dictated the Compact with

Maednac. And Caliburn. Everwar. The Lady's Demise. Carryon. Kindread. Which meant he could not return Flintmaw to the Armory simply by speaking the words of Loosing over Ardyth.

Another would have to be Bound.

Ardyth stood with him, silent in the Chamber. It had been hard and deadly serious work to get her into this chamber without anyone noticing. Aethal was still cursing himself for his earlier foolishness. *Yet now no one knows that Ardyth House Westerend has ever been a Wyrmguard.*

Aethal was not worried that anyone would wonder what had happened to Flintmaw's old mount. No one would miss *him*.

Before Ardyth had touched Flintmaw's grips, her face had been alive, and her eyes wild with the fear and heat of battle. Now all of that was drained away, and her face was carved ice. She eyed Aethal with a cool and calculating glance. "It would be kind of you, Last Sword, to return one of my idling brothers to service. In my stead, if you cannot do so concurrently."

"I do what I must. Under the Compact," Aethal answered, voice as dry as dust. "And I need your memories just now." His skin prickled with sweat under his fresh uniform's heavy black cloth. The smell of mothballs clung to it. He had not worn it since the death of one of his brother officers in a riding accident three years previously. The uniform was for funerals. Aethal would have worn the same uniform to sentence a man to die.

A task which might have been easier.

Aethal wondered at how his mind found distraction in minutiae. He traced the words engraved in the leadfoil in fascinated horror. They were not printed words, he had realized, the moment he glanced at the first sentence. They were *written*.

And by whose — by what — hand?

The words filled only the one page. The Binding. The Loosing. And there, at the bottom of the page, the Breaking. All the ceremonies began: *With thy right hand upon the barrel, speak thus*: For a single moment, Aethal imagined himself gripping Flintmaw's barrel and speaking the Ceremony of Breaking. And then returning to the Armory and breaking each of the Wyrmguard, one after the other. It would be treason, of course.

He looked up at the distant sound of a voice crying out, and found Flintmaw's gaze meeting him out of Ardyth's eyes. "You cannot simply break us, Last Sword. It is against the Compact."

Horrified, Aethal took a swift step back. The cries grew louder outside the door. Ardyth's brows rose. "I do not read your thoughts, Last Sword. All the Swords have considered Breaking us, at one time or another. Save the first. That was a hard man. And lived a hard time."

Article Nine stated: "Any Wyrmguard who shall commit any crime while mounted shall be Broken." None ever had. Aethal wondered if they really could. The same Thirty who had sworn to serve Maednac guarded him to this day. The muffled shouts had now turned to screams. The door opened.

Two Wyrmguard entered. Between them, they dragged a man smelling of sour sweat and urine. A young man, no older than Aethal himself, dressed in the cloth-of-gold that marked prisoners. It was ragged and stained, and the man's eyes rolled back under his mat of brown hair. "Oh, God-Beyond-The-World," he sobbed. "Oh, for His sake, Sir, don't make of me a deadwalker! Don't! Please!"

Aethal turned his face to stone and held out a hand. The nearer Wyrmguard handed him a scroll bound in a black ribbon. Aethal slid the ribbon off and the parchment unwound. "Gern Foeling of Sundwimmer," he said, praying that no one would notice the whiteness of his knuckles, "You have been found guilty of stabbing three of the City Watch while drunk and bloodthirsty in the streets, killing one."

"No!" Foeling screamed. "I never! Never!" He looked into Aethal's eyes and cringed. "'Tis the drink! I never did no worse'n get drunk like any other man! Oh, please, Sire! Don't damn me! Don't lock my soul in that thing!" He stared at Ardyth, eyes starting from his head. "And what's she done, eh? I know women! S'gotta've been worse'n me. It's gotta!"

"Foeling," said Aethal, quietly. Desperately, Foeling met his eyes, and the only sound in the chamber was his panicked breathing. "The lady is innocent. Victim of an accident, and her own bravery. And you have been sentenced to twenty years under the Gun. You have only been waiting in prison until you were needed." He held up the scroll. "Had you been unfit to serve, the penalty for your crime would have been death. You may yet survive. I would not see you go into your captivity bound and gagged. But I will if you cannot be silent. Will you face your fate with courage?"

Foeling's jaw worked. Then he hung his head. Aethal turned to Ardyth. She lay down on the spare camp cot in the middle of the room, raising the revolver in her right hand. Aethal placed his right hand on Flintmaw's barrel. The breathing behind him grew faster and more ragged. "By Table and Forge. By Nadesh Cor. By The Line of the King which is Forever. Be Loosed. Be Idle. Be At Rest."

Ardyth's hand released Flintmaw's grip and dropped to her side like a dead thing. Aethal held the Wyrmguard. Its mind pulsed under his hand, a hundred times more powerful than Gun's familiar presence. It was like a hole, a barely leashed hunger that he dared not examine too closely, lest it swallow him. He turned to Foeling, who began to struggle again, his breaths turning to ragged whimpers. Under the last vestiges of self-control, Aethal could hear him:

"No... no... no..."

Firestrike shoved the man's hand forward. Aethal closed his fingers around it. *Forgive me.* And of whom did he seek pardon? "By Table and Forge. By Nadesh Cor. By the Line of the King, which is Forever. Be Bound. Be Servant. Be Watchful." Aethal felt power surge under his hands, and the whimpering ceased. Gern Foeling immediately straightened. The Wyrmguard released him.

"Permission to bathe and request a new uniform, Last Sword?" Flintmaw asked.

"Granted," nodded Aethal, trying to forget the horror and despair in Foeling's eyes, erased now. He looked back at Ardyth, whose eyes were open, staring at nothing. "What did you do to her?" he snapped, anger and bile rising.

Flintmaw looked puzzled, then said, "She will recover momentarily, Last Sword. We do not often take mounts without the Binding. We may not, under the Compact, except in pursuit of our duty. When we do, the process is of necessity, less gentle. Our mounts require time to..." the weapon seemed to search for words, "once again... dominate... their bodies. Themselves." The Wyrmguard exited, and Aethal and Ardyth were alone.

Aethal could not look away from her eyes, that stared up at the ceiling, seeing nothing. The sun was very close to the horizon now, and he shuddered at the thought of standing forsworn before Lord Westerend. It was not a physical fear, though Westerend was frightening enough.

It is the thought of being seen as another in a long line of faithless Wrackbergs; like our island, we are rooted only in ourselves. She did not deserve this. Aethal wondered for an instant whether Flintmaw might have lied to him, but the Wyrmguard could not lie, except by direct order. *Lie, no, but could they be mistaken?* Aethal knew he had never met an ex-Wyrmguard, though he suspected that Flintmaw's former mount was the first one to be killed in the line of duty for decades. *Are women different from men? Are they, perhaps..?*

Ardyth sat up and screamed.

Aethal was on his feet in a moment, half-deafened. The sound came out of her like a wind from the Well, and continued in a single piercing note. He reached for her hands. Instantly, she stopped screaming and swung her right hand around in a roundhouse slap, eyes afire. Reflexively, Aethal caught her hand.

She collapsed onto his shoulder, sobbing.

She did nothing else for several minutes, and he began to rock her awkwardly, whispering empty reassurances. She looked into his eyes, frightened. "The Sleep," she whispered. "The Empty Core."

Aethal had no idea what this meant. "Lady Ardyth, House Westerend. Do you know where you are?"

She came more awake at this. "I... I know. I remember... I remember everything. Thank you." She sobbed again. "Thank you for making it go." Aethal had no idea what the panicked words meant. He should have thought to have wine present, or anything else of comfort. *More fool, I,* he thought. *But any other place would surely have been too public.*

Ardyth was sitting back on the cot, now, twisting her hands within themselves. "I couldn't stop it," she said, a note of hysteria rising in her voice. "I couldn't make it *stop!*"

Aethal looked her in the eyes. "No one can make it stop, my Lady. The Wyrmguard Revolvers were Wished from the Well to dominate men. No amount of will or faith can make one release its prey. Only the words of the Compact can do that."

She stared him in the face. "I would have shot my father. I would have pulled the trigger. It would have made me a murderess."

"No," said Aethal. "By Law no man is responsible for what he does as a Wyrmguard. He is released without fault or accusation. It is the Gun's will that rules."

A spark of loathing entered Ardyth's eyes. "You have no conception of what you speak of, Aethal Paaling. That... thing did not rule me. It did not direct me, or ride me. It *became* me. And I became it."

"It will never return to you," said Aethal. "And it never should have taken you in the first place. I never swore any oath more gladly than that I swore to your father."

Ardyth's face softened. "Thank you for freeing me, my Lord Wrackberg," she said, eyes downcast. "I... I truly had thought you would kill my father for what he had tried to do to you. Or even order me to do so." Her face was bleak with horror.

"I do not kill men except by necessity."

Ardyth seemed to nerve herself before she spoke next. "And why did you not take the advice of your Lieutenant Farnan? It would have been easy enough. To have left me the prisoner of your Wyrmguard."

"I suppose I might have," said Aethal. "But if I am false to your father, then I can hardly be true to the king. I am not my brother, Lady."

"Is your brother false to the king, then?"

Damnation, she is quick. Aethal resolved to watch his mouth. "My brother is as you have seen him. No more and no less."

"And you keep in your service a man who would counsel you to throw away your word simply for your safety?"

"Farnan is a man of honor. Perhaps more frightened than usual. I pray you do not judge him too harshly. He was not expecting to be ambushed in your father's house."

"It wouldn't have been much of an ambush if he had," Ardyth pointed out.

"And speaking of men who would throw away their words to gain an advantage, my lady," Aethal said, "Was that an example of your father's honor?"

She looked away. "Just so," Aethal said. "As your father would not abandon his... brother, Malcoor, so I would distrust myself before distrusting Farnan."

Ardyth fixed him with a disquieting stare. "Truly? I was there when you brought the news of Lotus to the King. This is the time when we are *not* to trust ourselves, yes?"

"Perhaps." Suddenly, Aethal was very tired. "And yet we must trust each other, in the end, or what are we fighting for? God-Beyond-The-World, lady, where did you learn to fight like that?"

Ardyth's smile was grim. "My father told me that any Lord Paramount's heir who walks the halls of power in Maednac Serpiin should be ready to cut herself free of them. I have trained with the blade since I was five."

"Indeed," Aethal could only wonder at the courage of this woman, slender and deadly as her blade. "Milady Ardyth, I must fulfill my oath to your father, and send you to him. He is surely very worried."

"He is more than that, Aethal Paal..." she blushed, as if aware that the situation called for something other than her father's custom of omitting Wrackberg titles. "My Lord. My father is nearly beside himself. For me and for my uncle."

"You should not make a habit of mentioning that outside your own house, milady."

She met his eyes with an exasperated frown. "All men know my father and Malcoor were friends. I've called him "uncle" since I could talk. Don't you do the same with Thane Pyk Imya?"

Aethal snorted. It was too easy to forget that deadly rivals were humans, too. "Yes."

"But my father fears for our people. The Lotus appeared on the borders of our domain, and we have not been seen there since. The people need us, but the King will not let us return."

"Lady Ardyth, I sympathize for your father's fears, but he tried to kill me today to assuage them. Both myself and Lieutenant Farnan. And he did kill a man. A man whose name I do not even yet know, but who bore the mastery of a Wyrmguard Revolver for much longer than you did, and I do not even know whether he was volunteer or convict. By rights I should charge him with murder."

Ardyth trembled. "You wouldn't?"

"Lady Ardyth," said Aethal evenly, "If I do that... make it known that Lord Vaughan Paramount of Westerend tried to perhaps...? slay a Wyrmguard, then a charge of treason against the crown follows automatically, and he must be tried and judged by the General States. All the lesser lords. All the High Overseers. All the Shireevs and Mayors. They haven't been called in a hundred years, but they are gathering now. And every moment they spend on your father's trial would be one more moment we were not fighting the Lotus. I will not charge your father with high treason, Lady Ardyth. Because we do not have the time. And the only other option would be for the King to use his power of Extreme Sanction, as Maednac did when he faced the Lotus."

Ardyth went white. "He can't."

King Maednac had once summarily tried and executed a dozen Imperial ship captains for cowardice because they had fled rather than fight ships full of Lotus-Eaters. *But the Westerend would surely believe the charges false.* "He can. Legally. But it would risk adding a civil war to our present chaos."

Ardyth swallowed. "To ambush you was surely wrong, Lord Wrackberg, but my father has been pushed beyond the limits of honor by despair. We seek only to return to our homes. I beg you, Lord Wrackberg..."

Aethal held up his hand. "Aethal, please," he said. "Or Lord Aethal, if you must."

"Lord Aethal," she began again. "I beg you speak to the king for us."

"The King keeps his own counsel much of the time. Your father is a Lord Paramount, and I am..."

"You are the King's cousin." Her eyes flashed. "My Lord."

"I will do what I can," he said, holding up a hand. Indeed he would speak to Cousin Paitir about this. The sooner Westerend was back at the Twin Fans, the better. An ugly thought struck him. *As long as Westerend is here, any enemies he's made at home can claim he is hiding beneath the King's walls. He can't exercise more than the most titular control of his realm. He's hostage against himself. Whose idea is this, truly?* It bore the hallmark of his father's schemes.

Footsteps sounded outside the door. A moment later it swung open. Aethal opened his mouth to rebuff the intruder when he recognized the angular good looks of Crown Prince Eraad, flanked by a Wyrmguard and another guard in the uniform of the Hydraxis garrison.

"Last Sword," said Eraad. "and Lady Ardyth. What are you doing here?"

Aethal launched smoothly into his prepared story, though his bowels had turned to water. What did Eraad know? But there was nothing else to do. "I have just Bound a man into the service of the Wyrmguard. A criminal who hailed from the Westerend originally. There was a Wyrmguard Revolver standing idle. Lord Westerend asked that the Lady Ardyth be present to observe your father's justice." And he had not told a lie. *Which will never save me if Eraad should learn the whole truth.*

But Eraad's focus seemed to be elsewhere. "And you thought it proper to do this here, alone?" he asked.

"We haven't been alone but five minutes," Ardyth protested, her voice still weak. "The Wyrmguard only just left."

"Wyrmguard are hardly fit as chaperones in the Hydraxis," said Eraad, glaring at Aethal. "They do not exactly take initiative where matters of propriety are concerned."

Matters of...? Aethal didn't know whether to burst out laughing or be insulted. Eraad was concerned not that Ardyth was in the Binding chamber, but that she and Aethal had been alone together unchaperoned. *Of course. All Eraad would have to do to find me is to ask a Wyrmguard. What one knows they all know. Yes, Eraad, most improper. And thank the Lord-Beyond-The-World for your nearsightedness.* And he had time for a brief moment of regret that *being unchaperoned* with Lady Ardyth was not something he had time to consider. But the Crown Prince was continuing. "Lady Ardyth, this whole ordeal must have distressed you greatly. Is there any comfort I can offer you? Clearly, you should not have been forced to see such a terrible thing!" he glared at Aethal, who caught the glint in Ardyth's eye. He hoped she was not about to break out in hysterical laughter. But her lip merely curled.

"Lord Prince, my father ordered me to be here to witness this event." Technically true. Her voice fell on her next sentence. "There is no more terrible punishment in the kingdom that a man may suffer than that of being bound under the Gun." She straightened. "We of the Westerend believe that if we pass such a sentence — even should the Crown do so in our name — we have a duty to look that man in the face as we do so. As my father was occupied with even more pressing matters, he sent me."

Eraad looked taken aback by this flat declaration. "Was this some man of note that was Bound? I heard nothing of this."

Aethal made his voice dismissive. "No, Sire. Simply a countryman of the Westerend territories. He was up for twenty years under the gun or hanging. I took him."

Eraad dismissed this with a wave. "In truth I did not come here to discuss the Wyrmguard with you, Last Sword, but to enlist your assistance. The Lady Ardyth may as well hear, this matter must soon be told to her father in any case. The Grassworms have breached the Treeline."

Aethal rocked back on his feet. "No. How?" The ground seemed to tilt up under him.

"The courier says that the clans have been infiltrating through the Tree-line by ones and twos at night. Apparently General Jeharok never thought of *that!*" The contempt in his voice was plain. *And did* you *think of it, Eraad? Or are you merely scornful now that the danger is obvious?* Aethal was quite sure, in fact, that Jeharok *had* thought of it. But thinking of it and being able to stop it were two different things. Of course, the Grass-worms weren't just going to sit outside the Treeline and wait to be caught between the swift death of Jeharok's prairie fires and the creeping death of the Lotus. But apparently, they hadn't been frightened into suicidal mass assaults on the Treeline, either.

"We'll need to re-convene the King's Council. Lord Prince, I believe that effective now, we must have another two companies sent to guard the Pass. And a company of rangers to occupy the length of the Serpiins. To broaden the search for Malcoor, but also to stop any who think to go around the Pass and over the mountains, mad as that would be..."

"Aethal!" snapped Eraad. "We did not come here to carry your orders but to give you ours!"

Aethal stopped. "How do my orders displease you, Lord Prince?"

"Firstly, this search for Malcoor must be abandoned. It's a waste of our resources that cannot be borne. Then, we..."

"But Uncle Malcoor knows the cure for the Lotus!"

Eraad stopped, mouth gaping open. "Have you gone mad?" he finally managed.

"Lord Wrackberg, tell him!" Ardyth's eyes were wild with hope. Aethal's heart sank.

"Aethal is this true?" Aethal looked into the Prince's blazing eyes. "Is this true, damn you?" Eraad shouted.

Aethal forced himself to meet Eraad's gaze. "I have just learned, from..." *not Lord Westerend, that practically begs for a charge of treason against the man, damn the girl,* "some archives Lord Westerend had never been able to make sense of, that General Malcoor — Commodore Malcoor, then — may have run across an island contaminated by Lotus. His observations hint at a weakness, though we have yet to discover it."

Eraad's eyes glowed with anticipation. "Do they really?" he said. There was an odd look in his eyes as they fell on Ardyth. To prevent this line of questioning going any further, Aethal took Eraad aside and said in a voice just loud enough for her to hear, "The Lady Ardyth is close to her uncle, and is desperately afraid of the Lotus, as are we all. I fear she hopes for too much, yet surely we should continue the search, my Lord?"

Ardyth drew breath and looked daggers at him. Aethal was surprised at how much that hurt. But before she could say anything, Eraad had taken her hand. "Of course, my lady; in my haste I misspoke. We shall surely be able to spare some men to find General Malcoor. We must apologize for Our Last Sword's behavior; he has been long in the field and has forgotten some of the delicacies young ladies should be used to." He turned to his guard. "Dafyd, please escort the Lady Ardyth to her father's manse." With a murderous glare at the back of Eraad's head, Ardyth allowed herself to be taken from the room. After the door closed, the Prince rounded on Aethal.

"Aethal, what do you mean by bringing a lady of her birth up here to witness a filthy thing like a Binding?"

"Her father insisted, my Lord Prince," said Aethal, "and indeed she took it very well."

"I will *not* allow such ugliness to be displayed before ladies. Particularly not this one. Even with Lotus in the land, we will observe some decorum. If her father insists on anything of the like in the future you are to do nothing until you have seen me first, is that clear?"

Aethal shrugged. "Of course, my Lord Prince." *Or your father, at least.* There was something in Eraad just now that had made him uneasy. A hunger for something unseen by any but himself. The way he had been looking at Ardyth was definitely proprietary. Was an alliance in the works? Surely not without his father the Chancellor's knowledge. Speaking of which...

"Does the king your father know of this news yet?"

"Oh, my father!" the Prince threw up his hands in exasperation, but Aethal thought he saw an uglier look in his eyes. "*He* is hanging his hopes on the General States to take this mess off his hands. There won't be enough for a quorum for at least two weeks more. We ought to close the Pass before they get here. If even one of all of those men is infected, and it slips past the Discipline of the Pass, what then? Besides which, the debate and discussion will take up at least a month that we don't have." Eraad turned to Aethal and, said in low tones, "This is really why I came to you, Aethal. Please try to talk my father out of this foolishness. As far as the Lotus is concerned... well, he trusts you."

As he does not trust you, Eraad? Aethal felt some sympathy for the young man, who was not by much his junior, the only surviving son of King Paitir, born late in his father's life. But didn't he see that the people needed to feel that their king was listening to them? That King Paitir had promised them this hearing?

"Your concerns are not entirely misplaced, Your Highness," Aethal said carefully. "But shutting the Pass now, after the convening of the General States has been declared, might be seen as an admission that his Majesty has lost control of the situation, and cause a panic."

"My father never had control of this situation!" snapped Eraad.

Well, that was certainly true. But did Eraad imagine he would have done better? Or was he simply frustrated by his superfluous role in events, and frightened of watching his kingdom burn under creeping green waves?

Perhaps I ought to give him a role, and see if he can bring some pressure to bear on Aerhan, too. They must have interacted socially; Eraad is the center of young men's society in the capital: he probably knows the little idiot's weak points better than I do. If Aerhan knows of Malcoor, then Eraad can bring pressure to bear on him that I can never match.

"I will discuss the matter with the King," said Aethal. And the King needs to know about this cure. That, above all else. Has Eraad thought of that?

But before Aethal could speak further, the Crown Prince only nodded and turned on his heel. Aethal waited for the footsteps to die away. Then he walked up the staircase, up past his own chambers, and presented himself to the Wyrmguard outside the royal apartments. "I need to see the king. Immediately."

****

Aethal threw back the doors of the Hydraxis with such force that the two guards flanking it jumped, then instantly resumed their forward-facing stare when they recognized him. They were younger and taller than he was, wearing baldrics over ribbed steel breastplates. The sun was fully down now, and their pikes gleamed redly in the torchlight, reflecting the light of the Ocean Court.

Aethal stood on a sloped path that ran between lines of trees. The path widened as it descended, until it ran out the Seagate and the walled avenue that led down to the Admiralty.

Aethal walked down the path, toward the great bronze statue of Maednac, its back a great black shadow limned in golden fire. Approaching it, he slowed.

It had been years since he had stood in the Ocean Court, though he remembered once, with Aerhan. Ten years old, Eraad had showed them that he could climb up the pedestal and sit at Maednac's feet. Neither he nor even Aerhan had quite dared follow. He'd been fourteen, then, and trying desperately to be as mature as everyone kept saying he should be.

Maednac stood with his left hand stretched palm out toward the harbor. His right hand clutched an aluminum crown to his breast. It was a denial, a repulsion, looking out over the sea. *Three hundred years ago, he stopped the Lotus and built a kingdom.*

But there had been other bronze sculptures then, Aethal knew. The ones from Paal's poem, ringing the harbor, the great cannon, now green with age and corroded by the salt.

When the Lotus had spread through the Old Empire and the Imperial subjects had fled, it had been Maednac who had taken the Imperial Fleet and fled to the far-off bay-fortress of Serpiin. Maednac who had ordered the cannon to fire on any ship that might break the quarantine. Maednac had established Verlaen as a Kingdom. Aethal did not need to read the words carved as deep as a dagger is long in the granite pedestal. *By My Word*, they said. Maednac had not been one to shy from taking responsibility.

For the first time since he was a little boy, Aethal wondered what it was like to truly pray. Church doctrine taught that God had been banished by the sinking of the Well. Only priests, those who had been sanctified, could reach beyond the world in prayer, so they might be heard by God. If God heard, did He give the Conversant any sign? Was there hope, echoing back from the Infinite?

Had it stopped?

Aethal shook his head. Whatever the truth, his own duty was plain before him.

There were guards flanking the statue's base. These carried lesser rifles. Their eyes were away from the flames, and they looked outward at the palace gardens that surrounded Maednac's statue.

Aethal found himself on the footpath that orbited the statue. Slowly, the great bronze figure showed its profile, left arm raised up, crown clutched in its other hand. The look on the statue's face was cold and forbidding.

Entranced by the great, burning face, he found himself walking closer. Step by step. You are still looking out to the Sea, thought Aethal. Scene of your triumph, where you stopped the Green Death, the Lotus that the Well threw up to destroy the Empire. Nothing has changed for you. Aethal searched for humanity in the glowing bronze face, but the sculptor had done his job too well, or not well enough. What would you do, now that your worst nightmare has come to pass?

A shape rose out of the darkness, and Aethal stumbled backward, shocked out of his reverie. "Good even, my Lord," said the strange Wyrmguard. For an instant, Aethal's blood froze. But it was Flintmaw. He had not recognized Gerd Foeling's face now that it was washed and shaven. "The Imperial Governor desires to be alone."

"Is that a command?" The guns would obey the King before they would obey Aethal, up to the limits of their judgment, as was proper.

But Flintmaw looked puzzled. "A preference," he said, finally.

"Then I must see the king." He passed by.

The King of Verlaen stood before Maednac's image, face ruddy and alight with the reflection of the bronze and the flames that lit it. He stared up at the statue like a starving man — like a Lotus eater, but unlike — there was none of the crazy hope of the Lotus eater's expression in the king's eyes. They were open like pits, and as empty.

"You coward," Aethal heard Paitir say, in an almost normal voice. Aethal looked around to see what luckless advisor the King was talking to, but then realized that his words were addressed to the statue.

"You Well-be-Wished coward," the King repeated, staring up at Maednac. "You never had to be a real king."

Aethal listened, entranced. The King stood trembling with rage before his ancestor, clutching his crown in mockery of Maednac's own stance. He spoke again.

"Where do I take my people, O Great One?" he whispered. "If you are the example for us all, then where do *I* run?" He turned away for a moment, but spun back almost instantly, shaking his crown up at the statue. "A real King does not run! Damn you! Damn you for being our hero! And blessed! And immune!" Tears streamed down the King's face, and Aethal felt ashamed to witness his nakedness in this night place, but he had no more power to leave than Maednac did.

"Now the Lotus comes, and what use are you, eh?" said the King. "There is no place left on the whole of the Earth to run, and you — three hundred years dead — can't even do that anymore! I Wish you had lived forever!"

Aethal felt his breath catch at the curse, but the King continued. "I Wish you still wore this crown and felt it heavy on your head. Take it back and die with the Empire you ran out on!" Aethal watched the king rear back and hurl the crown of Verlaen, Maednac's crown, at the statue, where it bounced with a hollow clang off Maednac's shins. It fell behind the King, rolling unevenly.

Aethal started forward and knelt beside the king, crouched in the dust between the two hedgerows, weeping softly. He looked up, and his eyes blazed. Then he recognized Aethal and his expression softened, sagged.

"I should have known it was you," he said, wearily. "Who else could find me by asking the Wyrmguard?" He made no move.

"Sire, I..." Aethal felt ashamed. He had found the king crying.

Paitir looked up at him. "Don't 'Sire' me, cousin Aethal. Not here. Not now. Sit down. Just be Aethal. And I will be Paitir, for awhile. Here at our nation's most impressive gravestone. Or go away."

Aethal sat. The King looked up at the statue. Aethal looked with him. Maednac took no notice. The pressure built in Aethal to say something. Paitir's crown lay ten paces ahead of them. The anodized aluminum gleamed golden in the light of the fires. It was beyond price.

"The situation is not yet hopeless, Si — Paitir," ventured Aethal. "Telerat guards the Skysil lands. And Uncle Falaar is a good man. He will not let the Lotus pass him. And there is still our own Pass, guarded by men who know Discipline like no other."

"Of course it is not hopeless. That would be too easy. When the situation is hopeless, I shall think myself at peace at last. Hope forces us to continue," said Paitir. "I suppose you heard me?"

"Yes, Paitir."

Paitir laughed once, utterly without humor. "And, Aethal? What do you think? Do kings run?"

Aethal was speechless for a moment. Was the king going mad? Or was he just terribly afraid? Finally, he said, "If Maednac had not run, it's likely none of us would be here to praise his courage."

Paitir gave him a sharp look. "You're more your father's son than either of you realize," he growled, and Aethal felt a cold stab of fear and rage pass through him. The insane fear that Paitir had somehow been watching himself and his father up there, that night on the Dragonmast... could the Wyrmguard know? Would they have told Paitir? Irontooth had heard all of their conversation but Paal's whispered threat, of that Aethal was sure. But Paitir continued, "So young and already a pragmatist. So, yes, we are here, a nation founded by cowards. Much good may it do us."

"Paitir," said Aethal. "Whether Maednac did right or not, we must stand. As you said, there is no place to run. The Weedrats' floating Tidetowns couldn't support us, and on all the Earth only Verlaen remains undrowned by the Well."

"So, you agree with Ilferth Simon, then?" said the King. "There is no hope for man?"

"I will never agree with Ilferth Simon," Aethal said. "Paitir, cowards or no, we stand a better chance fighting now than doing anything else. I am your Last Sword. I will die defending you. Even if that means hacking at Lotus blossoms until my sword arm falls off."

The King looked into Aethal's face and seemed to take some strength from it. "I have given you a thankless job, Aethal Paaling. No Last Sword has ever failed in his duty, not since Maednac landed. Through no fault of your own, you may be the first."

Aethal bowed his head. "Then at least none shall remember my shame," he said, smiling sardonically at the king.

Paitir snorted. "That's the spirit, boy." He coughed, shaking off his earlier weeping. "Do you know why I named you Last Sword, Aethal?"

Aethal shook his head.

"Because you brought the news to me. To me first. I know you're not your father's tool; that's been plain enough from the moment I divorced your mother from him. And you're no kin to those doomlovers that Ilferth Simon drags along after him." Aethal felt his heart sink, but Paitir continued. "I expected to be tripping over both you boys at court as fast as your father could shove you in front of me. But only Aerhan has had that distinction. You joined the cavalry and disappeared. Why?"

Aethal now studied the dirt. "Why did you divorce my parents, Paitir?"

Paitir sighed. "I'm the king, Aethal. I get my answers first."

Aethal's guts churned with fear. *He deserves to know if anyone ever did. But what about Farnan? What about the sergeant? He'll make good on his threats; I know he will.*

"Because I did not want to be my father's son, Sire."

Paitir gave him a cool look. "And what is it you see in your father, Aethal, that you hate him so? Are you certain it is him you hate?"

The words, when they came, were like pulling arrows from a wound. "Because he is a coward, Paitir. He's always been a coward. He holds people to him with secrets and threats, without any honor or principle. And..." Aethal felt the back of his throat tighten. "And so am I.

"Sire. Paal Haerling House Wrackberg intercepted me that day with the news of Lotus. And he blackmailed me with my inheritance not to tell you about Lotus then. Wish me dead, I almost listened to him. He is keeping news from you, Paitir. And there is more to the matter of General Malcoor than any man knows. I need to find him, Paitir; he may know a cure for the Lotus; I think Aerhan..."

"Enough!" Paitir roared. Aethal found himself speechless. Paitir shot to his feet and shook the dust off his robe. Bending over him, Paitir whispered, "Is that what you have come to say, Aethal? That your father is a traitor and a coward? That your brother is disloyal? Is that what you have been burning to tell me?"

"Sire, I..." Aethal stammered.

"And what else would you have me know?" asked Paitir. "That Ilferth Simon is a fanatic? That Lord Vaughan of Westerend is itching to use Lotus as an excuse to raise his banners in rebellion? That your Skysil cousins would do the same at the instant they thought it wouldn't play into your father's hands? That my Lord Mayor is a tool of anyone he thinks will advance him money and prestige? That my own son..?" His voice broke. When he spoke again, it was in measured and even tones. "That my own son aches to usurp my throne for its imagined power and glory and would rather be your father's child than mine? Do you think I'm a fool? D'you think I'm blind as him?" he asked, pointing up at Maednac. "I'm the king, Aethal. Kings are never surrounded by any other sort of man. But your father has supported me when no other man even did me the courtesy of pretending to. Did it ever occur to you that the other choices might be worse than your father?" He bent over Aethal.

"I did not invite you here so that you could use me to revenge yourself on your father and brother. You want to know why I divorced your parents, Aethal? It was because your Skysil uncles asked it of me. Because they threatened to start a blood feud over that affair with Kaelan and the Tidetown. And I needed them to hold Westerend in check; needed them ever since Malcoor sailed back on a wrecked ship only the Well knew what he planned to do with. Oh, and of course Ilferth Simon was so concerned at your father's undue influence. I am the king, Aethal. It is my duty to keep Verlaen alive, and whole, and as close to peaceful as it can ever get with Lords Paramount and their sons plotting murder and vendetta at every turn. So I destroyed your family because I was asked to, just as I created it, because I was asked to. For another year of peace. Another few months. I'm a coward, too, just like the rest of you. So get off your knees, Last Sword of Verlaen. Get off them now."

"Sire," Aethal muttered, dazed. "You said... you chose me as Last Sword because I was not my father's tool."

Paitir looked disgusted. "Because you balance him, not so you can use me to fight him. And perhaps to give him some hope of his own, that you are not entirely lost to him. But if you think I need you telling me all his faults or his treasons, you overreach yourself. I don't care about his faults; he's Chancellor and he can find his arse with one hand. As long as Lotus doesn't devour the kingdom, he can take the crown home and make love to it each night."

Paitir walked away, leaving Aethal frozen in the night. He turned. "If you think you're a coward, join me at council in the Ophidian on the morrow; you will be in good company. If you do not, then we have sore need of you."

The King swept away, and gestured savagely at the crown in the dust of the garden path. Aethal saw Flintmaw retrieve it and follow after the King in a silent glide. Aethal sat in the path at the feet of Maednac. The guards were shouting the next hour before he rose.

He made his way to his own apartments in a fog of too much worry and too little sleep. Osric sat in the antechamber, dozing. Aethal shook the valet gently by the shoulder. "Get to bed, Osric; I have need of you alert in the morning, not waiting up for me out of misguided duty."

Osric scrambled to his feet, blinking away the sleep. "Your pardon, Lord, but I was told to give you this. Into your hands, and none other's."

Aethal took the folded paper. It was sealed with a blob of wax, but there was no device on the seal. Breaking it, he read: THE WATER IS DRAWN AT LLHAWCAE CATHEDRAL TOMORROW AT MIDNIGHT.

"Who delivered this, and when?"

"It was delivered by some priest, my Lord," said Osric, yawning. "Vanished before I could get his name. Just after supper."

"Bring me a glass of strong wine. Then get you to bed."

So. The Guardians had something for him at last.

Chapter Thirteen

44th of Spring, 312 Exodus

The road to Llhawcae Cathedral was deserted, but even from there, Aethal and Farnan could see the lights burning dimly in the windows.

"Awfully bright for a few priests having a late prayer session," muttered Farnan.

Aethal muttered agreement.

He was weary. In the controlled chaos of helping to muster the next wave of reinforcements that would go out, he had reluctantly decided that the rest of the Wyrmguard would have to be activated. One by one, he had stared into the eyes of the condemned. Some had screamed, some had wept, and some had cursed him. And then they had just... gone away. He still didn't know which had been worse, the four criminals... or the two volunteers, their eyes burning with raw enthusiasm, right up until they had touched the guns... and their faces had gone blank and inhuman.

"And it's late for a service," he added, more to distract himself from his own thoughts than for any other reason. They were the only ones on the road. To their right, the evening tide lapped the pebbled shores of Maednac's Bay. The Madlands were a sloping darkness beneath the torchlight of Maednac Serpiin's beacons behind them. Aethal wondered if the Church had placed the cathedral just outside the Madlands to give the people the excuse of escaping their warrens once a week, or because the priests had refused to live in the Madlands. Beyond the cathedral lay a small inn, and the highway that led to the villages of the northern Bowl.

They reached the doors of Llhawcae Cathedral just as a priest admitted a cloaked figure. He turned to them.

"May I help you, gentlemen... my lords?" he corrected himself, recognizing Aethal.

"We are here for the service," Aethal said, as if it were an entirely ordinary thing.

The priest licked his lips. "This service, my Lord... is not open to the public."

"Then for whom is it open?" Aethal asked.

"It is for..." the priest hesitated... "select and devout lay members of the Church to petition God-Beyond-The-World for protection from the Lotus."

Aethal's lips compressed into a thin line. "I am a lay member of the Church as much as any other man in this Kingdom," he said. "In addition to which I am the Last Sword of Verlaen and the son of a Lord Paramount. Is it my devotion or my blood that you are questioning?"

The priest was breathing faster. "Neither, my Lord. Do enter." He opened the door and stood aside.

Within the cathedral stood only two dozen men, clustered near the elevated lectern beneath the high vault. All were cloaked and hooded, and many were in conversation. Aethal led the way down the nave of the cathedral. A few heads turned toward the two officers. Aethal recognized some: men that his father had introduced him to when he was a boy, at state functions. The nearest was the Baron of Penholt, a hunting community right at the edge of the Northern Serpiin range. The man met his eyes with a cold stare and turned away as if he did not exist. Others were local shire-reeves and magnates. Some refused to meet his gaze. Slowly, the conversation stopped. A couple of men walked away toward the back of the cathedral. One came back minutes later, accompanied by a hooded Overseer and a cantor, who took his position before the Shrouded Altar. The priest waited by the stairs to the lectern.

The Cantor began the service, singing:

"Before God, the Lord amid the Stars, we send our prayers to His heavens."

The men responded, weakly and raggedly:

"Intercede for us."

"And what shall we ask of God for you?"

"A safe return to us, for all those upon the sea."

"And what shall we ask of God for you?"

"A harvest of bounty for us, for those who till the lands."

The responses gained in strength as the men fell into the familiar weekly pattern, but sounded thin and weak in the large building. Aethal and Farnan mouthed the words along with the rest.

"And what shall we ask of God for you?"

"To Wish for nothing, but to live our days in contentment."

"And what do you fear, that God should deliver you?"

"From the storms and from the pirates, may He deliver us."

"And what do you fear, that God should deliver you?"

"From the blight and the drought, may He deliver us."

"And what do you fear, that God should deliver you?"

"From the spawn of the Well, may He deliver us."

The last was delivered with more emphasis than normal, and Aethal looked at Farnan, who returned his gaze grimly.

The Cantor sang again: "For all of these, and for all of you, we shall intercede."

Again, Aethal wondered what it would be like to pray. Or even to see men pray. Not that a priest would ever pray in a cathedral, of course, still less before the people, who had caused God to flee the world. Prayer was a mystery of the Church. Aethal vaguely pictured lit candles, darkened rooms, and faces lifted to the moons. Men and women, dedicated to bringing the hopes and the fears of the people before God.

And what Answer do they await? If He cares to give one?

The Cantor retired, and the Overseer climbed the steps of the lectern. Aethal looked around the cathedral, cursing the Lord Warden for the cryptic nature of his note. Did the man intend him to be met? Or was this mysterious, badly-attended midnight service the entire object? If we *are meeting someone,* he thought. *I'll have to hope that he recognizes us.*

The added heat of the incense-laden candles burning in every cornice was already causing sweat to runnel down Aethal's chest. He followed the thin wisps of smoke up to the stained plaster of the ceiling, where it collected against the skylight. The crescent of the Lesser Moon shone murkily through it.

Farnan was craning his neck, as though trying to see the faces of the heads whose backs remained turned to him. Aethal muttered aside, "Let's not be so obvious, Lieutenant."

Farnan glanced at him with an acid grin. "Because we haven't looked obvious at all, up to this point, sir."

Aethal made cutting-off gesture as the Overseer began to speak. He was a middle-aged man, his brown hair shot with gray. The Single Moon was picked out in silver thread on his black robe, the top half gleaming over the pulpit.

"Lost," he said, and the word echoed off the walls. Not loud, but pitched to carry. "Once, before Salnum's Wish sank the Well, we were not lost, for God dwelt in the World, and knew our names. But when that King, in his arrogance and pride, believed he knew better for the people than God himself, then God removed himself to Deep Heaven, and our people became, as we are now, so very lost." He bowed his head.

"Like a ship befogged, with no guiding star, without even the divided light of the moons to steer by, the people of Verlaen have become lost. But no longer becalmed. For now we see the green tinge of the coming storm. And we light fires in the rigging of the vessel, thinking it will give us light, and save us from the coming darkness. Gentlemen, what madness is this, to believe that we defend ourselves with such a feeble light?"

Aethal caught Farnan looking at him uneasily. *What does he have against the night-lamps? How else can we defend ourselves?*

"It is a storm of our own making," said the Overseer, flatly. "We have sent shiploads of our young men into the hungry sea, to drown unwedded in graves unmarked. We have sown fields far and wide from our homes, in the Grain Sea, rather than working in our own places, as men ought to do. Through all this, though we have seen the rest of the world fall to the spawn of the Well, we have not cleansed ourselves. Rather, we sow keepwoods along our borders and we arm our men from Well-spawned forges that work the likenesses of souls into their weapons."

the likenesses *of souls?* Aethal could see from Farnan's face that his weapon had doubtless echoed Gun's response. But his attention was torn away by the Overseer's final sentence: "We invite Wellspawn into our very homes and wonder that it now arrives to devour us."

Aethal glanced at Farnan, and knew his own face must reflect the disgust he saw there. Without the Keepwoods, the Grain Sea villages would have been raided daily by Grassworm savages and their Banshees. And Maednac Serpiin, let alone the entire Bowl, could not survive without the food harvested in the Grain Sea. Verlaen itself might not have been born if Maednac hadn't had Imperial Cavalry snipers to protect his shipyards from the masses of leafeaters while the Fleet was preparing for its Exodus.

"Yet we, perhaps, are not wholly to blame," said the Overseer, dropping his raised arms.

Yes, a little sanity, please, thought Aethal.

"It is not the people of Verlaen who have chosen this madness. We are not forgers of wizardry. It is not our business to push the borders of the kingdom ever outward. That foolishness cannot be laid at our feet. And you may rest assured that God, who sees all, though He is not with us, does not forget it.

"Nor does God forget that Maednac of blessed memory was a man, and one who was sorely tested, and so God gave him and his people, this land of Verlaen, that we might be saved.

"But where now is Maednac's likeness?" He made a show of looking around. "Where now is the King who will realize that, just as Maednac was called to leave the blind and corrupted Empire, so we are now called to lay aside all the spawn of the Well, and to face the world as God intended, sober in mind and ready for labor? That is what must be. Shall we ask this of God for you?"

"Yea!" The response came without hesitation from every man on the cathedral floor; Aethal and Farnan alone were silent.

"We shall send the King our message, and humbly pray that he hear the word of God in the Hydraxis, so that he may cleanse it of the Wellspawn haunting that tower. Shall we ask this of God for you?"

"Yea!"

Aethal gaped. Farnan's face was reddening. *Did I just hear him accuse the King of bringing the Lotus to Verlaen?* No. Not quite. The Overseer had only proposed to pray for the King to make the right decisions. While leaving no doubt whatsoever about what decisions those were, of course.

"And what shall we do, good intercessor?" rolled a new voice. Everyone, Aethal and Farnan, too, turned to see the speaker.

The Lord Mayor of Maednac Serpiin descended a narrow, iron stair from an upper balcony. How long had he been there? "What shall we do, we who have the people in our charge, so that God's eye may turn upon us with favor?" The Lord Mayor walked slowly toward the gathered men. As he passed Aethal and Farnan, he gave them an edged smile of acknowledgment. The faces of the men followed him as he approached the lectern, but some lingered with distaste on Aethal and Farnan and their Greater Rifles.

The Overseer nodded to him. "Purge any Wellspawn from your homes, my Lord. Be a good and dedicated protector of the people, and carry their petitions to the King, even as we carry their petition before God."

Aethal understood now what the Lord Warden had wanted him to see. *If this is what is being discussed among the prominent citizens, then what is being preached to the people?* This was surely no isolated incident. But with the Lord Mayor himself here, it was a special one. What exactly had they interrupted? How different would it have been without their presence?

Then Farnan turned to Aethal, and his lips moved. *Listen.* The applause was dying. From outside Aethal could — just — hear shouts and the irregular footfalls of men fighting. Farnan ran for the door, yanked it open, and was gone. Swallowing a curse, Aethal followed, flinging himself out into the night.

****

The cool air hit Aethal like wine after the heat of the cathedral. Farnan was running at full speed, angling right across the cathedral's thin strip of lawn. Aethal followed his course, and accelerated to join him.

Backed against a stone fountain was a man dressed in a much-too-heavy black cloak. He held a thin dueling sword in the manner of one who has once been trained and is trying to remember all his lessons very quickly. He was trying to keep the point between him and the four blocky men spreading out around him, brandishing knives and clubs. The lone man was shouting something. Without thought, Aethal felt Gun's mind slide into his just as easily as the polished stock and trigger slid into his hand.

Gun's sights bracketed the nearest thug's head. From the corner of his right eye he saw Farnan, much closer, take aim with Crow. Aethal felt Gun's barrel shift under his hand the merest fraction, making fine adjustments to the aim. *perfect shot.*

Or it would have been if the cloaked man hadn't then lunged at his attackers, screaming defiance. Smoothly, Aethal's target brought a sword-breaker up in his left hand, snapping the thin blade off short. He followed through by ramming the end of his club into the cloaked man's stomach with brutal speed. That motion took him directly between Aethal and his own prey.

Gun's soft, steel-coated balls were capable of punching through a man's chest from 200 yards away. The range was perhaps a fifth of that, but it was too late for Aethal to stop himself from shooting. Gun read the fear in Aethal's mind and its trigger suddenly became as immovable as stone. Aethal blessed his weapon's mind and corrected his aim. Farnan's gunshot echoed across the cobbles, and the assailant on the far left dropped as if punched by an invisible fist. The remaining three attackers whirled, and Aethal's shot took the nearest between the eyes.

Farnan charged in from the right, striking the nearest knife-wielder full in the chest with Crow's butt-end. With a yell, the man stumbled into his remaining companion, taking them both down. Aethal leveled Gun and charged, screaming. The men were up before he got there, and Aethal knew that these were no ordinary street fighters of the Madlands. For all their rags, these were soldiers, and they betrayed it in the way they stood to receive him, ready to fight.

Gun's bayonet slid out. His enemy parried with his knife, and a wicked *scring* of sound traveled up the rifle. Aethal's next thrust punched through the man's guard, but caught on some kind of armor. Aethal raised Gun for a finishing strike, but was forced to block a riposte from the knife. Aethal levered Gun's stock viciously up and under the man's chin. He fell back, gasping and spitting shattered teeth. Aethal whipped the butt down onto his enemy's skull. Bone crunched and the man fell dead.

From Aethal's left, he heard a shout of dismay. He turned to see Farnan's snarl of triumph, his dagger slicing a deep gash through his opponent's arm. The attacker dropped his own knife and sprinted, past the fountain in a breath. Aethal had just started to yell for him to stop when a foul wind blew past his face and the world exploded in sound. The running form pitched forward on his face and lay still.

Turning, Aethal saw Farnan calmly reloading. Fury built in him.

"Do you Wish me dead, Farnan?" he shouted.

"Unlikely," Farnan grinned.

Aethal drew breath to ream his friend out.

crow is an excellent rifle. Gun's thoughts cut across his own. *and farnan is a superior marksman. there was no danger. we would have taken the shot in the same circumstances*. Belatedly, it occurred to Aethal that having one of the men alive for questioning would have been useful.

you were unlikely to have caught him in any case, Gun told him. *panicked men run fast*. Aethal turned to the man he'd hit, but he knew the man was dead. They would learn nothing from their enemies today.

Aethal turned to the erstwhile victim, tangled in his black cloak, and helped the young man to his feet. He was not as tall as Aethal, and his dark hair was bound into the tail of a Guardian novice. He shut his eyes. "Did the Lord Warden send you?" *Wellspittle, this boy is younger than Aerhan. The Lord Warden's sent us a child. And didn't think to tell him how to disguise himself.* The boy looked mournfully at the hilt of his sword, and the three inches of steel that were still attached to it. He nodded, looking as if he were about to cry.

"I, a-am Magnei, yes, Seeker." He adjusted the weight of his black robe so that it settled more evenly on his narrow shoulders, then winced at the movement.

"And these men are..?" Aethal invited, gesturing at the three bodies.

"I don't," began Magnei, "don't..." his face twisted and he turned to the fountain behind him. Gripping its sides with whitened knuckles, the novice threw up into the fountain, again and again. Aethal moved forward and laid a hand on his shoulder to steady him, remembering the first time he'd stood on a field after a battle looking at the very real, very dead men around him and realizing how easily he might have lain among them. Finally, Magnei finished, and the racking rasps of his breathing filled the night.

A fit of wet coughing behind him brought Aethal's head around. Farnan stood over one of the attackers. It was the first man he had shot. Blood spread in a steady pool beneath him, yet the man raised his head, staring at Magnei.

"Si... sin... drinker." He raised his fingers in a last circling gesture, and spat feebly, but the spittle stuck to his lips. "Be damned. Sin... drinker." He fell back, dead.

Aethal tried, but could not stop a little shiver going up his back at the word. "Sindrinker?" he asked, keeping his voice light. The Sindrinkers were a foul presence on the borders of many tales of the Empire. It had been a Republican Sindrinker, so it was rumored, who had led the expedition that had Wished Lotus from the Well. The Sindrinkers actually claimed that the Well was good, and that God had truly given it as a gift to the people of the Earth. *Which makes God cruel, or mad, or perhaps both.* Aethal could see a faint revulsion at the name pass over both Farnan's face.

"Sindrinker," gulped Magnei, "is what all enemies of Ilferth Simon's are now being called." He shivered, clutching his broken sword-hilt to himself. "And even the walls of the Abbey are no longer safe. We stand on a knife edge of the Church's tolerance."

The sound of running feet interrupted all further conversation as a Lotus patrol, drawn by the two gunshots, rounded the corner. The City Watchmen carried studded clubs, and a pole-mounted lantern. Their officer wore a worked steel cap shod with silver, and carried a percussion shotgun. He recognized Aethal and saluted.

Aethal quickly ordered the bodies taken to cells and locked away. If the lieutenant of the patrol thought there was something odd about detaining corpses, he said nothing.

"One other thing," Aethal told him. "I need a Wyrmguard here, now. Take this," he twisted his mother's ring from his finger, "and give it to the first one you can find in the Hydraxis. Don't be afraid," he said, seeing the man's look of horror. "He will not hurt you." But Aethal, Farnan, and this Magnei needed to be out of the street, and needed firepower on their way back to the Hydraxis. "Tell him I will be..." He pointed to the inn across the square, "there and to run." As if in a nightmare, the officer took the ring and turned about, face white. He led his patrol off.

This is how the people think of the Wyrmguard. Wellspawn and killers. When had he stopped thinking of them like that? Was he rationalizing commanding

Wellspawn and killers, or was it just that he now knew how fragile and how breakable their power was? Aethal turned for the inn.

****

"Drink; you need it," said Aethal, as they piled into a dim corner of the inn's main room. The sleepy publican retired to his cot. Magnei shrugged his hands out of the long robe, accepted the ale from Aethal, and took a long pull.

"If you're in that sort of danger," asked Farnan, jerking his thumb toward the door, and by extension, the four bodies, "why are you wearing that get-up?" asked Farnan, gesturing at the swaths of black fabric.

"I didn't want anyone to recognize me, of course!" said Magnei, without the faintest trace of irony. Farnan rolled his eyes, and Aethal groaned inwardly. Wordlessly, Aethal removed the cloak and tucked it behind him. At Magnei's shocked look, he said gently, "They'll recognize you with it as quickly as without it, now."

"Ilferth Simon's Guard is training itself for war in the High Temple," Magnei said. We've known it for some time. I didn't expect to be almost their first victim, though."

Aethal schooled his face to blankness. Trained they might have been, but if those bravos had been the best Ilferth Simon could train, the Temple Guard wasn't worth much as a fighting force. But then, Sergeant Falk and his cadre had said as much. It was time to get to business. "The Lord Warden sent you to meet us here. Why?"

"I do not know. I was merely sent. I was told you would have the questions, and that I was to answer."

"The Lord Warden didn't tell you of our conversation?"

"Last Sword, uh, Seeker," the boy-man blushed at having involuntarily stepped out of his role, "the entire Abbey knows *of* your conversation, but only the Lord Warden and you know the substance of it."

"So, you are to answer my questions about the Well? What do you know about it?"

Magnei drew himself up and looked him in the eye. "I'm the Lord Warden's Scrivener. I've looked more deeply into the Abbey Records than any other man alive."

Farnan snorted. Aethal shot him a quelling look, but inwardly agreed. If this man had reached his twentieth year, he still looked young for it. "It's true," Magnei said defiantly, looking Farnan in the eye. "Languages are a gift to me, and there's no Record I cannot read. I can read pre-Fall Imperial texts, from Norrisk to Caalanese."

"No one speaks those anymore," Farnan said.

Aethal was impressed against his will; the old Empire had encompassed at least a dozen languages. "Those languages were never spoken within five hundred leagues of the Well," he said aloud.

"We Guardians have always had our own language," said Magnei. "It is part of our novitiate. Most of the Records are written in that tongue. But there are many in Sishandi, the language of the old Wish-kings. And even some in Avraic. I can read those."

"That language died with Salnum's Line," said Aethal. "It's a legend."

Magnei smiled thinly. "Well, the part about hearing it spoken giving you perfect pitch or its healing the sick are legend, but the language itself is very real, Seeker." A touch of arrogance crept into his voice. "Aside from the Lord Warden himself, I know more about the Well and the Guardians than anyone alive."

"And do you know more about the Lotus than any man alive?" put in Farnan. "That's what we need facts about."

Magnei tilted his head. "I have brought records of the Fall." He removed a slim volume from beneath his robes. "This is the best of them. But in brief: there is no cure for Lotus, at least none that the Empire or Maednac ever discovered. It's designed to be inconspicuous. The smell of it causes intense hunger and lust. The stronger the scent, the higher the intensity. It can be resisted, especially when people know what it is, but with difficulty. Lotus infection seems to go through several stages.

"When a man is first farmed, he is still more or less in his right mind, but is plagued by a permanent hunger that can only be satisfied — briefly — by eating more Lotus. He'll be happy to be around people, and will share it with others, as long as his own supply isn't threatened. If he can avoid the plant, he can live longer. His eyes will start showing the first hints of green within minutes to an hour. Of course, the Lotus starts growing in him from the first bite, and never stops.

"Eventually, victims begin to fear the un-farmed. By the time their eyes are solid green, they try to stay exclusively with other victims. They'll run from others, except to eat Lotus. The fear can manifest in rage, but they'll only fight if they can't run, or if they think the Lotus itself is threatened.

"By the time it starts showing in their skin, the victims are in a state of permanent euphoria. They don't really need to eat any more Lotus, it's growing in them so fast. It's hard to know what they think, because they don't talk anymore. The end is terrible. A convulsion of intense pain ends in death caused by the plant erupting from every part of the victim's body."

Farnan sat staring at the end of the gruesome monologue. "How long does this take?" he said, hoarsely.

"It depends," said Magnei, "on how much Lotus the victims eat. The more they eat, the faster it goes. A person who eats one bite of Lotus may survive several months to a year. A person who eats as fast as he can in a patch of the stuff may not last more than a few days."

"Is there anything in there about Greendels?" asked Aethal.

"About what?"

Farnan described his encounters with battle-mad warriors infected with the Lotus. Magnei shook his head. "Nothing like that is described in any records I have seen. But this is a Wish from the Well. They are," he hesitated, "known for doing the unexpected."

Aethal said. "General Malcoor, in his youth, saw what remains of the Free Republic," said Aethal. He outlined Malcoor's log entries. "Do you think it even possible that he might have discovered some sort of immunity?"

But Magnei shook his head. "There is no way of knowing that, Last Sword. Whether there was any immunity woven into the being of the Lotus depends on what whoever Wished it said to the Well. And they are unlikely to have Wished for Lotus."

"Dammit, the Lord Warden said the same thing, and I didn't understand it then," said Aethal. "What do you mean, 'they didn't Wish for Lotus?' The Lotus is here, and it's damned well not natural. They must have Wished for it."

Magnei sighed. "Of course Lotus came from the Well, Last Sword. That much is obvious. But from the records..." He lowered his voice further. "There are more and less dangerous ways of using the Well. No way is safe, of course. But in our records, all the most dangerous Wishes, are the ones in which the Well itself is the determinant."

"What do you mean?" asked Farnan.

Magnei groped for words. "The Well understands Wishes, Lieutenant, and fulfills the command of whoever addresses it. But the less specific the wish is, the more the Well — chooses, perhaps — how to fulfill it. Even very simple Wishes can go astray, as Eloras's Wish did. He wished for eternal life. So he lived forever, soul bound to an aging body that maintained only the strength necessary to keep it there. But even that Wish left very little to an inhuman imagination. Now, suppose you asked the Well to make you the King of Verlaen? But what defines Verlaen? This continent? The palace? Anywhere the King rules? And you didn't say how long. In these days, perhaps you would find yourself "King" for the space of a few weeks, over a few yards of sandy beach while everyone starved for want of aught but Lotus to eat."

Black silence covered the table. Magnei continued. "As it is, I'm not even certain what language the Republic's agent might have spoken."

"Why does that matter?" asked Aethal.

Magnei gave him an exasperated frown. "The agent was from the Free Republic, whoever he was, so he almost certainly didn't say, "'I Wish for a weapon to conquer the Empire,' with the Verlaisni *conquer's* connotation of *keeping for profit*. He might well have used Norrisk, the Republic's most popular language, and said '*zhermaistrin*,' which translates inexactly as "utterly dominate," a rather accurate description of what Lotus does. Or he might have been a scholar who knew Sishandi, in which case he might have said any of half a dozen words depending on his intentions. And, of course, his competence in the language."

"So far you've said exactly what the Lord Warden told us, and I doubt he sent you here simply to repeat himself," said Aethal. He let his voice drip scorn, now. "Unless he is, after all, only what he appears to be: an utterly cowed, feeble old man who lives in fear of Ilferth Simon and sends boys into mortal danger when he dares not go himself."

Magnei flushed red. "Seeker, you will not speak of the Lord Warden that way."

"Why not?" snapped Aethal, mimicking his father's most annoyed tones. "Is he something more, then? One of your guards told me he was as tough as a keepwood's root. Is he so tough or is he merely so dense?"

The defiance drained from Magnei's face. "He... we thought him to be so. Tough. Seeker, you cannot know how the Order has changed these last years." Then his face lit. "All my life, we could feel the Temple closing in, denying our traditional duties, mounting their own watches as if we were nothing. Then, when Old Lord Warden Furthark died, and Cledan took over, it all changed. I remember the first time Ilferth Simon swept into the Abbey like it was his own bedchamber, Cledan had him thrown him out so quick and smooth I thought he'd skip on the puddles in the walk. For the last year; it seemed we were coming back into our own, and the Lord Warden and Simon were coming to at least to some sort of mutual respect. Then something happened... we don't know what. The Lord Warden visited the Temple last winter. And since then, it's like Furthark is back. Ilferth Simon sweeps through the place like a high lord through some peasant's farm. It's like Ilferth Simon has some strange control over the man." The story came out as if the young man had been longing to burst like this for — well, half a year, if Aethal was any judge.

"We still believe in him, though," said Magnei, reddening at his own outburst. "He's a good man."

"And yet the good man is doing us a singular lack of good," Aethal said thoughtfully. "He sends you here merely to repeat hopelessness. There is no way to stop a Wish from the Well."

Magnei drew a deep breath. "I did not say that, my Lord."

"Then what did you say?" snapped Aethal.

Magnei looked at Aethal, and appeared to be carefully choosing his words. His voice dropped to a whisper. "The Wishes granted by the Well are the most dangerous things on Earth. But they are not invulnerable: this you know. Keepwoods can be chopped down, if you have enough men and axes. Men with Greater Rifles can themselves be shot, if you have the men and the courage."

"There aren't enough men, or axes, or courage in the world to destroy Lotus," Aethal said.

Magnei nodded. "And if all these fail, the Lord Warden says, there is one other remedy left for men to try, if they dare."

They stared at him, and Magnei met their eyes.

"Quite so. You must go to the Well, in the heart of the Dark Continent, and use your Wish. A Wish to destroy the Lotus."

The silence was absolute in the deserted common room. "Now what you have said," Aethal replied at last, "goes even beyond treason." His horror was a distant thing, somehow. Too awful to really be frightened of. The worst that could be said had been said, and nothing further could remain. "Who loses his soul, Magnei, in exchange for that Wish?"

"In the days of the Wish-Kings, instruments of torture were set up in the World's Core, and men gave their souls to have their families released from them.

It is a hard thing to ask," said Magnei. "But the Lord Warden hopes that such a man might be found, even in this latter day."

"A hard thing!" burst out Farnan, and lowered his voice at a glare from Aethal. "Do you know what's between here and there, even if anyone was mad enough to go?" He leaned over the table. "Five thousand miles of ocean between here and the Dark Continent. The only lands between are the Lotus-infested remains of the Empire and Republic — we can't land there. We might take a couple of Tidetowns and plunder them, but we'd lose men doing it. Have you ever seen Weedrats fight? They're the devils of Hell in those floating mats of garbage they call islands.

"But assume we survive all that, and we get to the Dark Continent itself. Ringed with mountains of gold that poison the very air with dust, to say nothing of the water! The resting place of every Wish ever spewed up from the Well. That's assuming, of course, that Lotus hasn't overgrown every square foot of soil, in which case, we will all die, slobbering our brains down our chins."

Aethal covered Farnan's hand with his own. It was shaking. "In any case," he said, "I thought Wishes from the Well were permanent. Lasted even beyond the life of the Wisher?"

"Permanent, yes, my lord," said Magnei, "but only if no one else Wishes against them. How could it be otherwise? People who Wish will often have conflicting desires. The Well must honor both of them. It grants the last Wish spoken to it, and grants one Wish to any person who asks."

Magnei lowered his voice to just a whisper. "These are the great mysteries of the Well, and the ones that have destroyed our world. One king asks for the eternal rulership of an Empire that will last forever, and puts a guard on the Well. So it lasts a hundred years, or a thousand, but how do you set guards on a Well that grants any man what he desires most? A thousand kings have held the Well, and not one has ever kept it. No Wish can stand before another.

"This is one of three things the Guardians know about the Well. No Wish can prevent another Wish from supplanting it. No Wish can grant a single person more Wishes. And no Wish can destroy the Well. To Wish for these things grants the Wisher instant death.

"In fact, this was almost the first secret the Well revealed of its nature. Eloras Wished to be King forever, and you know what happened to him. When his great-grandson Jehan took the throne and his Wish, he Wished to reign forever *at his present age*. That lasted for a good twenty years until his Heir, realizing he would never be King in any other way, got to the Well and Wished him dead. A Wish-King's power depends on absolute control of the Well. Wish for an eternity, and you must control it for just that long. No one has managed that yet."

Farnan laughed, a high, distorted sound. "So the Wishes of the Well are useless."

Magnei's lips thinned. "Not so. The Well gives, to everyone equally, what they say they want. But people want so many things. Even the Well finds itself hard-pressed to keep up."

Through the corner of his eye, Aethal saw that the Wyrmguard he had ordered to him had at last appeared. *And a king exchanged someone's soul for no more than that.* He focused his thoughts with an effort. "So, if I were to," he forced the words past his lips, "go to the Well. Exchange my soul. And Wish for all Lotus, everywhere, to die...?"

"Doubtless, it would," said Magnei. "It's a very good Wish as I understand the Well. There is no shadow of a doubt what you mean, and thus it would be hard for the Well to give you anything but exactly that. For your soul."

Farnan gripped Aethal's shoulder and turned him so they were face-to-face. "Aethal, what are you saying? This is madness! You are the Last Sword of the king. Your duty is to preserve his life, and yours! Not throw it away on some foolish errand to someplace no one could ever hope to come within sight of!"

Aethal turned to him and smiled wanly. "Farnan, only three hundred years ago, someone went to the Well and Wished Lotus to be. He had such hatred for us that he exchanged his own soul to see us die. In three hundred years, how much more perilous could it have become?" His mind raced ahead of his words. Whatever black heroism had fueled the unknown Wisher for the Lotus, his preparations would have had to be in the most absolute secrecy. The Empire would have stopped at nothing to prevent it, and even the Lords of the Republic could not all have been so mad. *I have the ear of the King of Verlaen, and we don't have to keep it a secret from anyone... except possibly Ilferth Simon.* Aethal turned and stood, gesturing to the Wyrmguard.

It approached. "Yes, Last Sword?"

"Get Magnei here to the Hydraxis, under triple guard. No one is to know he is there."

"There are eyes, Last Sword." said the Wyrmguard.

"Wyrmguard may know, then; no others. And tell the King; tell him I need to see him alone tomorrow at breakfast. Damn!" Aethal swore with feeling.

"What is it?" asked Farnan.

"I'd do almost anything to have one of those bastards alive to question." They left the tavern.

Outside, Llhawcae Cathedral was deserted and dark. Whatever the mysterious service had been meant to accomplish, it had. *I hope we are so fortunate,* Aethal thought. They turned for the Hydraxis, watching every shadow.

Chapter Fourteen

45th of Spring, 312 Exodus

King Paitir received Aethal and Magnei in the Sky Chamber after breakfast. Here the wall of the Ophidian swelled outward, and the chamber was roofed and walled in glass. The rich carpeting muffled their footsteps. King Paitir and Eraad looked up at their approach. Aethal stopped and bowed, and was relieved to see Magnei kneel smoothly, palm up and out. Aethal was relieved to find that proper behavior toward royalty had taken root in Magnei's social awareness. When Aethal had risen this morning, he had found Magnei still in the stinking cassock he'd worn last night. Delivering him into Osric's hands to be scrubbed and clothed had made all the difference. Magnei was now in a black silk robe with the royal colors worked into the piping, marking him as a guest of the king. Aethal was in full dress uniform.

"Sire," Aethal said, "May I present..."

"Not yet, you may not, Last Sword," said the King.

"Sire?"

Paitir leaned forward. "The Last Sword, Aethal, protects my interests, and that of my House. Is that clear?"

"Perfectly clear, Sire."

The king scowled. He leaned back with a grimace of pain, and Aethal saw again how his cousin had aged. The banked fires of anger shone in the old eyes.

"I have already had one Wrackberg drag my realm through the wreckage of a marriage between the Houses Paramount, Aethal. It will not happen again. Not while I live."

Aethal felt his face drain white. Eraad's eyes blazed triumph. Shit in the Well. Did Eraad really imagine that Aethal had arranged that scene in the Binding chamber as some sort of tryst? Nausea warred with embarrassment. The girl was comely enough, but it hadn't been *her* in that body for most of the time. Paitir pounced at his expression. "Your face admits it, so do not bother to deny. I have uses for Westerend's daughter. And Westerend himself. They do not include House Wrackberg. They do not include your father. But most especially, Aethal, they do not include, or even concern, you."

"Sire," Aethal stammered, his outrage choked by fear and a horrible urge to laugh. Eraad had not also guessed that Ardyth had been bound to a Wyrmguard pistol, had he? No, that would mean he'd also have discovered why, and then he'd have been crying out for charges of treason. "Sire, my only concern is destroying the Lotus and what is best for Verlaen. I have no other concern."

"Reduce your concern by half, Last Sword," said Paitir. "Your duty is to fight the Lotus. Surely that is enough. What best serves Verlaen is outside your mandate." He stole a glance at Eraad.

Ah, thought Aethal. *Paitir plans to marry Eraad to Ardyth.* Why did his stomach churn at the thought of that wedding? *Does my father know? He would never suggest such a thing.* "Sire," he said, "I did not mean to presume."

"Then don't!" The king's eyes blazed. "You said you never wanted your father's power; I have taken you at your word. Don't go back on it. I do not wish this conversation repeated. Not even among us. I trust that is clear."

Before Aethal could reply, the door opened, and the King's majordomo came in. "The Conversant Ilferth Simon and the Lord Mayor of Maednac Serpiin desire audience, Majesty. Quite urgently, it seems."

"Show them in," growled the king. "And summon the chancellor. He does hate to miss anything."

Aethal blanched. His father, too? Magnei swayed on his feet. *All I'd need now is for Aerhan to show up, and then all the men I fear would be aware of my so-secret plans.* Aethal steadied Magnei. "Sire, please: this man has risked much even in coming to me to warn..."

"Show. Them. In." commanded the king. "And you, Aethal, do your duty. Silently. Guardian Magnei, please you to remain with us while we deal with some unexpected business."

There was nothing more he could do. Aethal sent a Wyrmguard to fetch his father and sat the stunned Magnei on a chaise in the corner before taking up his position to the king's left.

Ilferth Simon entered. No longer playing the bland, easygoing priest, the Conversant wore the midnight blue robes of his office, symbolizing the Deep Heaven of God. It was emblazoned with a silver watersilk-embroidered Single Moon. On his head, he wore the great Shield Diadem, cut from a single pearl. He halted before the King and nodded as to an equal. Of the two, the Conversant looked far more regal than the graying man in the chair. Behind him, Rolf Hlafen trailed like a bright and fashionable shadow.

"King Paitir," began the Conversant, "I must report most grievous news. I have just received word that..." He paused. He took in Aethal and finally, he saw Magnei. His jaw firmed. Pointing a finger, he said, "May I ask, Sire, what that man is doing in your presence?"

King Paitir looked up at the Conversant, and said in tones of mild pique, "He has an audience with me at this time, Conversant Simon. It was just beginning when you arrived. I presume that I can trust my Last Sword so far that he would not have recommended granting such a request to any man who was a danger to my person."

Paal entered silently. His eyes passed over Aethal as if he weren't there, but settled on Magnei without a trace of surprise. Aethal realized the king was looking at him.

"No danger, Sire, and perhaps a very great help," Aethal said hastily. *A still greater help if Simon and my father knew nothing about it, though.* Why was his cousin being so dense today?

"Do you, your Holiness, have some reason to doubt that this Guardian of the Well has come to help us?" asked Paitir.

Simon took a step toward Magnei, who shrank back. Aethal tensed. "This man," Simon said softly, may be a greater danger to you than the Lotus itself. He is a Sindrinker, and seeks to pervert your Majesty, the last King of the True Faith on Earth. I only learned of his heresy last night, and unfortunately did so after his escape from the Church's justice."

"Sire, this is not true!" said Aethal.

"Peace!" said King Paitir, glaring at Aethal. He turned his gaze on Simon. "If this man is accused of treason, he must have a trial."

"A trial before the Church Council of Oversight," said Simon, "where he shall answer for the heresy of which he stands accused."

"No, Conversant Simon," said the King, and his eyes were steely. "You said it yourself. For him to hold heretical beliefs, you may try him for heresy. But if he intends to preach them to us, and so sway us from the True Faith, that is treason, and we shall try him for that. The Church shall have him after we are satisfied."

With an effort, Simon stepped back. "Very well, Sire. But act swiftly. Our land is already under the most fearful judgment of God. Entertaining heresy cannot bring His blessing."

Eraad looked as though he wanted to leap forward and strangle the priest with his bare hands, but a glance from his father quelled him for the moment. King Paitir's eyes narrowed. "I could, of course, try him here and now. As judge and jury. Are you *asking* me to try a Guardian under the Extreme Sanction?"

Hah. The Conversant would hardly want *that.* Allow that precedent, and the King could try Church members next.

The Conversant spread his hands. "Unnecessary, Sire." He speared Eraad with a cool look. "Why, my lord Prince, you look as though you had something to say to me. Pray speak. Nothing good can come of men in our positions concealing their thoughts from one another."

"My son has no time for further conversation," said the King. "He is leaving tomorrow for the Serpent's Pass, to help hold the Bowl, and drive back the Grassworms who have breached the Treeline. Send in General Vaagen." He nodded to the majordomo.

The Conversant nodded to the young man. "Such valor is indeed praiseworthy, especially considering that some of my own priests, who serve among the Grain Sea Peoples, have reported that the Green Death is among them."

"You have intelligence of Lotus among the Grassworms?" said Chancellor Paal, speaking for the first time. "You have not confided it in us."

The Conversant shook his head. "It is hardly intelligence, Chancellor. The news is weeks old, and I began receiving the reports not one week ago. I have only what my priests say or send, and it is difficult to pass news from the Grain Sea, where their people may be moving for days on end, far away from anyone to carry their messages. Many priests have returned to us, unable to master their fear of the Lotus. Others... we simply do not know what has happened to them. But any man might fall to Wellspawn." He looked directly at Eraad, who glared back. Before he could say anything, however, the general entered.

The King touched Eraad on the forearm. "General Vaagen, you will take the Tenth and Eleventh Guards Infantry north with Brigadier Garedder. My son will take up his position as Colonel of Maednac's Own Lancers which will be your vanguard. Colonel Jereg will be in operational command, of course. I want you to occupy the Serpent's Pass and arrest Colonel Sigrad for incompetence."

Vaagen nodded. "We'll use Serpent's Pass to stage our counterattacks. Then we'll advance to the Treeline." The King nodded.

Aethal felt his heart lift. Such a large force could block the Pass against any enemy, and would finally remove Sigrad from the chain of command.

Eraad shot to his feet. "Thank you, Father. I will do what is needed."

"I know you will, Eraad," said Paitir, then gave the ancient blessing: "May the spirit of Maednac guide you."

Aethal would have to assign Wyrmguard to the Crown Prince. He stepped over to Flintmaw, muttered two names. Then he added two more and stepped back.

four of them?

Gun's voice startled Aethal. It had been long since his weapon had ventured an opinion. But yes, he wanted four. Eraad might be in real danger. Almost certainly would be, in fact, given what he had said about the Telerati in Aethal's hearing. *At least I will not tell Paitir that his son died because of aught I did not do.*

Eraad bowed to his father, shook hands with the Chancellor, who said, "Good hunting, your Highness." The Prince nodded to the Lord Mayor and swept past the Conversant without a gesture. Ilferth Simon watched Eraad go, and turned back to the King with a thin smile.

The last time Eraad and Ilferth Simon exchanged words, the Conversant won a victory. All of us were here then, too. And now Paitir has dismissed the Crown Prince, with every sign of it being an honor.

Perhaps Paitir is not being as dense as I thought.

The Conversant turned to the Chancellor.

"You accused me once in this chamber of having planted Jehan Alfing in the office of Last Sword as a spy and assassin," Simon said calmly. "Now your son holds that title, and has done far worse. Alfing could only have slain the King, but your son reaches further still, seeking power over his majesty's very soul by bringing blasphemy into his court in the guise of hope."

Aethal forced his voice to steadiness in spite of rage. "If anyone must hold the life of the King, I would rather it be my father than you; he would at least save the Kingdom for his own honest love of power, rather than see it drown beneath the verdant tide of the Lotus because he thinks it the will of God!"

Paal inclined his head. "*Thank* you, Aethal," he said, voice heavy with irony.

The Conversant turned to Aethal. "You admit your family's treason," he whispered.

"I admit nothing of the kind," replied Aethal. "I am the king's man: he hung this sword upon my back. But let it lie." Aethal remembered Gun's words, so long ago, it now seemed. "For King's man or no, in this hour of need, I will fight the Lotus. It is in *that* fight that I have brought hope." He gestured in Magnei's direction. "Let King Paitir decide whether it is blasphemy or not."

The Conversant fixed smoldering eyes on Aethal. "Blasphemy is not for the king to judge. That is for God to decide, and for me to pronounce."

"It is for you to pronounce, but this is not your place to pronounce it," said Paal. "You keep forgetting, Holiness, that inside the Hydraxis Royal Law determines what crimes a man may be charged with."

The King nodded. "Quite. Aethal, present your guest, that we may examine him, and discover whether these charges the Conversant is so certain of are indeed true."

Aethal motioned to him, and Magnei rose, walking forward as a man might to meet his headsman.

"Sire, may I present Magnei of the Order of the Guardians of the Well."

Magnei bowed full from the waist. "It is an honor, Royal Seeker, to stand before you."

Paitir nodded. "And are you, as our Conversant claims, a Sindrinker and heretic?"

Magnei flushed. "No, Royal Seeker; I believe the True Faith. I come from my Lord Warden with a message for you, and for the Kingdom of Verlaen, in this dark hour."

"Let us hear this message, Guardian Magnei," said Paitir.

"It is this, Sire. 'Royal Seeker,' says the Lord Warden of the Guardians, 'for five hundred years the Guardians of the Well kept the world safe from the ravages of the Well, and during that time, even the Dark Continent lightened somewhat while the Hall of Desires lay under our watch in the bowels of the Kalidranym. We kept it sealed, for our order was founded upon the principle that no man or order of men could use the Well for good.

"'It is no secret that our watch failed, Your Majesty. It is the lasting shame of our order. Eventually, even our most sacred vows and the loss of our own souls were not enough to keep us from using the Well for our own selfish desires. And so we fell, driven from the Kalidranym and our duties, by the Apostate's Wish. But our fall did not happen all at once, and we give you a history of that time: our first step down that evil road.

"'It was in the days of the Sixth Lord Warden, two hundred years after our founding, that we first breached the Hall of Desires, because of the wrath of the Dragon King. He surprised us, for Dragons have not mixed with men since the death of their master, King Dyvad, the Last of Salnum's Line.

"'Now the Dragon King fell upon the Kalidranym, and the sudden fury of his descent was such that none could oppose him, for nearly all of our order was out in the fields gathering the harvest. The King, with a score of his mighty wyrms, struck in the heat of the day, and withered the fields in smoke and ash. They died in an instant, in a whirlwind of fire.

"'Had it not been for the Lord Warden, and a small company of the order inside the Kalidranym for the noonday prayer, all would have been lost, for the Lords Warden of our order, unlike kings and other fellowships of men, have never shunned work even of the lowliest sort, but have taken part in all the work of the people.'" Magnei looked sideways at the Conversant, who curled his lip.

"'The Lord Warden was faced with a terrible choice: Although the drag-ons and their king could roam the great halls of the Kalidranym, they did not know its paths, and the walls of that fortress had been Wished indestructible. Against them, all the Dragons' strength and fiery breath proved in vain.

"'So the Dragon King flew to the pinnacle of the Kalidranym and called to the Lord Warden to come out, promising that he would surely spare their lives, and even give treasure to all the survivors, if they would but come out and yield up the secrets of the fortress to them, that the Dragons might possess the Well.

"'The Lord Warden knew that his companions had food only for a few weeks. While the walls of the Kalidranym were invincible, he dared not trust them unguarded. "For nothing," he said to his companion, "prevents the King of the Dragons from waiting until hunger has slain us all, and if once they find the path to us, even a single century of men could easily overcome us, no matter what arms we possess."

"'And so, Royal Seeker, the Lord Warden ordered the Well unsealed, though it broke his vows. He went to the Well, and spoke his Wish, and every Dragon beneath the sun died that day, according to his word. At the cost..." Magnei gulped, "of his soul. So that the Well would not fall between the claws of the Dragon King.

"'The Lord Warden's choice preserved the Order's control of the Well for only another three hundred years, and gave its people another three centuries of peace before the Apostate (accursed be his name) rose to the Lord Warden's office and betrayed the world. His choice did not save the world. But it did preserve it, for a time.

"'You also are given a choice, Paitir, King of Verlaen, you who are beset by the Lotus. To remain here, where the defenses of sea and distance have at last failed to save Man from his own folly, or to return to the Well, and preserve the people that God-Beyond-The-World has given you.

"'You cannot know if any sent to the Well will succeed. And the Well may yet destroy all of mankind even if we do succeed. But until God returns from beyond the world, all any man can hope is to hold the darkness back, for a little while. For far less than that do men give their souls daily on this poor earth. I am at your disposal, even for a mission such as this, if I survive it, for I would not counsel any to do what I would not myself. Your obedient servant, Cledan.'

"These are the words of my Father the Lord Warden," said Magnei. "It is now for you to decide, Royal Seeker." There was an awful silence.

Aethal saw the faces in the room like statues, frozen in an endless moment of time. There was Ilferth Simon's set in horror and outrage. There was his father's, eyes locked on Magnei, masklike and unreadable. And there was Magnei's face, unaccountably relaxed, as though the worst had passed by. *What does my own face look like?* thought Aethal. Of all the faces, only the one mattered. King Paitir's, set in a single moment of indecision.

"Sire, the Church cannot countenance such an action." began Ilferth Simon

"The Church has countenanced far too much in this castle," replied Paal.

"Silence." The King's voice filled the room like a gunshot.

His eyes fixed those of his Chancellor and the Conversant in turn. "Do not, either of you, speak again unless I command it."

Both men shut up, and Aethal stared at his king. Paitir turned on Magnei. "Damn you," he whispered, passionlessly. "Damn you and your Lord Warden and your whole order together, for bringing me one more wild hope, one more incredible scheme to stop the Lotus from eating my people alive. And what unspeakable, vile threat will your master hang on my head if I do not do as he so kindly advises? Will he somehow mystically cause the Well to rise and drown the world?"

Magnei's mouth hung open. "N-no, Sire. He only seeks to be of help."

"Pity," sighed the King. "Only send a man to the Well, and Wish our troubles ended. Is that all? Find a man to buy my kingdom with his soul. And a way to get him there. Whom could I hate so much in the world, that I might ask this of him?" His eyes flicked from Ilferth Simon to Paal. Neither of them looked away. Aethal could not speak.

"Royal Seeker," Magnei's voice rose through the silence. "My Lord Warden begs permission to lead the expedition."

The Conversant took two swift steps, yanked Magnei around, and felled him with an open-handed blow whose sound echoed around the chamber. Aethal leapt forward, interposing himself between Ilferth Simon and the Guardian. But as quickly as he had struck, the Conversant stepped back and spoke to the

King. "I will see the Lord Warden damned before I see him approach the Well! I will see you…"

Aethal gestured. Flintmaw stepped forward and pointed itself at the Conversant's nose. Aethal rose to the balls of his feet, ready to hit Ilferth Simon if he moved another inch. But the Conversant trailed off, and the fire in his eyes settled back. Aethal let out a slight breath. *It is not a good day for martyrdom after all, it seems.*

Paitir's mouth was half-open, but Paal merely said, "Yes, Holiness? What were you saying to the King? You will see him..?"

Ilferth Simon's jaw worked. "The Guardians are a fallen and corrupt order," he snarled. "It was their Apostate who laid waste the Dark Continent. Their lust for power sends them clinging to any excuse to crawl back to the Well, and their repentance is the repentance of cowards, too afraid to face the consequences of it."

"I note, your Holiness, that it is a cowardice which you yourself do not share," shot back Magnei, wiping the blood from his lip. His eyes were cold.

The Lord Mayor touched Ilferth Simon's shoulder, and shrank back from the high priest's burning gaze. "Your Holiness, perhaps we should at least consider the Guardians' words. The people are frightened. Some hope... even false hope... may help calm the waters."

"That is what you have to recommend? False hope?" snapped Simon. "And why is that, *Lord* Mayor? Is it because your City Watch still does not know the Discipline? My Temple Guard officers report to me that they spend most of their watches disciplining your men for infractions!"

The Lord Mayor reddened. "Is that because the City Watch is actually spending time learning how to fight? With the Army leaving to defend the Grain Sea, we'll be relying on them to keep the Lotus from our walls. Half your so-called infractions are because of fights between Temple Guardsmen and City Watchmen. Which the City Watch win."

Simon ignored the Lord Mayor, but turned his face, dead and expressionless as any mask, toward Magnei. "You are excommunicated, Magnei. And your Lord Warden, for suggesting this blasphemy. You, and all your order."

Aethal's hand tightened on Gun. *Excommunication?* Then the Guardians would be disbanded and expelled from the Kingdom. *Mother.* But that thought came only dimly, to Aethal's surprise. Magnei's response cut through his fog.

"Shall you try our entire order before the Council of Oversight then?" asked Magnei, climbing painfully to his feet. "Or will you, Holiness, simply compel our obedience by force?"

"The Council shall be summoned," grated Ilferth Simon. "And your trial shall be short."

"I don't see how we could allow that, really," drawled Chancellor Paal. To the Conversant he said, "Lotus is spreading faster than we thought it could. I see no option but to restrict travel throughout Verlaen. Nothing should be allowed to enter Verlaen Basin. I think General Vaagen will agree; I'll make it part of his orders."

"So, you would use the Lotus to curtail the Church's power," said Ilferth Simon. "You can do this. We have a sufficient number of Overseers within the Basin to constitute a quorum. You cannot object to *that*, surely, Chancellor, unless your Discipline — or your faith — has actually failed to the point that Lotus is east of the mountains."

Paal looked as though he had bitten into something sour; Paitir spoke. "Simon, do not do this. Not now. The Kingdom needs every man and woman it can get." Aethal understood. If Paal or the King tried to object to movements within the Basin, it would be taken as admission of their failure to keep Lotus out. *And nearly half of our population is here in the Basin. That's why there is a quorum of Overseers here.* Aethal's nightmare of waves of people surging through the streets in panic, trampling all in their path, loomed closer.

"What will your Majesty do about this proposed expedition?" asked Ilferth Simon.

Paitir looked away. "Some decisions are too great even for the King to decide alone," he said at last. "The General States will decide this matter. Most of them are already here. We shall have a quorum there as well. And all shall abide by their decision."

Aethal nearly dropped Gun, but Ilferth Simon finished his thought before he himself had properly begun it.

The Conversant frowned, considering this. "The Church cannot promise to accept blasphemy by vote. We must stand against sin, or we stand for nothing."

"And will you, Conversant Simon," pressed the King, "further dismay the people by publicly excommunicating the whole of an ancient and respected order, when we have not yet made any decision regarding this proposal?"

Paal interjected. "The only conclusion that the average subject could come to, is that the Guardians of the Well were responsible for Lotus. The result of your decree would be rioting in the streets and mass murder."

The Conversant sighed. "We shall await the vote of the General States," he said finally. "In the hope that they shall hear the Voice of God-Beyond-The-World and heed His wisdom. But we cannot tolerate or accede to sin. When do you intend to call them?"

Paitir said, "One week from today. Chancellor, send out the final notice of the convocation."

Ilferth Simon smiled tightly. "Let it be even as your Majesty says." He walked out.

"With your permission, Majesty, I must withdraw to prepare for the Convocation," Paal said. The King nodded, and turned to Aethal.

"This man must be present to speak to the Convocation. See to it." Aethal dismissed Magnei, along with a servant. When he had gone, he turned to the King.

"Two nights past, Paitir, you said... is Eraad ready for this duty, your Majesty?" asked Aethal.

Paitir looked out the window. "Go away, Aethal," he said tiredly. "You are my bodyguard; not my judge. I owe you no answer."

"I am the bodyguard of your *line*, Paitir," said Aethal. "And you are sending Eraad, who is not known for his sensible caution, into the worst sort of danger imaginable. You are exposing the royal line to Lotus!"

"Vaagen can keep Eraad in check," growled Paitir. "Eraad will have two of the best officers in the kingdom to learn caution from. It's what he needs. And I cannot have it said that Maednac's line no longer leads his people."

"If you're the one leading the people, Cousin," said Aethal, "then why convene the General States? Why not just send the expedition?"

"I will not make that decision alone, Aethal," said Paitir.

"You'd give Ilferth Simon a voice in that decision?"

Paitir fixed Aethal with a cold eye. "If we're damned, Aethal, we're all damned together. King, Church, Lords Paramount and Commons. I won't be the sole voice responsible. Let them bear the burden with me, if they're good for nothing else, but I won't sink Verlaen alone."

"Yes, Sire." Aethal bowed himself out; he felt bloodless, drained. *Not alone, but with every soul of us to accompany you.* To Flintmaw, he said, "Get me Sergeant Falk and Lieutenant Farnan. Within the hour."

"Yes, Last Sword."

As they passed down the stairwells of the Ophidian, Aethal became aware of Magnei looking up at him, somewhat like an anxious puppy.

"What *is* it, Guardian?" he said, the words coming out harsher than he'd intended.

"Why did his Majesty do that?"

Aethal stopped. "Do what?" The young man before him looked as if he were ready to burst into tears or throw up. Perhaps both.

"Why did he let all those people in? Especially the Conversant. He... he damned me."

Not to mention struck you a solid blow on the jaw. But the young man wasn't complaining about that, Aethal noted with approval.

"If you believe he has the power to do that, why didn't you beg his forgiveness?" Aethal asked.

Magnei just looked at him for a long moment. "Because he's wrong," Magnei finally said. "Because the Well... Because this is the time to use the Well. But why did the King let Ilferth Simon know I was there? Does he believe him? Did he believe me?" His voice broke.

There were a million things Aethal needed to do. Comforting a grown man who had chosen the sheltered life of a scholar-monk was not among them. He opened his mouth to say...

you too wanted trust and leadership from the king your bearer.

Aethal blinked. The king his *bearer*?

All weapons together, are we? he thought, but Gun did not answer. Breathing deeply, Aethal forced himself to calm down, and speak softly. "The King is trying to decide whom to believe," he said, and grudgingly blessed his father for his lessons — both the purposeful and the inadvertent — in politics. "People lie to him regularly. I think that Cousin Paitir is tired of the lies, and decided to put you, and the Conversant and my father together in hopes that whoever was lying would be surprised into a mistake. It's difficult to keep track of lies when you're upset, and easy to be upset when you're facing multiple opponents. It's a dangerous game, but I think," Aethal paused, considering, "that Cousin Paitir may have just won a point." *Now, if he could just find the courage to make the decisions Verlaen needs. But if he does not, we must all surely find our own.*

"And Ilferth Simon?" asked Magnei.

"I believe he lost. He was forced to declare at exactly what point he would stand against the King. He certainly showed his true feelings about you." *That is also a weapon,* Aethal realized. *One we may all need a great deal.* He returned his attention to Magnei.

"Come. We must see to your quartering here. Osric is in my apartments; he'll know what to do. Hopefully, the day will not bring any more unpleasant surprises."

****

Aethal was proven wrong about this as soon as they reached his apartments two floors below.

Osric greeted Aethal as soon as he entered the antechamber. "Last Sword," he stammered. "The Conversant." He gulped. "He's here."

Aethal's eyes widened. "Here? You let him in?"

"He... he wanted to see you. He said he'd wait," the valet said, helplessly.

Aethal sighed. The Conversant had knocked on his door and demanded to see the Last Sword. What should Osric have done? Told His Holiness to make an appointment? What in the Well did the man want?

"I hope you made him comfortable," he managed.

"Yes, my lord; he's in your parlor now.

Aethal allowed Magnei to wait with Osric while he entered the parlor. "Your Holiness," he said, keeping his voice bland. "This is an unexpected honor."

"You need not stand on ceremony, my son." said the Conversant. "This is a matter of business." He rose. "The Lord Mayor, for all his rudeness, is quite right about the fighting capabilities of my Temple Guard. They are trained to stand up to bandits and to guard pilgrims. They are quite good at making the people feel at ease while inspecting them for the Discipline. They are not warriors, or even thugs like your brother Aerhan employs in the Crownguard." The Conversant let out a heavy sigh, as if making an admission he found distasteful. "I would like to suggest that perhaps the Temple Guard should, for the most part, enforce the Discipline in the City itself. Even in the Madlands."

Aethal hesitated. This could be seen as a concession. What would happen if he threw it back in the man's face? But it wasn't workable, and that was the only real consideration here. shook his head. "You don't have enough Temple Guard."

"In the meantime," the Conversant went on, "Rolf Hlafen's City Watch can take over the brunt of guarding the City from outside, and truly learning to fight as soldiers, which is a role they may well be forced into. As it is, they frighten the people. Many in the Madlands have committed offenses. How are they to know whether the City Watch wants to look in their eyes, or put them in jail? They will run. If they run from the Discipline, they will be shot. My Temple Guard reports that some are hiding weapons. You can see where this might end. People will hide weapons, hide themselves, and then what use will the Lotus Patrols be?"

Aethal nodded reluctantly. "I would have to confirm these reports for myself, of course."

"I will have the witnesses report to you," said the Conversant. "I *can* order My Temple Guard to carry guns, but they don't need them. The Kingdom needs them more. The Temple Guard will no longer carry them. So, the people will cease to fear us."

Aethal shook his head. "Every Patrol must have at least one firearm," he said. "You don't want your men forced to close with leafeaters, if that should ever happen."

"Of course not," agreed Simon. "So much is only sensible." He hesitated. "Thank you for listening to me, Last Sword. I... must confess that I had not expected it."

Aethal blinked. "Why would you not expect that, Holiness?"

The Conversant frowned. "Because you have not listened to my spiritual guidance, I suppose. Why should I expect you to follow my lead in organizing the defense of this city?"

"Because your advice, in this case, is both generous and sensible," said Aethal, as politely as he could. "Holiness, I am not a spiritual man, except insofar as I hope to be a good one, and I accept the Church's teachings. May I ask you a spiritual question?"

"Of course, my son?"

"What should that Lord Warden — the one in Magnei's story — have done? Spiritually?"

"Trusted God," said Simon, firmly.

"Trusted in God Beyond The World?" asked Aethal. "Forgive my ignorance, Holiness, but I understood that the Church taught that God Beyond The World had abandoned us because of our sin."

"That is true, Aethal Paaling. Yet He has a plan, made before the world itself was founded. And of course, He does hear — and occasionally respond — to the Church, when we pray to Him for guidance."

"But for this Lord Warden, he was alone, and without the Church. There was no one he could turn to pray for him, was there?"

The Conversant looked at Aethal. "Perhaps not. I don't see how this is relevant to our current situation. The kingdom is not without the Church. We are here."

"Spiritually, then, Holiness. Do you truly recommend that we let the Lotus take us?"

"No, of course not. What we have recommended is that we stay as far from sin as we can. That we cast away our Wellspawn, and that we should never approach the Well itself. Aethal Paaling, would you reward a man for breaking Discipline? Disobeying orders?"

"Ordinarily? No," said Aethal. "Occasionally, yes."

The Conversant's breath caught. "Explain."

"Holiness, the Discipline mandates that we must look a man in the eyes ten seconds before we let him pass our watch. But if a man was running for my gates being chased by a horde of leafeaters, I would let him pass. I would certainly not make him stop and stand there while the throng engulfed us both. The Discipline is there to make us better soldiers. Not worse ones.

"God has made me a soldier, and my only quarrel with your spiritual advice is when it threatens to make us worse soldiers. Be generous, sir. Allow us to serve God as He has made us."

For a moment, Aethal thought he saw a bit of recognition in the Conversant's eyes. "You are saying," Simon said, "that it might be like a priest lying to a heretic so that he could escape and warn the Church. Though lying is a sin."

"Yes, your Holiness. Precisely like that."

Simon sighed again, "I wish that you would trust God a bit more, my son. Perhaps, though, the fault is my own. Every man should serve God as best he can. I regret the ill-feeling there has been between us." He rose.

"What shall I ask of God for you?" he said, formally.

Aethal hesitated. But there was little to lose and everything to gain. "You will know best what to ask of God, Holiness," he said, in a rush, "but what I would ask is something of you: I was at Llhawcae Cathedral tonight." He detailed the message that he had heard. "Holiness, please remember that the king is more like a soldier than he is like an overseer. He must do what is proper as a king, without worrying that the Church may brand him a sinner, or cast the blame for Lotus at his feet. I beg of you, moderate your Overseers' words against him. The burden of his office lies heavy on him."

The Conversant's eyes widened at this. "Truly, Aethal Paaling? You heard this sermon preached?"

"Yes, Holiness."

The Conversant's lips hardened into a line. "This should not have been," he said. "The Church may not compromise with sin, but there are limits to what should be said in public. Please convey my regrets to His Majesty. I shall see that this is not repeated."

Aethal let out a breath of cautious relief. "Thank you, Holiness."

"Of course. In the end, I suppose we must stand together, mustn't we? You have opened my eyes, son, to things I had not considered. Thank you. Please, I shall show myself out."

****

It wasn't long after that Osric had Magnei escorted to his new quarters. Aethal was pouring himself a brandy when he heard the outer door open again. "Tell whoever it is that it must wait until morning, Osric," Aethal said.

His door opened anyway. "If you really mean that, I'll go away," said Farnan, gripping Osric by the shoulder of his tunic. "But I thought you might like to know who it was you were keeping out."

"Ah, Farnan! No, come in. Have a drink. No one else, Osric. Sorry about that." He shook his head and sat. "I just assumed I couldn't be lucky enough for it to be anyone I wanted to see." He took a swig of the brandy. "Can't imagine anyone else in that category right now."

"Well, I suppose I forgive you, especially when your last visitor appears to have been our good Conversant," Franan said. "What did he do? Come to describe in loving detail your own private hell for escorting poor Magnei into the presence of the king?"

"No, astonishingly enough. I think I may have possibly convinced him of something."

Farnan's eyes bulged. "You mean he actually listened to something you said? I hope it was something worth listening to for a change. Seriously, explain this miracle."

Aethal did, detailing the conversation as well as he could remember. By the time he was done, Farnan was shaking his head.

"Aethal the Un-bloody-likely," he chuckled. "I think you may actually save us all."

"God Beyond The World forbid it depends on me," said Aethal. Next, you just have to pull General Malcoor out from under your bed."

"I'm counting on Westerend's favor to help with that," Aethal replied.

"Or we could beat your brother to a quivering pulp."

"I doubt he truly knows anything, but I'm keeping my options open."

"Speaking of knowing things, what do you think of this Magnei fellow?"

"He knows things we need to," said Aethal. "That's all I'm certain of right now. And that we'll need to use every last one of them. The things he knows, and the people we have, in this fight."

"To defend Verlaen," asked Farnan, more grimly. "Or to go on his expedition to the Well?"

"I pray it won't come to that," said Aethal, fervently.

"But if it should?" asked Farnan. "Do we go? It's our souls, some would say."

Aethal took a breath, then looked in his friend's eyes. "It would mean our souls not to do it, wouldn't it?"

Farnan smiled. "That's the Aethal I know." He clinked his snifter on Aethal's. "Now, let's make sure we never have to."

"Even if we tried, we'd never bloody get there," Aethal said.

"After what you've done already, I wouldn't bet against you," said Farnan. "But... here's to home, and not leaving it."

"I'll drink to that." As they did, Aethal permitted himself the luxury of hope.

Epilogue

The room did not exist in any sense but the physical. It was doubtless that any other two men alive knew where it was. In the room with the men, who sat on simple stools, there was only a table, two goblets, and a bottle. Velvet curtains draped the windowless walls seen only as edgings of white stone. Had the room been discovered, only one thing of value to either of them could have been lost, and it was quite possible its discoverer would never realize its value. In an undraped square of cloth, a portal of black glass hung on the wall. Within it, as in a mirror, hung the sleeping face of Lord Warden Cledan. Blurred, as it always was in these times. The man's lips twitched in some dream that seemed unpleasant.

The elder of the men, moving stiffly, poured a dark wine from the bottle, first into the other's cup, and then into his own.

"He should be dead."

"He accomplished a part of his purpose. The rest is out of his hands. Death would only draw attention."

"Do you think he knows that?" The man took a sip of the wine he had poured.

"Quite likely." His colleague took his goblet. "But that is all he knows." He did not drink.

"Tell me: now the Lotus is discovered, what will the throne do for us?"

"Everything we wanted it to and more."

"And our other sources?"

The younger man replaced his goblet on the table. "It takes time to put them in place, especially since we didn't count on the Last Sword's actions." There was the slightest of stress on the *we*. "They have complicated matters considerably."

"Complicated matters," repeated the other. "If you are having problems with complicated matters, your life could be simplified." He waved his hand at the image, and it wavered, as if the dark glass were a deep pool, disturbed by a thrown pebble.

The new image was of a man smiling blissfully. Cords of muscle stood out on his throat, bulging as he chewed. Green froth burst from his mouth, black-green. Paler green tendrils ran beneath his skin, from the throat, up his cheeks, to his eyes that were solid green. He swallowed and plunged his face back into a wooden bowl, hard enough to bloody his nose, then reared back up, chewing. Chewing. He was tied in his chair, and the ropes had cut deeply, but the man felt no pain.

"Your predecessor had trouble with complicated matters, too. His life is now very simple."

The younger man's voice did not waver. "Your point, as always, is taken. However, I submit that hurrying doesn't always achieve a goal faster. Westerend is hurrying. Wrackberg is hurrying. For all the good it has done them."

"Their hurrying has made what was certain two weeks ago doubtful now."

"It hasn't. Wrackberg isn't nearly as clever as he thinks he is. I learned everything we needed to beneath the Pass. I said the situation was complicated. Not out of control. I am here, am I not?"

"Indeed. See that you are ready."

"Always."

To Be Continued ...

Acknowledgements

This book has been in the works since before I got married, and so I would be remiss not to thank my wife, Katie, for offering support and encouragement while I struggled with it. I would also like to thank Ben Pittman and Ralph Seibel who were the first people to read it twice voluntarily.

Thanks to J.F. Holmes and Cannon Publishing for taking a chance on this monster and showing me that sometimes it's best to chop a monstrously-long novel in half. Others who deserve credit include Jim C. Hines, who saw the most awful of awful first drafts and gave valuable advice. Also to Kim Wiggans, Felix Savage, and a host of others, my most heartfelt thanks.

Finally, a huge appreciation to Michael Morton and Bill Erwin, without whom this work would be a mass of inconsistencies, both story wise and grammatically. No novel comes into being without excellent editors, and I am grateful for their hard work.

PLEASE RATE AND REVIEW THIS BOOK ON AMAZON!

About the Author

For the next book in this series, follow G. Scott Huggins on Amazon!

G. Scott Huggins grew up in Wichita, Kansas and now lives in Wisconsin. At a young age, he fell in love with the worlds of Pern, Tran-Ky-Ky, We Made It, and many more. He studied all around the world, and speaks both German and Russian. He is a graduate of the Clarion Writing Workshop (1997) and sold his first story in 1999.

When he is not writing science-fiction and fantasy, Huggins teaches history. With his wife, he is in the process of raising children and tolerating cats. His favorite authors include G.K. Chesterton, Dan Simmons, C.S. Lewis, Lois McMaster Bujold, Larry Niven, and Terry Pratchett.

More from Cannon Publishing

Join the Crew!

Sign up for our newsletter for the latest news on new releases and more.

Follow our authors at their Amazon Pages!

Shane Gries (Dragon Finalist)

Lucas Marcum

Al Hagan

James Copley

Jason Kyle

G. Scott Huggins

Michael Morton

Charles Hackney

Jon LaForce

Jason Weiser

Kal Spriggs

Brian Gifford

Charli Cox

Dan Kemp

Jonathan Shuerger

J.R. Wise

More Books from Cannon Publishing

Irregular Scout Team One

In July of 2016 a plague swept the world, and the civilization collapsed and fell. For a lone National Guard sergeant, a veteran of the wars overseas who had settled down to a new life, the nightmare began on a hot summer evening at the barricades. Orders and chaos, gunfire and being overrun, his unit dwindles away in the face of the infected. Months later, living in the ruins, the thud of helicopter rotors followed by a crash and the rescue of a downed pilot leads Sergeant First Class Nick Agostine back into the arms of the US military. From his experience comes the idea of teams, military and civilians experienced in dealing with the undead and barbarism of the wilds. The first Irregular Scout Team leads the way for Task Force Liberty to advance down the Mohawk Valley in Upstate NY, making contact with survivors and clearing out the infected with stealth and firepower.

Volume 1

Volume 2

Volume 3: Civil War

Volume 4: Bad Company

The Line

When the world descends into chaos and anarchy with an unbelievably swift plague, turning victims into ravenous maniacs, the soldiers of America's storied 1st Infantry are asked to hold the line. From the brutal streets of urban combat to the bloodied, desperate defense on the plains of Kansas, they fight a war against an unrelenting enemy who used to be their fellow citizens. As civilization falls, can they hold the line?

The Thin Dead Line
Dead Storm Rising
The Big Dead One

Fallen Empire

What's a soldier to do when the war is over? When he's only known conflict his whole life? Since time immemorial the solution has been to find another war, this time for pay. Whoever has the credits and wins the high bid gets the experienced fighter. Sometimes, though, the credits aren't enough to cover the price. Empires rise, but Empires also fall. The Terran Union has spent five centuries under the control of the alien Grausians, like a barbarian tribe under the thumb of Rome. Now, after almost two decades of civil war and succession struggles, the formerly subject races have settled back in their ancient territories to lick their wounds and re-arm, leaving hundreds of settled planets to exist in a political vacuum. Into that space steps the free companies, mercenary units that fight for gold, honor, power and glory. Veterans who can't get the wars out of their souls, new recruits looking for adventure, corporations with their own agenda. Join us in a 27th Century that echoes history.

The Irish Brigade

Overrun

Silent Violence

Doom Company

Athenaeum, Inc

The Professor has problems, and not just what decades of soldiering did to his back and his knees. His boss just died, leaving him as CEO of the extremely discreet intelligence contractor Athenaeum, Incorporated. His old buddy the Operations Director is a highly skilled Army Ranger veteran but his finance chief is slightly unhinged and spends her money on highly inappropriate work outfits. The surviving old men on the Board of Directors are stuck in the 1970s. Running Athenaeum out of an old Cold War bunker and keeping their roster of experts together is expensive, but the government contracts are drying up or going to bigger, flashier corporate players.

Door Number Three

Doubling Down

When nuclear war erupts on Earth, the American colony in the Alpha Centauri system is left stranded. As the new day dawns, a furious attack by the native inhabitants threatens to overwhelm the colony's defenses. It's left to the thin red line of the US Army's 9th Regiment to stem the tide and ensure humanity's survival in this harsh new world. From two time Dragon Finalist and author of the best selling series "Irregular Scout Team One" and "Invasion" comes a new tale that tells of the struggle for survival on a brutal planet.

Offworld: Ragnarok

Offworld: Expeditions

Cannon Fodder: Tales From the Gun Crew

Fifteen stories from Cannon Publishing Authors, each taking from the universes of their novels to bring you perspectives and deepen their world. From 27th century mercenaries fighting on distant planets and young soldiers riding with Arthur to defeat Saxon hordes, to enchanted weapons dealing damage in hands of Fae, we bring you the best of Science Fiction and Fantasy!

Valkyrie

Humanity engages in a desperate struggle with an alien species for this side of the Orion Arm. Space ships die in instantaneous bursts of light and turn into vapor, but on the ground Marines scream and lie wounded in the mud and blood, praying for the Valkyries to come save them. They aren't wishing for death and a Nordic goddess to take them to Valhalla, the wounded are praying for the men and women of the '348th Field Hospital MEDEVAC to dive through fire and hell to come save them. Because they know that ...Valkyries never die!

Valkyrie
Valkyrie: Rebellion
Valkyrie: Attrition

High Caliber Awards

The Cannon High Caliber Awards are an annual contest for new writers. In it we ask them to submit a novella length story of Science Fiction, Military or Fantasy genre to challenge their skills.

2024

2025

The Wishkiller Saga

While on patrol Captain Aethal Paaling discovers evidence that an ancient terror has reached the rich soil of his home: the Lotus, a prolific growth whose addictive leaves devour their victims from within turning their hosts into horrible, terrifyingly violent mockeries of humanity. Created at the dawn of history by the twisted power of a godly relic called the Well, the return of the Lotus may be a harbinger of even more horrors to come. Carrying the fatal news to the capital, Aethal discovers that even in the face of death itself, the Lords Paramount of Verlaen will fight to keep their secrets and their power. With only the guidance of his legendary Greater Rifle and the aid of the Pheonix Lancers, the soldier must find his way through the halls of a forgotten holy order and into deep dens of crime seeking answers. He must find the truth as quickly as he can, because the Lotus may have already taken root among those he loves... and fighting it may cost him everything, including his soul.

A Cold and Mortal Spring

Hexen

When nine out of ten people in the world have died in a brutal plague, what do those who remain do to pick up the pieces? Does the creed, "Duty, Honor, Country" have a place any more if there's no country left? On his way across the devastated remains of Texas, Marine Corps veteran and survivor Eric Marten rescues a young woman from a vicious attack by men who have turned into savages. As Dani slowly learns to trust him, they try to stay alive in the deathlands that America has become, using all their wits to survive a post-apocalyptic nightmare.

90% Death Rate: A Post Apocalyptic Thriller
Angel of Death: A Post Apocalyptic Thriller
The Bloody Princess: A Post Apocalyptic Thriller

Hell Train

A single train carries what might be the last vestige of civilization through a hellish nightmare. A few hundred alive out of millions, lights going out all across what was once America as the possessed arose from the dead and murdered the living. A few hundred survivors travel across the country in an armored train, seeking some place to shelter in a fallen world. All that remains is a dystopian nightmare marked by rains of blood, impossible horrors, and portals to Hell opening in the skies.US Army Captain Jack Zamora is responsible for their safety, a self-imposed burden that wears on him every day. Fighting off undead, protecting the survivors, keeping the train running and supplied as his team desperately plans their next moves. Starvation and disease threaten. but it gets worse, because the ancient gods have sent their emissaries, horrific beings of myth and legend that walk the Earth. Things that can drain a man's very life essence or even that of an entire city.

Hell Train: All Aboard

Sometimes a hero isn't what you expect, and the one you need comes from the castaways of society. Nearly broken and at the end of his rope, former decorated scout pilot and prisoner of war, Red has finally accepted the inevitable. He and his kin have no future in the Human Confederation of Worlds, being gene mods and barely human themselves. With the help of his friend he flees Terra for adventure and fortune out in the reaches of the galaxy. Along the way he's dragged back into conflict that calls on all his piloting skills and he learns the deeper meaning of Kin, as his crew becomes his family.

Path to Freedom: The Path, Book One

More than a decade after the Confederated Earth Forces were defeated, their commanding general, a boyhood protegee, lives in exile and disgrace. His life on an isolated farm is forever changed when two strangers show up at his homestead, and the war comes crashing back down on him. The problem though, remains the same. How do you fight an enemy that is technologically superior and holds the high ground?

Invasion: Resistance

Invasion: Day of Battle

Invasion: Total War

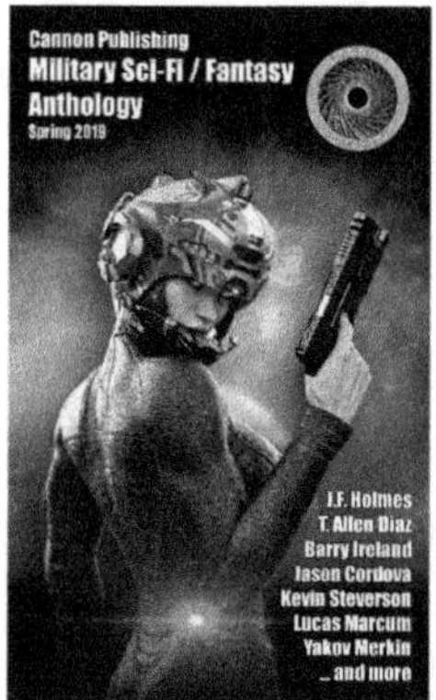

The military experience is timeless, and echoes down from our past and into our future. Along the way, not everything is as it seems. Thirteen stories from established and new writers in the field of Military Science Fiction and Military Fantasy bring you tales of the terrors of combat and the even greater fear of the unknown in Cannon Publishing's first Bi-Annual Military Anthology.

Fifteen classic Science Fiction stories from both masters of the craft and up and coming new writers! A tyrannical United Nations pulls the strings of its colony worlds, ruling with an iron fist. Corporate interests take precedence, and brushfire rebellions smolder on the edges. One system, home to the only alien species yet discovered, with human allies throws off the yoke and calls itself Independence.

MECHA

Feedback from the slight pressure of a hand closing sends a powerful mechanical arm smashing into an opponent. A neural link hurls blustering plasma fire from your suit's shoulder mounted cannon. Your reactor levels scream with overload as return fire smashes into your armor, and damage alarms wail while you hurl your twenty ton body sideways for cover. You're a Mecha, a mechanical fighting machine with a human pilot. The guy that the infantry curse at in training and pray for in combat. The machine that the last hopes of your people ride on. The construct that strikes fear deep into alien hearts as they hear your turbines power up. The one able to pass through hell and come out the other side victorious, or die trying.

In the near future, massive empires rule the stars, and west of the Reach, they are battling for control of new systems. In the no-mans land between the front lines, Captain Nate Meric and the crew of the privateer Lexington fight for prize money, and loyalty to their ship and their friends. Beneath it all, though, runs a hidden dream. To see America restored, and take her rightful place among the stars.

Brian Corel, former slave, gladiator, ex-fiance to an Empress, exiled Captain of the Taland Royal Guard and now owner of the frigate *Widowmaker*, does the best he can to balance the lives of his crew with his own desire to live life as a free man. Skirting the border between being a privateer and an outright pirate, Corel stumbles into a war with a religious cult intent on corrupting the kingdom of an old friend and has to set things right while grieving over his lost love. Along the way he signs a dragon into his crew and has to risk everything to rescue his brother from the grasp of a demon that has destroyed an entire continent.

Chosen by the Sword

There are some things a PhD doesn't prepare you for, like running two feet of steel through the guts of a flesh-eating monster straight out of a nightmare, while ducking razor sharp claws. Or having the sword critique your fighting style while you do it. Dave Howard had a problem. Last week, he was out looking for a teaching job in the middle of a wrecked job market. This week he was neck deep in green blood and hellfire. Dragged into it by the very sword, his grandfathers' mysterious possessed blade, that was now walking him through hacking up a ghoul without getting his own head cut off. This wasn't exactly what he had gone to school for, and the University he had just taken a job with seemed to be anything BUT an academic institution. More like some kind of monster hunting bunch of weirdo nerds. Maybe his degree in Personality Psychology might be useful there, at least. The fighting though ... as he dodged another swipe of claws and awkwardly tried to follow the instructions the sword was screaming at him, he shot back at it, "Hell, I'm Canadian! Swordplay isn't in my cultural DNA!"

The legions are but a memory, the glory of Rome only a shadow of crumbling ruins and broken walls. A darkening tide of barbarism was washing across Britain's shores and the lights of civilization were slowly flickering out into darkness, only kept burning by the legendary Red Dragons cavalry unit. Led by their Tribune, Arthur, who serves no kingdom but goes where the fight is hardest and most crucial, they wage desperate battles to keep back the tide. The Red Dragons ride the length of Britannia to fight the invading Saxons, Scoti and Picts, wherever they show, from across the seas or down from the Highlands. At sixteen years old Peredur of Gwynedd has listened all his life to the stories of his father Pelinor fighting with Ambrosius Aurelianus. When word comes that his older brother has been slain in battle with the Saxons, his desire for revenge leads him to follow in his father's footsteps as a warrior, becoming a cavalryman with the Red Dragons. Along the way he may either find himself a warrior and leader worthy of Arthur or be left lying forgotten in the dust of history.

Two souls collide in the middle of a deadly war.

Sergeant Sylvie Lyons of Her Majesty's Royal Engineers wishes she'd listened to her grandda's advice and stayed away from the military.

USMC Sergeant Hondo Cassidy wants nothing more in life than being a Marine and fighting. Hondo and Sylvie find themselves thrown together when his artillerymen are assigned to provide security for her engineers deep in the desert of Afghanistan.. Amidst death, destruction, cultural misunderstanding and the inevitable that happens when you mix an all male unit of Marines with an engineer unit that is mostly female, Sylvie and Hondo find in each other a reason to live. That is, if they can survive.

Semper Die

Semper Die

The dead rose expecting a feast. What they got was a firefight.

Sergeant Alex Slaughter and the Marines of Alpha Squad were on a routine training exercise near Quantico when everything went silent. No comms. No command. No clue.

What they find when they return to base is worse than anything they trained for: a bioweapon has unleashed a zombie virus that has shattered civilization, and now they must survive the Collapse.

But as the squad pushes deeper into hostile territory—through the death-choked streets of Arlington and into the rot-stained corridors beneath D.C.—they discover that the undead aren't the only threat. Desperate survivors, rogue military units, and darker truths buried beneath the weight of secrecy will test their loyalty, their mission, and their very humanity.

Written by USMC veteran Jonathan Shuerger and set in J.F. Holmes's brutal and unrelenting Irregular Scout Team One universe, Semper Die delivers pulse-pounding action, authentic military detail, and a terrifying vision of what happens when duty and apocalypse collide.

Lock. Load. Semper Fi. Semper Die.

More From the Fae Wars

Get the full series!

Onslaught

What would you do if America and the world were invaded tomorrow by a relentless and brutal enemy? In an alternate 2015, a US Army Special Forces Team, part of the legendary black ops unit "Delta", is in midtown Manhattan to take out a Chinese spy and his handlers, sending a message short of outright conflict. All goes smoothly until they find themselves in a full blown shooting war through the canyons of the City. Portals from another world have opened in Central Park, making a way for figures out of historical nightmare to invade. The Fae, creatures banished from Earth thousands of years ago and now only part of our legends, have returned with Dragon fire, spell and sword to conquer and take revenge. The first volume of The Fae Wars covers Team Three, G squadron, Special Forces Detachment (Delta) as they fight their way off Manhattan and then join the defense of the refugees as the Fae assault the bridges. The fabled 69th Infantry puts up an epic fight against superior weaponry and then the war descends into the asymmetric hell that the Delta Operators know so well. Along the way they find new allies and old powers that come to their aid.

The Fall

For the first time in two hundred years an enemy has stepped foot on American soil and war has come to our cities. The US military is rocked back on its heels and driven into a fighting retreat as each defense line falls. The foe is unstoppable and ... Fae. Creatures from a legendary past who have come to reclaim the Earth in the name of magic and revenge. In the hills of Pennsylvania a ragtag, devastated army prepares to make a last stand against dragon fire capable of melting an Abrams tank and wizardry that stops fifth generation fighter jets in mid-air. Inevitably it comes down to shining steel verses human will, and Sergeant Oliva Acevedo transforms from a hospital clerk to a hardened fighter. Volume Two of the best selling "Fae Wars" follows the fighting retreat of the US Army as the Fae establish control of a shattered America.

Futures Past

Two thousand years ago the Fae were banished from Earth and they've spent that time plotting return and revenge. When their portals open around the world and start crushing the human's military with spell encased steel and dragon fire, it becomes a massive stuggle between technology and magic. When the Fae Invasion hammers the West Coast, Captain James Powers and his California Army National Guard artillery battery is caught on its way home from Annual Training. In a running battle the unit is smashed by combat with orcs and elves, leaving their commander struggling to keep his people together and alive. Along the way a dying priest with a strange ability to see the future manipulates people and events to bring Captain Powers to his true calling as a Seer. As they run and fight, the humans gain new allies, Fea tinkerers who love all things mechanical and hate the elves. With their help they begin to take the war to the enemy in a brutal mayhem of ambush and assassination. Book Three of the Fae Wars series following the bestselling "Onslaught" (set in NY City) and "The Fall" (Pennsylvania)

Tales From the Occupation: A Fae Wars Anthology

Wars end, enemies are defeated and territories are conquered and the combatants have to return to a life changed. America and the rest of humanity have fallen to the Fae, ancient mortal enemies of mankind. After building their strength for two thousand years, the Elves have claimed their vengeance and now rule Earth with an iron fist and dragon fire. Down but not out, a human resistance is building, but first daily life needs to be lived. An anthology of stories exploring life during the Occupation in the best-selling Fae Wars universe.

Insurgent

Wars come and wars go. Eventually even the most belligerent of combatants will arrive at some kind of living arrangement, either through exhaustion or slaughter. Kill enough, down to the last child, and there will be no more war ... until the next one, of course. In August 2015, the war started, portals opening up between their world and ours, allowing the Fae to return to our (or their) home world in blood, fire and magic. Conventional forces fought back as well as they could, but the invasion had been planned to hit us in the middle of our civilization. America's military was scattered overseas or concentrated in large bases that were quickly overwhelmed by forces that were dropped right in the middle of their units. The fighting was brutal and horrific, magic overwhelming technology. It took six weeks, and the President surrendered to spare the civilian population. A puppet government was put in place and the Fae started to divide the conquered lands into principalities run by their Great Houses, slowly turning America into a land of feudal slavery. Thing is, though, the Fae had lived in their exile for thousands of years, fighting wars among themselves and against various races that populated their new home. Pitched battles where there was a clear-cut winner and loser. They had never fought an insurgency and had no idea how bloody it could get. Major David Kincaid. United States Army 1st Special Forces Operational Detachment–Delta, soldier of a defeated but unbroken nation, was going to show them. If, that is, he can keep the faith. The follow up novel to the bestselling "Fae Wars: Onslaught" by J.F. Holmes.

Ghost

There are wars, and then there's War. The all-encompassing thing that is fought on many levels, and with many kinds of weapons, many kinds of warriors. Even ghosts. Alex was no one, a man just trying to get by at his paperwork job at the new Homeland Security. A man grieving for his wife, who had died in the Invasion. Someone just trying to keep his head down while the elves appointed him to do the paperwork of putting their boots on the necks of a conquered American people. Thing is, even a nobody paper shuffling clerk has a weapon, one that had lit the fires of revolution in America hundreds of years ago. His mind, and his words. The internet was still up and running, somehow and someway, and Alex takes to his keyboard. Inspired by his hero Patrick Henry, soon the words of the "Ghost" start inciting attacks on the Fae and the District of Columbia rings with explosions, gunshots and cries of Freedom. The Resistance notices, and Alex is soon assigned a bodyguard and a handler, an ex-police officer who is running from her own hidden past. Together they work to keep the flame of resistance alive and escape from the tightening net of the Fae. The consequences are, as always, Liberty or Death.

Northwest Front

Fae Wars returns on a new front as war rages in the Pacific Northwest! Corporal Erik Doherty isn't some kind of special operations super soldier; he's just an infantry grunt trying to get by in what was once the United States Army, now an enforcement arm of the Fae overlords. When orders come down from a chain of command more interested in boot licking their new masters than protecting American citizens, he has to make the choice. To serve and live, or run and die? Ashleigh Greene is a teenage girl with a price on her head, the Fae looking for retribution for the killing of one of their nobles. As her hometown burns behind her, she flees into the mist shrouded forests of the Pacific Northwest, her family killed by dragon fire and her world destroyed. On separate paths, each human comes face to face with a haunting legend that has lived for thousands of years. One that has been waiting, watching, and hating the old enemy that has finally returned. Together, they bring war to the Fae in a battle for honor and revenge. Book seven in the best-selling Fae Wars series!

Vendetta

The echoes of the Fae Invasion have died out in the Midwest when a new thunder rumbles across the plains. Tukor, former warband leader of the Red Arrow Clan, now rides with a motorcycle club of humans and orcs against his former masters. It's hard to tell which challenges Tukor more though; being the new chief of all the orcs in the free city of Wichita Falls, Texas, or being engaged to the tough and lovely human woman Misty.

Throw in an elven duke that's still pissed at Tukor for murdering his sons, a motorcycle club that'll follow the chief to hell and back, and a newly arrived orc matron determined to prove Tukor and Misty wrong about their future. The Fae occupation of the Midwest just got way more bloody.

Featuring orcs on choppers, magic ammo and a whole crew of Army SpecOps, the tale of Tukor and Misty is a front seat view of the occupation in the Southwest that no one expected, least of all Tukor himself.

Relics of Empire

In a world shattered by elven conquest, where magic crackles and dragons soar, the Navajo Nation stands as a defiant refuge. Living there is Ben Yazzie, a battle scarred Marine veteran who wants no more war—until a brutal encounter with elven oppressors at a remote gas station ignites a spark of rebellion. Alongside Maria Hernandez, a grieving widow fueled by vengeance, and a band of unlikely allies, Ben is thrust into a fight against an empire wielding arcane power and ruthless ambition.

As ancient ley lines awaken, unleashing chaos across the American Southwest, Ben uncovers a legacy of resistance tied to his ancestors and a mysterious relic from a forgotten era. Magic surges and the earth itself stirs, forcing Ben to embrace his destiny as the Coyote, the elusive and mysterious warrior leading a desperate stand against an otherworldly tyranny.

From the dusty trails of Arizona to the neon-lit chaos of Las Vegas, *The Fae Wars: Relics of Empire* is a pulse-pounding tale of courage, sacrifice, and defiance against overwhelming odds. Will the old ways and a warrior's heart be enough to reclaim a shattered land?

The rebellion begins here.

John Holmes

J.F. Holmes is a retired Army Senior Noncommissioned Officer, having served for 22 years in both the Regular Army and Army National Guard. During that time, he served as everything from an artillery section leader to a member of a Division level planning staff, with tours in Cuba and Iraq, as well as responding to the terrorists attacks in NYC on 9-11.

From 2010 to 2014 he wrote the immensely popular military cartoon strip, "Power Point Ranger", poking fun at military life in the tradition of Beetle Bailey and Willy & Joe.

His books range from Military Sci-Fi to Space Opera to Detective to Fantasy, with a lot in between, and in 2017 two are finalists for the prestigious Dragon Awards.

In 2018, he launched Cannon Publishing, www.cannonpublishing.us specializing in military science fiction, fantasy and thrillers, with an emphasis on works from up and coming authors.

Lucas Marcum

Lucas Marcum is a critical care nurse practitioner and an officer in the US Army Reserve. When he's not working, or performing his reserve duties, he can be found hiking, reading, attempting to perfect his soft pretzel recipe and spending time with his family.

James Copley

James Copley is a former Non-Commissioned Officer of the U.S. Army, having served over twenty-one years in both Active and Reserve/Guard units, variously trained as Infantry, Communications, and Ordnance specialties before finally retiring from the Army National Guard in 2016. During his service, he deployed four separate times, twice to Iraq and twice to Afghanistan.

He is currently working as a software engineer in Central California with his wife, two children, and two dogs. Reading was his number one passion from a very young age, and more recently he decided to try writing his own. Feel free to join him on his writing journey!

Charli Cox

Charli Cox is a best-selling Military Sci-Fi and Horror Comedy author. She also writes Sci-Fi, Alternate History, and Military Fantasy stories.

If you enjoyed Fae Wars: Northwest Front and want to see more stories about Ash and "Gunny," Cannon Publishing has you covered. Burnt Mountain and Sasquatch will be coming to your Kindle later in 2025. Also, please be sure to leave a review!

Representing #teamandmore, Charli's first published short story is in The Phoenix Initiative: First Missions from Chris Kennedy Publishing. She has stories in Bureau 42 and Express Elevator to Hell, also from CKP.

Look for Whistles of the Wendigo, an Alternate History/Military Fantasy novel set in the Joint Task Force 13 universe from Three Ravens Publishing, due to release soon.

Charli's previous experience has been as a Realtor, HVAC Business Manager, IT Office Manager, and freelance bookkeeper. Professional skills such as drafting strongly worded emails transition surprisingly well into writing fiction.

An animal lover and #boymom, she lives in SW Oregon with her Leg husband, two sons, an Arabian mare, and two Husky mixes who think they are hooman.

Learn more about Charli and sign up for her newsletter on her website. Hang out with her on Facebook, Instagram, and/or TikTok.

Jason Weiser

Mr. Weiser has been a government contractor for the last eleven years, and before that, a writer working odd jobs trying to get by. He has a BA in History from CUNY Brooklyn. Mr. Weiser released his first novel in 2025, with Cannon Publishing, but before that, released a short story in their 2018 Spring Military Sci Fi Anthology.

Mr. Weiser is also an avid wargamer and has been published quite a bit in the hobby, having most recently run "Military Miniature" magazine as it's editor in chief from 2021-2023. Before that, he wrote for EpochXperience (a division of SJR Research) as a contributing writer for their blog on wargaming and military history topics from 2020 to 2021.

He also wrote two scenario books on Cold War wargaming topics, "Red Star, Burning Streets" and "Red Star, White Lights".

Mr. Weiser encourages all his fans to visit Cannon Publishing at their website

Brian Gifford

A military veteran with more than 25 years of service in the U.S. Air Force and Army (in an order that would surprise you!), Brian is a lifelong science fiction and fantasy nerd of the highest order. A student of the hard sciences and the arcane arts of cybersecurity and IT alike, Brian has spent a lifetime accumulating his unique view of the world, which he now insists on sharing with everyone else. He is a husband in awe of the magnificence that is his wife and the proud father of three awesome sons, and looks forward to retiring from the military in the near future to focus on his family and his writing.